# BLOOD
# CURSE

## Also by Emily Gee for Solaris Books

*Thief With No Shadow*
*The Laurentine Spy*

### The Cursed Kingdoms Trilogy

*The Sentinel Mage*
*The Fire Prince*
*The Blood Curse*

## More fantasy from Solaris Books

### The Chronicles of King Rolen's Kin Series
### by Rowena Cory Daniells

*The King's Bastard*
*The Uncrowned King*
*The Usurper*
*King Breaker*

### The Macht Trilogy by Paul Kearney

*The Ten Thousand*
*Corvus*
*Kings of Morning*

### The Chronicles of the Necromancer by Gail Z. Martin

*The Summoner*
*The Blood King*
*Dark Haven*
*Dark Lady's Chosen*

# THE
# BLOOD
# CURSE

## EMILY GEE

SOLARIS

First published 2015 by Solaris
an imprint of Rebellion Publishing Ltd,
Riverside House, Osney Mead,
Oxford, OX2 0ES, UK

*www.solarisbooks.com*

US ISBN: 978 1 78108 387 1

10 9 8 7 6 5 4 3 2 1

A CIP catalogue record for this book is available from the
British Library.

Designed & typeset by Rebellion Publishing

Printed in the US

*A big thanks to Moss and Jo,*
*who read this trilogy before anyone else.*
*Guys, I value your comments and insights.*
*Thank you!*

The Seven Kingdoms

Esfaban
(territory of
Osgaard)

Osgaard

Lundegaard

100 leagues
300 miles

Lomaly
(territory of
Osgaard)

Horst
(territory of
Osgaard)

Equator

Urel
Archipelago

Ankeny

Roubos

Sault

Gulf of Hallas

Vaere

Girond

Cornas

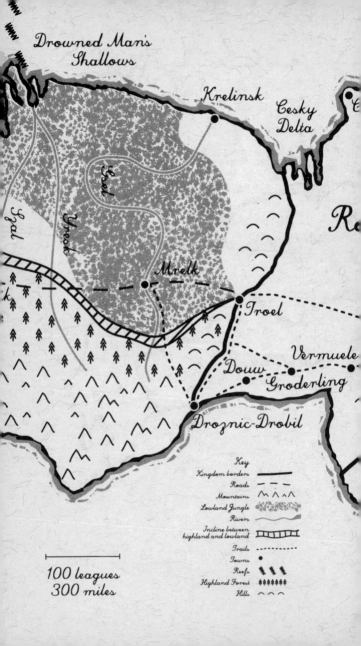

Urel
Archipelago

Vorshel

Beschiel

Kingdoms of
Roubos and Sault

os

Oudhees

Hansgrohe

Bloedel

Nime    Delpy

Widow Makers

Andeol

Furies

ult

Fenal

Vaere

# CHAPTER ONE

IT TOOK A week to walk out of the steaming jungle. There was no path that Jaumé could see, but Bennick rarely hesitated. Sometimes he used the compass, but mostly he used his eyes. "See here? A boot print." Or, "Look at the way those leaves are bent." Those were the only times Bennick talked. He was sour that the witches had saved Prince Harkeld's life. There had been honor in killing the prince, but none now that the prince was alive again.

Jaumé was glad the prince wasn't dead, but he didn't let Bennick see it. His relief was a soundless hum inside his chest. With the prince alive, the Ivek Curse could be broken. Bennick said that dead was dead, and it didn't matter when or how people died, but Jaumé knew he was wrong.

On the first day, Bennick found the pony Jaumé had ridden. Even Jaumé could see her hoof prints in the boggy ground. The pony came to their calls, pushing her way through the twisted trees and fleshy-leaved vines. She butted her nose against Jaumé's shoulder and snorted in his ear. When Bennick wasn't looking, Jaumé hugged her.

After that, he rode and Bennick walked. "Sleep,"

Bennick told him. "You'll need to watch for breathstealers tonight. Bastards will want to suck me dry."

Jaumé slept in the saddle, and stayed awake all night, guarding Bennick, but no breathstealers came floating in the mist.

Two days later, they came to the clearing where Odil and Steadfast lay dead. Jaumé woke in the saddle, and wished he hadn't. The pool bubbled and steamed, and the stink was more than just sulfur. He averted his eyes and hurried past on the pony. That night, he watched tensely for breathstealers, but still none came.

They passed Maati's body the next day. Kimbel's was gone. "Something's dragged him away to eat," Bennick said. It didn't appear to bother him, even though Kimbel had been his Brother.

*Dead is dead. Doesn't matter when or how.*

They found four of the horses they'd left behind, and the saddles and bridles and half-full saddlebags. Bennick rode, too, after that. The ground no longer steamed. The stink of sulfur faded behind them. "You can sleep tonight," Bennick told Jaumé. "Breathstealers can't reach me here."

The further they travelled, the less sour Bennick became. By the time they reached the river, he was whistling again. "I'll get him yet, young Jaumé," he said, slinging his pack down at the water's edge. "You'll see."

Jaumé said nothing. He didn't want Bennick to kill Prince Harkeld. But that was what Bennick did: kill people. He was a special type of soldier. An assassin. He did the All-Mother's work for her.

The river was wide and brown, turning slowly over on itself like a giant serpent. "What now?" Jaumé asked.

"Now we wait for the next boat. Upstream or downstream, it doesn't matter. Either way, we'll end up in the same place." Insects swarmed in a cloud around Bennick's face, but he didn't seem to mind; he whistled a few bars of a tune.

"Where's that?"

"Wherever the prince is." Bennick hunkered down and opened his pack. He rooted in it, pulled out a flask, slapped oil on his skin. The smell of cat's piss was strong. The cloud of insects thinned. "Let's hope this lasts us." He tossed the flask to Jaumé.

THEY SPENT THREE days at the river's edge, surrounded by the buzz of biting insects. Bennick seemed as strong as he'd ever been. When he practiced with his bow, his hands moved almost too fast for Jaumé to see. It was as if the breathstealers had never sucked the life from him.

Jaumé practiced, too. He could throw his bone-handled knife twenty paces, the blade flipping twice before it sank deep into its target, and he could hit a tree trunk at fifty paces with his bow and arrows.

"I'll start you with a sword next," Bennick said, clapping him on the shoulder.

Later that day, a boat came into view, laboring up the river, sail full-bellied, oars working like centipede's legs. Bennick grinned. He stood and stretched. "Time to go, lad."

# CHAPTER TWO

PRINCESS BRIGITTA CAME slowly back to consciousness. Her limbs were numb. Her eyes wouldn't open. Thoughts lurched in slow, confused circles inside her head. It took long minutes to realize what had happened: she'd been drugged again. All-Mother's Breath.

Time crawled past. It became easier to think. Sensation returned to her fingers and toes, to her face.

Britta kept her eyes closed, pretending to be asleep. Where was she? The surface she lay on seemed to dip and sway, but she was sure she was no longer aboard the assassins' ship. The sound the ship had made—a creaking, thrumming sound, as if the vessel lived and breathed—was gone.

She strained to hear.

Silence. She was surrounded by silence.

Her hands and feet tingled, came alive. Her hearing sharpened. She heard the coo of a pigeon, faint. A distant voice. The clatter of wagon wheels, barely audible. *I'm ashore. Where?*

Roubos. It had to be the kingdom of Roubos.

The iron weight of manacles was absent from ankle and wrist. Britta had a brief flash of memory:

the frantic scramble out the cabin window, the echo of her scream as the assassins hauled her back inside, the manacle being fastened around her ankle—cold, hard—the short chain bolted into the floor.

She'd pulled the bolt out, tugging day after day as the ship sailed across the vast Gulf of Hallas, had almost managed a second escape—or attempted suicide, or whatever one wished to call it. The second manacle had gone on, then, fastened tightly around her wrist. Punishment, not precaution. No precaution had been necessary; a Fithian had sat in her cabin every minute of the voyage after that, even when she used the chamberpot. Escape had become impossible, as had death. All she'd been able to do was wait. Wait until the ship berthed, wait until the men took her ashore—and then scream for help with all the air in her lungs. But they'd drugged her with All-Mother's Breath and taken that away from her, too.

What would passersby have done? Come to her aid? Turned away in fear?

The lingering effects of the All-Mother's Breath dissipated. Britta was aware of the rise and fall of her chest, the beating of her heart, the warm weight of a blanket over her. It was time to act. *If I'm alone, I try to escape. If escape is impossible, I kill myself.*

She held that thought firmly in her mind, let it become a solid intention, hard-edged and definite, and opened her eyes.

A Fithian assassin sat less than an arm's length away.

Britta felt rage and relief in equal measure. Rage because escape was impossible; relief because death was, too. No matter how many times she examined her choices and came to the same conclusion—that she must die rather than be used against Harkeld—she shrank from killing herself.

She stared at the assassin. He was maybe ten years older than her, in his late twenties, with curling brown hair and blue eyes. Curly, she called him in her head. He looked like a father, an uncle, a man who should have young children riding on his shoulders—until one saw the hard watchfulness of his eyes, the lack of expression on his face, the stillness in the way he sat.

A killer, this man.

He'd probably known the instant she woke. The Fithians were as observant as her armsman Karel had been, and even more dangerous.

Britta gazed at Curly as if he was a piece of furniture, trying not to let him see her emotions— rage, fear—and took in the room. Small, with a bare wooden floor. The door was closed, the window open a crack. Daylight.

She deliberately closed her eyes again. Eventually she would have to rise and use the chamberpot, while the assassin sat expressionlessly, but she would put that moment off as long as she could.

She went through her list. It was either that or allow despair to overwhelm her. She'd done this so often on board the ship that it came in a familiar sequence.

*One. We saved the boys.* Her little half-brothers were in Lundegaard, beyond Jaegar's reach. They would grow up loved and protected by their grandfather, King Magnas.

*Two. Yasma is free. She will never be a bondservant again.* That was her final memory from Lundegaard: Yasma slamming shut the bedroom door, bolting it, keeping the boys safe from the assassins.

*Three. Karel is free.* Karel, without whom she and Yasma and the boys would never have escaped Jaegar's palace. Karel, who was as impassive and watchful as the assassins, and almost as deadly.

Karel, who hadn't returned in time to save her from the Fithians.

*Which is a blessing, because they would have killed him. And how could I have borne that?*

She saw Karel's face for a moment behind her closed eyelids. The stern, hawk-like features, the eyes so dark they were almost black, the brown skin. Memory dressed him in a scarlet tunic and golden breastplate, but Karel was free now, as free as Yasma, and no longer wore an armsman's uniform.

*Four. Harkeld is alive and guarded by witches.* That was the item that gave her the most hope. Her half-brother Harkeld was still alive, he was destroying Ivek's curse, and he had witches to help him. Witches who could throw bolts of fire and change into lions and kill Fithian assassins.

Britta hugged that thought to herself. The assassin sitting soundlessly alongside her bed wasn't invincible. Witches could kill him. Would kill him. *Had* to kill him. Because Harkeld had to survive. He had to destroy the curse—or everyone in the Seven Kingdoms would die.

And she could not allow herself to be used as bait to catch him.

Escape or die. Those were her two choices. And now that she was on land again, a thousand leagues closer to Harkeld than she'd been before, it was imperative that she do one or the other.

# CHAPTER THREE

THEY CAME FOR her at dawn. Britta was led down a long, dark corridor and out into a courtyard of hard-packed dirt. Gray light lit the sky. The air was mild and damp.

A high wooden fence enclosed the yard. Britta saw a pigeon house in one corner and stables at the back. Horses waited in the middle of the courtyard, some saddled for riders, two harnessed to a covered cart. Men stood silently—five of the assassins who'd abducted her, six counting the man who held her wrists behind her back and pushed her into the courtyard—and a stranger, an old man with skin like leather and gray hair and a scarred mouth.

The old man was an assassin. One glance at him told her that. He watched her approach. There was no compassion in him, no empathy or kindness or humanity. His gaze was cold, hard, flat. He would kill her as casually as he'd swat a fly.

The hands gripping her wrists tightened. Britta halted obediently. Her gaze flicked to the horses, to the high fence. The sky was lightening. She heard birdsong. A wagon clattered past. *If I scream now, will anyone come to my rescue?* Best to wait until they were out on the street. Somewhere busy, where passersby might come to her aid, or even better, city guardsmen.

The old assassin spoke to the man who led her abductors. Short sentences, no wasted words. His voice was too low to overhear. He gestured with one hand, and she saw that it was wooden, fingers permanently curved, thumb sticking out stiffly. The rest of the assassins stood silent, waiting. They didn't speak much, Fithians. Their quietness made them even more frightening. The only human thing about them was the temperature of their skin. Britta was aware of the warmth of the hands gripping her wrists. It seemed wrong, a violation of nature. Fithian blood should be cold.

The old man stopped speaking. The leader of the assassins gave a curt nod. Leader, she called him in her head. He had a broad, flat-cheeked face and pale gray eyes.

Leader reached beneath his cloak and took something from a pouch. He stood half-turned from her. Britta saw his hands were busy, but not what he did. He turned and came towards her. Alarm spiked in her chest. It was suddenly difficult to breathe.

She'd made Leader bleed aboard ship, kicked his nose so hard that blood ran from it. Memory of that moment brought a little flash of triumph. Britta clung to it tightly, trying to smother her fear.

Leader halted so close that she could almost smell him. Pride kept her from cringing. She lifted her chin and met his eyes. *I made you bleed.*

The grip on her wrists tightened.

Britta couldn't control a flinch as Leader reached for her. She jerked her head away, but hard fingers grasped her jaw and hauled her head around. She saw what Leader held in his other hand: a cloth.

Britta opened her mouth to scream.

The cloth pressed against her nose and mouth. She inhaled the smell of vanilla. All-Mother's Breath.

Britta had time for a second's rage before plummeting into blackness.

# CHAPTER FOUR

THE SHIP SLID into the harbor of Droznic-Drobil. Karel
stood tensely at the railing, the captain's spyglass
to his eye. The harbor was busy, but nothing like
the harbor they'd sailed from. The bustle was an
everyday bustle. The panic hadn't reached here. No
chaos of refugees overflowed the wharves.

"There!" Prince Tomas cried, pointing. "That's it,
isn't it?"

Karel jerked the spyglass to the left. A sloop,
low and fast, built for speed. The Fithian ship? His
heartbeat sped up. He scanned the vessel. The sails
were furled, the deck empty. "Could be," he said,
and he sent a prayer to the All-Mother: *Let it be,
please*.

The minutes it took to find a mooring at the
wharf seemed interminable. Karel tried not to
let his impatience show. King Magnas had placed
leadership of this mission in his hands, and he would
prove the king's trust had not been misplaced.

"Tomas and I will speak with the harbormaster,"
he told the armsmen. Ten royal armsmen—the king's
best fighters—at his command. "Stay aboard. If
that's not the Fithian sloop, we sail immediately."

There were other, smaller ports on Roubos's south coast that the assassins could have headed for, but— All-Mother willing—this was the port, that was the sloop, and Princess Brigitta was here.

The mooring ropes were made fast. The gangplank slapped down. Karel strode down to the wharf, Prince Tomas at his heels.

THE HARBORMASTER WAS a thin, harassed man, but one of King Magnas's gold coins bought them his full attention. "Sloop?" The man flicked back a page in his register, running a finger down the scrawled entries. "Arrived yesterday mornin'. Early."

"From?"

The man peered at his handwriting. "Horst."

"How many passengers?" Karel asked, conscious of Prince Tomas standing tensely at his side.

"Uh..." The harbormaster squeezed his eyes shut. "Mebbe... half a dozen."

"What did they look like? Merchants? Soldiers? Refugees?"

"Soldiers," the man said, without hesitation, opening his eyes.

"Uniforms?"

"No. Just..." He shrugged. "The way they moved."

"Was there a young woman with them? With golden hair?"

The harbormaster shook his head. "Not so's I saw."

"No one came ashore but men?" Was it the wrong sloop, the wrong harbor?

"They carried some'un ashore, wrapped in a cloak. A child, I thought, sleeping."

"A child?" Excitement surged in Karel's blood. "How big?"

The man thought for a moment, then held out his arms. "So big."

Karel exchanged a glance with the prince. *Could be her.*

"Did they say where they were going?"

The harbormaster shook his head, and glanced at the gold coin Karel held.

"Did anyone meet them?"

Another headshake.

"What direction did they go in?"

The harbormaster pointed. "Up yon street."

"On foot?"

A nod. "They knew where they was headed."

"Their accents..." Prince Tomas said. "Were they from Roubos?"

The harbormaster shook his head again. "They was foreign."

"You must meet a lot of people, hear a lot of accents." The prince smiled, the scar creasing his cheek. "Where are we from?"

"You're from Lun'gaard," the harbormaster said, without hesitation. "And he's from Esfaban. Least, his face is. His voice is Osgaard."

Karel blinked, disconcerted by the man's acuity. He exchanged another glance with Prince Tomas. "Where do you think the sloop's passengers were from?"

"Not from the Seven Kingdoms."

"The Allied Kingdoms? The Dominion?"

"One or t'other," the harbormaster said. "Not from the Seven, at any rate."

"Has the sloop ever berthed here before?"

"I seen it a few times."

Karel turned the coin over in his fingers. The harbormaster's eyes followed the movement. "Could they have been Fithians?"

The man's gaze jerked from the coin. His face paled. "Fithians? I don' know what they sound like, and I don' never want to know!"

*Wise.*

"What about the crew?" Prince Tomas asked. "Local or foreign?"

"Foreign."

"Same accent as the passengers?"

The harbormaster nodded.

Karel glanced at the prince, lifted his eyebrows slightly. *Any more questions you want to ask?*

Prince Tomas shook his head.


KAREL STRODE BACK to the ship. The breeze from the ocean was mild, reminding him of Esfaban's warm, gentle winds.

"You think it's the right sloop?" Prince Tomas asked.

"Yes. You?"

"Yes." A fierce grin sat on the prince's scarred face. "What now?"

Karel glanced at him. Tomas was a year older than him, a royal prince, trained from birth to command. *And yet he abides by his father's wishes and awaits orders from me. Me. The son of bondservants.* But Prince Tomas didn't seem to resent him. There was no antipathy in the prince's manner, no hostility or bitterness, just a respect that was uncomfortably close to hero worship. *Because I killed a Fithian single-handed.*

Karel flexed his fingers. Killed a Fithian, yes, but that hadn't been enough to save the princess. "What now?" Karel halted. His body wasn't used to being on land; the wharf seemed to heave slightly beneath his feet. Princess Brigitta had been ashore a full day and a half. Was she even in Droznic-Drobil any more? "We try to follow their trail up that street. You and me and two of the armsmen. I'll send armsmen to each of the town gates to question the guards. If they have town gates, or guards. And armsmen to buy mounts and supplies. I want us ready to leave by first light tomorrow."

"You think the Fithians have left already?"

"Yes. But if they haven't... she's here somewhere." Karel turned and scanned the town. *I'm coming, princess.*

KAREL HAD TAKEN the Lundegaardan armsmen's measure during the weeks they'd been at sea. He'd fought with them, talked with them. He knew who were the fiercest swordsmen, the sharpest thinkers. The ten men were all superb fighters—they were King Magnas's personal armsmen, after all—but other skills were just as important on a mission such as this. Who could be trusted to ask the right questions, to listen, to observe, to not draw attention to himself?

He assigned tasks and handed out more of King Magnas's coins. The armsmen set about their assignments with swift efficiency, buckling on weapons, tying money pouches to their belts, heading down the gangplank and fanning out into Droznic-Drobil. They wore commoners' garb, plain shirts and trews; their forest green uniforms were buried in their packs.

Karel looked at the armsmen left on deck. Gunvald, lean, quiet, and lethal. And brawny Ture. Of the ten armsmen, these two were closest to him in skill. Gunvald had even managed to vanquish him at wrestling once.

"You two're coming with me and Tomas. We'll try to find where they took her."

AT THE MOUTH of the street the harbormaster had pointed to, Karel halted. "Sire, you and Gunvald take that side of the street. Ture and I'll take this side. Don't draw attention to yourselves. Ask a few questions, keep your eyes open. If there are Fithians here, we don't want to alert them."

He pulled Gunvald aside for a brief word. "Stay close to the prince. If we run into Fithians, keep him safe."

"Yes, sir."

Karel watched the two men go. Prince Tomas already bore the scars of an assassin's throwing star—the red slash across his cheek, the missing right ear. *What if I get him killed?*

But Tomas had begged his father to come on this mission, and the king had known the risks. Whose life was more important? Princess Brigitta's, or Tomas's?

*Neither. Harkeld is the most important.* And after him, Brigitta, because she was the bait to catch him.

Karel took a deep breath. "Let's go," he told Ture.

They took the left side of the street, strolling, pausing to talk with the people they passed— shopkeepers sweeping scraps into the muddy gutter, beggars crouched in alleyways, toothless old men smoking pipes on doorsteps. The town felt a long way from Osgaard. The buildings were wooden, crowded together like crooked teeth in a mouth, their upper galleries jutting over the street on stilts. Warm, thick air moved sluggishly in the street. Sweat trickled down the back of Karel's neck.

"Sir?"

Sir. He still hadn't got used to being called Sir, and, even less, to being called Sir by men who were older than him, and far more well-born. Both Gunvald and Ture were the sons of noblemen. *And I am the son of slaves.* But Lundegaard set less store in a man's birth than Osgaard did. King Magnas had shaken his hand, as if they were equals.

"Gunvald's waving at us, sir."

Karel glanced across the street, saw the armsman beckon, saw Prince Tomas grinning fiercely. His heartbeat quickened. He threaded his way through the oxcarts and wagons, Ture at his heels.

A young girl stood with Prince Tomas and Gunvald. Karel examined her as he approached. Perhaps ten years old, perhaps twelve. Long, dirty, tangled hair. Thin, smudged face. Threadbare boy's clothing too large for her. Bare feet. A street child. The girl's arms were crossed over her chest, her chin boldly lifted, but her feet were braced to run. *Brash façade, but wary.*

Karel ratcheted back his urgency. He slowed to a stroll, waved Ture back with one hand—*Don't crowd her*—made himself smile, ask casually, "What is it?"

"This is Goszia," Prince Tomas said. He rested his hand on the girl's shoulder. The girl stiffened slightly, as if hiding a flinch. "She saw half a dozen men carrying someone wrapped in a cloak."

"Did you, Goszia?" Karel tried to look relaxed and non-threatening. He hunkered down so that his eyes were level with the girl's. "When was this?"

Prince Tomas answered for her: "Yesterday morning, not long after dawn."

"How big was the person they were carrying?"

"Bigger'n me," the girl said.

"Did you see where they went?" Karel smiled encouragingly.

Goszia nodded, and glanced at Prince Tomas.

"The old one-handed merchant's house," Tomas said.

Karel blinked. "One-handed merchant?"

"Old, *scary*, one-handed merchant." Tomas's eyes met his for a moment. Karel understood the silent message. *Ex-Fithian. Possibly.*

Karel straightened to his full height. "Can you show us where his house is, Goszia?"

The girl nodded again.


THEY FOLLOWED GOSZIA down an alley, up a broad, busy thoroughfare, and along another alleyway, emerging into a street that ran down to the wharves. It was narrower and quieter than the one they'd started on. The girl halted. "Up there."

Karel crouched alongside her. "Which one, Goszia?"

"That one." Goszia pointed with her chin. Her bare feet shifted nervously. Her face was pinched, edgy, afraid. She didn't want to be here.

"What did the men look like?"

She lifted one shoulder in a tense shrug. "Like men."

"Old? Young?"

"Like you and him." She jerked her head to indicate the prince.

Karel stood and drew her back to the shelter of the alleyway. "Thank you, Goszia." He opened his money pouch and took out several coins.

Amazement flared on the girl's face. "Silver?" She snatched the coins from his hand and ran, her bare feet slapping on the ground, her tangled hair whipping behind her.

Prince Tomas went to the mouth of the alley and leaned casually there, gazing up the street. "High fence," he said. "Strong gate. No windows in the outer wall."

Karel joined him. The house looked no different from its neighbors: tall wooden fence enclosing a yard, upper story of a dwelling just visible, wooden shingles on the roof. Not dilapidated, not opulent. Ordinary. The house of a retired merchant. A retired, one-handed, scary merchant.

Karel flattened his lips to his teeth in a silent hiss. Fithian house.

His heart thudded loudly, insisting on action. He wanted to storm the gate, invade the house, rescue Princess Brigitta.

A pigeon swooped down to land within the walls.

"See that?" Prince Tomas muttered. "You said they communicated somehow."

"Yes." Karel took the prince's elbow and drew him back into the shadows of the alley.

"What now, sir?" Ture asked.

"Now we find out if she's still here."

"How?"

"Someone saw her arrive. Let's see if we can find anyone who's seen her leave. But discreetly. We must be *very* careful." One misstep, one question asked of the wrong person, and they'd be dead; however good the Lundegaardan armsmen were, Fithian assassins were better.

Karel eyed Prince Tomas. *Should I send him back to the ship?* If something went disastrously wrong, if they both died today, who would lead the mission to rescue the princess?

Ture took a step towards the street. Karel caught his arm. "No. We circle round till we're out of sight of that house. We don't go near it again unless we absolutely have to." Fithians would notice men loitering, staring. And if they noticed, they'd do something about it.


HE'D EXPECTED IT to be difficult, but it wasn't. The second person he spoke to, a vendor selling melons, told him all he needed to know.

Karel turned away from the man.

"Sir?" Ture said. "Prince Tomas is headed this way."

The prince was wearing his fierce grin again. "Half a dozen riders, all men. And a covered cart! Just after dawn this morning."

Karel nodded. "The vendor on the corner saw it, too. Dark brown canopy."

"Do you think she was in the cart, sir?" Gunvald asked.

"Yes." Karel ran through the equation in his head. *Half a dozen men arrive yesterday, carrying a person. Half a dozen men leave today, with a covered cart.* "They were never going to keep her here long. It's Harkeld they're after."

Princess Brigitta had passed this spot today. *Today.* He glanced at the sky. Dusk shaded it pink.

"Back to the ship!" He turned and headed down the street, almost running. They needed horses, supplies. They needed to know which gate she'd left by, which road she'd taken.

NIGHT HAD FALLEN by the time they reached the Lundegaardan vessel. The armsmen he'd sent to the town gates had returned. Karel listened intently to their reports, Prince Tomas at his shoulder.

"Six men and a covered cart, not long after dawn?" he said, when Lief finished speaking.

"Yes, sir." The man was massive, standing a head taller than the other armsmen.

"Any description of the men?"

Lief shook his head. "Didn't look like merchants. Not wearing uniforms. Could be anyone."

"Which gate?"

"The north-east, sir."

"Torkild, Arvid, you bought horses? Supplies?"

"Yes, sir. Twelve mounts. Supplies for two weeks and packhorses to carry them."

Urgency thrummed in Karel's blood. He wanted to order the armsmen to ride out now, this instant, even though it was pitch black outside. He took a deep breath. *Calm.* The Fithians were smart. He needed to be smarter, to make no mistakes.

"Excellent work, everyone." He looked around the cabin, meeting each man's eyes. "Tomorrow we go hunting."

# CHAPTER FIVE

BRITTA REGAINED CONSCIOUSNESS by degrees. Nausea first. Then hearing: the sound of wind in trees, men talking. Then smell: woodsmoke. Then, slowly, an awareness of each limb.

She lay for a long time, not bothering to open her eyes. Her stomach seemed to slosh from side to side. Her head ached. Her fingers and toes tingled.

After several hours, the tingle subsided. The headache didn't, or the nausea.

Finally she opened her eyes. Night. A blurry campfire that was tilted to one side.

Britta blinked, and blinked again. The campfire straightened itself slowly, became slightly clearer. Dimly, she saw long, dark shapes on the ground. It took several minutes before her sluggish brain recognized what they were: sleeping men wrapped in blankets.

Movement caught her slow attention. A watchman.

The watchman made two circuits of the fire and the sleeping Fithians, then halted beside her. Leather creaked as he crouched. A bowl and waterskin were placed beside her head.

The smell of food made bile rise in her throat.

The watchman stood with another soft creak of leather and resumed his soundless prowling of the campsite.

Britta moved stiffly, freeing her arms from the blanket she was wrapped in, pushing herself up to sit. She reached for the waterskin and lifted it with shaking hands. Water spilled on her face, trickled into her mouth, down her parched throat, and met the sloshing discomfort in her stomach.

She bent over, retching.

THE NEXT TIME she woke, it was dawn. Her head felt as if it had split in two. Her throat was too dry to swallow. Her stomach turned over and over inside her.

A figure stalked across the camp and stood above her, slanted at an impossible angle.

Pale gray eyes, flat face.

It took long seconds to recognize him. Leader.

He crouched. His hand reached for her face.

Britta reared back, scrabbling to free herself from the blankets, but he caught her easily. Fingers pinched her chin.

Britta bit Leader as hard as she could. Her teeth sank deep. The taste of blood blossomed on her tongue.

A cloth crammed against her nose. The smell of vanilla.

All-Mother's Breath.

Oblivion.

# CHAPTER SIX

KAREL AND HIS troop of armsmen reached the north-east gate not long after dawn. Karel spoke with the guard, and heard the same story Lief had told.

"Took this road, did they?"

"Yes, sir." The guard eyed the coin he held.

"Say where they were headed?"

"No, sir. I didn't ask."

"Anything stand out about them? One of the horses, one of the men, anything?"

"They had a cart," the guard said hopefully.

"What kind of cart?"

The guard shrugged with his face. "A covered one."

"What color was the canopy?"

"Brown. Dark brown."

"Were they carrying weapons?"

"Yes, sir. Looked like they knew how to use them, too."

"Young? Old?"

The guard's gaze flicked over the armsmen's faces. "'Bout the same as you lot."

Karel nodded. He flicked the coin in the air. It spun twice before the guard caught it.

They rode through the gate with a clatter of hooves. Karel fought the compulsion to spur his horse. He set their pace at a canter. There was no need to gallop. They'd catch up with the Fithians.

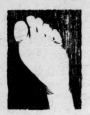

# CHAPTER SEVEN

MRELK HADN'T CHANGED. The mud-brick houses baking in the afternoon heat, the insects, the wrinkled, gray-skinned men sleeping with the dogs on the riverbank. Loomath hadn't changed either. He was as stooped and bald and bad-tempered as he'd been before. "Well?"

"The prince lives," Bennick said.

Loomath's mouth became even sourer. "Nolt?"

"Dead. They're all dead."

The old man grunted. "Here and gone."

"I need to send a message."

Loomath turned towards his house. His left arm hung bent and scarred at his side. "The boy waits outside."

Jaumé watched Bennick cross the dirt yard, his curly red-blond hair bright in the sunlight. When both men had disappeared into the house, he led the horses to the water trough. What should he do now they were back in Mrelk? Go with Bennick and become a Brother? Leave him?

Jaumé watched the horses drink. Being alone was frightening. People stole from you, hurt you. He remembered the youths who'd robbed him of his money. He remembered the hollow-eyed man who'd demanded his bread.

He didn't want to leave Bennick.

Jaumé stood in the dusty, humid yard. His feet were bare, and he almost thought he could feel the curse creeping through the soil towards him. Memories crowded into his head—Da's mad face, Rosa's scream, the scent of Mam's blood, the village burning.

Jaumé made a fist and pressed his knuckles hard to his forehead, forcing the memories out of his skull. He didn't want to remember those things. There was no curse in Mrelk. Not yet. Not ever, if Prince Harkeld lived long enough.

He glanced at the door Bennick had vanished through. Bennick had rescued him, fed him, given him his own knife and taught him how to use it. Bennick looked after him, and he looked after Bennick. That was how it worked. They were friends. They were almost-Brothers.

But he didn't want Bennick to kill the prince.


JAUMÉ HUNKERED DOWN in the shade, his back to the trough, and waited. It wasn't long before Bennick came out of the house. He was grinning.

"On your feet, lad. We're leaving immediately." He turned to Loomath. "You have a sword small enough for him?"

Loomath's mouth twisted. "He has a mark against him."

"Nolt erased it. He saved our lives."

"Nolt's dead."

"The boy saved us from the breathstealers." Bennick's grin was gone. There was a hard edge to his voice that Jaumé didn't recognize. "Get a sword."

Jaumé shivered. He didn't ever want Bennick to speak to him like that.

Loomath didn't shiver. His mouth twisted even more sourly. He turned away without a word and went into his house.

Bennick sniffed. "Old bastard." He examined the horses. "We'll take the pony and... none of these." He strode across to the stables. Jaumé trotted at his heels.

The stables were dark and smelled of hay. The horses they'd left behind were standing in the stalls. "Those two packhorses, and that bay mare for me," Bennick said, pointing. He swung around and crossed to the packsaddles piled by one wall. "We'll need our warm clothes, too."

*Where are we going?* But Jaumé didn't utter the words aloud. Bennick didn't like it when he asked too many questions.

# CHAPTER EIGHT

BRITTA FLOATED BACK to consciousness. She was a bubble rising through dark water. Slowly, grudgingly, clarity arrived. Woodsmoke. Silence. Tingling fingers. Aching head. Churning stomach.

Tonight, the watchman took longer to notice she was awake. Finally, she heard the crunch of soil beneath boots, the faint creak of leather as he crouched alongside her.

The assassin caught her head, anchoring her in place. Fingers pulled her mouth open. Water trickled down her throat.

Britta convulsed, retching. To her shame, when the paroxysms had finished, she was crying.

Whoever held her head let go. She was floating again.

Footsteps. The sound of men's voices. Snatches of sentences.

"—it's the All-Mother's Breath—"

"—no use to us if she dies—"

"Enough." That voice she recognized: Leader's.

She drifted away from them. The voices receded into silence.

# CHAPTER NINE

OUDHEES, THE MOST easterly of Roubos's northern ports. The harbor was chaotic beneath a sullen dawn sky. Ships jostled for space. The mages' ship inched its way forward, finally claiming a berth. Prince Harkeld stood at the railing and gazed down. Despite the early hour, the wharf teemed with people. The sound they made came to his ears, a babble that rose and fell. Ordinary noises—people shouting, children calling out, babies wailing—but with an edge of desperation to them, strident and off-pitch. The people milling on the wharf were refugees. Fleeing the curse that crept westward across the continent.

One of the mages came to stand beside him. Rand. "You see the curse shadows?"

Harkeld stared down at the refugees. "Yes." The curse shadows looked like black cobwebs, clinging to hair and skin. He'd worn those shadows himself, for years, and not seen them until today. It seemed impossible that he could have been so blind.

"When we set foot on land, the shadows will start to settle on us again."

Harkeld nodded. The shadows lay on everyone in the Seven Kingdoms, promise of the fate that advanced towards them: madness, death.

The curse shadows covered eyes, noses, mouths. How could the people down there breathe? Why were they not smothering to death?

"The shadows will rest lightly on us until we drink the water. Then, they'll darken. We'll look like them."

Harkeld's skin tightened in a shiver. *I won't drink the water*. But he had to. Water was life.

Except here, where water would very soon bring death.

"When we reach the curse itself, we expect the shadows to become even thicker and darker." Rand paused, glanced at him. "You have any questions?"

"No."

"Malle, Gretel, and I are going ashore. There are things that need to be done before we head east. You stay on board. Oren and Serril don't think there are any Fithians in the crowd, but that doesn't mean there aren't."

Fithian assassins. Harkeld touched his chest, felt the thin ridge of scar tissue over his heart. Fithians had tried to kill him, and Innis had saved him.

Innis.

Harkeld rubbed the scar. Deceitful, lying witch. Taking the shape of a man, pretending to be his armsman, Justen. Pretending to be his friend. He couldn't think of a name bad enough for her.

And yet he owed Innis his life. But for her, he'd have died, an arrow through his heart.

"I have your word you won't go ashore?"

"Yes."

He followed Rand with his eyes as the healer walked away. Rand was lean, middle-aged, as brown and weather-beaten as one of last year's oak leaves, with deep laughter lines creasing his skin. It was difficult to dislike Rand, but even so... *You deceived me. You knew Justen wasn't real.*

Most of the mages were on deck. Harkeld's gaze skipped from person to person. How fresh and pale their skin seemed without the curse shadows, even the male shapeshifters who were deeply tanned, Petrus and Hedín and black-bearded Serril.

Petrus. Harkeld scowled. Petrus had pretended to be Justen, too.

How could you trust people who lied to you? Who pretended to be people they weren't?

At least he could tell when the mages were shapeshifted now, could see the glimmer of magic surrounding them, glinting on feather or fur. They couldn't play that trick on him again.

Harkeld scanned the sky, looking for shapeshifters. There was one, a swallow, flying over the crowd in swift darts. Oren, perhaps, or the real Justen.

His scowl deepened. *Liars, all of them.*

He looked out across Oudhees. Wooden buildings. Forested hills. Dark thunderheads piling in the early morning sky. The weight of the clouds seemed to press heavily on town and wharf. The air was humid, heavy, thick. There was a sense of impending doom, as if soil and water and air knew the curse was coming.

None of the refugees could see the curse shadows covering them. They were what he'd once been: oblivious to magic. But they knew the continent was cursed, knew that death advanced westwards towards them.

Harkeld gazed down at the wharf. Were there any assassins in the crowd, looking up at him, eager to claim the bounty on his head?

Another shiver crawled over his skin. He pushed away from the railing and strode across the deck, ignoring the mages, and clattered down the ladder to the dark, cramped hold. He lay in his hammock and stared up at the low ceiling. Another month and his task would be done, Ivek's curse destroyed, the Seven Kingdoms saved.

The Fithians would stop hunting him.

He'd be rid of his magic. Rid of the mages.

*One more month. One more month, and it will all be over.*

# CHAPTER TEN

MID-MORNING, THEY came to a town. Douw was its name. Karel sent the armsmen to ask questions at the gates. Dag returned shaking his head, and a few minutes later, tall Lief. "Nothing, sir."

Karel waited, striving for patience. *Calm. Don't fidget with the reins.* But his mount had caught his mood, shifting its weight from hoof to hoof.

A cross-shaped wooden structure stood to one side of the market square. The crossarm was made of two pieces of timber, with rusted hinges and round holes. It took a few seconds before Karel recognized it for what it was: a pillory.

A dog trotted across the market square, lifted its leg against the pillory, then sat and began scratching itself, its tail thumping in the dirt, a grimace on its face.

"You heard the one about Ma Grondal and her dog?" Dag asked.

The armsmen turned their heads and looked at him expectantly. Prince Tomas sidled closer on his horse.

"Well, Ma Grondal was fetching water from the well when the watch captain came up to her and said, 'Ma Grondal, about your dog, you need to keep him tied up. Yesterday he chased a man on a horse.'

"'Oh, that can't have been *my* dog, captain!'" Dag placed his hand on his chest, fingers outspread, a gesture so feminine that Karel grinned.

"The watch captain said, 'I'm certain it was him, Ma Grondal.' And Ma Grondal said, 'But, captain, my dog can't ride a horse!'"

Karel laughed, turned his head, saw Ture trotting towards them, and sobered instantly.

"Six men and a covered cart, sir," Ture said. "They took the east road."

"When?"

"Yesterday, sir. Early afternoon."

*We're gaining.* Karel glanced at the armsmen, counting them—four, six, nine. Who was missing? Solveig. He scanned the market square. It was hard to lose a man six feet tall with a long, blond plait down his back. "Anyone seen Solveig?"

"Pissing," Bjarne said, with a jerk of his thumb, and sure enough, there was Solveig, half-hidden in the shade, pissing against a crumbling wall.

"You heard the one about the man who pissed on an ants' nest?" he heard Dag say, as Solveig hurried back and swung up into his saddle.

Karel clicked his tongue, urging his mount forward. The dog stopped scratching and watched as they trotted past, harnesses jingling.

# CHAPTER ELEVEN

BRITTA SLOWLY WOKE. The surface she lay on rocked and swayed beneath her. A rattling noise reverberated in her ears. Her eyelids were almost too heavy to lift. She saw brown fabric stretched above her head. For a moment she stared at it blankly, and then understanding arrived. She was in a cart.

She blinked gritty eyes. Her throat was raw, her head throbbing, her stomach aching, but it was daytime and she was awake. They hadn't drugged her with All-Mother's Breath.

Because they didn't want her to die?

Britta closed her eyes and lay unmoving, exhausted, while the cart rattled and lurched its way towards Harkeld. *I can't just let them take me to him. I have to fight, run away, do something.*

Run away? How could she run when it took effort just to lie here and breathe?

The cart halted. She heard the crunch of footsteps on gravel. A pause. Then the sound of fabric being drawn aside. The daylight came brighter. She had a sense that it was late morning. The cart swayed as someone clambered aboard. A face loomed in her vision. The Fithian with brown curly hair.

An emotion flickered across Curly's face when he saw she was awake. Relief?

Curly cupped a hand behind her head and pressed the mouthpiece of a waterskin to her lips. Water trickled into her mouth, slid down her parched, painful throat.

Britta drank thirstily. Her stomach churned for a moment, uneasily, and then settled.

Curly gave a grunt, an almost soundless exhalation, and poured more water down her throat. Then he lowered her head, crawled out of the cart, closed the flap.

A few words, spoken too fast for her to hear. Footsteps. The cart lurched forward again.

Thoughts crawled in Britta's head, slowly coalescing into a solid purpose. She must not let them drug her again.


SHE DRIFTED IN and out of sleep, while the cart rocked and swayed and rattled. Bait. Her thoughts kept returning to that word: bait. She was bait, and the Fithians were going to use her. How?

She remembered Jaegar's words: *Harkeld was always fond of you. He'll pause his little quest long enough to save you.*

Jaegar was right. Harkeld would try to save her. And the assassins would kill him. And Jaegar would use Harkeld's hands and blood to hold the other kingdoms to ransom: yield sovereignty to him, or be overrun by the curse.

The movement of the cart lulled her towards sleep. With effort, Britta hauled herself back, focused. How to escape?

It would be easier if she was on horseback, not in a cart. But how could she make the Fithians give her a horse?

Her thoughts looped slowly, pondering this question. After a while, an answer drifted by: Carriage sickness.

THE CART HALTED. The flap drew back. She caught a glimpse of sky. The sun was high. Noon. A Fithian clambered aboard. Not Curly this time, but the one with pox scars pitting his face. As well as a waterskin, he had a slice of bread and cheese.

Britta's stomach squeezed with hunger.

She levered herself up on one elbow. Pox held out the waterskin.

Britta took several thirsty gulps. Water slopped down her chin.

Pox put the slice of bread and cheese down on the floorboards and turned to go.

*Quick, while he's still here.*

Britta grabbed the food, chewed hastily—and gagged as best she could, spilling the half-chewed bread and cheese from her mouth.

Pox turned back, a frown on his face.

Britta retched again. Her stomach obliged with a genuine heave. She coughed, gagged, retched—and lay shakily back on the blanket, hugging her stomach.

Pox retreated from the cart, but the vehicle didn't lurch forward. The flap opened again. Leader climbed aboard.

Britta closed her eyes. She tried to lie limply, to not tense.

She heard a faint sound, as if Leader breathed out through his nose with impatience, then a rustle, then the noise of someone jumping down from the cart, the crunch of boots on a gritty road.

Britta slitted her eyes open. The mess she'd made was gone; Leader had wiped it up.


THE CART STOPPED again in the afternoon. This time it was Leader who brought the waterskin and food. Britta's chest constricted at sight of his flat-cheeked face, his cold, gray eyes. *I can't do it. He'll know I'm pretending.* And then she saw the bandage on Leader's right hand, where she'd bitten him yesterday.

The fear dissolved. A tiny sliver of glee took its place. *I hurt him.*

Leader thrust the waterskin at her.

Britta obediently drank.

When she lowered the skin, Leader held out a piece of bread.

Britta shook her head.

Leader's face became even flatter, his eyes even colder. "Eat."

Britta hesitated, then took the piece of bread. She bit into it.

Leader watched, narrow-eyed.

Britta chewed until the bread was paste in her mouth. Her fear returned, growing in her stomach, rising up her throat. Now was the moment, now she had to fool Leader.

*I can't.*

She'd duped her half-brother Jaegar, and Jaegar had been as dangerous as Leader, would have killed her just as easily.

Britta heard the memory of Karel's voice in her ear: *You can do it, princess. I know you can.*

Britta pretended to swallow, to gag. She opened her mouth and spat the bread-paste out, coughing and heaving, hugging her stomach, then sank back on her blankets.

She risked a glance at Leader. He was staring at her, even more narrow-eyed than before. A gob of chewed-up bread had landed on his trews.

"Carriage sickness," Britta mumbled, wiping her chin. She closed her eyes, trying to look wretched.

There was a long moment of silence. Leader was watching her, she knew. She felt his gaze boring into her. Her skin seemed to stretch tightly with apprehension. If he touched her, she would split open.

Leader made a rustle of movement. Britta flinched. Her eyes opened.

Leader's back was to her. He swung down from the cart. She saw a wedge of sky before the flap dropped down. The cart lurched forward.

Britta's tension slowly released. Her skin stretched less tightly, her stomach unclenched.

It took a few moments to realize that Leader had left the waterskin and the rest of the bread.

Bread.

Hunger cramped painfully in her belly, as if her intestines wrapped themselves around one another and squeezed. How much longer would she have to refuse food before they let her travel on horseback?

Britta closed her eyes, shutting out sight of the bread. She held tightly to Karel's voice. *You can do it, princess.*

# CHAPTER TWELVE

As DAYLIGHT DRAINED from the sky, a village came
into view. They rode through the gate at a weary
trot and halted in the market square. Karel glanced
around. Wooden houses, dirt streets. "Gunvald, find
us an inn. Solveig, Lief, Bjarne, ask questions at the
other gates. Meet back here."

He dismounted stiffly and led his horse to the
well at the center of the square. Hooves clopped on
packed dirt as the rest of the armsmen followed.

The well was built of stone and had a small,
peaked roof of slate tiles. Half a dozen battered tin
cups sat on the rim.

Karel lowered the bucket to the bottom with
a splash and hauled it up several times, filling the
water trough. The horses snorted and shouldered
one another, jostling for space, drinking thirstily.

Karel pulled the bucket up again, set it on the
stone rim, and reached for one of the cups. He held
it out to Prince Tomas. "Drink?"

"After you."

Karel snorted under his breath. He might command
this mission, but Tomas would always outrank him.
He put the cup down in front of the prince and

picked up another one for himself. He examined the square as he drank. A large bell hung from a post. Buckets were stacked upside down alongside. He looked at the bell and the buckets for a moment, then realized what they were: fire bell, fire buckets.

Karel drained the cup, and inspected the four corners of the market square. Had the Fithian assassins halted here? Drunk from this well? Had the princess?

Solveig trotted up, wearily slid from his horse. "They didn't leave through the northern gate, sir."

Karel nodded, and gave the armsman his cup.

Next was Bjarne, with a shake of his head. "Nothing, sir."

Lief rode up, his grin visible in the gathering dusk. "They left through the eastern gate, sir. Cart covered with brown fabric, and six men. Mid-afternoon."

THEY ATE IN the taproom—thick sausages bursting out of their skins, stewed cabbage, mashed potatoes— and washed the food down with golden ale.

Karel leaned back in his chair, and glanced down the table. Dag and Ture had found a game of King's Leap. They were making a show of it, jumping each other's pieces rashly, baring their teeth in mock aggression. The other armsmen laughed, urging the players on. Even quiet Gunvald was leaning over the board, making suggestions.

There was no division between the armsmen that he could see, even though their backgrounds differed markedly. Several were the sons of noblemen, but most were commoners. Bjarne's father was a stonemason, tall Lief was the son of a baker, and Dag and Solveig came from fishing villages.

In Lundegaard, men were judged by their merit, not their birth. He remembered King Magnas, remembered the way the king had clasped his hand.

"We stand out like seagulls in a rook colony."

Karel glanced sideways at Prince Tomas, shrugged. "Can't be helped."

It wasn't the armsmen's high spirits that made them stand out; it was their coloring. One tall, blond man would be conspicuous in this taproom, let alone ten. And then there was Solveig's long plait of hair. And Bjarne's beard.

Karel eyed Bjarne. The armsman had washed his beard and combed it and plaited it into two short braids. "It's Bjarne," he said. "Without that beard, we'd blend right in."

Prince Tomas snorted into his ale.

"Think I should tell Bjarne to cut it off?"

Tomas grinned. "Good luck with that."

Karel grunted and leaned further back in his chair. His relaxation was on the surface, no deeper than his skin. His muscles, his ligaments, even his bones, were tight with tension. He counted the miles separating them from the princess in his head. How many more days before they caught up with her? He glanced around the taproom again, his gaze skimming over the locals—dark-haired, olive-skinned—before coming to rest on the armsmen. As he watched, Ture jumped his way across the board and let out a crow of triumph.

The armsmen laughed. So did Prince Tomas.

Ture began to set up the board again. Dag picked up his tankard, drained it, wiped his mouth. "Did you hear the one about the man on his deathbed? Cocky little bastard called Ture, he was."

Ture glanced up and grinned, but didn't pause in laying out the pieces.

"So Ture was on his deathbed breathing his last, and his beautiful young wife, Anka, said, 'Ture, please tell me... is there anything I can do for you?'"

Ture glanced up again. The wary gleam in his eye told Karel that there really was an Anka.

"'There *is* something,' Dag said, in a croaking voice. "'After I die, it would mean so much to me if you would marry my best friend, Dag.'"

Ture snorted and turned his attention back to the pieces on the board.

"Anka took Ture's hand and clasped it to her breast. 'My dearest darling'"—Dag's voice was a high-pitched coo—"'You have nothing to worry about. We've been planning that for a long time now.'"

Even Ture joined in the laughter, grinning and shaking his head.

Karel didn't laugh. He thought about the look in Ture's eyes. Was Anka his sweetheart? His wife? Would Ture ever see her again?

His gaze slid over the armsmen's faces. The men had all volunteered. They knew what they were up against. They knew some of them would die.

And some would live.

He glanced at Prince Tomas, saw the scarred cheek, the missing ear. The prince had faced Fithians before. Faced them and survived—and volunteered for more. *Because he sees this as a heroic quest. Rescuing the beautiful princess.* And then he looked down at his ale and wondered if he was being too harsh. Princess Brigitta had saved Lundegaard from invasion. Perhaps Tomas felt he owed it to her to rescue her?

*Or maybe he wants to win her hand?*

For a moment he almost hated the prince—then common-sense asserted itself. If Princess Brigitta ever married again, Tomas would be a good husband. A thousand times better than Duke Rikard had been. Tomas was good-humored, courageous, honorable. He'd never bed the princess forcibly, as Rikard had done.

# CHAPTER THIRTEEN

THE CART HALTED. From the clink of harnesses being removed, they were stopping for the night. Britta reached for the waterskin, gulped a few mouthfuls, then lay back in her dirty nest of blankets, curled up like a child. Half an hour passed before someone climbed into the cart. She kept her eyes closed.

A Fithian gathered her up in her blankets and passed her down to someone. She was carried a dozen paces, laid on the ground, and left. From nearby came the low murmur of voices and the scent of meat cooking. Her mouth watered. Her stomach tied itself in a knot of hunger. After several minutes, she opened her eyes fractionally. Darkness, a campfire, the shapes of seated men.

Britta closed her eyes again and lay as if asleep. Her long plait was uncomfortably coiled beneath her, digging into her arm.

Her hunger grew more intense with each passing minute, and, matching it, her resolve. She would starve to death, if that's what it took to get out of the cart and onto a horse.

But she knew the Fithians wouldn't let her starve; they needed her alive.

Footsteps approached. Two people. They crouched alongside her with a creak of boot leather. The smell of meat wafted to her nose. The knot of hunger in her belly twisted tighter.

A hand gripped her shoulder, shook her.

Britta stayed limp and unresponsive.

Whoever it was made an impatient sound. He took hold of her plait, dragging her head up. Hard fingers gripped her jaw, opened her mouth. A spoon pushed between her lips. Liquid spilled onto her tongue, warm and fragrant.

Broth. Meat broth.

Britta swallowed, a greedy instinctive gulp, and then intellect took over: *No. Don't eat.*

The spoon pushed into her mouth again. Britta tried to spit the broth out, to gag. Her pretend choking became real for several seconds. She coughed and spluttered, fighting for breath, struggling weakly in the men's grip, trying to pull away from the hand holding her jaw, the hand holding her hair.

Britta caught her breath, then willed herself to go limp, to pretend she was sliding back into unconsciousness. She sagged, her plait pulling painfully in the assassin's grip.

The spoon didn't invade her mouth again. Instead, the two men laid her on the ground, pulled the blankets up around her throat, and left.

The plait was even more uncomfortable beneath her now, but Britta didn't move. She lay as if dead, savoring the taste of broth on her tongue.

\*   \*   \*

THE NIGHT PASSED with agonizing slowness. Hunger gnawed at Britta's innards, keeping sleep at bay. The plait grew more and more uncomfortable. It was an iron chain, digging into her arm and ribs, but she dared not move. *Unconscious. I'm unconscious.* Once or twice she thought she heard the faint creak of boot leather as a watchman prowled past, but no one tried to make her eat again. At last, dawn arrived. Faint light filtered through her closed eyelids. Britta lay listening to the sounds of horses being harnessed.

Footsteps approached. Someone crouched and gathered her in his arms, blankets and all. Britta willed herself to stay limp.

She was lifted high, higher—the Fithian carrying her grunted with effort—someone else took her, settled her into... a saddle. An assassin's arm was tight around her waist, her head lolled against his chest.

Elation fizzed in her blood. *I'm on horseback!*

# CHAPTER FOURTEEN

HARKELD STOOD NEAR the head of the gangplank, waiting. The deck was wet, the thunderheads gone from the sky, but the early morning air was as thick and heavy and humid and full of impending doom as it had been yesterday. *They call this winter?*

The horses, hardy survivors of desert and jungle, had been unloaded. Mages clustered around him. Shapeshifters circled as birds in the sky. He could tell who the hawks were by their size and color. Small and dark: Innis. Large, with pale underwings and breast: Petrus. The swooping swallows were harder to distinguish, the flitting sparrows impossible. He knew they were mages by the magic glinting on their feathers, but not who they were. Serril, Justen, Hedín, Oren.

He glanced at the circling hawks again. Innis and Petrus were the last survivors of the mages who'd come to his father's palace three months ago. The mages who'd turned his life upside down.

Harkeld grimaced and looked away from the birds. His gaze skimmed the mages surrounding him. Three healers, four fire mages, two water mages. How many of them would still be alive next month?

"You know your places?" Rand asked.

Harkeld nodded. He'd go ashore second to last, trailing at the end as if he was unimportant. Thayer, the young, dark-haired healer, would disembark in the middle. *Pretending to be me.* He glanced at Thayer. He seemed unconcerned by his role as decoy.

"Let's go," Rand said.

Harkeld watched the mages file down the gangplank. Thayer set foot on the wharf. No one darted from the crowd and tried to kill him. A fire mage disembarked, a water mage, a healer, another fire mage, and then it was his turn. He walked down the long, swaying gangplank and stepped ashore. The noise and smell of the crowd enveloped him. He breathed shallowly, trying not inhale the odor of desperation and fear and people gone too long without washing. Curse shadows surrounded him. Someone buffeted him on his right and he jerked sideways as if burned and almost lost his balance. The mage behind him stepped closer, the shapeshifters swooped low, but no attack came.

They pushed their way slowly through the crowd. Harkeld kept his arms close to his sides; he didn't want to touch any of these curse-shadowed people. But it was impossible not to. He flinched each time he brushed past someone, flinches he tried to hide, but couldn't. He imagined the shapeshifters laughing scornfully as they hovered overhead and gritted his teeth, felt his cheeks grow hot with mortification— then noticed that the fire mage ahead of him, Gretel, also shied from the curse shadows.

Once past the press of people, they moved faster, off the wharf, along a side street, into the stableyard of an inn. The horses waited—riding horses saddled, packhorses loaded with the supplies Rand had bought yesterday.

Harkeld went to the bay mare he'd ridden in Ankeny. The horse huffed a breath at him and nuzzled his shoulder. He stroked her neck. Poor beast. She had no inkling of the journey that lay ahead. She didn't understand Fithian assassins, or curses that sent people mad with bloodlust. She headed into danger without knowing it.

Or perhaps the mare was to be envied? Perhaps it was better not to know what the future held?

# CHAPTER FIFTEEN

THE ASSASSINS STOPPED mid-morning. Britta allowed herself to stir to alertness, to blink her eyes open and look around. The arm holding her tightened, and the man—she couldn't see his face—handed her a waterskin. She drank thirstily.

One of the other riders nudged his horse close. Curly. He held out another waterskin. "Broth," he said. "Drink."

Britta obeyed.

The broth was lukewarm, fragrant. Its flavor filled her mouth.

Britta gulped it hungrily.

SHE DIDN'T FEIGN sleep again, but watched the countryside, leaning into the assassin's body heat. It was uncomfortably intimate—his arm warm and strong around her, her cheek resting against his chest—and also oddly protective. Britta felt safe, as if it was Karel who held her, and he would shield her from anything. But this man would protect her only until her usefulness had been served—and then he would kill her.

Kill her, and kill Harkeld, and take Harkeld's blood and hands back to Osgaard, so that Jaegar could force the other kingdoms to bow to his rule.

Britta shivered. *I have to escape.*


IN THE AFTERNOON, they passed through a town. It wasn't until several hours later, when they halted in a copse not far from the road, that Britta realized the cart and one of the assassins were no longer with them.

The Fithian whose mount she'd shared lowered her from the saddle. Britta leaned against the horse and clung to the stirrup, pretending to be weaker than she was. She glanced up. The man was nondescript: mouse-brown hair cut close to his skull, an unremarkable face. She had no name for him yet.

Curly took her arm, his fingers pinching like a manacle around her elbow, and walked her to the trees. Britta staggered and clutched at him, feigning dizziness. Curly halted. "Sit."

Britta sat, a half-collapse.

Curly handed her a waterskin. "Broth," he said. "Drink it." There was no compassion in his voice, no compassion in his eyes. *I am a thing to him, not a person.*

Britta obeyed, sipping the broth when her stomach demanded that she guzzle it. She watched the Fithians unsaddle the horses, light a fire, set up their camp. Each man worked quietly, efficiently. They rarely spoke, seeming to use gestures as often as words. A secret, silent assassin language?

Leader's right hand was still bandaged. He favored it as he worked. Britta felt a bubble of glee in her chest. She'd hurt him. And she would hurt him again, if she could. Kill him, if she could... Here, her thoughts faltered. She hadn't the skill to kill any of these men. They'd laugh at her if she tried.

But she could escape. *Would* escape.

Her gaze skipped over the men. Leader. Curly. She needed names for the others. The nondescript Fithian could be Plain. And the one missing several front teeth, Gap-Tooth. The fifth Fithian was pale and skinny, his muscles ropy, his cheekbones sharp. But Skinny wasn't a name that suited him; he was almost as frightening as Leader. His ice-blue eyes had an edge of madness to them. Looking at him made the tiny hairs on the back of her neck prick upright.

Killer. That was the name that suited him.

Leader had never set Killer to guard her. Was he the least predictable of the men? The most dangerous?

Britta averted her eyes from Killer and scanned the campsite. Pox was gone, along with the cart. Why? She puzzled over this question while she sipped the broth.

The question was answered not long afterwards. Pox rode out of the dusk. Instead of the cart, he had a second horse with him, a small, sturdy piebald mare.

Britta's heart gave a kick in her chest. *For me?*

POX DISMOUNTED. HE tossed a sack to Leader. Britta tried to guess what was inside. Food? It didn't look heavy.

Leader strode to her and dropped the sack at her feet. He unsheathed his heavy throwing knife and crouched, reaching for her head.

Fear squeaked in Britta's throat. She recoiled instinctively.

Leader snatched her plait and wrapped it around his fist, holding it painfully taut. "Don't move." He sawed through her hair, so close to her skull that she almost felt the blade.

The painful pull ceased. Leader rose from his crouch. He kicked the sack towards her. "Clothes. Get changed, or I'll strip you and do it myself." He walked away, the plait dangling like a dead snake in his hand.

Britta touched her hair. It was short, ragged, the longest strands finger-length. She should be horrified, feel violated, but instead there was a strange sense of... liberation? No one could bind a crown to her head now. *I'm no longer an Osgaardan princess.*

BRITTA OPENED THE sack. Inside it were trews, a shirt, a sheepskin vest, a cloak. Thick woolen socks and leather boots. *I'm to be a man.*

She stripped out of her stained, stinking gown and chemise, trying not to feel self-conscious. The Fithians didn't see her as a woman, there was nothing sexual in the way they looked at her, but even so, she tried to hide her nudity beneath the cloak as she struggled into the shirt and trews. With sleeves and trouser legs rolled up, the clothes fitted. The fabric was a sturdy cotton. Britta pulled on the socks and shrugged into the sheepskin vest. The hide faced outward, cured but undyed, and the wool curled warmly against her shirt. Peasants' garb, practical and warm and hard-wearing—and more comfortable than the heavy silks and stiff gold-embroidered robes she'd worn as a princess. She buttoned the vest, snuggling into its warmth, and looked at the piebald mare.

*Tomorrow I escape.*

# CHAPTER SIXTEEN

HARKELD RODE HUNCHED beneath his cloak. Moisture trickled down the back of his neck. His hair was wet beneath the hood, his clothes were soaked. The woolen cloak hung from his shoulders, saturated and heavy. His breeches clung to his thighs, his boots were filled with water, rain dripped off his nose. The mare's hooves made sucking sounds as she slogged across a muddy field and through a copse of sodden trees. Harkeld clenched his teeth and stared at his horse's ears, and endured. *One more month*, he told himself. One more month and he could go wherever he wanted. No mages, no curse, no Fithian assassins. And no rain. He imagined a crisp Osgaardan winter, with blue skies and white snow. Fur-lined boots. Roaring fires. Hot, spiced wine.

But he couldn't go back to Osgaard or Lundegaard, not now he was known to have witch blood. Even once the healers stripped his magic from him, as they'd promised they would, he'd still be thought of as a witch. He'd have to sail north to the Allied Kingdoms, where mages weren't hunted and killed.

The mare halted.

Harkeld raised his head. Ahead, the riders had come to a standstill in the middle of a bare field. Through the encroaching dusk he saw a naked shapeshifter standing in the mud, gesturing as he talked. Petrus, his white-blond hair plastered to his skull.

The mages conferred. Harkeld didn't try to get closer and listen.

Petrus shifted into a hawk again. His feathers were saturated, bedraggled. He flapped slowly up into the darkening sky.

HARKELD HAD EXPECTED they'd pitch wet tents in the mud, but Petrus led them to a cart track, and then a wretched, dripping hamlet. A barrel-chested black dog barked once at them, then trotted alongside the horses, its tail held high. Magic shimmered over its muddy flanks. It was the big, black-bearded shapeshifter, Serril.

The hamlet boasted a tavern, a ramshackle wooden building with a stableyard of filthy, churned mud. A peasants' tavern, little better than a hovel. Harkeld thought of the marble and gold palace he'd grown up in and gave a silent, sour grunt of laughter.

Rand nudged his horse alongside Harkeld's. "Serril and Petrus have searched the village. There's no sign of assassins. Petrus says the inn is half-empty. Two families fleeing Sault, and that's all."

Harkeld nodded.

The black dog was gone, but three crows perched on the wooden shingle roof, staring down at them, magic glinting on their wet feathers.

Harkeld dismounted. His waterlogged boots squelched in ankle-deep mud. Cursed rain. They'd had enough of it in Ankeny. Why couldn't it snow? Clean, crisp snow, like they had in Osgaard.

He helped with the horses, brushed them down with handfuls of straw, fed and watered them, then followed Rand and the gray-haired water mage, Malle, inside. The sleeping quarters were cramped and primitive, a dark room lined with hard wooden bunks. The room smelled of mold and sweat and urine. *A bedchamber fit for a prince*, Harkeld thought, then snorted under his breath. Who was he kidding? He wasn't a prince. He hadn't been one since his father placed the bounty on his head. He was an outcast. A mixed-blood fugitive. He didn't even have his own name any more. Too risky, with every Fithian assassin in the Seven Kingdoms hunting him. The mages called him Flin. Flin, a safe, peasant-like name no assassin would recognize. And this was a safe, malodorous bunkroom in a safe, filthy hovel no assassin would expect to find him in.

EVERY ITEM IN Harkeld's packsaddle was wet. He stripped off his sodden clothes, dressed in damp ones from his packsaddle, and headed for the taproom. A fire burned in the grate. Woodsmoke stained the low ceiling black. Dirty straw lay on the floor. A party of men, women, and children ate around a long wooden table. Their clothing was travel-stained, but the decorative embroidery at cuffs and hems was expensive. They ate silently, their faces weary beneath the curse shadows.

Harkeld sat at the only other table in the taproom. Two of the new fire mages, both women, were already there. Signy and Gretel. He sat as far from them as he could. They hadn't lied to him yet, but that was only because he hadn't given them the chance. Mages were all liars. He'd learned *that*.

The table filled up. Rand. The other two fire mages, Bode and Davin. The healers Nellis and Thayer. The water mage, Malle, and her journeyman, Adel. Harkeld ignored them all.

Serril joined them. He was built like a draft horse, tall, broad in the shoulder, broad in the chest, with a black beard trimmed close to his jaw. He shared leadership with Rand, although he was only in his thirties. Harkeld ignored him, too.

An unkempt serving woman brought tankards of ale and bowls of thick, steaming soup.

Harkeld stared at the soup. Chunks of meat and turnips floated in it. His stomach was hollow with hunger, but he didn't pick up his spoon. Soup was made with water, wasn't it? And so was ale? His skin was already gray with the shadow of Ivek's curse. If he ate the soup, drank the ale, his curse shadow would become dark.

Someone sat opposite him at the table.

Harkeld glanced up. Petrus and Justen. The real Justen. The person the shapeshifters had pretended to be for three months.

Justen grinned at him. "Ach, it's good to be out of the rain, isn't it?"

Harkeld looked back down at his soup. Justen— this Justen—had only joined them two weeks ago. He'd had nothing to do with the deception. But it was his face the shapeshifters had used, his accent, and seeing him, hearing him say "Ach" brought Harkeld's humiliation flooding back.

*They played me for a fool.*

Harkeld picked up his spoon and stabbed the steaming soup. He still had half a waterskin from the ship. He could skip dinner, keep his curse shadow faint for one more night.

The smell of meat and vegetables drifted up. His stomach knotted, telling him he was hungry.

Harkeld put the spoon down and glanced at the refugees. The curse shadows shrouding them were thick and dark. Several of the mages had dark shadows, too; they'd drunk the water here. Others, like Petrus, glowering at him, and Justen, who'd lost his grin, still had gray curse shadows; they'd only drunk water from the ship.

Innis entered the taproom. The curse shadow covering her was thin and gray.

Harkeld looked back down at his soup. Innis had been Justen most of the time. She'd ridden alongside him, slept in his tent, pretended to be his friend.

The humiliation turned over in his belly. He'd said things to Justen that he would *never* have said to a woman, done things he would *never* have done. He'd bathed in front of her, pissed in front of her.

And—even more humiliating—he'd dreamed of her.

In his dreams, they'd been lovers. He'd become closer to Innis than he had to any woman. In her company, he'd felt happy.

Happy? *What a fool I was.*

Harkeld shoved his soup bowl away and pushed to his feet, elbowing his way past Innis.

Humiliation fermented sourly in his chest as he stepped outside, into the stableyard. A lantern hung on a hook beside the door, casting faint light. Rain streamed down.

"Whoreson." Petrus pushed through the door behind him, and slammed it. "Think you're better than us, do you? Think you can treat us like we're dogshit?"

Harkeld ignored the shapeshifter. Another lantern hung outside the stables, a blurry beacon. He headed for it through the rain. The ankle-deep mud was as sloppy as gruel, stinking of horse manure and rotting straw.

Fingers gripped his elbow, swinging him round. "It's you who's dogshit."

Harkeld lifted his upper lip in a sneer and used his palace voice, disdainful and cold: "Release me, witch."

Petrus sneered back and obeyed, shoving Harkeld so hard that he lost his balance and sprawled in the mud.

Harkeld had an instant of shock—he was a prince; no one shoved him—before fierce, joyous rage ignited in his chest. He surged to his feet, hands clenched, teeth bared in a snarl. He was going to beat the crap out of this deceitful, lying mage. He was going to beat the crap out of him and *enjoy* it.

A hard fist struck his jaw, snapping his head back, sending him sprawling again. Harkeld hissed a curse and rolled, shook his head to clear it, scrambled to hands and knees. He dimly saw the dark blur of Petrus's raised arm. Knuckles bounced off his cheek, a glancing blow.

Harkeld shoved to his feet, a roar in his throat, and grabbed Petrus in a bear hug, grappling with the mage, forcing him back. He'd wrestled hundreds of times, thousands of times, but never with such rage before, his muscles bunched with fury, his teeth bared. If he could get Petrus on the ground he was going to rip his head off—

Petrus shifted his weight, twisted, hooked a foot around Harkeld's ankle.

They fell together, rolling in the mud, wrestling for dominance, grunting, snarling. Harkeld heaved himself on top. He laid a forearm across Petrus's throat and pressed with his full weight, forcing the shapeshifter's head back, choking him.

Petrus's knee took him in the groin, hard enough to make him yelp. Harkeld jerked back. They rolled again in the mud. This time, when they stopped, he was on the bottom. Fingers fisted in his hair, yanked his head back. Rain stung his eyes. The stink of mud and horseshit filled his mouth and nose.

"You're not better than us. You're *one of us.*" The words were punctuated by a knee in his belly that made the breath whoosh from his lungs. "Innis saved your rutting *life.*" The knee dug painfully into his belly again. "You should be *thanking* her, not treating her as if she's—"

Harkeld bucked his hips and twisted, dislodging Petrus. They rolled again, grappling awkwardly. Harkeld tried to catch his breath, tried to gain dominance.

They thudded hard against the stable wall. Lantern-light fell across them. Petrus's face was inches from his. The mage looked almost beast-like in his rage, lips pulled back from his teeth. "You might be a prince, but you are *worthless*." The words hissed into his face. "We should have killed you that first night in Osgaard. Taken your hands and blood and left the rest of you to *rot*." Petrus head-butted him, cracking their foreheads together.

For an instant, Harkeld saw only darkness—then the stableyard snapped back into focus: lantern-light, rain, fetid mud. He shoved away from the stable wall, trying to force Petrus onto his back. Petrus shoved back. Teeth snapped together half an inch from Harkeld's ear.

Harkeld kneed Petrus in the genitals.

The mage gave a strangled cry and released him.

Harkeld rolled away. He scrambled to hands and knees, panting. Petrus's savage, unrestrained fury was startling. *He's as angry as I am. He wouldn't mind killing me.*

And yet Petrus had saved his life more than once.

He looked at Petrus, doubled over in the mud. Even as he watched, the mage straightened. Dimly, Harkeld saw the gleam of bared teeth.

Harkeld hurriedly stood. He raised his fists, dodging Petrus's first blow and taking the second in the mouth. He lurched back several steps, tasting blood.

"Arrogant whoreson, looking down your nose at us." Petrus swung again.

Harkeld sidestepped and punched, connecting solidly with the mage's cheekbone.

Petrus retreated a few steps, shaking his head, panting. "We risk our lives for you, and you treat us like we're less than human."

Harkeld spat blood. "I was right, wasn't I?" His voice was as fierce as Petrus's. "You *are* less than human. Stinking, lying *witches*."

Petrus snarled and charged.

Harkeld hit him hard. The mage's nose broke beneath his fist in a spray of blood. Petrus lurched back, lost his balance, fell.

Harkeld bent, grabbed a handful of wet, muddy hair, and hauled the mage's head up until it was inches from his own. "You *lied to me*."

"We were trying to save your life." Petrus jerked his head, spraying blood, trying to break free.

Harkeld tightened his grip on the shapeshifter's hair. "You rutting *lied*—"

Petrus kicked him solidly in the chest.

Harkeld heard the crack of ribs breaking. He released Petrus and sat down hard in the mud. A sound between a scream and a groan choked in his throat.

Petrus rolled over and struggled to one elbow, panting, his face a mask of blood, then staggered to his feet. "That was for breaking Innis's jaw." His voice was thick with rage, thick with blood. "And this is for almost killing her in Lundegaard. Whoreson." He kicked Harkeld's chest again.

Agony knifed through him, but Harkeld had no breath to scream. Pain blanked his mind. For several seconds, the world vanished. When it returned, he became aware that Petrus had lurched back half a dozen paces. The mage sat heavily in the mud and cupped his hands over his nose.

Harkeld cradled his ribs, struggling to breathe.

Long minutes passed. Rain streamed down. The pain didn't ease. Waves of agony expanded in his chest.

Each breath stabbed. Getting to his feet, walking back to the taproom, were impossible tasks. He imagined pushing open the door, imagined the mages turning their heads to look at him, imagined the humiliation of asking one of the healers to mend his ribs.

He glared in Petrus's direction, hating him. Hatred was good, rage was good; it would give him the strength to climb to his feet. But his rage kept sliding away, swamped by the sheer agony of breathing.

The lantern cast enough light for Harkeld to see that Petrus had his hands cupped over his nose. Healing himself.

He knew better than to ask Petrus to heal him. In fact, it would be prudent to leave before Petrus got to his feet again.

*If I can stand.*

Harkeld levered himself slowly to his knees, and halted there, dizzy with pain, wheezing shallowly.

Petrus turned his head. His eyes glittered darkly. "Not so full of yourself are you, now?"

Harkeld didn't bother to reply. He concentrated on breathing.

Petrus wiped blood and mud and rain from his face, and carefully felt his nose. "You broke my nose, whoreson."

"Good." Harkeld tried to stand. For a sickening moment he thought he was going to pass out. Or vomit. Or both. He lurched back down to his knees, eyes squeezed shut. *Breathe. Slowly.*

He heard a sucking sound in the mud—footsteps— and opened his eyes.

Petrus crouched in front of him. "If you set yourself on fire, I wouldn't piss on you to put you out. You're an arrogant, foul-tempered son of a whore. We risk our lives for you, we *die* for you, and you treat us like dogshit."

"You are dogshit," Harkeld said. His voice was faint, wheezing. "Lying to me, laughing at me behind my back."

"Laughing? None of us were laughing. You think we *wanted* to be Justen? You think we *enjoyed* it?" Petrus spat into the mud. "We did it to protect you, whoreson, All-Mother only knows why. Should have just let you die. Would have been a lot easier."

Harkeld shut his eyes again. *Breathe slowly.*

"Treat Innis or Justen like that again and I'll cursed well break *all* your ribs. Do you understand me?"

Harkeld didn't reply. It took all his effort to breathe.

"Do you understand me?" A hard finger stabbed against his sternum.

It was one agony too much. His chest was on fire. Harkeld bent over, retching.

# CHAPTER SEVENTEEN

"WELL?" KAREL DEMANDED, trying to keep impatience from his voice. He wanted to grab Solveig by the shoulders and shake the man's words from him.

"No covered carts passed through the eastern gate this afternoon, sir."

Karel turned on his heel, surveying what he could see of the town. Its name was Groderling. Torches burned in brackets, lighting some of the doorways. Wooden galleries loomed above, some dark, some warm with lamplight.

They were close to the princess. He knew it. Only an hour or two behind. Was she even in this town? Had the Fithians chosen to stay here for the night?

The gelding he'd been riding snuffled his shoulder with a dusty muzzle and blew out a weary breath. Karel patted the animal's neck.

"Maybe they're still here?" The voice was Prince Tomas's.

Karel glanced at him. In the flickering torchlight, the prince's scar stood out, bisecting his cheek.

"Maybe."

Hooves clattered as another armsman rode up. Arvid. "A covered cart passed through the western gate a couple of hours ago, sir."

"West?" Karel frowned. "How many men?"

"The guard couldn't remember exactly. A handful, he said."

"The canopy was brown?"

"Yes, sir."

West? Why west now, when the Fithians had been heading east and north for three days?

The last armsman he'd sent out returned. Bjarne. "Nothing at the northern gate, sir."

"West," Prince Tomas said, bafflement in his voice. "Why west?"

"Could be they're meeting someone." More Fithians? "A couple of hours ago, Arvid?"

"Yes, sir."

Two hours. He was two hours behind the princess. Karel wanted to throw himself on his horse and gallop after her.

*Prudence. Rest the men. Rest the horses.*

"We'll stay here the night," Karel said. "Leave before dawn. Catch them tomorrow."

# CHAPTER EIGHTEEN

HE MUST HAVE passed out. He woke lying on his back, rain pattering on his face. Petrus crouched alongside him, his face shadowed, his wet hair silver in the lantern-light.

Harkeld blinked rain from his eyes. Breathing was easier. His ribs still hurt, but nothing like they had before. He tasted blood in his mouth, and bile. He lifted a hand and gingerly touched his chest. Pain, but not agony. "You mended them?" His voice was a hoarse whisper.

"Some." Petrus rose to his feet. "Do the rest yourself. You're a healer."

"Healer?" Harkeld pushed slowly up to sit. "No, I'm not."

"Only healers can share dreams."

Harkeld's head jerked back. He stared up at Petrus. "*What* did you say?"

The mage scowled at him.

"Share dreams? What do you mean, share dreams?" But Harkeld knew the answer, even as he asked. The dreams he'd had in Ankeny, the ones with Innis in them. The private, intimate dreams. They'd been *shared*.

"Didn't Rand tell you?"

Anger swelled in Harkeld's chest. The pain in his ribs seemed to fade. "No."

Petrus shrugged and turned towards the taproom. "Ask him."

Harkeld lurched to his knees, grabbed Petrus's leather belt, and hauled. The mage sat down hard in the mud. He scrambled round to face Harkeld, fury stark on his face. "Want more broken ribs, whoreson?"

Harkeld matched him glare for glare. Cursed mages, never telling him the whole truth. "Sharing dreams," he said. "*Tell me.*"

Petrus hissed between his teeth. "I'm not one of your bondservants, to be ordered about like a slave."

Harkeld wrestled with his temper for several seconds, clenched his jaw, unclenched it, and said, "Please."

For a long moment, Petrus didn't react. Then he snorted. "Remembered your manners, have you?"

Harkeld gritted his teeth and waited.

Petrus looked away. He scowled at the lantern hanging by the taproom door. "Healers sometimes share dreams. It's extremely rare. One healer has to be exceptionally strong, like Innis. The other..." He shrugged. "Maybe you have a little healing magic, maybe a lot. But if you're sharing dreams with her, you *are* a healer." He pushed to his feet and headed for the taproom again.

Harkeld stood too, with clumsy, painful haste. "How do you know we're sharing dreams? *I* don't even know that!" But he did know, deep down. The dreams had been so unusual, so *real*.

Petrus halted. He stood motionless for a long moment, then breathed out sharply through his nose and turned back to face Harkeld. "Innis told me."

"Well, she didn't tell *me*."

Petrus shrugged again, a movement jerky with anger. "I thought Rand had. He said you needed to know."

Outrage dulled Harkeld's pain. He almost didn't feel his ribs any more. "Rand? She told *him* about the dreams, but not *me*? Why?"

"She wanted to know what they mean."

Harkeld fastened on that last word. "Mean? What do they mean?"

Petrus's lips pressed together. He looked away. The silence lengthened until Harkeld thought the mage wouldn't reply.

Petrus inhaled deeply and turned his head. He stared at Harkeld, his eyes black in the darkness. "Mages who share dreams develop a strong bond. They usually marry."

Marry? Harkeld opened his mouth, and then shut it again. Marry Innis?

His response was instinctive: *Never*. Innis was a *mage*. She'd lied to him. Deceived him.

But on the heels of that thought, came memory of the dreams: the deep intimacy between them, the companionship, the pure contentment he'd felt in her company...

Harkeld understood the bitterness on Petrus's face. *But you love Innis*. He didn't say the words aloud.

"If you have any questions, ask Rand," Petrus said flatly. "Not me."

Harkeld nodded. "Thanks."

Petrus snorted. "I should break your ribs more often. It's improved your manners."

Harkeld touched his chest with both hands, lightly. The faint pressure brought pain. He tried to hide a wince. "I don't like being lied to."

"We were trying to keep you alive."

Harkeld lifted one shoulder in a shrug, conceding this point. Shame trickled into the void where his anger had been. The mages had deceived him—but at the same time they'd risked their lives for him. And they'd died for him. "I know. And I am grateful. Truly."

Petrus snorted again. The sound was followed by a sigh. "Rut it. Let me finish fixing those ribs."

"Thanks," Harkeld said again. "I... um... would appreciate that."

They went into the stables and hunkered down in an empty stall amid the scents of hay and dung and wet leather. Rain drummed steadily on the roof. Petrus's healing magic was rough and blunt and slow, quite different from Innis's complex, subtle magic. *I wonder what my healing magic is like?*

He thought about this for several minutes, while Petrus methodically worked his way down his ribcage. "Can I find out how strong my healing magic is?"

"You want to?"

Harkeld considered this question. Did he want to become more of a mage than he already was? More of an abomination, more of an outcast? "Maybe."

"There's a test—breath and blood—that shows what kind of magic you have."

"Jussi's Oil," Harkeld said. "Ebril told me about it." He fell silent, remembering red-haired Ebril.

Petrus was silent, too. The patter of rain on the shingle roof was loud. Nearby, a horse shifted its weight and sighed, a heavy sound.

"The test gives an indication of how strong your ability is." Petrus's voice had a harsh edge. He'd been thinking of Ebril, too. "But it's not always accurate. The instructors do their best, but some people never learn to use their magic."

*The instructors...* Harkeld frowned. His instructor in fire magic had been Cora. He remembered the terror he'd felt lighting his first candle, and he remembered Cora as he'd last seen her: dead in the rain, a throwing star buried in her skull.

Petrus worked his way along another rib. The pain in Harkeld's chest eased to an ache. His thoughts slid sideways, to Innis. *She knew we were sharing dreams, but she didn't tell me.* She'd told Rand, though, and Petrus.

A spark of anger flared alight in his chest. Harkeld snuffed it, as he would snuff a flame with his fire magic. He was tired of being angry, tired of hating the mages.

*We're companions in this nightmare. Their lives are forfeit too, not just mine.*

Nine mages dead already. He could recite their names. Dareus. Susa. Frane. Gerit. Ebril. Katlen. Hew. Linea. Cora.

Some he'd barely known. Others...

Dareus, he'd come to respect. And Cora. And laughing, red-haired Ebril had been his friend. Harkeld thought he could probably be friends with Petrus, too, and the real Justen, if he let himself.

His attention slid back to what Petrus had told him. Innis had been inside his head, he'd been inside hers. They'd dreamed together. The conversations, the sex, the companionship, the sense of connection, the bone-deep happiness—Innis had experienced those things, too.

*And she didn't tell me.*

The spark of anger re-ignited. Harkeld quenched it. He examined his thoughts, trying to decide how he felt about Innis. *Do I trust her? Do I love her?*

In the dreams, the answers were easy: yes, and yes. Here, sitting in the stables, his clothes sodden and filthy, with rain streaming down outside and Petrus mending his broken ribs, Harkeld wasn't so certain.

Petrus lowered the shirt. "There," he said. "You're done." And after a beat: "Whoreson."

Harkeld grunted. *I could be friends with him.* "Thank you," he said, and after a beat: "Whoreson."

Petrus stood. "You're welcome. Witchspawn."

Harkeld climbed to his feet. Witchspawn. It was a good insult. He filed it away, and followed Petrus back to the taproom.

# CHAPTER NINETEEN

BENNICK WAS SINGLE-MINDED, driven, leaning forward in
his saddle, straining to see past the next rise in the road,
the next bend. They rose before dawn and didn't halt
until long after night had fallen. Jaumé had no time to
practice with his throwing knife, or the new sword.

"Where are we going?" he dared to ask, on the
second evening. They sat hunched over a small fire,
chewing dried meat and tough bread. Bennick had
boiled half a billy of water and scattered tea leaves
in it.

"Bloedel." Bennick strained the tea leaves from
the water and offered the billy to Jaumé.

Jaumé shook his head. He didn't like the tea the
Brothers drank. Too strong, too bitter.

Bennick shrugged, and swallowed a long mouthful
of tea and smacked his lips.

"Are we going to Bloedel to find the prince?"
Jaumé ventured.

Bennick glanced at him. "To meet someone."

Jaumé bit his lip. Dare he ask a third question? "A
Brother?"

Bennick looked away. "To bed with you, lad.
We've a long day ahead of us tomorrow."

# CHAPTER TWENTY

Karel and his men rode out of Groderling before dawn and pushed west at a hard pace. A blustery wind pushed clouds like gray tufts of wool across the sky. After two hours, they came to a village. The Fithians' cart had passed through twenty minutes ago. "Twenty minutes!" Prince Tomas said, his eyes alight. "We'll catch them soon!"

*Prudence*, Karel told himself. *Prudence*. It took all his self-control not to leave the village at a gallop.

The road wound up a wooded slope, then dipped west, and there—*there*—in the distance was a covered cart and a handful of riders.

Karel reined in.

Tomas halted alongside him. "How do you want to do this?"

*Six of them. Twelve of us.*

"We split in two," Karel said. "Six of us overtake them, six ride behind. Then, we attack. Sire, you and Gunvald and Ture concentrate on the cart. Get her out, and get away. Don't wait for us, don't engage, just head for Groderling as fast as you can."

Prince Tomas grimaced, but made no protest.

\* \* \*

KAREL CANTERED TOWARDS the cart, five armsmen strung out behind him. His heart hammered in his chest, pushing his blood fiercely through his arteries.

The cart moved at an unhurried pace, the horses ambling. As he drew closer he heard the riders talking among themselves, laughing. One of them was whistling.

Karel slowed to pass the cart at a trot, the gelding's hooves kicking up puffs of dust.

The man driving the cart stopped whistling. He gave a cheerful wave. "Good day to ye."

Karel lifted a hand in response, and examined the Fithians. They weren't what he'd expected. None of them had the hard, lean savagery of the man he'd killed in Lundegaard. One was young enough to be called a boy, another middle-aged, with a jowled face and large belly. They all appeared unarmed.

The cart was older than he'd thought it would be, the canopy sun-faded and patched. The front flap was tied back. Inside, Karel caught a glimpse of turnips.

His heart seemed to stop beating. *It's the wrong cart.*

# CHAPTER TWENTY-ONE

BRITTA SAT DROOPING in the saddle, feigning exhaustion. Lumpy hills surrounded them. Straggling herds of goats foraged on saw-leafed grass and twisted thorn trees. The air was cool, crisp. They must have climbed during the days she'd spent in the cart. The settlements they passed were small. Villages, not towns, enclosed by rough palisades. Inside the palisades were wooden houses with wooden shingles on their roofs, and dirt streets. There were fewer refugees on the roads than she'd expected—the odd cart, some wagons, a few donkeys piled with household goods. She remembered what Prince Kristof had said: Roubos's king, Salavert, had told his people not to flee, that the All-Mother would protect them. It seemed most of them were obeying him.

But Kristof had also said that Sault was evacuating as fast as it could. Where were those refugees?

She pictured Sault in her head—a rough square, with impenetrable mountains along its eastern coast—and tried to imagine she was a refugee. If she came from the south or west of the kingdom... she'd flee to Sault's western coast and sail to Lundegaard.

And if she lived in the north... she'd head for the ports on Roubos's northern coast, and from there to the safety of the Allied Kingdoms.

Viewed like that, the empty roads made sense. The exodus was happening north of here, south of here.

Britta glanced beneath half-lowered eyelids at Plain, riding alongside her, holding her reins.

*Next time we pass through a town I'll tear the reins free, bolt, scream for help.*

But Fithians killed without remorse. They'd have no hesitation in slaughtering innocent townspeople. Men. Women. Children.

*Next time we pass close to some trees, I'll jump off the mare and hide among them.*

But the stands of thorn trees—dense and tangled though they were—wouldn't hide her for more than a few minutes.

Britta let her head loll on her neck. She examined the road, the ditches, the rocky hillsides and meager creeks, the farmhouses, the villages inside their palisades. She felt alert. She felt hopeful. The Fithians were no longer drugging her. She had a mount of her own. The opportunity to escape would come. She just had to recognize it when it did.

# CHAPTER TWENTY-TWO

IT WAS LATE morning by the time they reached Groderling again. Karel dismounted in the main square and tried to appear calm, but panic fizzed in his veins. *I've lost her!*

"What now?" Prince Tomas looked as grim as Karel felt. "Have we been following the wrong cart the whole time?"

That was the fear that nestled beneath his breastbone, making it difficult to breathe. "No," Karel said, with a certainty he didn't fully feel. "The cart that arrived here yesterday afternoon was the right one. We lost it here." He turned on his heel, surveyed the town square. "We ask questions at the gates again. And the inns. Someone saw that cart and knows where it went."

He gave orders rapidly and the armsmen obeyed as promptly as they always had, but Karel thought there was a difference in the way one or two of the men looked at him. An edge of doubt. *They've lost confidence in me.*

He'd made a mistake. A *big* mistake. He shouldn't have headed blindly west. He should have checked Arvid's information, cross-examined the gate guard.

How big a mistake he'd made, how catastrophic, remained to be seen.

He led his horse to the nearest water trough and looped its reins around one of the posts. "Leave your horse here," he told Prince Tomas. "We're going for a walk. See if we can find any houses that have pigeons."

Tomas's gaze sharpened. "You think there's a Fithian house here?"

"It's a possibility."


THE ARMSMEN HE'D sent to the gates returned with the same news they'd brought back yesterday: no carts covered with brown fabric had left Groderling heading north, south, or east.

The news was no better from any of the inns. A few refugees fleeing Sault, but no one matching the description of the Fithians.

Gunvald was the last armsman to return. He crossed the square, his steps fast, almost running, his face alight with excitement.

"What?" Karel demanded.

"I found it, sir! The cart. They sold it to a cartwright."

"Sold it?" Karel blinked, frowned. "Why?"

"Said they didn't need it any more."

"But the princess—"

"The man who sold it asked where he could buy a horse."

"And?"

"The cartwright sent him to one of the inns. Where he bought a piebald mare. The hostler said it was a woman's mount."

Silence followed these words. Prince Tomas turned to Karel. "She's riding?"

"She's riding." Elation filled his chest. He hadn't lost her. "Gunvald, did you get a description of the man who sold the cart?"

"He was armed. Looked like a soldier. The cartwright was scared of him."

"Fithian," Tomas said.

Karel took a deep breath, felt his ribcage expand. They'd lost a whole morning, but they hadn't lost the princess.

He strode to his horse and swung up into the saddle. "We need to find which gate that piebald mare left by."

# CHAPTER TWENTY-THREE

THEY CRESTED A muddy hill and looked down on a settlement. Rand brought his mount alongside Harkeld's. "Hansgrohe. On the border with Sault."

Harkeld looked past the town to the wide, bare sweep of highlands beyond. No forest cloaked that broad slope, just tussock and lone trees sculpted by the wind.

Sault. Where the curse already had a grip. Where bloodlust walked the land and people died.

Harkeld shivered, an involuntary reaction, and glanced sideways to see whether Rand had noticed. He hadn't.

"How far to the curse?"

Rand shrugged. "A hundred leagues, at a guess, but it could be closer than that. Depends how fast it's advancing."

The healer studied the town, frowning. Harkeld followed his gaze. "You think there're assassins down there?"

"It's possible. Keep your face covered. Lag behind; the shapeshifters will guard you. Thayer'll ride up front with me."

"No," Harkeld said. "I won't have him used as bait. If there are Fithians—"

"Of all of us, you are the one who must survive."

"I don't want any more mages dead because of me."

"I know." There was compassion on Rand's face. "The sooner we cross into Sault, the sooner we end this. Stay at the back."

HANSGROHE HAD A frantic, desperate edge to it. The town was small, shabby, with muddy streets and sagging wooden buildings, and refugees, hundreds of refugees, heading for Roubos's ports. Harkeld rode near the back of the mages, picking his way through the throngs of people and wagons and carts and donkeys. They halted at a crowded tavern, where the desperation seemed to have reached fever-pitch. Harkeld's gaze skipped from face to face: the distraught mother, the grim-faced father, the screaming child.

He looked down at his hands, resting on the saddle pommel. *Only I can stop this. My hands, my blood.*

"We need to buy a wagon here. And barrels for water."

Harkeld glanced to his left. Rand was there, astride his horse.

"We'll be half an hour, an hour at the most. Try to look unimportant."

Harkeld grunted a faint laugh.

"Wander off with Adel. Visit the market. Buy yourself lunch." Rand held out some coins. "The shapeshifters will guard you."

Harkeld took the coins and dismounted. He glanced around for Adel. The journeyman water mage sidled diffidently towards him.

Harkeld made himself smile at Adel. He deserved the hesitancy, the diffidence; he'd made no attempts at friendship during the voyage from Ankeny, had kept to himself, aloof, seldom speaking to anyone.

Adel cautiously returned the smile.

They left the tavern stableyard. Harkeld glanced back once. Thayer was in the midst of a circle of mages, pretending to be a prince, the most important person on the continent. Harkeld lifted his eyes to the gray sky and prayed to the All-Mother. *Let him be alive when we return.*

THE MARKET SQUARE was three streets away. Harkeld set a brisk pace, weaving through the refugees, his belly growling with hunger. Adel followed. The water mage was tall and gawky, with long arms and a thin throat in which his Adam's apple bobbed nervously. He hadn't the fighters' physique of the other Sentinels, or their confidence—but he must know how to fight, or he wouldn't be here. It was part of their training—to fight as well as soldiers. Ebril had told him that.

Ebril, who was dead.

Harkeld plunged into the market square, Adel trailing a half-step behind. It was hard to feel safe with Adel as his guard, but a glance showed him that shapeshifters were also there. The sparrow hopping across the rooftops was a mage, the dog sniffing the gutters, the swallow swooping above the square. And Innis was there too, browsing the skeins of wool displayed in a wagon.

Harkeld picked up a leather belt and tried to look as if he was examining it, while his gaze rested on her.

Innis was slender, tomboyish, almost as shy and quiet as Adel, and yet she was the strongest shapeshifter in a century—and the youngest mage ever to take the Sentinel's oath. Ebril had told him that too.

Strong magic, but not yet certain of who she was in the world. Too young to be a Sentinel, killing people, being killed. But she'd been his armsman for several months. She'd not been shy, then. She'd wrestled with him often—and won often. She'd defended herself against two soldiers at the pass in the Graytooth Mountains, and killed one of them. She'd killed a Fithian assassin.

And she'd been Justen when Harkeld had broken the armsman's jaw. And Justen in King Magnas's castle, when he'd believed the armsman guilty of rape and nearly killed him.

Harkeld lowered the belt. He remembered cornering Justen in the stairwell, remembered squeezing the armsman's throat between his hands. *I almost murdered her.* His stomach turned over on itself, a queasy, curdling sensation.

"Er... Flin? Are you all right?"

He glanced at Adel. The water mage was watching him, his head slightly ducked. Adel was the same age as Petrus and Justen, ready to take his oath as a Sentinel, but he looked years younger, an adolescent yet to grow comfortable in his body. *A Fithian would kill you in half a second*. Harkeld forced a smile to his lips. "Fine."

He moved on, to a stall selling meat pies. Adel followed. The water mage reminded Harkeld of a half-grown puppy, hands and feet too big, clumsy in his movements, eager to please.

Harkeld bought pies for himself and Adel, then stepped into a quiet space between two stalls. "Want one?" he asked the barrel-chested black dog that was Serril. Shapeshifters weren't allowed to eat when in animal form—it was one of their Primary Laws— but Sentinels were allowed to break those Laws if necessary, and Serril had to be hungry.

The dog shook its head.

Harkeld shrugged and bit into his pie. He ate quickly, scanning the crowd while he chewed. The pastry was tough, the meat dry, but his stomach stopped growling. His gaze skipped over faces, ignoring the women, examining the men. Were any of them Fithian assassins? *If I was an assassin, this is the kind of town I'd be in.* A border settlement, a place that people and information flowed through. All headed in one direction, now: into Roubos. Anyone crossing into Sault would stand out. *And if the Fithians have even one agent here, every assassin in the Seven Kingdoms will soon know where I am.*

When he'd finished the pie, Harkeld moved further into the market square. He ignored Adel trailing diffidently behind him, and kept his awareness on Petrus and Justen—overhead—on Serril—trotting nearby, ears pricked—on Innis—half a dozen stalls away.

In the dreams, he'd had sex with Innis; in real life, he'd barely spoken to her. *Except when she was Justen, when we were friends.*

He watched Innis examine a fur cloak, watched her scan the crowd. She didn't know Petrus had told him about the dreams; her awareness of him would be different, if she knew. Conflicting emotions fought in his chest. He missed her, curse it. Missed the dreams. Missed talking with her. Missed the contentment of holding her in his arms, and yes, missed the sex. But mixed with the longing was a resentment edging towards anger that she'd pretended to be Justen, that she'd lied to him for months, that she hadn't told him the truth about the dreams. *She told Rand and Petrus, but not me!* And overriding those emotions, was an anxious protectiveness. Innis shouldn't be here. It was too dangerous. She was too young. She should go back to the Allied Kingdoms, where mages weren't reviled and killed. Where there was no curse.

Something nipped his calf.

"Ouch." Harkeld bent and rubbed his leg. He frowned at the black dog.

Serril wasn't looking at him. His gaze was fixed on something on the other side of the market square. He growled, his hackles rising.

The hairs on Harkeld's scalp stood on end. He slowly straightened, his hand on his sword. He followed Serril's gaze. A man stood beside a cartload of iron pots. Amid the clamor of the market his demeanor was calm and watchful, alert. He leaned against the cart, but his hand wasn't far from his sword hilt. His physique was lean, his hair clipped short, his jaw clean-shaven.

His gaze was on Innis.

Harkeld tensed. "Fithian?"

The dog gave a curt nod.

Harkeld's protectiveness surged into something close to panic. Innis didn't look like the other women in the marketplace. It wasn't her garb—the refugees wore a miscellany of clothes; some of them dressed in men's trews, like Innis, and a few even had swords strapped at their waists. But none of those women carried their swords with ease, as if they knew how to use them. And none of them moved the way Innis did. She lacked the edgy desperation, the fear. She was like the Fithian: calm, watchful, alert. And the man had noticed.

"Does she know?" He pushed through the crowd towards Innis.

The dog nipped his calf again, almost drawing blood.

"Stop that," Harkeld said, and elbowed his way past a stocky farmer.

The dog sank its teeth into his trews, halting him.

"Serril!" Harkeld hissed, wrenching his leg free with a sharp tearing of fabric. "He's seen her! We don't have time for—"

The dog moved to block his way, teeth bared, snarling.

*I'm important, not Innis. I'm the one Serril will save.*

The realization made his panic spike. Harkeld shoved past the dog. "Innis!" he shouted. "Get—"

A hawk screamed warning overhead, drowning his words. A flash of steel sliced through the air. Throwing star.

Harkeld grabbed his fire magic—scorching hot—and hurled it. The weapon flared alight with a white-hot burst of flame and sharp thunderclap of sound.

For a moment there was utter silence—and then the marketplace erupted into chaos.

Harkeld threw himself back against a stall and crouched, his sword clenched in his hand. Around him, people screamed and pushed to flee. Serril stood at his shoulder, hackles up, a low growl rumbling in his chest. Adel hunkered behind them. The crowd surged past. What did they fear most? The assassin's weapon, or the magic that had destroyed it?

Harkeld gripped his sword, straining for a glimpse of Innis, for a glimpse of the Fithian. He shoved aside his panic. Innis would have shifted. She'd be a bird now, a dog, a lizard. She'd be safe.

"Serril, how many of them are there?"

The black dog wrinkled its lips, pushed its lower jaw out, uttered a growl that sounded like...

"Two?"

The dog nodded.

"Adel," Harkeld said, his gaze fixed on where Innis had been. "Stay here."

The water mage uttered a squeak of dismay. Harkeld ignored it. He gripped his sword tightly and headed in the direction he'd last seen Innis.

Serril gave a deep-throated growl.

Harkeld ignored that, too. He needed to see that Innis didn't lie dead on the ground. She was a shapeshifter, but Fithians could kill shapeshifters. Gerit and Linea were proof of that.

The crowd parted and there—*there*—was the assassin, staring directly at him, a throwing star gleaming in his hand.

Harkeld held the man's gaze for an instant, and saw the Fithian bare his teeth in a grin and hurl the star. He grabbed for his magic as the weapon flashed towards him. *Burn.*

The throwing star burst alight.

Harkeld crouched low, blinking away the after-image of flames. A roar resonated in his ear. He flinched as a thickly-muscled lion barreled past him.

The fight was over in a handful of seconds, quick, savage, brutal. The Fithian lay dead, his throat torn open. The lion turned to face Harkeld, blood dripping from its mane.

Harkeld tightened his grip on his sword. "The other one?"

Serril lashed his tail, fastened his gaze on something to Harkeld's left, and bounded off.

Harkeld glanced at Adel. The water mage crouched behind him, sword half-extended, eyes wide with fright, Adam's apple bobbing in his throat.

Harkeld cautiously straightened to his full height. He scanned the marketplace. It was almost empty. He could hear individual voices now. To his right, a mother screamed for a child. Beneath her cries were the frantic squawks of hens and the high, terrified yelping of a dog. "Innis!" Harkeld bellowed.

There was no reply.

Produce lay scattered on the ground. He headed for the stall where he'd last seen her, crushing apples beneath his boots, trying not to panic. Innis would be fine. The first hint of danger and she'd have changed shape. She wasn't lying dead. She was flying high in the sky. A sparrow, a swallow, a hawk.

He looked up at the gray sky. Only Justen flew there.

A lion's roar sounded behind him. Harkeld jerked around. Was the lion Innis?

He ran, pushing past abandoned stalls and overturned carts, stumbling over bolts of fabric and iron pots and pumpkins the size of his head.

In a muddy space between stalls, a lion crouched over the body of a man. The corpse lay in a widening pool of blood with one hand outstretched, a razor-sharp throwing star inches from his fingertips, as if even in death he tried to reach for it.

The lion was male, its pale mane streaked with blood. Petrus.

Harkeld met the lion's eyes. "Thank you."

The lion nodded, shifted into hawk shape, and flapped up into the sky. A black dog came to stand at Harkeld's side. But where was Innis?

"Innis!" he bellowed again.

"Here."

She stood beside a cartload of coal, sword in hand.

Relief surged in his chest. Harkeld crossed to her at a run. He wanted to hug her, instead he said, "We need to get back to the tavern."

# CHAPTER TWENTY-FOUR

THEY WALKED WITH cautious haste. Innis looked up, and saw Justen and Petrus flying overhead. Serril trotted beside the prince. "Serril, you only saw two Fithians?" the prince asked.

The black dog nodded.

"Two at the market," Innis said, scanning the street. "But maybe more elsewhere. Fithians always turn up when you least want them to." That was the last thing Cora had said to her—her exact words—before a throwing star had buried itself in her skull. Innis touched the hilt of her sword. The mood of the town had been anxious before; now it was in the grip of full-blown hysteria. Did the people shoving past them even know why they ran? Or did they think the curse had arrived in Hansgrohe?

A cry caught her attention, a toddler screaming in open-mouthed terror. And then she saw why, saw the blood.

Innis halted instinctively. Healing magic surged inside her, tingling in her palms, in her fingers.

The prince halted, too. He followed her gaze, and hissed between his teeth. "Can you help her?"

"Yes. But the Fithians—"

"Do it." The prince took her elbow and pulled her across the street, cutting through the tide of people.

In the dozen strides it took, Innis assessed the situation: the woman lying sprawled, her long plait caught in the spokes of a wagon wheel, her scalp half-torn from her head; the man screaming at the wagoner; the abandoned child shrieking his terror. Her thoughts moved with lightning-fast clarity. Her magic gave another surge, the tingling in her hands became stronger.

Innis dropped to her knees, cradled the woman's head. "Flin, cut her hair!"

The prince drew his sword and severed the braid in a swift movement, releasing it from the wagon wheel.

The woman's scalp had peeled back from her brow to the back of her head, revealing the gory dome of her skull. Blood streamed from the wound. Grazes marked the left side of her face. Her abdomen was rounded, a firm and definite swelling. Seven months pregnant, was Innis's guess. She sent her healing magic swiftly to the wound, halting the terrible loss of blood. "You're going to be all right."

The woman didn't respond. She gazed up at the sky, not blinking as rain fell in her eyes, lost in pain and shock.

Innis took hold of the scalp—limp, warm, heavy with wet hair—and inspected it for dirt before smoothing it over the exposed skull. She focused on her patient, ignoring the child's piercing screams, ignoring the shouted altercation between the wagoner and the woman's husband, ignoring the crowd surging past her.

"Can you heal her?" The voice was Prince Harkeld's.

"Yes." It would be rough and hasty, the scar wouldn't be pretty, but the woman would live—as long as there was no infection. Innis coaxed the skin to refasten to the skull. There was no time to match capillary with tiny capillary; the major blood vessels, those she could mend. Everything else, she'd have to trust to fate.

Her magic couldn't tell her the woman's name, but it told her who she was: practical, kind-hearted, not clever, but with a strong streak of common-sense.

The shouting stopped. Dimly, she was aware of the woman's husband turning towards them. "What d'y think y're doin'?" he snarled.

"Helping her," the prince replied.

"She cain be helped." The man was a farmer, young and burly, armed with a thick wooden stave. "She dead! Her head tore off."

There was a skirmish—she glanced up and saw Prince Harkeld grappling with the man, saw his skill outstripped the farmer's, and looked back at her patient, pouring magic into the woman, urging the scalp to bond to the skull, creating a ridge of scar tissue along the woman's hairline. When she next glanced up, Prince Harkeld had the farmer pinned to the ground. "It's not as bad as it looks," he told the man, panting. "Head wounds bleed a lot. She'll be fine. Now see to your son!"

The farmer clambered to his feet and obeyed. After a long moment, the high-pitched shrieking died to a whimper. She heard Prince Harkeld talking again. "The skin's back in place. Your wife will be fine. But we'll need a bandage to hold the wound tight. Give me your shirt."

Half a minute later, the prince crouched opposite her, a rough cotton shirt in his hands. "Don't look at it for three days." The words were for the farmer, not her. "Three days, do you hear me? It needs a chance to heal."

It was healed already, hastily, roughly, but she met the prince's eyes and nodded to show that she understood: he was hiding her magic.

Prince Harkeld wrapped the shirt around the woman's head, a bulky, concealing bandage. "Time to go," he said, in a low voice.

The woman was shivering, still dazed. A contraction rippled across her distended abdomen. Innis's attention fastened on that movement. "Not yet." She reached to touch her patient's stomach. The muscles tightened beneath her hand, a fierce spasm.

The farmer knelt alongside his wife. "Lemme see."

"No!" Prince Harkeld reached for the man's wrist.

Too late. The farmer pushed the bandage up from his wife's bloodied brow, exposing the fresh, pink scar along her hairline.

There was a moment of silence, and then the man reared back. "That ain natural!" His gaze fastened on Innis, fierce with fear. "Ye're a witch!"

# CHAPTER TWENTY-FIVE

HARKELD SAW THE farmer raise his wooden stave, saw Innis scramble backwards. Too late, too slow. The stave hit her head with a sound like an ax splitting wood.

"Witch!" the farmer screamed, swinging the stave again.

Harkeld uttered a roar. He seized the man, wrestled him to the ground, beat him with his fists.

Someone grabbed the back of his cloak, dragging him off the farmer. Adel. "Run!" the water mage yelled.

"Innis—" Harkeld looked for her. Serril cradled Innis's body in his arms. The shapeshifter was in human form, black-bearded, naked.

"Witches!" The farmer pushed to his feet, reaching for his stave again. His shout lifted above the crowd, raw-throated. The current of people faltered; some turned towards them, others still pushed to flee.

"Witches!" someone else cried. "Witches!"

A dozen voices picked up the cry. "Witches!" And above that word, someone shrieked, "Kill them!"

Adel yanked on Harkeld's cloak again, pulling him towards the mouth of an alley. "Run!"

Harkeld ran, staggering slightly, numb with disbelief. Innis was dead. Dead. No one could survive a blow like that.

The roar of voices swelled behind them. The sound held a baying note. Then, the deep bellow of a lion cut across it. Harkeld glanced back, stumbling, almost falling. A lion with a dun-colored mane stood between them and the mob. Justen.

A stone struck the lion's side, drawing blood. Justen stood his ground. He roared again.

"Run!' Adel yelled in Harkeld's ear.

Harkeld ran, along alleys and down side streets, following Serril, his eyes on the shapeshifter's naked back, on Innis's body in the man's arms.

The cries grew fainter behind them, yet still they ran, panting, weaving through the backstreets of Hansgrohe, following the hawk that was Petrus. They turned left, and left again, doubling back on themselves. Finally, in a deserted alleyway, Petrus landed and shifted into himself. "Let me see her," he demanded.

Serril laid Innis's body on the ground. He was wheezing for breath.

Petrus crouched and cupped her face in his hands. His eyes closed, his brow furrowed with concentration.

*You can't heal her*, Harkeld told him silently. *Mages can't reverse death.* He blinked his eyes fiercely and looked away.

"We need Rand," Petrus said.

Harkeld's head snapped around. "She's alive?"

"Barely." He'd seen Petrus look grim before, but nothing like this. The mage's eyes seemed to blaze in his ashen face.

Serril bent to pick Innis up again.

"I'll carry her." Harkeld pushed forward, crouched, and carefully took Innis in his arms. She was as limp as a corpse. No pulse seemed to beat in her throat, no breath to pass her lips. "How far to the tavern?"

"It's two streets away."

A swallow darted down and landed. Justen. Blood trickled from a cut on his ribs. "We're not to go to the tavern." His face was grim, too. "There were assassins. Thayer's dead, and Oren. And Davin and Gretel are hurt bad."

*Thayer's dead because he was pretending to be me.* But Harkeld couldn't think of that, not while he held Innis in his arms and there was a chance she might live. "We need a strong healer!"

"Rand's coming," Justen said. "Wait here." And he shifted and leapt up into the sky again.

Harkeld carefully laid Innis on the ground. "Petrus? Can you do anything?" Damp strands of hair were plastered to Innis's face, but he was afraid of touching her, afraid of hurting her more badly than she already was. The sound the stave had made echoed in his ears. How could she still be alive?

Petrus knelt alongside him. "She's bleeding inside her skull. And her brain's swelling." He laid his hands very gently on either side of Innis's face.

Harkeld remembered how Petrus's healing magic felt in comparison to Innis's: rough, blunt. "Could you harm her, trying to heal her?"

"No," Petrus said. "But I don't have the precision to fix most of this. Innis is the one with that kind of skill."

Harkeld watched, feeling helpless. The things he was good at—fighting, throwing fire—were no help to Innis. He jerked around at the slap of running footsteps, his hand going to his sword.

It was Rand. Blood stained the healer's cloak. Not Rand's, as far as Harkeld could see.

Petrus yielded his place to Rand. Harkeld watched the man's face intently as he bent over Innis. *Will she live? Will she be all right?* He bit his tongue to hold back the questions.

The clop of horses' hooves and rattle of wagon wheels echoed in the mouth of the alley. Harkeld swung to face this new threat. A covered wagon, riders. He reached for his sword again.

A swallow landed, changed into Justen. "They're ours."

HARKELD HELPED LIFT Innis into the wagon. Inside were half a dozen empty barrels. Gretel and Davin lay on the wooden floorboards. He couldn't tell what Gretel's injury was, but Davin's was obvious: a throwing star buried in his abdomen. A killing wound. But the blonde healer, Nellis, was bent over Davin, and perhaps magic could save him. At the back of the wagon was a man's body. Thayer. And alongside it, the huddled shape of a dead bird. Oren.

Harkeld gazed for a long moment at Thayer and Oren. A heavy weight of guilt settled on him. Two weeks they'd travelled together, and he'd scarcely spoken to them, and now they were dead because of him.

Outside, Rand was issuing orders: "Serril, Justen, in the sky. Not you, Petrus. We need your help here."

Petrus climbed into the wagon. Rand followed him.

"Petrus says I'm a healer. Can I help?"

Rand shook his head. "No."

Harkeld leapt down from the wagon and ran for his mount. He scrambled into his saddle, clumsy with haste, clumsy with fear.

THEY PUSHED SOUTH and west along roads clogged with refugees. Their progress was slow, little more than walking pace. Sometimes they had to halt altogether, while people streamed past on either side of the wagon.

Towards dusk, a large black hawk swooped low, a dead pigeon gripped in its talons.

The hawk hovered above Malle, dropped the pigeon, and climbed back into the sky.

Harkeld nudged his mount closer to the water mage. "Fithian messenger bird?"

"Yes." Malle was the oldest of the Sentinels, her hair iron-gray. She squinted at the tiny leather pouch tied to the pigeon's leg, then held the bird out to him. "See if you can get that knot. My eyes aren't what they used to be."

Harkeld hastily untied the knot, slipped the tiny pouch off the pigeon's leg, and opened it. A small scrap of paper was tucked inside. He unrolled it. Two lines of marks and symbols. Some of them he recognized. The symbol for a target. The symbol for a mage. "Here." He held the message out to Malle.

The water mage took it, held it at arm's length, squinted at it, then tucked it into her pocket.

It wasn't so much what it said, as what it told them. *Someone in Hansgrohe is informing other Fithians where we are.*

AT NIGHTFALL, THEY turned off the road into a muddy patch of ground surrounded on three sides by twisted trees and on the fourth by a creek. Harkeld swung down from his horse and hurried across to the wagon. Stubble crunched beneath his boots as he strode; this had been some poor farmer's field.

He pulled back the covering. "How are they?"

The healers were dark shapes. He couldn't see who was who, couldn't see the patients.

"I'll get some light." He jogged across to the packhorses, fumbled hastily through the bundles, found the brass soldiers' lanterns, found candles, ran back, lit the candles with a flick of his fingers.

The shadows drew back into the corners of the wagon. He saw the healers, saw the patients, saw Thayer and Oren dead at the back. Gretel was sitting up, half-propped against a barrel, Petrus crouched alongside her. The shapeshifter was still naked. He glanced at Harkeld, glanced away. Davin lay as motionless as a corpse. Nellis, bending over him, didn't look up. Deep furrows of concentration were carved on her face.

Harkeld's gaze fastened on Innis. She was as still as Davin, her skin bloodlessly pale. His eyes told him she was dead—her heart didn't pump, no breath filled her lungs—but if she was dead,

Rand wouldn't be cradling her head in his hands, wouldn't be trying to heal her.

Harkeld swallowed. "How are they?"

"Still alive." Rand's eyes were dark hollows in the candlelight. He released Innis's head, smoothed her hair gently from her brow, and sat back with a sigh, rubbing his face. Harkeld heard the rasp of stubble.

"I need to learn how to heal."

"Not now." Rand crawled to the tailboard and climbed stiffly down. "Petrus, get dressed. Gretel will be all right."

Rand walked a few paces, and stretched wearily. Harkeld followed him. "I need to learn how to heal," he said, more urgently.

"Not now," the healer repeated. Around them, was the bustle of riding mounts being unsaddled, packhorses being unloaded.

"Yes! Now!" Agitation filled him. He couldn't stand still. His feet were pacing, carrying him back and forth in front of Rand. He gestured fiercely at the wagon. "Davin and Innis are dying and I can't just do nothing! I'm a healer. Let me help! Please!"

"Not without training. I'm sorry." Rand looked upward. "Serril!"

An owl swooped out of the darkness and landed at their feet, changed shape.

"That pigeon, where was it headed?"

"Same direction as us."

"Ah, rut it."

Harkeld knew what that meant. *There are Fithians ahead of us somewhere.*

The knowledge didn't scare him. In the morning it might, but right now he wasn't afraid of assassins; he was afraid of what was happening in that wagon. Innis and Davin were dying, while he stood back and did nothing. He wanted to grab Rand by the shoulders, shake him, bellow *Let me help them!*

Instead, he crossed to the horses, found his mount, and unbuckled the saddle, wrestling with his agitation. His heart beat loud and fast in his chest, as if he'd been running.

"Help me dig the graves." Bode thrust a shovel at him.

"The horses—"

"The others'll deal with them."

Harkeld followed the fire mage to the edge of the trees. They worked without speaking. He didn't know Bode, had spoken only a few words to him on the voyage to Roubos. The fire mage was in his late thirties. A blunt-mannered man who'd made no effort to be friendly. *But I made no effort either.*

By the time Thayer's grave was dug, the horses had been picketed, the tents pitched, and a stewpot hung over the fire. Harkeld leaned on his shovel, panting, sweating. His agitation, his urgency, had faded. *They'll be all right, Innis and Davin.*

Bode clambered out of the hole and reached a hand down.

Harkeld pulled himself up. "Thanks."

Bode nodded.

It took only a few minutes to excavate a grave for Oren. A few shovels of dirt, a rock levered out, and it was done.

Bode stared down at the small hole. He sighed.

Harkeld understood the sigh. Dying in animal form was what shapeshifters feared most. "Did you know him well?"

"Yes."

There was nothing in Bode's manner to suggest blame, but Harkeld still felt responsible. *Oren wouldn't be dead if he hadn't been protecting Thayer, and Thayer wouldn't be dead if he hadn't been pretending to be me.*

Footsteps crunched across the stubble field towards them. Petrus, his hair moonlight-pale. The shapeshifter carried a shovel.

"It's done," Bode told him.

"No, it's not. Davin died."

It took a few beats of Harkeld's heart before the words sank in. *Not Davin, too.* He felt as if Petrus had kicked him in the chest again.

Abruptly, it was too much. Harkeld made an inarticulate sound. He hurled his shovel aside and swung away from Petrus, swung away from the graves, and pushed his way into the dark trees. Branches slapped at him, tore at him. He bulled his way forward, stumbling over roots and fallen branches, almost running.

A dozen yards in, he tripped over a log and sprawled headlong. He lay where he'd fallen for several seconds, then pushed up to hands and knees. His heart hammered in his chest. Each breath had a faint hitch in it, as if he was about to cry.

*What am I doing? Running away?* There was no running away from this.

He heard the *pad pad* of paws, the snap of a twig breaking, and then an animal came to stand alongside him. A dog. A shapeshifter. Probably Serril.

Harkeld felt stupid. He lurched upright, groped for the log he'd tripped over, sat. "I'm not going anywhere. Please leave me alone."

After a moment, the dog did. The soft *pad pad* of its paws died away.

His breathing settled. The wood wasn't completely dark. He saw the glow of firelight through the tree trunks.

A figure moved, silhouetted against the light, one of the mages, coming through the trees towards him, walking slowly, pushing through the undergrowth. Twigs snapped and cracked. Branches crunched underfoot.

The man reached the log and halted. He was too tall for Bode, too broad-shouldered for Adel. Petrus. After a moment Petrus sat on the log alongside him. Not close enough that Harkeld could feel his body heat, but still close.

Harkeld rubbed his face, looked away from Petrus. "Sometimes it gets too much, you know?"

"I know."

They sat in silence for a long time. "How's Innis?" Harkeld asked finally.

"Not good. But Nellis is working on her too, now that Davin's dead. I can't. I used up all my strength on Gretel."

Harkeld leaned his elbows on his knees and stared down at the ground. He could dimly make out the shapes of his boots. He grew cold. His stomach told him he was hungry. Petrus had to be cold, too, and hungry and tired, but he made no move to leave.

*Does he feel the same way I do? Sick with it all?*
*Wishing it was over. Wishing it had never started.*

Petrus could be in the Allied Kingdoms now,
where Sentinel mages were respected, but instead
he was here, halfway across the world, in a land
that reviled magic, watching his friends die,
burying them, wondering if he was going to die
too, wondering if he'd ever see his home again.

Harkeld clasped his hands together, felt the
shapes of his fingers, his thumbs. *My hands and
my blood. That's what this is all about.* "You were
right. You should have cut my hands off, back in
Osgaard." Dimly, he saw Petrus turn his head.
"It's not too late, you know. We could do it now."

Petrus was silent for a few seconds. "You mean
that?"

"Yes." Right now, he did. Whether he'd have
the courage in the morning was another matter.

Petrus turned his head away and looked towards
the distant firelight. "Be a waste, don't you think?
After we've tried so hard to get you through this
in one piece."

"It's already a waste. I'm not worth anyone's
life, let alone so many."

Petrus said nothing. Harkeld took his silence as
agreement.

"You'd only need one of my hands now, and a
bit of blood. It's not like you have to kill me." He
tried for some flippancy: "I'll even let you cut it
off."

Petrus snorted, shook his head. "No."

"I thought you'd want to."

"Not really." Petrus sighed. "You know, it's not

actually about you. It's the Seven Kingdoms we're trying to save. You're just the tool we need to do it."

A tool bred by mages. But he couldn't muster any anger. Not this time. Not after the events of today.

They sat side by side in silence for a few more minutes, then Petrus sighed again and pushed to his feet. "Come on. Davin's grave's not going to dig itself."

Harkeld followed the shapeshifter back through the trees. Bode was standing in a foot-deep grave, driving his shovel into the ground, tossing soil to one side. Petrus bent and picked up a shovel.

"No," Harkeld said, taking it from him. "Go eat."

Petrus opened his mouth to argue.

"You're a trained healer, I'm not. Go and eat. Sleep. And then you'll be able to help with Innis."

Petrus closed his mouth. After a moment, he nodded and turned towards the fire.

Harkeld stepped down into the hole. Bode made room for him. In silence, they dug Davin's grave.

THERE WAS LITTLE talk around the campfire. The three deaths, the possibility of there being a fourth, hung over them. It was as if the night sky had substance and weight and was pressing down. Harkeld ate slowly, without appetite.

Rand clambered down from the wagon, stretched stiffly, and came across to the fire.

"How is she?" Adel asked.

Rand filled a bowl with stew. "Her skull's in one piece again. We've dealt with the bleeding and the worst of the swelling. There's a lot of bruising, though.

Bad bruising. And brains are just so... intricate. Delicate." His voice was weary, almost defeated.

There was a long moment of silence, and then Adel burst out: "All Innis did was heal his wife! Why'd he try to kill her?"

"Because that's what they do here," Serril said.

"But she was *helping*."

Serril shrugged. "Doesn't matter. He saw a mage, so he tried to kill her. It's what they've been doing here for centuries."

Harkeld looked down at his empty bowl. Before he'd met the mages, before he'd become one himself... he would have tried to kill Innis too. *The only good witch is a dead witch*. It was a truth. A fact. Everyone knew that spring followed winter, that the sun always rose in the east, and that witches were evil and had to die.

"But she was *helping*," Adel persisted. "Why harm someone who's helping you?"

"Ignorance, fear." Serril shrugged. "They're a dangerous combination."

Rand nodded. "All of this..." He waved his spoon, indicating the Seven Kingdoms, the Ivek Curse. "All of this is because of those two things. Ivek was a healer. He only helped people, too. Until the purge."

"Who is most to blame for Ivek's curse?" Serril asked Adel. "The ignorant and fearful, who decide to hunt mages to extinction? Or the healer driven mad by the slaughter of his wife and young children?"

Harkeld put down his bowl. He'd never thought of it like that. Ivek had been a healer, a husband, a father. Victim of a terrible purge. And in revenge he'd created a purge of his own, even bloodier and more violent. It had taken three centuries for Ivek's curse to come to fruition, but once it passed through the Seven Kingdoms, there'd be no survivors.

"The people were to blame," Adel said.

"You won't get folk here to agree."

Harkeld studied his hands. The skin had grown back on his left palm, but he remembered how it had looked, remembered the blood. The blood of a Rutersvard prince, the blood of a mage. *My ancestors led the purge. Rutersvards. And now I am a mage myself.* Ivek had understood irony. It was why he'd crafted the anchor stones the way he had.

He closed his hands, clenched them, looked across the fire at Serril. "You could leave the curse to destroy the Seven Kingdoms."

Serril shook his head. "The people here... they're ignorant, not evil."

"And no one knows exactly what the curse will do once it's consumed the Seven Kingdoms," the water mage, Malle, said. "It *should* stop advancing, but... it may not. It may poison the world."

Rand scraped his bowl clean, put it to one side, and leaned forward. "For those of you who don't know, the pigeon Serril caught was headed this way. Which means that somewhere between us and the anchor stone are more Fithians."

For a moment, no one spoke. Harkeld found himself watching Adel. The journeyman water mage's face seemed to grow paler, his eyes to get bigger.

"It'd be easy for them to pretend to be refugees," Serril said. "They could get right up alongside us. So from now on, when we travel, we'll have two shapeshifters guard us, plus one flying ahead, searching the road, looking at everyone, and I mean *everyone*."

"Do we have enough shapeshifters for that?" Malle asked quietly.

Serril's grimace said *Not really*, but what he said aloud was, "We'll be pushed for the next day or so, but once Innis is better, we'll have the numbers."

RAND DISAPPEARED BACK into the wagon. Harkeld wanted to follow him. He wanted to push back the canvas and clamber inside and talk to Innis while she was still alive, even if she couldn't hear him.

He stayed at the campfire until it burned down to glowing embers, then crawled into his tent. He never slept alone, always shared his tent with a shapeshifter—Cora's rule. Tonight, it was Hedín, as lean and weather-beaten as Rand. Hedín was already asleep. Harkeld wrapped himself in his blanket, and lay staring at the dark.

The sound the stave had made echoed in his ears. *Thock*. Like an axe splitting wood. *Thock*.

HARKELD JERKED AWAKE. Dawn. He flung aside his blanket, crawled out of the tent, and hurried across to the wagon. His ribcage felt as if it had shrunk overnight; tight with hope, tight with fear. *Let her be alive.*

Innis was still alive, but Rand and Nellis looked half-dead, their skin almost gray, their eyes bloodshot. Rand lurched when he climbed down from the wagon and nearly fell. "You, sleep,"

Serril ordered. "And you too, Nellis. Petrus'll take care of her."

*Let me help.* Harkeld bit back the words. He knew the answer: not without training. He peered into the wagon and saw Innis, saw her curling black hair, her pale face. He recognized that she was deeply unconscious.

"There's not much left to do," Rand told Petrus, rubbing his face, yawning. "Keep an eye on her right forebrain. There's a chance it might hemorrhage again."

# CHAPTER TWENTY-SIX

WHEN POX BROUGHT her food that morning, Britta hid some bread in her pockets. What else could be useful when she escaped? She scanned the ground where she'd lain. Stubbly grass, stones, twigs.

A short, snapped-off twig about six inches long caught her eye. One end was as sharp as a spear. She picked it up, tested its strength. Would it pierce skin if she stabbed hard enough?

Perhaps.

Britta slipped the twig into a pocket.

Plain came for her. Britta clung to his arm, stumbling as they walked to the horses. *Weak and exhausted, that's what I am.*

Plain boosted her up into the saddle, then mounted himself and came up alongside her, taking the mare's reins.

Leader swung up onto his horse and headed for the road. Plain tugged the reins. The piebald mare obediently fell into a trot. Britta sat drooping, her eyes half-closed, her mind racing. She had a weapon in her pocket. She had food. Today, she'd escape.

# CHAPTER TWENTY-SEVEN

KAREL HEARD THE same story in each village. Seven riders, one mounted on a piebald mare, had passed through the previous day. "A young woman?" he'd asked in the first village.

This question was met with a blank look and a headshake. "Woman? Ain't no woman with 'em. They was all men."

*Have I made another mistake?* "Can you describe the piebald mare's rider?"

A shrug was his answer. "Small lad. Short yeller hair. Looked a bit wean."

"Wean?" Prince Tomas asked.

"Sickly."

"When did you see them?"

Another shrug. "Mornin', it were. Near on a day ago."

After that, Karel stopped asking for a young woman. "A lad with yellow hair? Riding a piebald mare? Passed through here in the last day?" And in each village the answer was the same: yes.

# CHAPTER TWENTY-EIGHT

THE MAGES PUSHED their way through the tide of refugees, moving slowly. Sometimes it seemed to Harkeld that the press of people even pushed them backwards.

Sounds filled his head—tread of feet and clatter of hooves, rattle of cart wheels, voices—and beneath all those things was the sound of Innis's skull breaking. *Thock*. It was imbedded in his memory. It wouldn't go away, wouldn't leave him alone.

The road climbed steadily. No rain fell, but a wintry wind blew from the south. The grass became sparser, the trees smaller and more gnarled, but the refugees kept coming. A few called out warnings, urging them to turn back, but most were silent. Harkeld saw emotions on their faces: fear, desperation, grief. Rarely did anyone look at them with curiosity. These people were focused on fleeing.

Mid-afternoon, they halted briefly at a crossroad. Harkeld dismounted, jogged across to the wagon, and pushed aside the canvas covering. "Innis?"

Nellis was asleep, but Rand was awake, crouched alongside Petrus, holding Innis's head, his gaze unfocused.

Harkeld glanced at Petrus, alarmed. "Is she hemorrhaging again?"

Petrus shook his head.

Rand's eyes refocused. He released Innis, smoothed her hair, sat back on his heels. "Well done, Petrus."

"She's all right?" Harkeld asked.

Rand tilted his head, a half-nod. "No bleeding, no bruising, no swelling."

"The gland in her brain, the one that gives her magic...?"

"Wasn't damaged." Rand smoothed Innis's hair again. "Now, we just need her to wake."

"She will, won't she? If everything's healed?"

"Brains are tricky things. Trauma this bad... Even once it's healed, some people never wake."

Harkeld glanced at Petrus again. The shapeshifter's face was somber.

# CHAPTER TWENTY-NINE

LATE IN THE day, they came to a town. Britta tried to ride as if she was exhausted, barely awake in the saddle, head nodding on her neck, but every muscle in her body was tense with a painful mixture of anticipation and fear. This could be her opportunity.

They passed through the town gate and rode down a street of wooden buildings. Plain moved closer to her on one side, Curly on the other, hemming her in, their knees touching hers. Plain held her reins tightly in one hand.

Britta's gaze darted left and right. What if she stabbed Plain's hand, wrenched the reins free, and plunged down that alley? What if she threw herself from the piebald mare and ran into the crowded market square, hid beneath one of the stalls?

No. They'd be seconds behind her. Her escape would last less than a minute. And people would be killed. Innocent townspeople. Children.

She scanned the town desperately, her gaze jerking from one object to the next: the tall houses with wooden galleries jutting over the market square; the songbirds in cages hanging from the upper windows; the farmers haggling over flocks of geese; the covered well at the center of the square.

Throwing herself into the well seemed the only option she had. Death, not escape, but with the same result: she couldn't be used to kill Harkeld. But would she reach the well in time to jump in, or would the Fithians catch her first? And if she did jump in, would they haul her out before she drowned?

She hesitated too long. The busy hum of the market died behind them. There, at the end of the street, another town gate stood tall. Desperation rose in Britta's chest. *Jump off the horse. Jump and run.*

But where could she run to? An image flashed into her mind of herself scurrying down the street, beating on closed doors, begging someone to let her in, while songbirds looked down at her from their cages and the Fithians closed leisurely around her.

Up front, Leader spoke a few words. Pox nodded and trotted ahead, turned into a street to the left. Britta tensed. Were they stopping in this town? Was there a Fithian house here?

The rest of the party didn't slow. As they passed the street, Britta glanced down it.

Pox had halted outside a house with a tall wooden fence. He rang the bell dangling at the gate. Half a dozen pigeons perched on the fence, watching him.

Who lived there?

They passed the street. The gate grew close, closer. Britta's desperation increased, pushing up her throat in a silent scream.

The gate loomed above them. They were through it. She'd failed to escape.

* * *

BRITTA SAGGED IN the saddle, her exhaustion unfeigned. Dusk was drawing in. She closed her eyes, swaying, longing for hard ground to lie on, for sleep.

She dozed lightly until the clatter of wheels jerked her awake. An oxcart piled high with household goods passed them, heading towards the town.

Britta rubbed her eyes. They were past the last of the straggling farmsteads, climbing a rocky hillside. A forest of thorn trees and scrub surrounded them. Surely they'd stop soon? Eat. Rest.

Movement caught her eye, about a hundred yards ahead. Men riding towards them. Armed men.

She stiffened. Bandits?

No, from their colored vests they were a local militia.

Britta's exhaustion evaporated. She counted the approaching riders. A full score of men.

A quick, cautious glance at the assassins told her that Pox was still in the town. Five Fithians against twenty militiamen. She'd never get better odds than this.

Britta fumbled in her pocket for the sharp twig. The militiamen were thirty yards distant. Twenty yards. Ten.

The Fithians drew to one side of the road to let the militiamen pass. Plain was at her side, his knee touching hers, the reins fisted in his hand. Britta's heart beat hard and fast in her ears. Her chest was tight with terror. It was a struggle to fill her lungs.

Five yards. Two yards. The first militiamen were level with her.

Karel's voice whispered in her ear: *You can do it, princess.*

Britta drew in a sharp breath, stabbed the stick deep into the web of flesh between Plain's forefinger and thumb, wrenched her reins free, and dug her boots into the mare's flanks. "Help me!" she screamed. "They're kidnapping me! Help!"

She plunged into the militiamen. Horses shied on either side of her. Riders shouted and hauled on their reins, reaching for their swords.

"They're kidnapping me!" Britta shrieked. "Help!"

The piebald mare collided with a huge black stallion, almost unseating her. The stallion's rider grabbed her arm. He was a massive man, with bristling eyebrows and beard.

"Help—!"

A throwing star buried itself in the bearded man's forehead. He jerked backwards, releasing her arm, toppling from the saddle.

The rest of Britta's cry choked in her throat. She jerked a glance behind her. The road was a chaos of horses and riders. Shouts bellowed in the air. She heard the fierce clash of sword blades.

She tried to push deeper into the militiamen, to burrow between them, but there were too many horses, too many men. A bandaged hand snatched at her reins, and missed. Leader's. Their eyes met. Fury was stark on his face. His mouth snarled at her. Britta's heart kicked against her ribs. *Run.*

She slid off the other side of the mare and ran, pushing through the tangle of horses' legs and stirrups. Above her, men shouted. Someone snatched at her cloak. A militiaman. "What—?" he yelled at her.

Britta wrenched free, falling to her knees. *Leader's after me!* She scrambled to her feet and plunged deeper into the turmoil, dodging horses. The sounds of battle came from all around her. Someone screamed, a sound full of agony.

Britta crouched low, her heart thudding hard in her chest. *Where to run to?*

The forest. Downhill.

She caught her breath, took a moment to orient herself, and ran again, low, almost on hands and knees. Horses buffeted her, swords clanged—and then she burst from them and bolted into the trees on the far side of the road. *Run. Run.*

DARKNESS FELL, AND still Britta ran, scrambling, sliding, crashing through thickets of thorn trees, falling to her knees, dragging herself upright, plunging deeper and deeper into the forest. Stones tripped her and branches slapped at her, tore skin and clothing.

When she had no breath left, she halted, sinking to the ground, shaking, laboring to drag air into her lungs.

Had anyone followed her?

She strained to hear sounds of pursuit, but heard only her own harsh breathing and the loud gallop of her heart. Gradually, her heartbeat slowed. Her breath came more easily.

The forest was silent around her. No crunch of feet. No shouts.

Britta relaxed. *Safe. Free.*

She groped on hands and knees, found a tree trunk to lean against, and fumbled in her pocket for the bread she'd hidden there. She was lost, completely and utterly. But that was good. If she had no idea where she was, how could the Fithians find her?

Elation filled her. *I escaped!*

Britta broke off a small piece of bread and tucked the rest safely in her pocket for tomorrow. The elation faded. She saw the bearded militiaman's face for a moment, saw the throwing star sink into his skull, saw him fall.

Men had died because of her today.

# CHAPTER THIRTY

INNIS WAS STILL unconscious in the morning. "Don't worry," Rand said, when Petrus checked on her. "Sometimes it takes time."

The words were reassuring, but Rand's expression wasn't. He looked deeply worried.

"Eat," Rand told him. "Then I want you in the air. Stay close to us. Keep your eyes peeled. Serril'll fly ahead, see if he can spot any Fithians."

Petrus ate his gruel fast and stripped out of his clothes, trying not to worry about Innis. But it was impossible not to. What if she never woke?

"Justen, you ride this morning," Rand said. "Change your hair color. I want you to have the same brown as Flin."

"No," the prince said.

"Just until we're past the last of the refugees—"

"We didn't do it yesterday. Why do it today?"

"An oversight," Rand said. "If there are assassins—"

"No."

Rand looked past the prince to Justen. "Justen, change your hair color."

Justen obeyed. His hair became dark brown, his eyebrows, his stubble.

"Change it back, Justen, or I'll break your rutting nose," the prince said fiercely, his fist cocked to punch.

Justen took a step back, holding up a hand to ward off a blow.

"Flin," Rand's voice was curt, impatient. "It's only until we pass the last of the refugees."

"No! Hew's dead because he was pretending to be me. Thayer's dead because he was pretending to be me. I will not have Justen—or anyone!—do it again. Do you hear me?"

"We can all hear you, son," Serril said, his voice a low rumble.

Prince Harkeld swung to face him, fist still raised.

"Suppose I make myself look like you... You plan to break my nose, too?"

The prince wasn't cowed by Serril's size, by his authority. "Yes," he said, not lowering his fist.

Petrus halted, one leg out of his trews. Was the prince going to hit Serril? *He's a braver man than me.* No one beat Serril in a fight. The man was stronger than an ox.

Serril met Rand's eyes, shrugged.

Rand blew out a breath. "Fine!" He flung up his hands and turned away.

"Change back, Justen," Serril said.

Justen's hair became dun-colored again.

Petrus finished undressing. He watched Rand clamber into the wagon. He'd never seen the healer lose his temper before.

"I APOLOGIZE FOR threatening you," Harkeld said.

Justen shrugged. "Ach, forget it."

They rode in silence for several minutes, side by side, then the shapeshifter grinned. "Would have liked to see you try to hit Serril. He'd swat you like a fly."

"Probably." Harkeld glanced at Justen. The shapeshifter was almost the person Innis and Petrus had pretended to be. Friendly. Patient. Good-humored. "I... uh, I'm sorry I've been such an ass. It wasn't your fault they used your face."

Justen shrugged again. "Ach, forget it."

Harkeld looked at the wagon ahead of them. "All this would have been much easier if I was a shapeshifter, not a fire mage. The Fithians would never have found me."

"Wouldn't have helped," Justen said. "Takes years to learn how to shift safely."

"It does?"

Justen nodded. "Lot of studying. Got to understand the anatomy of what you're shifting into. You make mistakes, otherwise."

"What kind of mistakes?"

"Well, birds' bones are different, see? If you don't give yourself the right bones, you might *look* like a bird, but you can't fly."

"Huh."

"And they have different types of feathers, too. Flight feathers and down feathers. Get the flight feathers wrong, and you can't fly either."

Harkeld looked up and found Petrus gliding above them, his underwings and breast creamy white. "Do you *like* being a shapeshifter?"

"Love it," Justen said. "Especially flying."

Harkeld considered this answer, following Petrus with his eyes. What would it be like to ride the air currents? To rise up on the wind?

To have feathers instead of skin? Talons, instead of fingernails? A beak, not a nose and mouth?

He shivered. No, he didn't want to be a shapeshifter.

# CHAPTER THIRTY-ONE

BRITTA WOKE BY slow degrees. She opened her eyes
and saw light filtering through tree branches. At
first she had no idea where she was, or why she was
there—then memory returned.

*I escaped!*

She pushed up to sit, suddenly alert, tense, listening
for sounds of pursuit.

She heard birdsong and the rustle of leaves in the breeze.
No twigs snapping, no stealthy footsteps, no voices.

Britta relaxed. She yawned and rubbed her eyes.
Scratches and dried blood crisscrossed her face and
hands, thirst burned in her throat, but none of that
mattered. She was *free*.


BRITTA DECIDED NOT to eat breakfast. No more bread
until she'd found some water to drink. She headed
downhill, walking as quietly as she could, picking
her way through the thorn trees and scrub, stopping
often to examine the forest, to listen. But she heard
nothing, saw nothing.

Within half an hour she found a small, boggy
creek fringed with bright green reeds.

Britta crouched and drank greedily, gulping handfuls of water. Then, she sat back on her heels and wiped her chin and looked around. Thorn trees. Scrub. Stones. Reeds. Creek. She had no idea where north and south were, no idea where the road lay, or the town they'd passed through yesterday. But that didn't matter. It didn't even matter if she walked in circles until her strength gave out and she died in this forest. What mattered was that the Fithians couldn't find her. That she couldn't be used against Harkeld.

She pushed to her feet. She would follow the creek. At least she'd have water then. There was bread in her pocket, but she wouldn't eat until she absolutely had to. Until she was starving. A few crumbs at a time.

Britta took two steps and halted. Someone stood alongside the nearest tree, his teeth bared in a silent grin.

Killer.

Britta's heart punched against her breastbone. She turned to run—and froze. Pox stood with his boots in the creek.

Terror rooted her legs to the ground.

Pox stepped out of the creek. He struck her hard across the face.

Britta fell, tasting blood in her mouth, rolled and tried to scramble to her feet, but Pox grabbed a fistful of her hair, his knuckles digging into her scalp, and held her down.

Footsteps crunched across the stony ground. Someone crouched in her field of vision. Killer. His ice-blue eyes glinted. She saw how much he wanted to kill her.

Pox hauled her to her feet. Killer stood, too. He stepped closer. He held a rope in his hands.

Britta kicked out in panic. Her boot sank into Killer's groin.

Killer uttered a strangled grunt and curled in on himself, collapsing to the ground.

Pox grunted, too. He released Britta's hair, shoved her to her knees, and tried to haul her arms behind her.

Britta flailed and kicked and clawed, fighting Pox with all her strength.

Pox hooked an arm around her throat and squeezed.

Blood roared in Britta's ears. She plummeted into blackness.

# CHAPTER THIRTY-TWO

THEY RODE INTO a town called Vermeulen in the afternoon. Something had happened here recently. Something bad. Karel knew even before they passed through the gate. It was in the way the gate guard looked at them, tense, his hand gripping his sword. It was in the busyness of the main street. Townspeople clustered together, grief on some faces, excitement on others. The men were all armed. The voices he heard were high-pitched. Karel caught words as he passed. *Dead. Fithian.*

He dismounted in the market square. "We need to find out what's happened here."

"What do you mean?" Prince Tomas asked, glancing around.

"Can't you feel it?" The air seemed to bristle with emotion. Tension. Fear. People were watching them. A babble of noise rippled outwards, shrill with alarm. He scanned the crowd, saw women catch children and hurry away, saw men step back, loosening their swords in their sheaths. *They're afraid of us. Afraid we're Fithians?*

"Keep your hands away from your swords," he told the armsmen quietly, and then raised his voice:

"We need to speak with your watch captain. Where do we find him?"

Silence met his words. A silence filled with hostility and fear.

"Your watch captain," Karel repeated loudly. "Where is he?" He stood with his feet slightly apart, as relaxed and unthreatening as he could be, but he knew what he looked like, what the armsmen looked like. Like soldiers. Like Fithians.

There was a stir in the crowd, someone pushing through. A man almost as tall as Karel, solidly built, with thick dark hair and a beard graying at the edges.

"I'm watch captain here." The man stopped three paces from Karel. His chin was up, his voice level, but the skin was taut across his cheekbones. *He thinks we'll kill him.*

Karel stepped slowly forward, keeping his hands well away from his sword belt.

The watch captain's fingers twitched, but he didn't unsheathe his own weapon.

"You've had trouble here recently," Karel said, in a low voice. "What?"

The man blinked, and considered the question. "Why should I tell you, stranger?"

Bravado, or caution?

Caution, Karel decided. He lowered his voice still further, so no one in the watching crowd could hear. "We're looking for some people. They'd have ridden through here yesterday. Does your trouble have anything to do with them?"

"What kind of people?" The watch captain's voice was as low as Karel's.

"Men." Karel examined the man's face, assessed him, decided on honesty. "Fithian assassins."

The watch captain's face tightened in a grimace. "They passed through."

"What happened?"

The man assessed him in turn, his gaze flicking over Karel, over the prince, over the armsmen. "Why should I tell you? Who are you?"

"Not Fithians," Karel said. "You can search us if you want. You'll find no throwing stars."

"Why are you following them?"

"They have something of ours."

"What?"

"A person."

The watch captain stared at him for a long moment, then gave a curt nod. "You'd best come with me. Leave those men of yours here."

KAREL TOOK PRINCE Tomas with him. He left the armsmen behind with orders to look as harmless as they could. If ten strong, well-armed men could look harmless.

The watch captain walked at a brisk pace, not speaking. Along a street, then left, and left again. The building he led them to wasn't Vermeulen's watch house. The All-Mother's circle held in cupped palms was carved into the wood above the door: the town's infirmary.

The watch captain halted on the step. "Yesterday, close on dusk, a troop of our militiamen met some riders, about six miles east of here."

"What happened?"

The man pressed his lips together, flattening them against his teeth, and shook his head. "I'll let Eckel tell you."

THE CAPTAIN LED them down a wooden corridor scented with herbs. They entered a dormitory. Karel counted twelve beds. Only two were occupied. In one, an elderly man slept. In the other, a younger man lay. A woman sat alongside his bed, holding his hand.

The watch captain led them to the second bed. Karel and Prince Tomas followed, their boots clattering on the wooden floor. The scent of herbs was stronger in here.

The woman looked up, released the man's hand, stood. "Rohmer?"

The captain nodded at her. "Good day, Mistress Tersa. I need to talk with Eckel here. Can you give us a moment?"

The woman ducked her head in a nod, gathered her skirts, and left the room.

Karel watched her go. Mother? Sister? Or the patient's wife?

The captain, Rohmer, sat in the chair the woman had vacated. "Eckel? I need to talk with you again."

Karel examined the man in the bed. Bandaged head, bandaged arm, flushed with fever. Younger than he'd thought, perhaps even younger than he himself was. The woman must be his mother.

"Cap'n." The word was slurred. Eckel's pupils were dilated, his gaze vague.

"Poppy syrup?" Karel asked, crouching alongside the bed. "How bad are his injuries?"

"He'll live," Rohmer said. "Unlike the others." He pressed his lips together again, grimaced. "Twenty militiamen. Eckel here's the only one still alive."

"What?" Karel heard shock in Prince Tomas's voice. "Nineteen dead?"

Rohmer didn't answer, instead he turned to the man in the bed. "Eckel, tell me what happened again."

Eckel didn't answer for several seconds. He lay blinking, his eyes glazed and unfocussed. *Too drugged*, Karel thought, rising from his crouch. But even as he stood, Eckel opened his mouth and spoke: "On dusk, it were. We was headed home, just passed the six mile marker." He rubbed his face, smearing his eyes with a clumsy hand. "Were these riders comin' towards us. Didn't look at 'em. Wasn't thinkin' of anything 'cept my dinner."

Karel crouched again. "What happened?"

Eckel was silent for a moment, his brow creased below the bandage. "Hard to remem'er. Happen so fast." He blew out a breath scented with poppy syrup, rubbed his face again. "One of them rid right into us. Yellin', she were. Shoutin' for help. Said she'd been kidnapped."

Karel's pulse picked up speed. "She?"

"Then it was jus'..." Eckel blinked, his confusion clear to see on his face. "It jus' happen so fast. One minute we was ridin', the next we was fightin'. There was swords and them star things. And then we was all dead on the road."

"She?" Karel said again. "You're certain it was a woman shouting for help?"

"Thought she were a boy," Eckel said, squinting up at Karel. "Tried to grab her. Got her cloak, got a look at her. Not a boy. A girl. Yeller hair. Pretty face."

"That's her?" the watch captain asked. "The person you're looking for?"

"That's her," Karel said.

"Who is she?"

Karel exchanged a glance with Prince Tomas. "A kinswoman."

"What do the Fithians want with her?"

"I can't tell you."

"Can't, or won't?" There was a note of anger in the watch captain's voice.

"Can't," Karel said, meeting the man's gaze. "I would, if I could, but more lives than just nineteen depend on it." *The lives of everyone in this kingdom, yours included.*

Rohmer stared at him, his mouth tight.

"I can't tell you who we are," Karel said quietly. "I can't tell you who she is. But I need to know what happened on that road."

"They killed everyone," Eckel said, the words slurring together. "Tha's what happened. Killed us all."

Karel turned to him. "Except you."

"'Cept me." Tears filled Eckel's eyes. "'Cept me."

"What happened?"

"Got knocked off me horse. Can' remem'er much after that, 'cept... 'cept it was all over. The fightin' had stopped and they was... they was killin' the wounded." Tears spilled from Eckel's eyes. "Saw them kill Lobel, and Ren. Knew they'd kill me soon as they got to me. So's I got to me feet and grabbed the nearest horse an' headed for Vermeulen. They follered. They was right behin' me. One of them star things hit me in the arm. But it fell dark, an' I knew the road and they didn'."

"And you made it home."

Eckel nodded, and wiped the moisture from his eyes.

"And the girl? The one with yellow hair?"

"She were gone."

"Gone? What do you mean, gone?" Prince Tomas leaned eagerly over the bed.

"The one in charge of 'em, he were screamin' at 'em to find her." Eckel shivered. "In a murderous rage, he were."

The prince turned to Karel, his eyes shining with excitement. "She got away!" His attention swung to Rohmer. "Did you look for her? Did you find her?"

"No," the watch captain said. "We did not look for her. We lost nineteen men yesterday. We're not looking to lose any more. You want her, you find her."

Karel met the man's gaze, saw the anger there. "Fair enough," he said, pushing to his feet.

"But—"

"No." He cut the prince off. "This isn't their fight, it's ours."

Tomas closed his mouth.

Karel turned away from the bed, and turned back. "Eckel? How many Fithians were there?"

"Didn' see, didn' count. Mebbe five, six?"

"Any of them die?" He glanced at Rohmer. "You find any bodies you didn't recognize?"

The watch captain shook his head.

*Six against twenty, and the six win.* Karel grimaced. He walked quietly from the dormitory, careful not to wake the elderly man, then lengthened his stride in the corridor.

Princess Brigitta had escaped. Escaped from Fithian assassins. He felt like whooping until the corridor rang with his voice. His pride in her was enormous.

Karel stepped outside and halted on the stoop. Prince Tomas followed him out, and Rohmer. "Thank you," Karel told the watch captain.

Rohmer acknowledged this with a curt nod and turned away.

The prince came to stand alongside Karel. "Nineteen dead." His voice was dismayed. He didn't utter the words, but Karel heard them clearly: *We haven't a chance.*

The watch captain, Rohmer, heard it, too. He halted and looked back. "Our militia are farmers and shopkeepers. They're volunteers, not soldiers. Not like you."

*We're armsmen and a prince, not soldiers.* But Karel didn't correct the mistake.

"Twenty to six, we hadn't a chance. Twelve to six, you do."

Karel studied the man's face. He saw anger there, and bitterness. "Any of your kin die yesterday?"

Rohmer's mouth tightened. "Two nephews."

"I'm sorry."

Rohmer's lips pressed together. After a moment, he nodded. "My deputy's in charge out there, at the six mile marker. Steppen. Tell him I said you could look around."

"Thanks," Karel said.

"Get the bastards."

"We will."

"All-Mother's blessing go with you." With that, the watch captain strode away.

Karel stood on the stoop, watching until he was gone.

"Nineteen dead," Prince Tomas said again, in a more neutral tone.

"Untrained. Not expecting a fight." Farmers and shopkeepers, the watch captain had said. Dressed in uniforms and with swords on their belts, playing at being soldiers. "We're trained. We're ready."

The prince glanced at him. "You forget, I've seen them fight." He touched the stump of his right ear, ran his fingers along the scar bisecting his cheek.

"Seen, and survived."

"Because we had witches with us." Tomas lowered his hand. "You're the only one of us capable of killing a Fithian, one on one."

*And even I wouldn't survive for long.* He'd had surprise on his side in Lundegaard. And the advantage of higher ground. Take those away, and the next Fithian he fought would probably be his last. "The rest of you are close."

Prince Tomas snorted. "You'd beat me in a fight, a hundred times out of a hundred."

Karel didn't deny this. "Gunvald beat me once."

Tomas snorted again. "Once. Out of how many times?"

Karel shrugged. He started walking towards the market square.

Tomas caught up with him, matched his step.

"Were you Esger's best?"

Karel considered this question. "One of them. I didn't win every training bout. There were a couple of others who sometimes beat me."

"Sometimes."

"Sometimes."

They walked in silence for the length of one street. Karel heard the twitter of birdsong, glanced up, saw birdcages hanging from the upper windows of a house.

"Are there many Esfaban armsmen?" the prince asked, when they turned the corner.

"I'm the first. There are others training."

Prince Tomas gave a grunt of satisfaction. "Thought you might be the first. The best of the best. That's what you tried to be. Am I right?"

Karel glanced at him.

"Your fighting skills. You have something to prove."

"My family's loyalty." To save them from servitude again.

Tomas shook his head. "Not just that. You're proving your people's worth. Fighters, not slaves."

Karel hesitated, and then nodded.

"And you threw it all away for Princess Brigitta."

Karel felt himself flush. "Jaegar was going to murder those boys. And her, if she tried to stop it."

They turned the next corner. The market square came into sight. "What now?" Tomas asked, his pace quickening.

"Now, we ride out to the six mile marker. See what we can find."

\*     \*     \*

THEY CAME ACROSS signs of the battle well before the six mile marker: two wagons laden with dead horses. The prince counted the carcasses under his breath as the wagons lumbered past. "Seven," he said.

Next, were a man and woman, both gray-haired. The woman wept quietly as she rode. The man was grim-faced. Not refugees; they carried no belongings with them. Mourners, Karel guessed. On their way back from seeing where their son had died.

No bodies lay on the road where the fight had taken place, but there was blood. Lots of blood. And half a dozen men, who reached for their swords.

Karel signaled for the armsmen and Prince Tomas to halt. He slowed his mount to a walk, his eyes skipping from one hostile face to the next. His gaze fastened on one man. "You Steppen?"

The man gripped his sword more tightly, his knuckles whitening. "What of it?"

*He's afraid the next blood spilled on the road will be his.*

Karel swung down from his saddle, but made no move towards the men. He stood quietly, his hands relaxed at his sides. "Rohmer sent us, said we could look around."

"Why?" Steppen said, his grip on the sword still white-knuckled.

"We're hunting the men who did this."

Steppen examined him with a quick flick of his eyes, head to toe, and then the prince, and then each of the armsmen. "Hunting Fithians? Why?"

"To kill them."

Steppen stared hard at Karel, eyes narrowed, then sheathed his sword. He swept his hand out in a broad, angry gesture, indicating the mess of hoof prints and boot prints, the dusty marks where bodies had lain, the discarded fragments of tack and clothing, the blood. "Look as much as you want."

"Thanks."

The armsmen dismounted quietly behind Karel.

"You seen anyone you can't place here today?" Karel asked the watchman. "A young woman with golden hair? Dressed like a man?"

Steppen's mouth twisted. "The one who started this?" He turned his head, spat into the dirt. "No."

"And you've not seen any Fithians." It was a statement, not a question. Steppen would have looked hard at every person who passed, every farmer, every refugee.

Steppen shook his head. "The men who did this, they're long gone."

Karel nodded. That was what his instinct told him, too.

Prince Tomas stepped up alongside him. He looked at the bloodstained road, and then turned to survey the ground on either side. "What now? We search for her?"

Karel glanced left and right, taking in the terrain. A rocky hillside clothed in thorn trees and scrub. The ground rose to the east. The princess would have run downhill, away from the road, into those dense thickets of trees. And the Fithians would have followed.

He imagined her running, imagined her fear.

"We search for her?" the prince said again, turning on his heel, examining the hillside as if trying to decide where to start looking.

"No," Karel said.

Tomas frowned. "No?"

"These men are professionals. They know how to track people. They lost her. They found her. They left."

"But—"

"We ride to the next village, ask questions, see who passed through. I'd wager the Fithians did some time this morning. If not, we come back here and search."

Prince Tomas was still frowning. "But if she's still here, we risk losing—"

"She's not," Karel said, his certainty gut-deep. "She escaped. They caught her." He examined the scene again: the hillside, the thorn trees, the bloody road. Princess Brigitta was resourceful and courageous. She'd escaped from the Fithians, slowed them down, delayed them. "We'll catch up with them soon."

# CHAPTER THIRTY-THREE

THE FITHIANS DIDN'T punish her. They didn't buy a cart at the next village and bundle her into it. They didn't use All-Mother's Breath on her. Leader simply tied her hands together, fastened them to the pommel of the piebald mare's saddle, and let her ride.

*My escape isn't worth comment? Or warnings of dire punishment if I try again?*

It made Britta angry. She'd ridden with three things: the painful ache of her throat where Pox had throttled her, the hot, swollen throbbing where he'd struck her face, and anger. She'd *escaped*. Had injured Plain. Brought Killer to his knees. How dared they not even mention it?

Beneath the anger, was a gray eddy of defeat. She'd escaped; they'd caught her.


THE ANGER—AND the defeat—stayed with her all day. It flavored the dried meat she painfully swallowed for dinner. It blanketed her as she lay down to sleep. Britta closed her eyes and felt exhaustion weigh her down. Her wrists were still bound. Leader hadn't untied them. Punishment? Her throat ached. Her cheek radiated heat, radiated pain.

Footsteps came towards her.

Britta opened her eyes.

Curly knelt, pulled a length of rope from his belt, and grabbed one of her ankles.

Britta tried to jerk free.

Curly's fingers tightened, biting into her ankle, pressing flesh against bone. His gaze lifted to her face for an instant. The threat in his eyes was unmistakable.

Britta froze, held her breath.

Curly swiftly bound her ankles together. He stood and walked away without a word.

Britta lay wrapped in her cloak, feeling the tightness of the rope around her ankles. *They're afraid I'll escape again.*

A fierce bubble of exhilaration expanded in her chest. The ache in her throat, the throbbing heat in her cheek, evaporated. She grinned to herself. By the All-Mother's name, they *should* be afraid, because she was cursed-well *going* to escape again.

And next time, they wouldn't catch her.

# CHAPTER THIRTY-FOUR

"SEE IF INNIS will respond to your voice, Petrus," Rand said, when they halted for the night. He'd napped in the wagon; his eyes looked brighter, his face less haggard.

Petrus climbed into the wagon. Innis lay in a bed of blankets. She looked as pale and fragile as porcelain. He knelt, took one of her hands, held it in both of his. Her fingers were limp, cool.

He bent his head, spoke softly in her ear. "Innis? Innis, can you hear me? You need to wake up."

There was no twitch of her fingers, no change in her breathing, no flicker of her eyelids.

He tried again. "Innis, wake up!"

But no matter whether he spoke softly or loudly, no matter whether he couched his words as an entreaty or a command, Innis didn't stir.

Finally he sat back and looked at Rand.

"Don't look so upset, son. We'll wake her."

"How?" He heard desperation in his voice, took a breath, tried to speak calmly. "At the Academy they said that the longer a patient is unresponsive, the less likely—"

"I have an idea," Rand said. "Something we can try."

"What?"

"You said you'd told Flin about the dreams?"

Petrus nodded.

"How did he react?"

"Uh... he was angry Innis had told you and me, but not him. But then he asked some questions. I think he wants to know more."

"Good."

"You're going to ask him to share a dream with her? Try to wake her up that way?"

"If he's willing. Stay with her, will you?" Rand clambered down from the wagon.

Petrus looked down at Innis. He touched her cheek lightly, let his fingertips rest on her cool skin. The strongest shapeshifter in living memory, a powerful healer—and yet not an ounce of arrogance or conceit. Kind. Shy. Brave. Quiet. He thought about her solemn, dark gray eyes, thought about the flashes of mischief that sometimes lit her face, thought about how much he loved her.

The familiar, bitter jealousy surged in his chest. He remembered what Innis had told him in Ankeny. *You're my family. I will always love you.*

But not as much as she loved the prince.

Footsteps approached the wagon. He heard Prince Harkeld's voice. "Of course I will. Now?"

"Once you've eaten."

THE PRINCE BROUGHT his bedroll and blankets. "How close should I be?"

"Best be right alongside her," Rand said. He turned his head, and peered across at the campfire.

"Won't be a minute. Need to talk to Malle before she turns in." He disappeared into the dark.

The prince laid his bedroll next to Innis and spread out his blankets. Petrus's bitterness returned. He tried to smother it, but Prince Harkeld must have sensed it. He stopped what he was doing, sat back on one knee, met Petrus's eyes in the candlelight.

For a long moment, they stared at each other, and then the prince said, "I'm sorry."

Was that pity in Prince Harkeld's voice? Petrus felt his face stiffen. "For what?"

"I know how you feel about her."

Petrus's face seemed to become even stiffer. "No, you don't," he said, turning away, hot with anger, hot with humiliation. Pity? Rutting *pity*?

"Petrus..." The prince scrambled after him and grabbed his arm. "Don't go."

Petrus tried to wrench free, but Prince Harkeld's fingers dug in. He turned his head and glared at the prince. "Let go of me." *Or else I'll break your face.*

"Hedín's slept with me the last two nights; tonight I want it to be you. If Innis wakes up, you should be here."

Petrus glared at him, hated him.

The prince released his arm. "I'm sorry," he said again. His mouth twisted wryly. The expression on his face wasn't pity. What was it? Fellow-feeling? Friendship? "Please stay."

Petrus looked away. He wrestled with his pride, with his temper. "All right," he said finally.

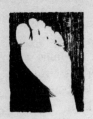

# CHAPTER THIRTY-FIVE

DUSK DISSOLVED INTO night, and still they continued, the pony putting one hoof in front of the other. Stars shone, pinpricks of light, and a bright sliver of moon rose over the horizon.

The night was half gone before Bennick halted.

Jaumé stumbled when he dismounted. His legs trembled with exhaustion. *Do we have to travel so far, so fast?*

Bennick gripped his arm, steadied him. "Only a couple more days at this pace, lad. Sit. I'll see to the horses."

Jaumé sat, his legs folding bonelessly. His head flopped forward, his chin resting on his chest. He heard the jangle of bridles and stirrups as Bennick unsaddled the horses.

He must have fallen asleep. He woke to Bennick shaking him.

"Eat this." Firelight flickered over Bennick's face, over the food he held out.

Jaumé wolfed down the bread and cheese and dried meat. When he'd finished, Bennick reached out and ruffled Jaumé's hair, like Da had used to do. "Better?"

Jaumé nodded.

"Good lad." Bennick tossed him his sleeping mat and blanket. "We'll slow down once we've caught up to Vught."

Vught? Jaumé glanced at Bennick.

"He's a Brother."

Jaumé hesitated, and then blurted: "We'll travel with him?"

"Him and his men."

Jaumé unrolled his sleeping mat, digesting this information. He'd liked traveling with Nolt and his band of Brothers. There'd been a camaraderie, a sense of belonging. "Is Vught like Nolt?" He remembered Nolt's grizzled beard, his sternness.

Bennick shook his head. "Younger. Tougher."

Tougher? Jaumé wrapped his blanket around himself. He couldn't imagine anyone tougher than Nolt.

"Smarter," Bennick said, half under his breath.

Smarter? Jaumé glanced at him.

Bennick caught the glance. His lips compressed, as if he sensed the silent question and wanted to rebuke him for it, and then he seemed to relax. He reached for his billy of tea. "Vught has something the prince values. Bait."

"Bait?" Jaumé tried to imagine what bait could catch a prince. Ropes of jewels? Golden ingots?

Bennick grinned, his teeth catching the firelight. "The prince's sister."

# CHAPTER THIRTY-SIX

HARKELD WALKED FOR a long time—around the palace gardens, up to the highest parapet of King Magnas's castle, through Masse's red desert and the muddy wasteland of Ankeny's milled forest and the steaming, stinking jungle—but Innis was nowhere to be found. Anxiety built inside him. "Innis!" he shouted. But his dream remained empty.

He repeated the circuit. Osgaard, Lundegaard, Ankeny. All the places they'd been together. "Innis!"

Still nothing.

He tried the street in Hansgrohe where she'd been attacked. He found the blood where the woman had lain, found the stave. But no Innis.

Harkeld kept walking. He was in unfamiliar territory now. Plains. Forests. Mountains. Coast.

He followed the coastline for a long time. A fishing village came into sight, houses built of red stone, boats bobbing in a small harbor. The village was silent, empty of people. Past it was a headland and a broad sweeping bay, with a fishing fleet and a town and orchards on the hillsides. And people. He heard voices, laughter, children singing. Seagulls hung in the air above him, uttering mewing cries. Dogs barked. Donkeys brayed.

Harkeld walked faster. *She's here.*

His feet led him through the town square, up a cobbled street so steep it had steps cut into it, past the last red stone house, along a donkey track winding up the hillside, into an orchard. He didn't recognize the trees. They had leaves that were dark green on one side and silver on the other, and hard pale green berries.

A young woman sat beneath one of the trees, in a patch of sunshine, looking out over the town and the harbor and the sea. She was slender, dressed in men's clothing, with long, curling black hair. Innis. She turned her head when she heard his footsteps. A smile lit her face, lit her eyes. "Harkeld."

*She remembers who I am.* That was a good sign, wasn't it?

Harkeld sat down alongside her, uncertain what to say. "Where is this? Which kingdom?"

"Lirac."

He reached out and took her hand. With that touch came the familiar sense of deep connection. He could feel her emotions. Calmness. Contentment. She was happy sitting here.

He was the one who was worried. Innis wasn't worried at all.

"Why are you here?"

"It's home."

"I thought you were from Rosny."

Her contentment faltered slightly. "I grew up in Lirac. My parents were posted here. They were Sentinels."

"Sentinel mages?" he said. "Both of them?"

"Yes." Her contentment evaporated. In its place was distress. Innis released his hand, got to her feet, and began climbing the hillside, pushing through the trees.

Harkeld followed. Soon, he was panting. "What are these trees?"

"Olives."

At the top of the hill, Innis halted. She hugged her arms and stared down at the harbor glittering in the sunlight.

"They both died here. Mother first. And three months later, Father."

"Ah..." Harkeld stepped up behind her, put his arms around her, rested his chin on her hair. "I'm sorry."

"I was sent back to Rosny. To the Academy." She shivered.

Harkeld tightened his hug. Innis hadn't changed shape, but somehow she felt smaller, younger, like a child in his arms. "How old were you?"

"Twelve."

Yes, a child.

"You feel like Petrus," Innis said. "Protective."

"Petrus looked after you?"

"He became my brother." Innis slipped out of his embrace. "Come on, I'll show you the grotto. You'll like it. There's a spring coming up out of the rock, and a pool."

"Innis, wait—"

"Come on." She took his hand. "We can bathe."

Harkeld's heart seemed to turn over in his chest. She'd never looked at him like this in real life, her eyes warm and smiling.

"We need to talk, Innis. It's serious."

Her smile dimmed slightly. "How serious?"

"This is a dream. We're sharing it. You know that, don't you?"

Her smile died. "Ah... Someone told you."

Harkeld nodded.

Innis released his hand. "I'm sorry," she said, turning away, hugging her arms again. "It should have been me who told you."

"Why didn't you?"

She was silent for a long time, staring down at the harbor. "I didn't know how to. You've been so angry."

"I'm not angry now." Harkeld stepped in front of her, took hold of her shoulders, caught her gaze. "Innis, listen to me. This is serious. You were hurt. Really bad. You've been unconscious for two and a half days. You need to wake up."

Her brow creased. "What?"

"Do you remember Hansgrohe? The pregnant woman whose scalp was torn off?"

The crease between Innis's eyebrows deepened. She shook her head.

"Someone hit you, and it broke your skull, and Rand and Nellis healed it, but you haven't woken up. Innis—you *need* to wake up."

She stared up at him. Harkeld felt her confusion, her bewilderment.

"Innis, wake up!"


HE HEARD PEOPLE talking quietly. He smelled food. Stew?

Harkeld opened his eyes and saw candlelight flickering on canvas, turned his head and saw Rand and Petrus and Innis. Petrus had an arm around Innis's shoulders. An empty bowl rested in her lap.

Harkeld pushed aside his blankets and sat up hurriedly. "You woke up!"

Petrus's expression stiffened. He removed his arm from Innis's shoulders.

"About an hour ago," Innis said. "I don't know why I didn't wake earlier. I've checked and I can't find anything wrong." She touched her temple.

"It took me forever to find you. What's the time?" It felt like morning.

"Nearly dawn," Rand said.

"I'll get the gruel on." Petrus took the empty bowl from Innis's lap and clambered down from the wagon.

"No patrolling for you today, Innis," Rand said. "I want you to rest. We'll see if you're up to a shift this evening." He followed Petrus from the wagon.

Harkeld folded up his bedding, wishing Rand and Petrus hadn't left. The silence between him and Innis felt awkward, self-conscious.

He looked up and met her eyes. *What do I say to her?* It was so much easier in the dreams, when he could sense what she was thinking. "How do you feel?"

"Fine."

The awkward silence fell again. Harkeld found his boots, pulled them on. "Innis... we need to talk."

She nodded warily.

He examined her face. Too thin, too pale. She wasn't ready for this either. "But not now. When you're feeling stronger."

"I'm perfectly all right."

"I think not." He reached for his sword belt. "I'll help them with breakfast. You stay here. Rest."

Outside, Rand crouched at the fire, hanging a pot on the tripod. Petrus was going through the packsaddles, looking for gruel. Harkeld walked across to him, buckling his sword belt. "Need a hand?"

"No," Petrus said. "Found it." He straightened, turned away, turned back. "Thanks for waking her."

"You're welcome."

Petrus gave a short nod and headed towards the fire.

Harkeld caught his arm, halting him. "Don't stop hugging her. Not because of me."

Petrus turned his head to look at him. His green eyes were black in the pre-dawn gloom.

"Innis needs you."

Petrus shrugged Harkeld's hand off his arm. He shook his head. "Your bond with her is stronger than mine."

"Not stronger. Just different. She says you're her brother."

Petrus grimaced and looked away again, at the dark line of the horizon and the graying sky.

"If I see you do that again—stop hugging her because of me—I swear to the All-Mother I'll break your nose again."

Petrus snorted. "You could *try*."

Harkeld stepped closer and lowered his voice. "I don't know what's going to happen between me and Innis. I don't even know if we'll both be alive in a month's time. But I *do* know how she feels about you, so for *her* sake, don't do that again. All right, whoreson?"

There was a long moment of silence, and then Petrus said, "I should break your rutting ribs again."

"You could *try*."

Petrus snorted, was silent, then said, "All right, you've made your point. Whoreson."

"Good." Harkeld waited until Petrus was several strides away, and then called, "Wrestling tonight?"

Petrus glanced back, bared his teeth. "You're on."

"WANT TO TRY today?" Serril asked Rand, during breakfast.

Rand glanced around, counting the mages. No, just the shapeshifters. His gaze came to rest on Petrus. "How tired are you?"

"Not tired at all," Petrus said.

Serril and Rand exchanged a glance, and then Serril nodded and went to fetch a map. He sat down beside Petrus and unrolled the calfskin. "We need to know where the curse is. And we need to know how fast it's moving."

Petrus's pulse picked up. He leaned forward, studying the map.

"We're about here." Serril tapped the calfskin. "We think the curse is somewhere between here... and here."

"How will I know where it is?"

"The people. If there are any left alive. If there aren't, you'll have to land, change into yourself. You should be able to tell by the curse shadows. They'll be darker and thicker than they are now. But if you *do* land and change into yourself, for the All-Mother's sake make certain no one sees you. They'll kill you if they have the curse, and they'll kill you if they haven't."

Petrus suppressed a shiver.

"Animals can't get the curse," Rand said. "So theoretically you can't catch the curse if you're shifted."

Petrus's attention jerked to him.

"The issue's been debated back and forth at the Academy for decades," Rand said. "The general consensus is that that shapeshifters in animal form can probably drink cursed water and be unaffected."

A feeling of panic rose in Petrus's chest. Was Rand going to ask him to break a Primary Law and drink while shapeshifted? *But I don't want to drink cursed water!*

"You are absolutely forbidden to try. Do you understand me, Petrus?" Rand looked as stern as Dareus ever had, no humor on his face, not the slightest hint of a smile in his eyes. "*Absolutely* forbidden."

"Yes, sir," Petrus said. The panicked feeling in his chest subsided.

Rand held his gaze for a long moment, and then nodded.

"You remember that, son," Serril said, and there was a grim note in his deep voice. "Or I'll personally flay you. Now, take a good look at this map..."

PETRUS STUDIED THE map while the others dismantled the tents, loaded the packhorses, saddled the riding mounts. When he felt satisfied he knew where he was going, he rolled up the calfskin and gave it to Rand.

"Petrus..." The voice was Innis's.

He turned and found her standing behind him.

"I won't drink a drop of water, I promise." Petrus put an arm around her. He wasn't sure whether to be angry with Prince Harkeld for giving him permission to hug Innis, or not. *Permission? Like I'm one of his bondservants.*

Innis hugged him back fiercely, then stood on tiptoe and kissed his cheek. "Be *careful*."

"I will."

Petrus stripped out of his clothes and stuffed them into one of the packsaddles.

The prince wandered over. "You heard her," he said. "Be careful."

"Don't worry, I'll be back. I'm planning on breaking some of your ribs tonight."

The prince grinned. "You can *try*."

# CHAPTER THIRTY-SEVEN

POX UNTIED HER ANKLES when he brought her breakfast: bread and cheese. He left her wrists bound. *So this is how it's going to be. Tied wrists.* A hindrance to escape, yes, but nothing she couldn't overcome.

Britta chewed her food, and looked around. A broken stone with a jagged edge lay less than an arm's reach from where she sat in her nest of blankets.

*Why not?*

Britta finished her bread and cheese. She climbed to her feet, picked up her blankets and shook them, dropped one, picked it up again and curled the stone into one palm.

She slid the stone into the pocket of her cloak. Escape was possible again.

# CHAPTER THIRTY-EIGHT

PETRUS FLEW SOUTH and east, following the roads he'd memorized from the map. For the first thirty or so miles they were clogged with refugees, then the numbers dwindled. These were the stragglers, the people too poor to have horses and too elderly or infirm to walk fast.

A strong headwind slowed him. He had to work hard for every mile gained. The road climbed, winding up valleys and over ridges, passing through a village, cresting finally at a high plateau. This was poor land, eroded into gullies and hillocks. Crumbling stone walls marked out an uneven patchwork of small fields. He saw solitary farmhouses, small hamlets. In the distance, smoke smudged the sky. Beyond the haze of smoke were snowy mountains to the east and south.

The headwind didn't ease. It came from the south, sweeping across the plateau and funneling down the valleys to the northern lowlands. *Rut it*. The next few hours were going to be tough.

He followed the main road—a cart track, really—laboring to make headway. A lone farmer was trying to bully a flock of goats northwards. Once Petrus passed the man, the road stretched empty.

A hamlet came into sight. It was tiny, little more than a dozen buildings around a dusty market square with a well at its center. Petrus flew low, circled the square, landed on the edge of the well. He folded his wings, cocked his head, listened. Utter silence, apart from the wind.

After several minutes, he glided down to the ground and changed into himself. The curse shadows on his skin didn't appear to be any darker or thicker than they'd been before.

Petrus changed back into a hawk, spread his wings, and headed into the wind again. The smoke in the sky had spread.

He followed the road south-east, towards the mountains. He saw goats grazing in stony fields, hens pecking in the dirt around abandoned farmhouses, a flock of gray geese, but no people.

The next village was almost large enough to be called a town, fifty or sixty houses clustered together, bounded on one side by a river. Delpy, was the village's name—if he was where he thought he was.

Delpy wasn't empty. His hawk eyes saw movement when he was almost a mile away: two men crossing the market square.

He flew faster. Were they cursed?

The men kicked a door, broke it open, vanished inside. They emerged as Petrus glided down into the square. He stared at them intently, looking for signs of madness and bloodlust. The men kicked open another door, pushed inside.

In the middle of the square was a covered well. Off to one side was a whipping post. Petrus landed on the whipping post and waited for the men to come out. All around the market square, doors sagged open.

He examined the men when they emerged into the sunlight. Unshaved faces, ragged clothes, each with a sack slung over his shoulder. Their curse shadows seemed no darker than normal.

Looters.

He launched himself skyward again. The source of the smoke was closer now. His sharp hawk-eyes told him what it was when he was still several miles away. A barn and a farmhouse burning.

Petrus circled for several minutes, examining the scene. The barn had collapsed in on itself, but two walls of the house still stood. Embers glowed and acrid smoke billowed upward in great clouds, pushed north by the wind.

There were no people that he could see, no animals, yet the fire was no more than a few hours old. If the farmhouse had been abandoned... why the fire? Was it accidental, or deliberate?

Instinct told him it was because of the curse. Someone—someone cursed—had torched this farm.

But who?

Petrus glided cautiously down to land and shifted into the shape of a dog. He lifted his muzzle and sniffed. Smoke, yes, and also... blood.

He trotted around the house and barn, ears pricked, hackles up. His nose told him that blood had recently been spilled, that several bodies lay roasting in the remains of the house, and that one body was in the charred barn.

He padded warily across to the well and sniffed. Nothing.

Petrus sat down in the dirt, trying to piece together what had happened.

Someone had killed the inhabitants of the farmhouse and burned it down.

Had the killer lived here, or come from elsewhere?

Was the curse here?

Petrus shifted into himself, and rose to standing. He looked down at his body. Thick, dark curse shadows swathed him.

Fear prickled across his scalp, prickled down his spine. Cold sweat broke out on his skin. His heart was suddenly galloping. Every instinct he had clamored for him to change shape, to flee.

Petrus inhaled a shallow breath, a second breath. Nothing threatened him here. The only people in the smoldering ruins were dead.

He sidled two steps to the well and peered over the lip. He couldn't see anything.

Rand and Serril and Malle would want to know what the water looked like.

An empty leather bucket sat beside the well. Petrus hooked the handle on the rope and lowered it into the well, let it fill, hauled it back up.

Water dribbled from the leather bucket. Sight of it made his heart beat even faster.

Petrus took a deep breath. Touching the water wouldn't infect him, only drinking it would. He reached out and unhooked the bucket, put it on the ground, crouched and examined the water. It looked ordinary, clear, the surface shimmering in the sunshine, except... The water reflected the light oddly.

He tilted his head to one side, looked at the bucket out of the corner of his eye. Yes, that reflection was wrong, as if an oily substance lay on the water.

PETRUS FLEW BACK to Delpy, gliding mostly, with the wind behind him. Creeks came down out of the gullies. All of them had the oily reflection of Ivek's curse.

The creeks flowed into the river that ran through Delpy. Dread swelled inside him as he approached the village. Did Delpy have the curse, now? Did the looters?

Petrus made two circuits of the village. The men weren't in the market square breaking down doors, nor on any of the roads leading out of Delpy. So, where had they gone?

He spiraled down, landed beside the well, and shifted into a dog. The sound of glass smashing echoed across the square.

Petrus pricked his ears. Where had that come from?

The sound came again, and this time he located its source. The tavern on the south side of the square.

Petrus trotted cautiously across to the tavern. A sign hung above its door, creaking in the wind—a goose with its wings outstretched.

The door stood ajar.

Petrus halted on the doorstep and sniffed. Ale. And blood.

His hackles rose. A growl filled his throat.

Petrus nudged the door open a few more inches and slipped inside, slinking low to the floor. Smells invaded his nose—moldering straw, sweat, piss—but the strongest were ale and blood.

His ears twitched. Someone was giggling softly.

Petrus crept forward, his belly almost brushing the straw-strewn floor. His ribcage felt tight, his lungs tight, his throat tight. Past a bench lying on its side, past an upturned table...

There were the looters. One dead, one alive.

The smell of ale came from the tankards lying in the straw—and the smell of blood came from the man sprawled alongside them with his throat ripped out. The second looter sat beside his dead companion, giggling as he licked his fingers. Blood stained his face, his hands, his teeth. And beneath the blood was the curse shadow, so thick and black that Petrus could barely make out the man's features.

Every hair on Petrus's body stood on end. His lungs squeezed shut. *Run*.

ONCE IN THE air, Petrus felt only slightly safer. He wanted to get as far from Delpy as he could. But Rand and Serril had given him two tasks. The first one he'd completed; the second, he hadn't.

He had to measure how fast the curse was advancing.

Petrus hovered, looking at Delpy and the river and the road, remembering the map.

The curse was travelling westwards, so that was the direction he needed to measure it in. Unfortunately, the river flowed north and the road ran north-east. Finally he found a line that went directly east-west, an old stone wall bisecting a paddock that had grass as sparse as an old man's hair.

He paced out two sections of the wall, each an eighth of a mile long, with twenty yards between them, checked them twice, marked them, and sat on the wall to wait for the curse. The wind blew, carrying with it the smell of smoke and the chill of the snow-covered mountains to the south. After a few minutes he crouched down in the lee of the wall, shivering, wishing he could be a wolf, with a nice, thick pelt. But the Ivek Curse didn't affect animals. He wouldn't be able to see when—

The curse shadows covering his skin darkened.

Petrus's heart seemed to stop beating for an instant. The hairs on his scalp felt like they were standing on end. *It's here.*

He pushed to his feet. He wanted to run, but instead he made himself count. *One second. Two seconds.* He shifted into a hawk, flew an eighth of a mile along the wall, shifted back into himself. *Eleven seconds. Twelve seconds.*

Petrus hunkered down behind the wall and counted steadily. Not slow. Not fast. Just steady. He marked each minute with a pebble. The pebbles began to pile up. The wind couldn't reach him behind the wall, but the stones were icy against his back and the dirt cold beneath his bare feet. The chill seemed to seep inside him.

He was almost relieved when his curse shadow darkened.

Petrus quickly counted the pebbles. Nineteen. And fifty three seconds. Close enough to twenty minutes.

For accuracy's sake, he should do that again. *But my balls will freeze off.*

Petrus jogged along the wall to the second section he'd marked. Less than a minute after he'd got there, his curse shadow darkened again. "One second. Two seconds." He changed into a hawk, flew to the last marker, landed. After two minutes of shivering, he gathered a handful of pebbles, laid them in a line, and changed into a wolf.

He lay in the lee of the wall, counting in his head. Not fast. Not slow. Just steady. When each minute passed, he pushed a pebble out of the line with his paw. At sixteen minutes, Petrus changed back into himself. The air, the stones, the dirt, were colder than he remembered. Seventeen minutes. Eighteen minutes. Nineteen.

At twenty minutes and six seconds, his curse shadow darkened. "Thank the All-Mother," he said aloud. His feet were numb, his teeth chattering, his shivers convulsive.

NINETEEN MINUTES FIFTY-THREE the first time, twenty minutes and six seconds the second. Call it twenty minutes. Twenty minutes to cover an eighth of a mile...

Petrus tried to work it out in his head while he flew. If an eighth of a mile took twenty minutes, then three eighths would take an hour, and... He stuck there for a while, wishing he had a slate and piece of chalk, until he realized that if three eighths of a mile took an hour, then three miles would take eight hours. Which meant that the curse was advancing nine miles westward a day. Three leagues. Which was a lot.

With the wind behind him, he flew fast, skimming over the ragged patchwork of fields.

He spied movement on the road ahead. The farmer with the goats. The man had stopped and was sitting on a rock eating his lunch, his goats milling around him.

Lunch. Petrus was abruptly aware of how hungry he was, and even more than that, how thirsty. He put more effort into flying. The sooner he got back, the sooner he could eat. An hour and a half, he reckoned. Maybe less.

He swept over the farmer, flew half a mile further, and then swung back. If the curse was advancing three leagues westward a day...

*It'll catch up with him soon.*

Petrus circled above the man, torn between prudence and altruism. Altruism won.

He glided down to land a few yards from the farmer.

The man stopped chewing and looked at him.

Petrus shifted into himself.

The man's mouth dropped open. He fell backwards off the rock he was perched on.

"The curse has passed Delpy. You need to move faster!"

The farmer scrambled to his feet and snatched up a wooden stave.

Petrus stepped back a few paces, holding up his hands. "The curse has passed Delpy. It'll catch you if you don't move faster. Forget the goats, they'll only slow you."

"Ye're a witch," the man snarled, brandishing the stave.

"Yes," Petrus said. "And the curse is—"

The man bent, seized a stone, threw it.

The stone struck Petrus's chest. *Ouch.* So much for altruism. "You need to move faster," he told the man, and changed into a hawk and flapped up into the sky. Another stone hurtled past him.

A quarter of a mile down the road, Petrus circled briefly, looking back. The farmer hadn't moved. He was still standing behind the rock, a stone in one hand and his stave in the other.

# CHAPTER THIRTY-NINE

AHEAD, THE ROAD forded a boggy stream. An oxcart laboriously navigated the marshy ground. Britta heard the sucking sounds of the animals' hooves in the mud, the sucking sounds of the wheels. The Fithians drew to one side of the road and halted. Britta's gaze slid sideways to Pox, mounted alongside her, holding her reins. He was watching the oxcart, not her.

Britta released the pommel. The coarse rope securing her wrists to the pommel was long enough that she could scratch her nose, if she bent her head. She did just that—scratch her nose—then pretended to pull her cloak closer around her, and slipped the broken stone from her pocket. Another glance at Pox. He was scanning the hillside, his gaze skimming over thorn trees and scrub.

Britta clasped the pommel again, making sure the cloak fell over her hands, concealing them.

The oxcart passed, the driver lifting his hand in a wave.

Pox tugged at her reins. The piebald mare started forward.

Britta examined the stone carefully with her fingers. It was blunter than she'd thought, but she found the sharpest edge, laid it to the rope, and started sawing. She tilted her head to the left, gazed listlessly at thorn trees and scrub. Her chin sagged, her shoulders sagged. *Defeated. Not thinking of escape.* But her hands were busy.

A mile passed. Two miles. Three. And still Britta sawed.

# CHAPTER FORTY

THEY REACHED BLOEDEL in the late afternoon, as the sun was sinking towards the horizon. The town straddled a gorge with a roaring river deep in its gullet. A bridge crossed the river, the tallest bridge Jaumé had ever seen, with legs like stilts that disappeared into the dark chasm.

He glanced at Bennick. *Are we going to cross that?* It looked too spindly, too precarious.

Bennick wasn't afraid of the bridge. He rode onto it, whistling. Jaumé gulped a breath and followed. The pony's hooves clattered on the wooden planks. Jaumé peered over the railings and caught a glimpse of white water a long way below.

The Brother lived on the far side of Bloedel. His house had a high wooden fence and a bell hanging at the gate. Bennick rang the bell.

Jaumé looked east. A rough palisade ringed Bloedel and beyond that the ground rose in a broad sweep towards the gray sky. He saw thorn trees and scrub and tussock and rock, disappearing into the distance. A cold, scouring wind swept down from the highlands. It twitched at his cloak and slid into the gaps between his shirt buttons, making him shiver.

He remembered crossing the plateau with Nolt, how cold it had been. Bennick had bought him a sheepskin jacket from an old woman. And then Odil had killed her when she'd tried to steal the pony.

Jaumé screwed his face up. He saw the old woman's body, the gaping slit beneath her chin, the blood drying black. He heard Bennick's voice in his head: *Don't snivel, Jaumé. There's nothing wrong with dying. We come, we go. She's with the All-Mother.*

He didn't want to become a Brother if it meant killing people, even if they were thieves and even if they went to the All-Mother once they were dead.

The gate opened.

Jaumé blinked and stared. The man standing in the gateway had only one leg.

The man ignored him. He frowned up at Bennick, his eyes narrow beneath beetling brows. "What do you want?"

"A place to stay for the night, Brother."

The man's scowl didn't lessen. His fingers moved in a series of rapid gestures.

Jaumé dragged his gaze from the man and saw that Bennick's fingers were moving, too.

The man stepped back from the gate, and jerked his head at them. "Come in."

Jaumé followed Bennick into the Brother's yard, craning his neck, staring around. Like Loomath and Kritsen, this Brother had a pigeon house and a place for stabling horses.

The man bolted the gate and led them across the wide dirt yard. He walked with a swaying gait, one silent step with a leather-booted foot, one sharp thumping step with his peg leg. His face was creased and weather-beaten.

The Brother halted at the stables. Bennick dismounted and had a low-voiced exchange of words with him. What he heard seemed to please him. He turned to Jaumé, grinning, and clapped him on the shoulder. "We made it in time, lad. Vught's not passed through yet."

# CHAPTER FORTY-ONE

INNIS SAT AT the campfire, hugging her knees, watching Petrus and Prince Harkeld wrestle in the dusk. The bouts were rough, fast, brutal. She winced as the prince took Petrus down hard. *He'll break his ribs!* But Petrus merely rolled and leapt to his feet, grinning.

Beside her, Rand and Serril were muttering over the map. "Three leagues a day," she heard Rand say. "That's faster than we thought."

"We'll meet it soon," Serril said, his voice a low rumble. "Maybe tomorrow night."

"We need to fill the barrels first thing tomorrow morning," Malle said.

"Absolutely," Rand said. "We daren't risk—"

A loud thud captured her attention. Prince Harkeld lay on the ground, apparently winded. Petrus said something that her ears didn't quite catch. From his tone, it was rude.

The prince pushed up on one hand, wheezing, and said something back that made Petrus laugh. She watched as the prince stood, as he caught his breath, as he crouched ready to fight.

"No sign of any Fithians," Serril said. "Spent the

whole day looking for 'em. Must know the face of every refugee between here and the plateau."

"Innis..." Rand waited until she'd turned her head. "How do you feel? Can you help patrol tonight?"

Innis nodded. "Yes."

"Take the first shift. Swap with Justen after dinner."

She nodded again.

Bode stirred the stewpot. "Dinner's ready," he bellowed.

Petrus and Prince Harkeld stopped wrestling. They wiped their faces, pulled on their shirts and boots, and came to the fire, sweating and breathless. Innis watched as they grabbed bowls and sat alongside each other. *They're friends*, she thought, astonished. When had that happened?

# CHAPTER FORTY-TWO

KAREL EXAMINED THE map of Roubos in the firelight. "This mission is the All-Mother's way of teaching me geography," Prince Tomas muttered alongside him.

Karel nodded agreement, his eyes flicking over the names of towns and rivers and mountain ranges. "They're moving faster, without the cart."

"We're gaining, though. Couple more days and we'll have the bastards," Tomas said.

"Three days," Karel said. "Maybe four. I reckon we'll be into Sault before we catch up to them."

"You reckon?" Tomas peered at the map.

Solveig leaned over to study the map, too, his shoulder nudging Karel's for a moment. "Cesky Delta. I've heard of that. That's where they've got those swamp lizards, isn't it?"

Cesky Delta? Karel searched the map, and found the delta in the northwest, on the border with Ankeny.

"Swamp lizards?" Bjarne said.

"You know, giant lizards, six foot long. Got hides thick as armor and teeth like daggers. Live in the swamps."

"Never heard of 'em," Bjarne said.

"I have," Dag said. "Heard a joke about them once."

Prince Tomas looked up from the map. "Remember it?"

Dag grinned. "Course I do." He put down his mug. "See, this man walks into a tavern up in Cesky and discovers they're holding a contest. The tapster tells him the details: First you got to drink a half-tankard of scallywater. Second, you got to go out back and pull a sore tooth out of the mouth of his pet swamp lizard. And third, you got to go upstairs and have sex with the oldest, ugliest whore in Cesky. If you do all that in under an hour, you win six whole barrels of scallywater. Enough to last you a year."

"Scallywater?" Lief asked. "What's that?"

"Liquor. Made with potatoes. Real strong stuff."

"Potatoes?" Solveig pulled a face. "Doesn't sound nice."

"You want to hear this joke or not?"

"*I* want to hear it," Prince Tomas said. "Tell."

"So, three tasks. Drink the scallywater, pull the tooth out of the swamp lizard's mouth, and tup the ugly whore. Got it?"

Tomas nodded.

"The man decides to give it a go. He drinks a half-tankard of scallywater, then staggers out the back to find the swamp lizard. After half an hour of crashing and screaming, he crawls back inside, and says..." Dag paused, picked up his mug, drank from it, wiped his mouth. "Where'sh the whore with the bad tooth?"

Tomas laughed.

Solveig groaned. "Wasn't worth it."

Karel shook his head, grinning, and looked at the map one last time before rolling it up. *Getting closer.*

# CHAPTER FORTY-THREE

IN THE MORNING, Bennick went through the packsaddles. He pulled out the rabbit-fur cap Jaumé had worn in Sault, and the boots and the sheepskin jacket. "You'll need these from now on," he said, tossing them to Jaumé.

Jaumé piled the clothes at the end of his bed. He remembered how warm the jacket was—and he remembered the old woman's face and the black puddle of dried blood.

Bennick repacked, and they went out into the yard and Jaumé practiced with his weapons, throwing the bone-handled knife at a mark painted on a wooden post, piercing a straw-filled target with his arrows. Bennick practiced, too. He could stand at the far end of the yard—fifty strides, Jaumé counted—with his back turned and the knife in its sheath, and turn and throw in a single movement, not pausing to take aim. The heavy knife always thudded deep into its target, making the timber shudder. And he could send arrow after arrow into the straw butt, nocking and releasing so swiftly that Jaumé's eyes couldn't follow the movement. His arrows always landed within the same square inch. Twice, an arrow landed on top of another, splitting its shaft neatly in two.

Bennick put away his bow and brought out the sword Loomath had given them. He hefted it in his hand, feeling the balance, then held it out to Jaumé. "Try this."

Jaumé's heart fumbled a beat with excitement. A sword. His very own sword. He eagerly took it.

Bennick unsheathed his own sword in a smooth movement. "Hold it like this, see?"

Jaumé obediently wrapped his fingers around the hilt. He looked from his sword to Bennick's, and was disappointed. His sword seemed like a toy alongside Bennick's.

"What?" Bennick said.

"It's small."

Bennick studied him for a moment. "You'd rather have one like mine?"

Jaumé nodded.

Bennick held his sword out to Jaumé, hilt first. "Go on. Have a try."

Jaumé laid the small sword on the hard-packed dirt. He took hold of Bennick's sword. It was heavier than he expected. The blade dipped towards the ground for a moment before he steadied it.

"Swing it," Bennick said.

Jaumé took a deep breath and swept the sword in an arc. The blade wobbled in the air, the tip dragging down.

"Careful." Bennick grabbed the hilt before the blade touched the ground, his hand wrapping around Jaumé's. "That's why you start small. We all did. There's no shame in a short blade. Not if you can use it properly."

Bennick took his sword back. Jaumé picked up the little sword and glanced at Bennick. Was he cross?

Bennick winked at him.

Jaumé felt better. He gripped the hilt the way Bennick had shown him.

"Stand like this, your feet apart."

Jaumé obeyed. He raised the sword, mimicking Bennick, concentrating hard.


AFTER HIS SWORD lesson, Jaumé retreated to the stoop in front of the Brother's house, where he sat and sharpened his throwing knife, and then Bennick's. Bennick stripped down to his breech-clout despite the cold wind and exercised in the yard, leaping and kicking and twisting his body in the air. The Brother joined him. His name was Ifrem. He was lean, his muscles like hard knots beneath skin the color of old oak. Jaumé tried not to stare at the man's wooden leg. Instead, he counted the tattoos on Ifrem's chest. Eighteen daggers. Eighteen battles.

Bennick only had six dagger tattoos. Would he earn another dagger for killing the prince?

Jaumé tested the edge of Bennick's knife with his thumb. He remembered Bennick's arrow thudding into Prince Harkeld's chest, remembered the prince falling. And he remembered the prince climbing into a boat afterwards, brought back to life by witches. *Stay alive*, he whispered in his head, and then he glanced at Bennick and felt guilty.

After the exercises, Ifrem and Bennick wrestled, grunting with effort. Ifrem was almost as good as Bennick, even though he was old and had only one leg. Twice, he threw Bennick to the ground. Bennick didn't seem to mind. He leapt to his feet, wiping dirt from his face, grinning.

The men gripped hands when they were finished. Both were sweating. They turned and came towards the house. Jaumé scrambled to his feet. He hoped Bennick would ask if he wanted to learn how to wrestle.

Bennick didn't. He scooped up his throwing knife, tested the sharpness of the blade, nodded at Jaumé. "Good lad."

# CHAPTER FORTY-FOUR

THE VILLAGE OF Nime bustled with frantic activity; those inhabitants who'd not already fled were being turned out of their homes. Dust and noise hung in the air. Children cried, dogs barked, donkeys brayed, and hens ran clucking with their wings outspread. Innis saw a gray-haired woman arguing with a mounted soldier, her voice shrill with despair, but most of the villagers were abandoning their homes without protest, piling belongings into carts and onto donkeys. There was fear on some faces, grief on others.

In the market square were four more mounted soldiers. They looked as if they'd been traveling hard for weeks; men and horses were whipcord-lean. Another rider blocked the southern gate.

"You!" one of the soldiers bellowed, trotting towards them. "You can't take that road." His uniform was grimy, his face unshaven.

Rand halted. "Why not?"

"We're evacuating."

Innis could see Rand thinking through his options. "Who is your commanding officer?"

"I am."

"And you are...?"

"Captain Jerzy, King's Riders," the man snapped. "Turn around and head back the way you came."

"I'm afraid we can't do that, captain."

"King's orders. Now turn around or I'll *make* you turn around." Captain Jerzy reached for his sword.

Innis tensed, and Petrus and Hedín swooped low.

Rand opened his shirt and took something from around his throat. He held it out to the captain. Innis saw a silver disk, hanging from a chain. Recognition was like a physical slap: she'd last seen Dareus wear that disk.

The captain scowled. "What's that?"

"Diplomatic seal. From the Allied Kingdoms. Take a look, captain."

Captain Jerzy kneed his horse closer and inspected the seal, then shot Rand a narrow-eyed glance, and, for the first time, ran his gaze over the rest of them. His eyes were full of suspicion.

"You need to let us pass," Rand told him quietly. "For the good of Sault and the rest of the Seven Kingdoms."

Captain Jerzy examined them all again. His gaze paused on Gretel, noting her sword, her short hair. Innis held her breath. What rumors had this captain heard? If he realized he was looking at mages...

*Will he aid us, or try to kill us?*

Innis summoned her shapeshifting magic, let it tingle beneath her skin.

Captain Jerzy's gaze lingered on Justen for several seconds, then on Prince Harkeld. Was he trying to recognize a prince? Innis slid her boots from her stirrups, her magic spiraling even closer to the surface, stinging over her skin—ready to change into a lion—and the captain turned his head and bellowed: "Let them pass!"

The King's Rider blocking the gate hesitated, then moved his mount aside.

Rand rehung the diplomatic seal around his neck. "Thank you."

"Go with the All-Mother's blessing." A scowl still furrowed Captain Jerzy's forehead. Innis realized the expression was mostly exhaustion and strain. How many weeks had these men been riding, trying to empty this corner of Sault, afraid Ivek's curse would catch up with them?

She found her stirrups, but didn't release her magic. It hummed in her bones.

"The curse is close," Rand told the captain. "It passed through Delpy yesterday. And if it's in Delpy, it'll be in Hansgrohe, too."

"Delpy?" Innis saw disbelief on the man's face, followed by dismay. "Hansgrohe?"

"It's moving fast. Three leagues a day, westwards. It'll be here tomorrow."

Captain Jerzy glanced at the frantic, bustling villagers, and back at Rand. His dismay had become something grimmer. *He knows most of these people won't make it.*

"Head west," Rand said. "Fast as you can."

"We will." The captain kneed his horse to one side. "Go!"

# CHAPTER FORTY-FIVE

AFTER NIME, THE press of refugees dwindled. The road was clear for long stretches, winding its way up dry hills tufted with tussock. Serril flew a mile ahead, and Petrus and Hedín circled above them. Most of the refugees were clearly harmless—the elderly, families with women and young children—but mid-morning, four men came into view, walking fast. Above them, a swallow swooped and dived as if hunting for insects. The bird's feathers shimmered with magic. Serril.

Petrus and Hedín glided protectively lower.

Harkeld loosened his sword in its scabbard. He called up his fire magic and let it lie just beneath his skin, sizzling hot.

The eldest of the four men stepped in front of the wagon, forcing Bode to halt.

Harkeld tensed, and half-raised his hand.

"Turn back," the man cried. "While you still have a chance!"

Harkeld's gaze jerked between the four men. Who was going to hurl the first throwing star?

"Come along, Da," one of the younger men said. "We don't hurry, it'll catch us." He took the older man's arm, tugged him. "We got no time to stop, Da!"

Harkeld didn't lower his hand until the four men had gone from sight. Serril landed briefly. "There's only one man between here and the plateau who looks possible. These are the stragglers, now."

Stragglers, they were. Walking with their few possessions slung on their backs. The poorest of the peasants. The sickest and oldest.

"Do you think they'll make it?" Harkeld asked Justen, riding alongside him.

Justen shook his head. "The curse'll get most of 'em."

Urgency prickled in Harkeld's chest. *We need to travel faster!* But they were constrained by the pace of the wagon and its six barrels of precious, uncursed water.

The single traveler passed them, a gaunt-faced man with a sword belted at his waist. His glance at them was sharp, curious, but he didn't pause, didn't offer either greeting or warning, just hurried past.

Rand ordered Innis into the air. "Follow that one, make sure he doesn't turn back."

Harkeld turned in his saddle, watching the disappearing figure. "You think he's Fithian?"

Rand shrugged. "Don't know what to think. Someone, somewhere, knows we're coming."

"Perhaps not," Malle said. "Perhaps that message didn't get through. Or if it did, whoever received it is dead."

Harkeld watched Innis flap into the sky. Anxiety eddied in his belly. He hoped she'd keep her distance from the man.

"Or perhaps they're waiting for us somewhere ahead," Justen said.

Rand grimaced. "That, I can believe."

So could Harkeld. He needed to continue his lessons, needed to learn how to throw fire with his left hand. Which fire mage should he ask? Middle-aged Gretel? Blunt-spoken Bode? Or Signy, the youngest of the fire mages?

He studied Gretel and Signy, riding ahead of him. Gretel, fair-haired and stocky, Signy, dark and angular. Gretel's hair was as short as Katlen's had been, but she was quiet, not bossy. She reminded him of Cora. Calm. Even-tempered.

Signy had been close to Thayer. Harkeld remembered seeing them together on the ship, sitting side by side, shoulders touching, heads close together, talking, laughing. Had they been lovers? He thought they might have been. Signy hadn't spoken to him since Hansgrohe. *Does she blame me for Thayer's death?* If she did, she was right.

So, not Signy. Either Gretel or Bode, then.

They rounded a bend and saw more refugees—two men, grizzled and gray-bearded. One was limping heavily, leaning on a stick.

Harkeld examined them as they approached and felt pity. Neither of the men was hale. The one who limped had a shriveled socket where his right eye should have been, the other man had an arm that ended in a stump. *They won't make it.*

The limping man stopped and leaned on his stick. He swayed with each breath, looking ready to collapse.

Harkeld halted. "Would you like some water, father?"

A horse and rider pressed close on his left. Nellis. She held out a waterskin. "Here."

"Thank ye kindly," the old man said. He took a long swig from the waterskin, wiped the mouthpiece with grave dignity, and held it out to his companion. "Drink, Udo."

The one-handed man drank, maneuvering the waterskin with surprising deftness. "All-Mother bless you." He gave the waterskin back to Nellis.

"And may she bless you, too," she replied.

"She already has," the limping man said. His single eye wasn't faded and rheumy, but bright and fierce. He reached under his cloak in a swift, fluid movement and flicked something at Harkeld.

Harkeld reacted without conscious thought. Fire magic detonated in front of his face, so close the heat scorched him. His horse reared. He grabbed for the reins—missed—tumbled from his saddle and hit the ground hard. All around him was a chaos of brightness and moving shadows, of shouts that sounded like the chirping of birds. He was as helpless as a newborn kitten, unable to see, unable to hear. Something struck him in the head. A horse's hoof. He curled himself up as small as he could.

Gradually the chaos became less confusing. Harkeld uncurled slightly. The imprint of flames still blocked his vision, but he knew someone stood over him, a shadow against the brightness. Friend or foe? He groped for his sword. A hand grasped his shoulder. Someone spoke words he couldn't make out.

"I can't see," Harkeld said, wiping moisture from his stinging eyes, trying not to panic. "I can't hear."

Whoever it was released his shoulder, crouched, and cupped his face in their hands. He felt calloused fingers against his cheeks, smelled someone's sweat. Rand. He squinted, trying to see the healer.

"Keep your eyes closed." Those words, he heard faintly.

Harkeld obeyed.

Slowly, the ringing in his ears faded. Sounds began to come clear: people talking in low voices; the crunch of boots on dirt; a horse's nicker.

The gritty stinging of his eyes eased.

"Open your eyes," Rand said.

Harkeld cautiously obeyed. His vision was blurry, still marked by the imprint of flames, tears still leaked down his cheeks, but he could see Rand.

"Better?"

"A lot better." Relief unfurled in his chest. *I'm not blind.* He wiped his eyes. "Thank you."

"You're welcome." Rand's smile was lopsided. "Next time you burn something that close to you, shut your eyes."

"Was it a throwing star?"

"It was." Rand stood, held out a hand, pulled Harkeld to his feet.

"Those men were Fithians? But... they were *old*." He looked for the bodies, but found only bloodstains and scorch marks on the ground. A faint smell of roasted pork lingered in the air. "Is everyone all right?"

"Three dead."

"What?" Harkeld swung to face Rand, lurched, almost lost his balance.

"Nellis, Hedín, and Signy."

Harkeld stared at him, open-mouthed, unable to speak, almost unable to breathe. "But... there were only two of them and they were *old*!"

"One-eye had fifty-six kills," someone said behind him.

Harkeld turned unsteadily and almost lost his balance again.

The speaker was Justen. The shapeshifter took Harkeld's arm, steadied him. "Is Flin all right?" he asked Rand.

"Concussion," Rand said. "Perforated eardrum. Flash burn. He'll be fine with a bit more healing."

"Fifty-six kills?" Harkeld said, wiping his eyes again.

Justen nodded. "Serril says it's the most he's ever seen."

"What about the other one?"

Justen grimaced. "Too badly burned."

"Nellis? Signy? Hedín? Where are they?" Harkeld headed for the wagon, listing as he walked. Justen kept grip of his arm.

Nellis and Hedín and Signy lay side by side on the floorboards of the wagon.

"Throwing stars, all of them." Justen released Harkeld's arm. "At least Hedín had time to change into himself before he bled out."

Harkeld stared at the three bodies. The tears in his eyes were no longer solely due to the stinging. "But... Nellis gave them *water*."

"That's Fithians for you," Rand said, flatly.

"Is everyone else all right?" He turned too fast, almost fell, grabbed hold of the tailboard. He could see Adel and Gretel calming the horses, and there were Malle and Bode, and the black hawk was Serril... "Where's Innis? Where's Petrus?"

"Fine," Justen said. "You're the only one injured. That throwing star... It just *exploded* in your face. I thought you were dead."

No. Not dead. But Nellis and Hedín and Signy were. Harkeld turned back to the wagon, and looked at their bodies. A bloodstained ivory disc was visible at Signy's throat. "She was from Groot," he said. "Like you." His voice broke on the last word and to his horror he began to cry.

"It's the concussion," Rand said. "Justen, help him into the wagon. Bode! Let's get moving."

"Come on, Flin," Justen said gently. "Up with you." He put an arm around Harkeld, steadied him as he clambered into the wagon.

# CHAPTER FORTY-SIX

HARKELD WOKE SLOWLY. He lay on wooden floorboards that rattled and jolted beneath him. The wagon. He knew without opening his eyes that it was Innis who now healed him, not Rand. Her magic felt different.

The hands cupped over his ears lifted. "How do you feel?"

"A lot better." Harkeld opened his eyes and stared up at her. Gray eyes, black curls, freckles on her nose. A mage. A shapeshifter. Something he'd been taught to fear his whole life. Monstrosity. Abomination. Creature unhuman. *Do I love you?*

"You look a bit sunburned," Innis said. "But that'll pass in a day or two."

Harkeld pushed up on one elbow and rubbed his face. The wagon swayed and lurched around a corner.

"How's your vision?"

"Fine," he said. "Fine." How could he be certain whether he loved Innis or not? He didn't *know* her.

"And your eyebrows and eyelashes are only a little singed."

*The only good witch is a dead one.* The tenet he'd grown up believing, something he'd known with his whole being to be true. So, how had Innis become so important to him?

"Good," Harkeld said. "Um... look, Innis... we need to talk."

She looked down at her lap. "I know."

"Not, you know... not..." Not declarations of love, or anything. "It's just..." Just what? "I don't know anything about you. I don't even know how old you are."

She glanced at him, met his eyes.

"I thought I knew Justen, but he wasn't real. He wasn't anyone. He was just a mix of you all. *We*'ve never talked. You and me. Face to face."

"We talked in the dreams."

"*I* talked, most of the time. And the thing is, Innis, they're just *dreams*. They're no more real than Justen was. They're make-believe. We *can't* know what each other feels. That's impossible! No one can do that."

"I can. When I heal."

He stared at her. "Healers feel *that*? Petrus, and Rand—"

Innis shook her head. "Most healers don't. Only ones as strong as me."

He sat back, unsettled. "I didn't know that."

Innis lifted her shoulders in a faint, almost apologetic, shrug, and looked down at her lap again. She plucked at an unraveling thread on the hem of her cloak, wound it around one fingertip.

Harkeld examined her face. Frustration surged in his chest. How had he fallen in love with someone he didn't *know*? "I know nothing about you! I don't know who you *are*."

Her gaze jerked to his. For a long moment they stared at each other, and then Innis unwound the thread from her finger. "What would you like to know?"

Everything. "Well for a start, how old you are."

"Twenty. Two weeks ago."

"While we were sailing from Ankeny?"

Innis nodded.

He remembered how angry he'd been during the voyage. And he remembered Thayer and Signy sitting on deck, heads bent together, shoulders touching, talking. He didn't remember Innis celebrating a birthday.

Harkeld glanced at the front of the wagon, where Signy lay dead. Someone had covered her with a blanket.

He looked back at Innis. "How did your parents die?"

"Ah..." She looked down at her lap, picked up the hem of her cloak, turned it over. "My mother was a shapeshifter. She was killed hunting down a fire mage who'd gone rogue."

"Rogue?"

"Some mages decide the Primary Laws don't apply to them. They misuse their magic, harm people." Innis began pleating the cloak hem, lining the folds up neatly. "Father was a healer. He... There was a ship came into harbor, but the captain wouldn't dock, refused to let the passengers off. Said he had an outbreak of cow pox onboard and they'd wait at anchor until it passed."

"Your father went out to help," Harkeld guessed.

She glanced up at him. "Not to cure the pox. Healers can't cure plagues. We can heal flesh and bones, we can alleviate some of the physical symptoms of diseases, but the causes..." She shook her head. "If it's in the blood, if it's all through the body, there's not a lot we can do."

"Like that soldier who was stung by a scorpion."

She nodded. "I could ease his cramps, but I couldn't get rid of the poison. It had to work its way out of his system."

"Dareus said..." Harkeld narrowed his eyes, trying to remember. "He said it would take many mages many days to remove a poison from the bloodstream."

Innis nodded again.

"So... if your father didn't go out to the ship, what happened?"

"Oh, he went out. One of the passengers was in labor. And father had had cow pox. He thought there was no risk." She folded a few more inches of hem, pinched the folds together.

"It wasn't cow pox?"

She shook her head.

"What was it?"

"Have you heard of a kingdom called Torborgen?"

"No."

"It's small, Torborgen. Way out in the ocean, almost off the edge of the map."

He waited, wondering what Torborgen had to do with ships and her father's death.

"Have you heard of the black pox?"

"Yes." He pulled a face. "Was it...?" -

Innis nodded.

"I heard... four out of five people died."

Innis nodded again.

"I'm sorry."

Innis lifted one shoulder in a shrug and went back to folding the hem of her cloak. "They figured out later that three ships left Torborgen with the black pox aboard. Two never made landfall. Everyone perished at sea. The third one made it to Lirac.

"If the captain hadn't stayed out at anchor, if he'd let his passengers disembark... Lirac would have been infected, and if Lirac had been infected, most of the Allied Kingdoms would have been, too. Four out of five people. That's a lot of people. He saved thousands of lives."

*But not your father's life.* "Did the captain survive?"

She shook her head, pleated more of the hem.

Harkeld studied her face. There was a tiny furrow between her eyebrows. Her mouth was tight. Was she remembering what it felt like to be twelve years old and orphaned? "You were sent to Rosny?"

"Yes. To the Academy." The furrow didn't disappear.

"How did you become friends with Petrus?"

"Oh..." The furrow vanished. "I met him the first day. My parents tutored me, you see. I knew all of the basic theory—ethics of magic, and human anatomy, and animal anatomy, and, oh, lots of things—and the instructors weren't sure whether to put me in a class with students my own age or not, and in the end they decided to try me in an older class."

"Petrus's class."

She nodded. "The master introduced me, and they were all so much bigger and older than me, and I felt so... so overwhelmed and intimidated, and all I wanted to do was run away, and then Petrus winked at me." She glanced at him. "It sounds stupid, I know. But he winked, and made space at his bench, and after that everything was all right."

"It doesn't sound stupid." Harkeld tried to imagine what it had been like for her. A long way from home. Feeling lost and alone, afraid, shy, homesick, grieving. And then, Petrus had winked.

He felt a deep surge of gratitude towards the shapeshifter.

"Petrus became my brother. I followed at his heels like a puppy all that first year. It must have annoyed him sometimes, but he never showed it. He was just so nice and so kind and he made me laugh and... and I love Petrus more than anybody."

She glanced up again. Their eyes met.

Innis's cheeks colored and she looked down at her lap. She unfolded the pleats, smoothed the hem of her cloak.

The subject of the dreams loomed between them. Harkeld remembered what it felt like to kiss her, hold her, make love to her.

If what she said about the dreams was true—if they truly could sense each other's emotions—then she loved him. Differently from how she loved Petrus, but as deeply.

The wagon swung to the left, halted.

Alarm spiked in Harkeld's chest. "Is something wrong?" More Fithians? He scrambled to the tailboard, pushed back the covering, and looked out, his hand on his sword hilt.

He saw riders dismounting, a stubbly paddock, a creek, a crumbling stone fence climbing a hillside towards a smoky gray sky streaked with orange.

"Stopping for the night."


HARKELD HELPED DIG the graves for Hedín and Nellis and Signy. The ground was hard, dry, stony. A cold wind flavored with smoke blew incessantly. They laid the dead mages in the graves and covered them. Rand spoke the words to the All-Mother.

*Fifteen dead because of me.*

And then he remembered what Petrus had said. *It's not about you. We're trying to save the Seven Kingdoms. You're just the tool.*

He tried to believe it, but those three mounds of dirt and stones felt personal. Nellis and Hedín and Signy had died instead of him.

Harkeld turned away from the graves. He walked across to the two fire mages, Bode and Gretel.

"Um... Cora was teaching me how to use my magic." He felt awkward, diffident, emotions he'd rarely experienced when he was a prince in his father's marble and gold palace. "I'm all right with my right hand, but I've no control with my left. I was wondering if... if one or other of you would be prepared to help me learn?"

Bode and Gretel exchanged a glance.

He'd made no effort to be friends with either of them. Would they refuse?

Gretel shrugged. "We can both help. What do you need from us?"

"I need help practicing," Harkeld said, absurdly relieved. "Cora threw sticks in the air and had me burn them. And then arrows. Then throwing stars. And then I learned to burn clothes off a scarecrow."

Gretel shrugged again. "Let's start with the sticks, then."

HARKELD PRACTICED FOR an hour, holding his right hand behind his back, throwing fire with his left. It was frustratingly difficult at first, but gradually his aim improved, his speed and precision. By the end of the hour, he was able to burn sticks from the sky faster than Bode and Gretel could throw them, incinerating each one with a tiny, economical burst of flame.

He was sweating, exhausted, almost shaking from the effort of concentrating so hard. "Can we try with arrows tomorrow?"

Gretel nodded. "If you want to."

He did. If they encountered Fithians again, he needed to be able to fight with both hands.

# CHAPTER FORTY-SEVEN

"GATE GUARD SAYS they passed through three to four hours ago," Solveig said. "Heading east."

Karel nodded.

"He also said... the piebald's rider had a bruised face."

Karel nodded again. It wasn't new information—but every time he heard it, it made him want to kill someone. He kept his face impassive. "Good work."

He looked around the market square, counted ten armsmen plus one prince, and swung up into his saddle.

They left the village at a canter. Prince Tomas brought his horse up alongside Karel. "Can't we ride faster?"

Karel glanced at him, saw his impatience. The prince wanted to push ahead at a gallop.

"Two more days, sire, and we'll be breathing down their necks. And the men and horses won't be too tired."

Prince Tomas made a sound of frustration and set his mount prancing in a tight circle, kicking up its hooves. Then, he came up alongside Karel again. "This is why Father put you in charge," he said.

"Knows me too well. Bull at a gate. Don't like waiting for things to happen."

Karel didn't like waiting either. Someone had hurt the princess. There was rage in his blood, a compulsion to gallop. He held it sternly in check.

THEY PUSHED ON until dusk. Once the horses had been tended to, Karel set the men to wrestling one another. He tossed aside his cloak, stripped off his jerkin and shirt, unlaced his boots. *Don't go too hard*, he told himself. The mood he was in, he could easily injure one of the men.

He had a bout with each armsman. Gunvald pressed him hard, tossed him several times, and Karel was able to relax some of his self-control and push hard back.

After Gunvald, he fought with Ture, and tall Lief, and Prince Tomas last of all. The prince was red-faced and sweating.

They came together, arms locked, forehead to forehead, circling, each trying to tip the other. Karel dipped a hip and threw the prince, but Tomas rolled and leapt to his feet, came at him in a rush. Karel let the prince's weight propel them both backwards, and twisted, bringing Tomas down. They rolled, struggling for dominance. He got a knee in the prince's stomach—

Tomas tore free and sprang to his feet. "Almost," he said, grinning, panting. "But not quite."

They circled again, grappled again, broke off again. Karel saw the prince inhale, saw his muscles tense. He dropped to one knee as Tomas charged, drove his shoulder up into the prince's midriff, heaved him over his shoulder.

Tomas hit the dirt hard. "Oof."

Karel pressed one knee between the prince's shoulder blades and hooked an arm around his throat. Tomas was wheezing, half-winded. "Yield?"

"Yield," the prince croaked.

Karel released him.

Prince Tomas rolled over slowly, caught his breath, pushed up to sit. "You're not even sweating!"

"I am," Karel said. "Gunvald nearly got me."

Prince Tomas snorted. "Nearly means nothing." He wiped his face with one hand, squinted around the circle of armsmen, found Gunvald, pinned him with a fierce stare. "You beat this whoreson and I'll pay you the weight of my sword in gold. That's a promise."

Gunvald's lean face broke into a grin. "Yes, sire."

Prince Tomas levered himself slowly to his feet.

"It's the charge," Karel told him. "You do it every time. I can see it coming."

"Bull at a gate," the prince said, still wheezing. "Didn't I tell you?" He groaned, and hobbled towards the campfire, hamming it up, making the armsmen laugh.


"HAVE I TOLD you the one about the chastity belt?" Dag said, after they'd eaten. He glanced around the campfire, saw the headshakes.

"So there's this king, see? Osgaardan. The one who conquered Lomaly. Who was that, sir?"

"Hildur the third," Karel said.

"So Hildur the third wants to do some more pillaging in Lomaly, get himself some more plunder, but there's one problem. He'll be gone for a while and he's worried about leaving his beautiful young queen home alone." Dag glanced around, grinning.

Karel didn't grin. After Lomaly, Osgaard had gone on to conquer Esfaban.

"Hildur orders ten of his best armsmen to stay behind to guard her, but he's more worried about her virtue than her safety. You see, she's a war prize, a Lomalian princess, and he's pretty sure she'll jump at the chance to cuckold him. And while his armsmen may be able to resist her for a while, he doubts they can hold off for very long." Dag outlined a buxom figure with his hands. "Just looking at her makes a man want to bed her."

Karel looked away. This wasn't the sort of joke he wanted to hear. Hildur's queen had been as helpless as a bondservant, forced to marry a man she hated, forced to share his bed, forced to bear his children.

"So, the king goes to his blacksmith and the blacksmith makes him a chastity belt out of steel, but with a large hole exactly where it shouldn't be.

"'Blacksmith,' Hildur the third says. 'Thy device cannot protect my queen's virtue!'

"The blacksmith picks up a wooden stave, pushes it into the hole and—*snick*—a steel blade cuts the stave in two." Dag sliced the air with his hands. "Hildur's delighted with the blacksmith's device and sails off to Lomaly knowing that any armsman his queen seduces will be in for an unpleasant surprise."

*Hildur should have used the chastity belt on himself*, Karel thought sourly. There'd have been no King Vallus, then. No invasion of Esfaban.

"Hildur returns home several months later with two score of ships laden with gold and jewels and slaves.

He's well-pleased with himself—until he notices that most of the ten armsmen he left behind are walking... oddly."

The armsmen were grinning, firelight glinting off their teeth.

"Hildur assembles the ten men in the courtyard and orders them to strip. And he discovers that all but one of them have, uh... *swords* that are cut off at the hilt."

Solveig barked a laugh.

Karel grimaced. Queen Aramis hadn't seduced her armsmen while Hildur had been absent; she'd planned her own death.

"Hildur does have one consolation, though. A fine-looking young armsman called..." Dag's gaze flicked from face to face before settling on one. "Called Gunvald has a *sword* that is entirely unharmed."

A chuckle of amusement went around the circle of armsmen.

"Hildur is overjoyed that one of his men managed to restrain himself, and he offers Gunvald a reward. All Gunvald has to do is say what he wants, and if it's within Hildur's power, he'll grant it."

Dag paused, glanced around the armsmen again, grinned. "But despite Hildur's urging, Gunvald can't answer. You see, for some reason, Gunvald is missing his tongue..."

A shout of laughter went up. Lief thumped Gunvald on the back. "That's why you don't talk much, huh? Tongue too tired?"

"*And* why you're so popular with the ladies!" Bjarne said, grinning.

Karel glanced sideways, and found Prince Tomas watching him.

The prince leaned closer. "It's just a joke," he said quietly in Karel's ear.

"I know." *But once you see a woman being raped, you never forget it.*

The prince gripped Karel's arm—Sympathy? Friendship?—and stood. "Right you mangy lot, who's taking first guard shift tonight?"

# CHAPTER FORTY-EIGHT

MORE BROTHERS ARRIVED an hour after dusk. The
bell clanged loudly at the gate and Ifrem went to see
who it was. He didn't return. Instead there was a
bustle in the yard, a clatter of hooves, the sound of
men's voices. Bennick put down the map he'd been
studying. "That'll be Vught." He rose to his feet.

Jaumé followed him. A lantern hung at the door,
and another by the stables, casting light. Bennick
stepped out into the yard; Jaumé stayed in the
doorway, watching.

Horses and men milled in the wide dirt yard.
Jaumé counted the riders swiftly. Seven men. Where
was the princess?

It took him several minutes to realize that the
smallest rider was a woman, and that her hands
were tied to the pommel.

He watched as she was lifted down from her
mount. She swayed when her feet touched the
ground, stumbled and caught herself. She looked
tiny alongside the Brothers. Tiny and weak.

The princess lifted bound hands and pushed back
the hood of her cloak. She had a small, pale face,
and hair chopped as short as a boy's.

Jaumé was disappointed. That was a princess? Princesses were supposed to be pretty. Where was the long rope of hair? The eyes like jewels?

One of the new Brothers took the princess's arm and walked her to the door, one step behind Ifrem.

Jaumé hastily moved aside.

Ifrem ignored him. So did the Brother leading the princess. So did the princess.

Jaumé stared at her as she passed. Someone had hit her. A dark bruise mottled her cheek.

He swiveled his head and watched her disappear down the corridor. It was hard to believe she was a princess.

Jaumé wondered how the Brothers were going to use her as bait. He remembered one of Mam's tales: a princess tied to a stake, and a great winged beast swooping out of the sky to eat her. A gallant huntsman had saved the princess, and married her, and become king, and it was a tale, because there were no winged beasts in the sky... but the stake could be true.

Jaumé turned his attention back to the yard. Bennick stood a few strides in front of the stoop. His stance, the way he clasped his hands behind his back, made Jaumé uneasy, but he wasn't sure why. Bennick looked relaxed, but Jaumé knew he wasn't. Was Bennick scared? Wary?

One of the new Brothers walked across to Bennick. He spoke to Bennick, seemed to ask a question. Bennick answered. Jaumé heard their voices, but not the words. After a moment, the two men clasped hands.

Bennick turned back to the house. Jaumé caught a glimpse of his face. Bennick looked like he was trying not to grin.

THE NEW BROTHERS gathered around the long table in Ifrem's main room. Ifrem had bread and cheese for them and a thick, spicy stew and the bitter tea the Brothers liked. Jaumé learned the new Brothers' names while he ate. Vught was their leader, a flat-faced man much younger than Nolt had been. And there were Krey, Doak, Soll, Luit, and Hetchel. Hetchel was with the princess, guarding her.

Ifrem laid three curling scraps of paper on the table in front of Vught. "Messages from Oudhees, Hansgrohe, and Vermeulen."

"Oudhees?" Vught frowned, as if he was surprised.

"Came in first." Ifrem tapped one of the messages.

Vught unrolled the message, held it close to a candle, and read. When he'd finished, he said a word Jaumé didn't recognize. It was a swearword; Vught's tone told him that. "They sailed to Oudhees."

Jaumé glanced around the table. The new Brothers were all frowning. "When did they arrive?" one of them asked.

"Message came in five days ago," Ifrem said.

"A problem?" Bennick asked, his voice neutral.

"Puts them ahead of us. We'll have to move faster." Vught scowled, and read the message again. "Konrad counted thirteen mages. That's more than we thought."

He tossed the message aside and reached for another one, read it. His expression changed, became less of a scowl. "Passed through Hansgrohe. Bought a wagon. The roads are jammed with refugees. Werner says their pace'll be slow."

One of the Brothers nodded. "Good."

"Even better, our Brothers killed three Sentinels. When did this come in?"

"Four days ago," Ifrem said.

Vught unrolled the third message, read it, gave a sour grunt. "Twelve men behind us."

The mood around the table changed. The new Brothers weren't frowning; they were sitting up, looking alert. "Following us?" one of them asked. Luit, Jaumé thought his name was. He was missing several of his front teeth.

"Following *her*." Vught screwed the paper up and tossed it in the fire.

"Mages?"

Vught shook his head. "Our Brother doesn't think so. Soldiers, he reckons. From Lundegaard."

There was a moment's silence, then Bennick shrugged. "Twelve soldiers. What's to worry about?"

"Nothing," Vught said, reaching for his mug. He swallowed deeply, wiped his mouth with the back of his hand, put the mug down with a thump. "We're seven, now that you've joined." His eyes flicked over Jaumé, dismissing him. "They haven't got a chance."

Bennick grinned. "No, they haven't." He stretched his arms over his head and leaned back in his chair, looking relaxed.

"How far behind are they?" one of the Brothers asked. Jaumé tried to remember his name. Soll? He had curly brown hair, like Da's.

"Less than a day." Vught leaned back in his chair too, like Bennick. "Not that it matters. They're no match for us." His grin was sharp, full of teeth. It reminded Jaumé of the shark that had once washed up on the shore at Girond.

"What about the boy?" Ifrem said. "Want him with you? I can send him to Fith."

Fith? Jaumé looked at Bennick in alarm.

Vught shrugged. "Why not? He'll just slow us down."

"He didn't slow Nolt down," Bennick said, still sprawled in his chair, relaxed. "He saved our lives."

Vught's gaze swung to Jaumé. The pale gray eyes seemed to pin Jaumé to his seat. He sat absolutely still, holding his breath.

"Fast learner," Bennick said. "Good marksman."

Vught stared at Jaumé a moment longer, then shrugged. "He can come if he wants."

"Well, lad?" Bennick said.

"I want to stay with you." The words spilled fast from Jaumé's tongue.

Vught shrugged again, looked at Bennick. "He's your responsibility."

Bennick nodded.

Vught glanced around the table. "Luit, change with Hetchel."

The Brother with the missing teeth pushed back his stool and left the room.

"Bitch keeps trying to escape," Vught said. "Given us a lot of trouble."

Jaumé's ears pricked.

"Escape?" Ifrem said. "How?"

"Loosened the bars on her cabin window, tried to jump overboard. We manacled her after that, but she pulled the bolt out of the floor. Since then we've kept a watch on her, day and night, even when she pisses."

Bennick snorted, a sound of amusement. "Bet she likes that."

"Doesn't seem to care. Looks through us, like we're those slaves they have in Osgaard."

Bennick snorted again. This time he didn't sound amused.

"Three days ago, she stabbed Doak here with a stick and rode into a band of militiamen, screaming that she was being kidnapped. We had to kill them all. Took us all night and half the next morning to track her down."

Jaumé blinked, impressed by the princess's daring.

"Why don't you use All-Mother's Breath?" Bennick asked. "If she's such a handful."

"Can't," Vught said. "We tried, but she couldn't keep any food down. Came close to dying on us. We need her alive."

Bennick nodded, grunted.

A Brother entered the room. His face was pitted with small, round scars. He sat on the stool Luit had vacated, reached for a bowl of stew, and started eating.

"We used a covered wagon for a while. Kept her tied up, but she gets carriage sick. Can't eat." Vught drank deeply from his mug. "Bitch."

Bennick grunted again.

"You've seen the prince?" curly-headed Soll asked. "You know what he looks like?"

"I do. And some of the mages he's with."

"Mages." Vught scowled again.

"Most of 'em seem to be shapeshifters, though there's at least one healer. Healed the prince when I killed him. Arrow through the heart. Dead. Then a couple of hours later he's walking around like nothing happened." There was disgust in Bennick's voice.

Vught's scowl faded. He looked almost amused.

"Probably got fire mages, too. But I didn't see any."

"Best to assume they do." Vught scratched his ribs. "But magic or no magic, we got the advantage now. This time, the prince isn't going to walk away."

Bennick leaned forward. "How're you planning to use her?"

Vught grinned his shark's grin again. "It's good." And then he glanced at Jaumé.

Bennick glanced at him, too, and jerked his head. *Leave us.*

Jaumé went to the far end of the long table, even though he was burning with curiosity. He rinsed his hands in the wooden basin there, and dried them.

Bennick and Vught were still talking.

He imagined the princess tied to a stake, and Brothers crouched in the bushes all around, and Bennick with his bow, and he imagined Prince Harkeld galloping towards her...

Jaumé shook his head, chasing away the image.

Ifrem had placed a basket of soft, wrinkled apples on the table. Jaumé spent a minute choosing one. When he glanced up, Vught and Bennick had stopped talking.

Jaumé went back to his seat. Bennick was chuckling under his breath.

Jaumé bit into his apple. He wished he'd heard Vught's plan.

WHEN HETCHEL HAD eaten, Ifrem cleared the table and laid out maps. Jaumé stayed quiet in his chair, trying not to draw attention to himself. He squinted at the closest map. It looked like a quilt, with patches of blue and green and snaking lines. How did one make sense of it? He dared not ask Bennick; he didn't want to be sent to bed.

"We're here," Vught said, placing a finger on one of the lines. A bandage wound around his hand, trailing a frayed end over the map. Vught uttered a wordless sound of impatience and stripped the bandage off, tossing it into the fire. Jaumé saw a curving line of scabs, like teeth marks.

Bennick saw it too. "Someone bite you?"

Vught scowled. "That bitch. Got infected. Had to cut it open."

Jaumé's gaze jerked to Vught's face, to the flat cheekbones, the thin mouth, the cold eyes. He shivered. He would never dare bite Vught. But *she*'d dared to. And she'd tried to jump out her cabin window, had stabbed Doak with a stick and ridden into a troop of militiamen. Maybe there *was* something special about her.

"We're here," Vught said again. "Any idea how far away the curse is, Ifrem?"

Ifrem leaned forward. "Oudhees fell a couple of days ago; Konrad managed to send pigeons out.

Hansgrohe'll go soon—if it hasn't already. I reckon it'll be in Bloedel in a fortnight."

Bennick uttered a low whistle. "It's covering ground." His eyebrows were raised, but he looked interested, not scared.

"Moving directly west?" Vught asked.

Ifrem nodded. "Seems to be doing exactly what the storytellers said it would."

*The curse shall rise in the east and pass across the kingdoms until it sets in the west, like the sun.* Jaumé remembered that from the tales. And he also remembered, *Those who drink the water shall thirst for blood. They shall be as wild beasts.*

He shivered again, to the pit of his stomach.

"What about the Urels?" Soll asked. "Curse get them, too?"

Ifrem nodded. "All the eastern isles had it, last I heard. Haven't had any news since Oudhees fell."

"No panic here," Hetchel said. "Seems calm."

"They don't know about Oudhees yet," Ifrem said. "They'll panic soon as they hear. Dumb goat-rutters."

Vught grunted a laugh.

The Brothers bent over the maps and talked. Jaumé curled up in the chair, hugging his knees, trying to stay awake.

# CHAPTER FORTY-NINE

"THE CURSE IS less than a mile away," Rand said, after they'd eaten dinner. "You all know this, but I'll say it again: any water on the ground is cursed. Don't get it anywhere near your mouths."

Less than a mile? Harkeld glanced over his shoulder, and saw only blackness.

"Both Petrus and Serril have landed on cursed ground and they're fine. We don't anticipate any problems, but... to be safe we'll have two mages on guard tonight."

"We can only guess what's going to happen," Serril said, his voice rumbling deep in his chest. "And because we can't be absolutely certain, we've decided all shapeshifters will sleep as animals tonight. The curse doesn't affect animals, so it shouldn't affect us when we're shifted."

For the first time, Harkeld found himself wishing he was a shapeshifter.

"You don't sound certain," Gretel said.

"We're not," Serril said. "It's a theory that hasn't been tested. But we're fairly confident we can't get the curse if we're shifted, so tonight, those of us who can, sleep as animals."

"It's a Primary Law broken," Rand said. "But under the circumstances..."

"Under the circumstances, breaking Primary Laws is the least of our worries," Malle said briskly. "At least until we reach the anchor stone."

"Within reason," Rand said. "Shapeshifters, be careful near cursed water. It shouldn't affect you if you're shifted, but it's one theory I don't wish to test. Take no risks. Is that understood?"

Harkeld looked across the campfire at Innis. Her gaze was on Rand. She nodded, her expression grave.

"Any humans nearby?" Bode asked.

"There are some in Delpy," Serril said. "Petrus's looter and a couple of others, running as a pack. We'll have to deal with them tomorrow. If they haven't eaten each other."

A shiver ran down Harkeld's spine.

"How much further to the anchor stone?" Adel asked. His voice was pitched higher than normal, as if his throat was tight. His fingers fiddled with his empty bowl.

*He's scared.*

But everyone around the fire was scared. They just hid it better than Adel, looking stoic, like Bode, or grave, like Innis.

"At least a week. If we don't encounter any problems."

Harkeld glanced at Petrus, seated alongside him. Petrus didn't look stoic or grave; he looked worried.

\*    \*    \*

No one made a move to turn in. They sat around the campfire, waiting for the curse to arrive. Harkeld expected to feel something—a prickling running over his skin, or perhaps underneath it, or in his blood, *something*—but he didn't realize the curse had reached them until Malle stirred and spoke. "Look at our shadows."

Harkeld glanced at the faces around the campfire and saw that the curse shadows were thicker, darker.

Now, his skin prickled. It felt like every hair on his body stood on end. His heartbeat sped up. The Ivek Curse.

The shadows looked too thick to breathe through, too thick to see through, but they weren't. He felt no different than he had before. Except more afraid.

They waited another half hour, another hour. No one seemed to want to go to bed. *How can I sleep knowing the curse is here?*

Finally Rand stood. "Adel, you're on watch now, with Justen. Petrus and Gretel are next. Then, Innis and Bode. Flin, Serril will sleep in your tent tonight."

"Sir... do I still need to be called Flin?"

Rand halted and turned back to face him.

"There's no one to hear us now," Harkeld said.

"Fithians," Serril said.

"But the curse—"

"Do you *know* there are no Fithians between here and the anchor stone?" Rand asked.

Harkeld hesitated. "No." If they could carry safe water with them, then so could Fithians. "But even if there are, surely it's no longer necessary—"

"If it makes a Fithian doubt who you are—for even half a second—it's worth it. For all of us."

Harkeld drew breath to argue, and looked at Rand's face, weary beneath the thick curse shadows, and released it.

# CHAPTER FIFTY

JAUMÉ MUST HAVE fallen asleep. When he woke, it was dark and he was in bed, with the blankets pulled up to his chin.

For a moment he was confused. Was he at home? Were Mam and Da in the next room? Was Rosa asleep in the little cot by the window?

And then he remembered: Mam and Da and Rosa were dead. He'd run from the curse and Bennick had saved him. It was Bennick who'd put him to bed.

Jaumé snuggled deeper into the blankets. Memory of Mam and Da and Rosa nibbled at the edges of his mind. He could see Da's face, mad with the curse, could hear Rosa screaming, smell Mam's blood, feel it slippery beneath the soles of his feet—

He pulled the blankets over his head and fastened his attention on the one thing that mattered: he was staying with Bennick. Bennick, who whistled and whose eyes smiled the way Da's had and who was teaching him to use a sword.

By holding Bennick in his head, Jaumé was able to forget Mam's blood and Rosa's scream and Da's mad face.

He went to sleep again.

# CHAPTER FIFTY-ONE

HARKELD CRAWLED OUT of the tent. A cold wind gusted. The dawn sky was as smoky and orange-streaked as dusk had been. A black hawk drifted in lazy circles above them. Innis, not Serril. Serril was eating breakfast.

The water mages and Rand were at the creek, crouching, looking at the water.

Harkeld rubbed his face, combed his hair roughly with his fingers, and walked across to them, hugging his cloak around himself.

"... very interesting," he heard Malle say. She scooped some water up in her hand, looked closely at it. "Can you see that, Adel? Each particle is affected."

Adel bent his head and peered at the water in Malle's hand. "I see it."

"And the surface, that film, like a curse shadow..." Malle released the water and wiped her hand on her trews. "I'd like to make some notes. I brought some vellum."

"I'll get it," Adel said. He trotted over to the pile of supplies, gangly and gawky and puppy-ish.

Rand saw Harkeld, and beckoned. "Can you see it?"

"See what?"

"Look at the water."

Harkeld hunkered down alongside Rand and stared at the creek. What was he looking for? The water looked perfectly normal, clear where it wasn't reflecting the orange dawn. "See what?"

"Look at it out of the corner of your eye."

Harkeld obeyed, but all he saw was water and reflections and... He frowned, squinting. "Kind of oily on top?"

"Yes."

"What is it?"

"The water's curse shadow," Malle said. "Or its equivalent. I've never seen anything like it. What Ivek did is unprecedented! All-Mother only knows how he managed it."

"Can it be undone?" Rand asked. "Without the anchor stone? Could you take a cupful of this water and return it to its natural state?"

Malle opened both hands in a shrug. "I don't know. I shall certainly try."

Rand frowned thoughtfully, and pulled on his lower lip. "Is it worth Innis trying too? She's strong enough to lay curses. Maybe she's strong enough to uncurse some of this water?"

"Again, certainly worth a try."

Harkeld frowned. "Wouldn't that be dangerous for her?" A question Petrus would have asked if he was there.

"No more dangerous than dealing with any other curse. What's cursed—or unhealed—can usually be healed, although the results are always best if the mage who laid the curse can be, er, *induced* to reverse it." Rand looked at the water, and shook his head. "No one's ever managed to curse a kingdom before, let alone a whole continent. How did he get his curse to bond with the water?"

Malle shook her head.

Adel hurried back to them, clutching a roll of vellum, a quill, and a flask of ink.

"Excellent," Malle said. "We'll start with a description of the water's properties." She leaned over the creek. Beside her, Adel hurriedly uncorked the ink flask. "Odor, normal. Color, normal. Flow, normal. Surface tension..." She cupped water in her palm, dipped a fingertip into the water. "Surface tension, normal."

Rand caught Harkeld's eye. "Go have breakfast. We'll be a while."

PETRUS WAS AT the fire, eating gruel. Harkeld grabbed a bowl and sat alongside him. He knew the gruel would have been made using water from their barrels, but he still wanted to ask, to double check, to make *absolutely* certain. He bit the words back on his tongue. It was the sort of question Adel would ask. A nervous question. Revealing his fear.

Determinedly, he began to eat.

"What're they doing?" Petrus asked.

"Examining the water. Malle's going to try to uncurse some of it."

He watched Serril strip off his clothes, shove them in a packsaddle, and change into a hawk. Serril took a moment to shake out his feathers, then sprang up into the air, climbing with great sweeps of his wings. The two black hawks circled in the sky together, their feathers shimmering with magic. Serril was twice the size of Innis.

Innis glided down and landed.

Harkeld looked away to give her privacy while she dressed. "What's the shimmer?" he asked Petrus.

"Huh?"

"The shimmer." He pointed at Serril with his spoon. "What is it?"

"No one really knows. It's magic, obviously, but what or why...?" Petrus shrugged. "Philosophers have been debating it for centuries. There are dozens of theories, but only a couple of 'em make sense to me. One is that shapeshifters give off magic when they're shifted, kind of like how we all give off body heat. The other..." He shot Harkeld a glance. "It's kind of complicated. Do you really want to know this?"

Harkeld nodded.

"All right." Petrus put down his bowl. "You see..." He paused, frowned, seemed to be figuring out how best to start. "Air isn't just air. The same as rock and water aren't just rock and water. They're made up of particles that are too small for us to see."

Harkeld looked at him dubiously. "They are?"

Petrus nodded. "And we're made up of tiny particles, too. Not just blood and bone and skin and hair and all that, but tiny, *tiny* particles that no one can see."

Harkeld felt his forehead wrinkle. "We are?"

"So the philosophers say. And the theory is that when we change shape, those tiny particles somehow alter, too, and that causes the shimmer."

"It sounds... far-fetched," Harkeld said.

Petrus shrugged. "Far-fetched or not, most philosophers agree on that part of it. What they argue about is *why* the change in our particles causes the shimmer. Is it because of how our particles interact with the particles in the air? Or is it because of how they reflect light?"

Petrus was looking at him as if expecting an answer. Harkeld shook his head.

"Exactly. No one knows. It happens when we shift shape. Only mages can see it. Those are the facts. The rest..." Petrus shrugged. "Just guesses." He picked up his bowl and began eating again.

Harkeld stared at Serril, circling in the sky. Tiny particles?

He looked down at his gruel and stirred it. Some things were unexplainable. Like why the sun always rose in the east and set in the west. And why compasses always pointed north. Although the mages probably had theories for both of those.

"What's she doing?" Petrus said, his tone sharp.

Harkeld looked up, saw Petrus frowning, and followed his gaze. Innis knelt alongside Malle at the creek.

"Seeing if she can uncurse some of it."

"What?" Petrus put down his bowl and pushed to his feet.

"Rand said it was safe."

"Nothing to do with that water's safe."

Harkeld watched Petrus stride over to the creek.

Justen crawled out of his tent, yawned, wrapped his cloak tightly around himself, and came across to the fire. Harkeld nodded a greeting to him.

Thick, dark curse shadows covered Justen—covered them all—but the shadows didn't seem as threatening as they had last night. Already his eyes were used to them. *It won't be long before I stop noticing altogether.*

After a few minutes, Petrus came back, his expression sour. "She wants to try." He sat, picked up his bowl, and scowled at it.

"Try what?" Justen asked.

"Uncurse the water."

"Huh." Justen looked at the cluster of mages beside the creek, shook his head, went back to his gruel.

"She shouldn't be here," Harkeld said to Petrus. "It's too dangerous."

Petrus glanced at him. "Finally, we agree on something."

"Well," Harkeld said, putting down his empty bowl. "We also agree that I'm a better wrestler than you."

Petrus almost choked on his last spoonful of gruel. "Better?"

Harkeld tried to look modest. Across the fire, Justen was grinning.

Petrus shook his head, snorted. He scraped his bowl clean and licked the spoon. "You know, you wasted a lot of weeks being a surly son of a whore."

Harkeld conceded this with a shrug. "Another thing we agree on."

# CHAPTER FIFTY-TWO

BLOEDEL WAS BUILT on both sides of a ravine. The ravine marked the border with Sault. The gate guard said that a party of seven horsemen had arrived at dusk the previous night. One of the men had been riding a piebald mare.

Karel tossed him a coin. "How many gates does Bloedel have?"

"Uh... eight, sir. Counting this one."

"Where's your market square?"

"Other side of t' ravine, sir."

Karel sent armsmen to check the town gates and waited in the market square, trying not to let his edgy impatience infect his mount. Prince Tomas didn't bother to hide his impatience. He paced the dusty ground, kicking stones out of his way. "How can you stay so cursed calm?" he demanded.

Karel shrugged. *Because I have to.*

Prince Tomas's gaze fastened on something behind him; he stopped kicking stones. Karel turned his head. Lief, returning from the southern gate. The tall armsman shook his head. "Nothing."

Gunvald, Dag, Solveig, Ture, and Arvid all reported the same news. Karel built a map of

Bloedel in his head; only the north-eastern gate remained.

The prince resumed kicking stones.

A buxom housewife bustled past, a gray goose clamped under one arm. Dag's eyes followed her until she disappeared from sight. "Have you heard the one about the lord and his goose?" he asked.

Prince Tomas swung towards him. "No."

"Well, there's this lord, see, and he comes home to his wife and he's holding a goose. The lord says, 'This is the dog I lay with every night.' And the wife says, 'That's not a dog, 'tis a goose.' And the lord says, 'I wasn't speaking to you.'"

Prince Tomas groaned and shook his head. "Why do I listen to you, Dag?"

Dag shrugged, grinning.

"Here comes Bjarne," Solveig said.

They all turned to look. Bjarne rode across the market square. He was frowning.

"What?" Karel said. "They didn't leave through that gate?"

Bjarne tilted his head in a movement that was neither nod nor shake. "Not sure, sir."

"What do you mean, not sure?" Prince Tomas demanded.

"I mean that a party of nine left this morning. Nine." Bjarne swung down from his mount. "Eight men, one riding a piebald mare, and a young lad on a pony."

Silence met these words.

"Nine," the prince said, turning to Karel. "Nine?"

Karel turned possibilities over in his head, frowning. "When did they leave?"

"Just after dawn."

Less than two hours ago. *We're close!* But was it the right party? Nine travelers, not seven...

Karel shuffled through the possibilities. Why nine? Why now?

"What do you think?" Tomas asked.

"They stayed the night," Karel said. "Which means that either they put up at an inn—or there's a Fithian house here."

The prince glanced over his shoulder. "Fithian house?"

"Bloedel's large. A border town, on a crossroad. Perfect place for one." Karel rubbed his forehead, still thinking. If there was a Fithian house here...

"We could look around," Lief said. "Ask questions."

"We could," Karel said. "But we run the risk of alerting the Fithians we're here." Was the risk worth it? They were so close to their goal, now. *Two hours from the princess!*

If it had been her on the piebald mare.

He shoved his hands through his hair, thinking. Princess Brigitta could be right here, in Bloedel. Or she could be miles away. He lowered his hands, turned on his heel, scanned the market square, the buildings, the rooftops—and made some decisions.

"Dag, Bjarne, Lief, Solveig, ask questions at the inns. Discreetly. Not pushy, not drawing attention to yourselves. Casual conversation, casual questions, that's all. Gunvald and Ture, you're with me and the prince. We're looking for men who keep pigeons. The rest of you, you're looking for piebald mares. They may have sold it. Check the stables, check anywhere you can think of. Meet back here in one hour."

The armsmen dispersed. "Sire, Gunvald, take the western half of the town. Other side of the gorge. Ture and I'll do this side. Be careful. If there is a Fithian house, if they think you're looking for it, you could end up with a throwing star in your back."

Karel watched them go. *I hope neither one of them gets killed here.*

He shook the thought aside and headed across the market square, examining the sky, examining the rooftops, looking for pigeons, Ture close on his heels.

# CHAPTER FIFTY-THREE

"THEY ARRIVED LAST night, stayed at a Fithian house, left this morning with two extra people. A man and a boy." Karel met Prince Tomas's eyes. "You agree?"

"I agree."

"Who are they, sir?" Bjarne asked. "The man and the boy?"

"My guess is the man's Fithian. The boy?" Karel shook his head, shrugged. "Recruit? Prisoner? We'll find that out when we catch up with them."

He swung up into the saddle and clenched the reins in his hand. Seven assassins to deal with now, not six.

*The advantage is still ours*, Karel reminded himself. They outnumbered the Fithians nearly two to one. And the assassins didn't know they were behind them. "Let's go." The horse caught his excitement and pranced a few steps.

They rode through the gate at a sober pace. Karel raised his hand to the gate guard. A man with a wooden leg, leaning heavily on a stick, watched them go, his expression sour, as if he dreamed of days when he'd had two legs.

Karel urged his mount to a canter. The road stretched ahead. The princess had traveled this way only a few hours ago. *So close.*

They'd catch up with her soon. Not today, and maybe not tomorrow, but definitely the day after that.

# CHAPTER FIFTY-FOUR

A NEW FITHIAN had joined them. It was easy to find a name for him: Red. Beneath the bright, curly hair he had a face made for smiling. He didn't look like an assassin. But he carried a throwing knife strapped to his belt, and a sword, and there was a hardness in his eyes when he looked at her, a hardness to his mouth. Yes, he would kill her without hesitation or remorse.

Red had a child with him, a boy no more than eight or nine years old, wearing a miss-match of clothes. The boy carried a throwing knife too, and a small bow. An apprentice assassin?

The boy rode by Red's side and didn't speak much, but Britta caught him looking at her several times, his expression quizzical, as if trying to figure out who she was.

*Who are you, child? Where is your family?*

Harkeld would have looked like this boy, when he was young. The olive tone to his skin, the dark brown hair, the hazel eyes bright with intelligence. Did the child have any understanding of what Fithians were? Did he know he would become a killer if he stayed with them?

*When I escape, I must take him with me.*

But, no, she couldn't. The fate of the Seven Kingdoms hung in the balance, tens of thousands of lives. Her own survival was irrelevant, this boy's survival was irrelevant. All that mattered was that Harkeld lived long enough to end the curse.

*I must escape. I cannot be the bait to catch Harkeld.*

Whatever the Fithians planned, it would be cunning. And deadly.

Britta glanced at Plain, riding alongside her, holding her reins. She bent her head and scratched her nose, and carefully fished the broken stone from her cloak pocket.

THE ROAD WOUND its way up a stony hillside. Britta let her gaze drift across the hill, while her hands worked furtively, sawing the rope that bound her wrists to the pommel. She saw stunted thorn trees and outcrops of rock. Nowhere to run to, nowhere to hide.

A gray thunderhead loomed over the line of hills. It looked like an anvil, squat and asymmetrical. A damp, cold wind swept down from the east, whimpering between the rocks, lifting her cloak, exposing her hands. She jerked a glance at Plain. Had he seen the stone she clutched?

No. Plain was scanning the road ahead, his eyes narrowed against the wind.

The wind grew stronger, tugging at her cloak, uncovering her hands again, flipping her hood off her head. Too risky to keep sawing.

Britta slid the stone into her cloak pocket, but the wind caught the fabric, made the cloak billow like wings around her, and the stone tumbled to the ground.

She almost cried out—and clamped her tongue between her teeth. *Draw no attention.* But she couldn't stop an anguished backwards glance at the road, at the stone.

A sinewy gray mare followed behind her. Its rider was watching her. Killer. Britta shivered, a shiver that had nothing to do with the wind. She turned her head and stared at the road, but she could still see Killer's eyes, see the edge of madness, see how much he wanted to kill her.

# CHAPTER FIFTY-FIVE

HARKELD RODE TENSELY, his hand resting on his sword hilt. Ivek's curse surrounded them. The sense of danger, of threat, was palpable. He smelled it in the smoke-scented air, tasted it in the back of his throat, acrid.

But the day passed without incident. They encountered roaming flocks of goats, rode through abandoned hamlets, skirted a burning village that Petrus said was Delpy, saw empty farmhouses in empty paddocks. Innis, and later Petrus, flew overhead, keeping close watch on them, while Serril roamed miles ahead, miles behind, scouting.

They halted just before dusk. Smoke smeared the sky. Harkeld dismounted and examined the paddock, the creek, the crooked stone walls, the twisted thorn trees, his hand still on his sword hilt. He felt on edge, certain that at any moment something terrible would happen.

He unloaded the horses and helped pitch the tents. Gretel crossed to him as he was banging in the last stake. "Want to burn some arrows before it gets dark?" she asked.

"Yes." And maybe it would burn off some of this nervous energy. He raised his voice, "Rand, you remember those cheap arrows Cora bought? You know where the last hundred are?"

"I do," Innis said. "I'll shoot, if you like. I was Justen when you did it before."

They set themselves up in the neighboring paddock. Harkeld stood with his right hand behind his back and his left hand slightly raised. Bode and Gretel were off to one side. Innis was at the opposite end of the paddock, a quiver slung over her shoulder. Behind her, the sky looked like a giant, smoldering fire: swirls of orange clouds, streamers of smoke. "Ready?" she called.

"Ready."

Innis started as she had in Ankeny, letting the arrows arc up into the sky. *Burn. Burn.* His magic incinerated the arrows, leaving small puffs of smoke and specks of ash drifting down. After he'd burned half a dozen, she began reducing the angle. Soon the arrows were speeding past him. *Burn. Burn.* He wasn't quite as deft as he was with his right hand, but he wasn't struggling either.

Innis lowered the bow. "Shall I aim at you?" she called.

He looked at Bode and Gretel. "Ready?"

The fire mages stepped forward and positioned themselves ahead of him and to the right. Bode cupped a hand to his mouth, "Go, Innis."

Innis raised the bow, nocked an arrow.

Harkeld shifted his weight forward, exhaled, focused. He couldn't see the arrow leap from the bow at this distance, but he saw Innis reach for the next one. *Burn.* A tiny burst of white-hot flame flared alight halfway between him and Innis. *Burn.*

He was slower with his left hand. It hadn't been obvious before, but it was obvious now. Not a lot slower, but enough that it made a difference. He tried to aim faster, but the harder he tried, the harder it became to focus his magic. The explosions of flame crept across the paddock towards him, each one a little closer than the last. Curse it. His heart was beating fast, his breathing was shallow, and despite the cold wind, sweat was forming on his face. *Too slow, too slow—*

His right hand instinctively reached out and incinerated an arrow, an easy flick of flame that required no thought, no effort.

"Rut it," he said, out loud. "Stop a minute, Innis!"

Innis lowered the bow.

Harkeld drew his sword and gripped it in his right hand. Now, he wouldn't be tempted to cheat. "All right!" he called.

She reached for an arrow, raised the bow.

*Burn.* Harkeld tried to relax into the exercise, to not focus so intently, to let instinct rule, not effort. For the first few arrows it seemed to work—*burn, burn*—and then he noticed that the explosions of flame were creeping closer to him again. He concentrated harder, tried to speed up. *Burn. Burn.* Sweat stung his eyes. His grip on the sword hilt was so tight his fingers were cramping. The arrows were getting closer. Much closer. Any closer and they'd—

He dropped the sword and used his right hand. There was a loud crack of sound, a bright flare of white and yellow flame, then silence.

At the other end of the paddock, Innis lowered the bow.

Harkeld and Bode and Gretel looked at each other.

"I think we all got that one," Gretel said.

Harkeld nodded. He bent and picked up his sword, sheathed it, flexed his cramped fingers, shook out his hand. "Can one of you tie my hand behind my back?"

The orange in the sky was fading. Another ten minutes and it would be too dark for this exercise.

Harkeld stared at the smoke stain in the sky while Bode tied his hand to his belt with a leather cord. *I need to not try so hard. Not get tense.* But it was impossible *not* to get tense when there was an arrow leaping across the paddock at him.

Bode stepped back.

*So what if I miss one? Doesn't matter. Bode and Gretel'll get it.*

Harkeld planted his feet, blew out a breath, and gazed down the paddock at Innis.

"We're ready," Bode called.

Harkeld watched Innis reach for an arrow. *Relax*, he told himself.

They practiced while the light faded from the sky. Harkeld kept his attention on Innis, on the movement of her hand reaching back for each new arrow, kept his attention on his breathing, slow and steady. *Burn. Burn.* He was still a little too slow. Bursts of flame crept across the paddock towards him, a gradual advance. *Burn.* An arrow flared alight two thirds of the way up the paddock.

Innis lowered the bow. "That was the last of the arrows," she called. "Do you want to burn the bow?"

Not with Innis holding it. Not if he was using his left hand. "No," Harkeld shouted back.

Bode untied the leather cord. "Better that time."

"Better," Harkeld conceded. "But still not as good as my right hand."

"But good enough to save your life. Or someone else's," Gretel pointed out.

He glanced at her. "True." He didn't have to be perfect with his left hand. Not yet. Just enough to save a life.

They walked back across the paddock together. Harkeld's jitteriness was gone. He felt tired, not edgy. He glanced around at the dark humps of hillocks and gullies. The curse had emptied this plateau, and the emptiness made it safe. Anyone still alive would stand out. The shapeshifters would see them from miles away.

They clambered over the stone wall into the next paddock, where the horses were picketed. Bode tripped on a rock, putting out a hand to catch himself.

"You all right?" Gretel asked.

Bode climbed to his feet and grunted a laugh. "Horseshit." He held up a palm dark with dung. "Just wash it off." He veered away from them, towards the creek.

"Is that safe?" Harkeld asked.

"As long as he doesn't drink the water."

Even so, he watched Bode out of the corner of his eye. The fire mage crouched at the creek and washed his hands. Malle and Adel were there, too. They seemed to be talking, Bode asking questions, Malle answering.

Serril and Rand were at the fire. The smell of food made Harkeld's mouth water.

"How'd it go?" Rand asked, filling a bowl and handing it to Gretel.

"Moderately well," Harkeld said.

"Flin's too hard on himself," Gretel said. "Extremely well, is what he meant to say."

Harkeld shrugged and sat alongside Gretel. Where was Innis? He frowned and looked around. There she was, putting away the bow.

"Flin." Rand handed him a bowl of stew.

"... still have no idea how he did it." The voice was Malle's. "It's bound so tightly to the water as to be inseparable from it."

Harkeld stirred his stew, blew on it, watched as Malle and Adel and Bode sat opposite him. Bode held his hands out to the fire to dry them.

"No luck?" Rand asked.

Malle shook her head. "It's quite a puzzle. In theory it should be possible to unbind the curse from the water. What can be done can almost always be *un*-done. But I can't do it, and Innis can't, and—"

"Bode," Gretel said sharply. "Your hand!"

Everyone's attention jerked to Bode, with his hands held out to the fire. The curse shadow around his right hand was thick, dense, black.

"What—?" Bode said, but even as he spoke the blackness flowed up his arm like a tide. He lurched to his feet. "I've got the curse!" He swung to the nearest mage, Adel. "Kill me!" he screamed.

# CHAPTER FIFTY-SIX

THE BLACK SHADOWS enveloped Bode's head. He stood motionless for the space of one heartbeat, then uttered a sound that made the hairs on Harkeld's scalp rise— guttural, edged with insanity. His hands reached for Adel, claw-like.

Adel scrambled backwards, panic on his face.

Harkeld dropped his bowl and lunged to his feet, snatching for his sword.

A sword swung out of the darkness, reflecting the firelight, and cleaved Bode's skull in half.

Bode swayed, and fell solidly, scattering embers.

Harkeld stood frozen with shock, unable to speak, unable to move. After a moment, he remembered to breathe. The smell of blood filled his mouth and nose.

His eyes fastened on the person who had killed Bode. Serril, his face grim.

Still no one spoke. The only sound was Adel's gulped breaths, half-sobbing, half-panting.

Harkeld looked for Innis. She stood near him, both hands pressed to her mouth.

An owl swooped down, scattering more embers, and changed into Petrus. "What in the All-Mother's name just happened?"

"The curse infected Bode." Rand's voice sounded rusty. "Somehow." He squeezed his eyes shut, pressed the heels of his hands to them, as if trying to erase the sight of Bode lying dead.

"He washed his hands in the creek." Malle pushed to her feet, her movements agitated. "But that shouldn't have done it! I've touched it, and Adel, and Innis and Rand! I don't see how..." She turned to Bode's body.

"It started with his right hand," Gretel said. "I saw it."

"I did, too," Harkeld said.

"Then let's examine him." Rand lowered his hands. "Serril... thank you."

The big shapeshifter shook his head.

Rand cautiously approached Bode's body and crouched.

Harkeld looked at Innis again. Like him, she hadn't moved. Her hands were still pressed to her mouth.

He crossed to her and hugged her. His arms and legs moved stiffly, as if shock had thickened his joints.

"Promise me you will never touch that water again." His voice was gritty, harsh. "Promise me, Innis. You'll *never* touch it again."

She nodded against his chest. He felt her trembling and tightened his grip on her.

"There's a small graze on his knuckles," Rand said. "Fresh."

"He fell over," Gretel said. "Maybe five minutes ago. Just before he washed his hands."

Rand tipped his head to look up at Malle. "Could that have done it?"

"It's a blood curse." Malle paced, agitated. "It infects the blood, that's how Ivek crafted it. But the water's meant to be *drunk*. No one ever thought it could do anything like *this*." She stopped pacing, took a shaky breath, pressed her hands to her temples, as if trying to hold her skull together. "I beg your pardon, Rand. Let me think about this. If there was an open wound, a *fresh* open wound... and if water got into the wound... I suppose it's possible the curse could infect a person's blood."

"No supposing about it," Serril said flatly.

"No." Rand levered himself slowly to his feet. He looked haggard. He gazed down at Bode and sighed. "Let's bury him."

# CHAPTER FIFTY-SEVEN

THE ASSASSINS HALTED at dusk in a wide, muddy cleft between two outcrops of rock, out of the wind. Others had sheltered here; the ground was churned with hoof prints and scattered with the blackened remnants of old campfires.

Plain untied the rope that fastened her to the pommel, led her to a spot away from the horses, pushed her down to sit. Britta surreptitiously examined her bound wrists while the Fithians unloaded the horses. Had she cut halfway through the rope?

No. Not halfway. Not even a quarter. Not even— if she were honest with herself—an eighth.

Britta gritted her teeth. Another stone, that was what she needed. A stone that was sharper, one that would cut through the coarse rope like a knife.

Her gaze wandered across the muddy ground. Pebbles. A discarded horseshoe. Charred sticks. Ash. A ring of blackened stones. Barbed twigs from thorn trees. More ash.

Her eyes skipped from pebble to pebble, stone to stone, looking for one that was broken, looking for a sharp edge. Around her, the Fithians attended to the horses. There was an edge of dampness in the wind, as if a squall might come through. The boy was busy building a fire, working with quiet, unsupervised efficiency. Britta watched him for a moment, then resumed her search. There *must* be something sharp here. A stone. A nail. A piece of broken crockery. Anything. Her gaze skimmed across the cold ash of someone else's campfire, a yard to her left—and halted. Was that a discarded arrowhead?

Britta's heart beat faster. Yes. An arrowhead, half-buried in old ashes.

An arrowhead would be as sharp as a knife. An arrowhead would cut through rope easily.

She glanced around. None of the Fithians had noticed the arrowhead, and soon it would be too dark for them to see it.

Britta let her gaze slide back to the arrowhead. She stared at it hard, marking its position, then looked away. The boy had lit the fire and was setting a pot on a tripod over the flames.

Should she inch her way across to the ashes and make a stealthy snatch at the arrowhead? Or wait?

Instinct told her to wait. Usually, wherever she sat was where she slept. It would be easy to roll over in the night, sift through the ashes with her fingers, hide the arrowhead in her cloak. If she was quiet enough, careful enough, the sentry wouldn't notice.

But what if the Fithians decided she should sleep closer to the fire tonight? Or closer to the sheltering overhang of rock? Or—

The boy was watching her while he unwrapped bundles of food, with the puzzled expression he wore whenever he looked at her.

Britta stiffened, and forced herself to relax, to smile at him.

The boy looked hastily away.

She watched him for several minutes, but he didn't look at her again. Who was he? What was his background? Why was he with the Fithians?

Her curiosity was laced with an emotion that she had to look at from several angles before she understood what it was: protectiveness. *I want to protect this boy. I want to keep him safe.*


DARKNESS FELL. THE assassins sat around the fire. Gap-Tooth brought her two tough, spicy, smoked sausages and a waterskin.

It was difficult to drink with bound wrists, but Britta knew better than to ask for her hands to be untied. She ate, savoring the spices on her tongue, drank. The wind picked up. A speck of rain struck her cheek.

If it rained, would they move her under the overhanging rock?

Was it a risk she could take?

Britta glanced to her left. She couldn't see the arrowhead in the dark, but she knew precisely where it was, knew how far she needed to move if she was to get it.

She took a deep breath and dropped her waterskin, spilling a great spurt of water on the muddy ground. "Oh!"

She looked up. The Fithians were all watching her.

Britta made a show of shuffling sideways, away from the spilled water. The arrowhead was less than a foot away now, buried in the old ashes. She glanced at the Fithians. Only the boy was still watching her. He looked hastily away when he saw that she'd noticed.

Wind gusted into the cleft. Rain began to patter on the ground.

Britta reached sideways. Her fingers closed around the arrowhead. Quickly, she shoved it into the pocket of her cloak.

Leader stood, scowled into the wind and the rain, spoke curtly. Men moved to obey. Plain and Pox strode to her, grabbed her by the arms, hoisted her to her feet, pulled her towards the overhang.

Britta made no protest. She let them tie her ankles, then burrowed as far back under the rock as she could, snuggling into her cloak and blankets. After several minutes, she felt in her pocket for the arrowhead and examined it with her fingers. The haft was broken, but the edges... Almost razor-sharp.

*With this, I can escape.*

# CHAPTER FIFTY-EIGHT

HARKELD WOKE AT dawn, stiff and cold and tired. The second bedroll in the tent was empty; Petrus was already awake. Harkeld crawled outside and wrapped his cloak tightly around him. There'd been a frost overnight. The camp was stirring. Petrus and Rand sat hunched by the fire and the water mages were at the creek. As he watched, Adel uncorked the ink flask and began making notes. Malle knelt, leaned over the creek, poked the water with a finger.

"She's not touching it, is she?" Harkeld said, alarmed.

"I checked her hands," Rand said. "No cuts, no grazes." His voice was as rusty as it had been last night. He sighed and rubbed his face, a harsh scratching of bristles, then climbed to his feet. "Dawn exercises. Come on, Petrus. We'll feel better afterwards."

Petrus grimaced, but he stood, shrugging off his cloak, unbuckling his sword belt.

"May I do them, too?" Harkeld asked.

"Of course."

He dropped his cloak and sword belt alongside Petrus's. "You'll need to talk me through them. Ebril only showed me once."

They started slowly, a flow of lunges and stretches. After five minutes, Harkeld's body woke up. The advances and retreats, the twists, the blocks, came more easily. He was no longer cold. Sweat began to bead his face.

"Rand!" Malle called excitedly. "Look at this!"

Rand straightened from a lunge. He wiped his face and headed for the creek.

Harkeld paused for a moment. What had Malle discovered? A way of un-cursing the water?

Petrus didn't stop. He turned and lunged in the opposite direction.

Harkeld followed, a beat behind him, his attention half on Rand and Malle, half on the exercises. He almost overbalanced, almost fell flat on his face. He caught himself with one hand. *If you're going to do this, concentrate.* A smooth lunge, a gliding turn, another lunge—

A commotion at the creek snapped his head around. Malle and Adel were wrestling on the ground. "What the—?"

Malle began to shriek, a high, keening sound.

Harkeld pushed out of his lunge, ran for the fire, snatched up his sword. Malle and Adel were flailing on the ground by the creek, bucking and rolling, Rand trying to pull them apart. Malle's shriek rose in pitch, sharp enough to splinter glass.

Harkeld ran faster, gripping his sword. She had the curse. No sane person could scream like that.

A huge black hawk swooped down, but before it could land Malle's shriek died.

Harkeld slowed, halted. Petrus halted alongside him, also gripping a sword, also panting.

For a long moment, no one moved—the two water mages on the ground, Rand leaning over them—and then Rand straightened. Adel shrugged Malle off him and scrambled backwards. Malle didn't move. Harkeld looked at her body—limbs awkwardly sprawled, eyes half-open—and knew she was dead.

The hawk landed and changed into Serril. "What happened?" he demanded.

Rand shook his head. "Don't know. Adel, are you all right?"

Adel huddled on the ground, shaking convulsively, his face as white as parchment.

Rand crossed to him, took his elbow. "Petrus, help me get him to the fire. He's going into shock."

Petrus silently handed Harkeld his sword and took Adel's other elbow. Harkeld looked around for Innis. She stood just behind him, her face almost as pale as Adel's. "What happened?"

"Malle got the curse."

They were a silent procession back to the fire. Malle's shriek still seemed to hang in the air.

Rand sat Adel close to the fire and busied himself putting herbs in hot water. "Wake Gretel and Justen," he said.

Innis hurried across to the tents. "Gretel?" he heard her call. "Justen? Wake up!"

Harkeld slowly sheathed his sword, and Petrus's. Shock reverberated inside him. Two dead at this camp. *I was a fool to think we were safe here.*

Rand poured the tea into mugs and passed them around. "Drink it, Adel," he said, when the water mage stared at his mug blankly. "It'll make you feel better."

Adel didn't respond. He was shivering, white-faced.

Rand guided the mug to Adel's mouth. "Drink." He rested his hand on the nape of Adel's neck, an expression of concentration on his face. Calming him?

Harkeld sipped his own drink. It tasted of herbs. Not the dried peppermint leaves the mages often used, but something milder, soothing.

Adel's violent trembling seemed to be easing.

Rand kept his hand on Adel's neck. "Tell us what happened, son."

Adel gulped a mouthful of tea. "I don't know."

"Malle had discovered something, hadn't she?"

"I don't know!" Adel's voice slid upwards in pitch. "She didn't tell me what she was doing. She just... she just..." He gulped for air, seeming on the verge of tears.

"It's all right if you don't know." Serril's rumble was surprisingly gentle. "Just tell us what you saw."

Adel wiped his eyes with his knuckles. "She was trying to figure out how Ivek bound the curse to the water, and she said... she said, 'I wonder if that would work?' and she put her hand in the creek and... and I don't know what she did because I was busy writing!"

"Why did she call me?" Rand asked.

Adel gulped a breath. "Because... because whatever she did worked. She said, 'Look, Adel! Look!' and I did and there was her handprint in the water, a perfect handprint, where the curse shadow was gone. And then the curse sort of flowed back into it and it went oily again. But it was *there*. I saw it."

No one spoke for a few seconds.

"Did she say anything about what she'd done?" Rand asked. "Anything at all?"

Adel shook his head. "She said, 'So *that's* how he did it,' and called you, and then... and then she said my name, and her voice was funny, like something was wrong, and... and she was looking at her hand, and it was all black with the curse, and she said 'Run, Adel!' and then... and then her curse shadow changed all over her and she attacked me."

Rand frowned. "So... Malle discovered a way to uncurse the water, but whatever she did transferred the curse to her?" He glanced across the fire at Serril.

The big shapeshifter nodded. "Sounds like it." He rose from his crouch, naked, and jerked a thumb skyward. "I'd best get back up there. Justen, relieve me when you've eaten."

There was silence around the campfire after Serril had gone. Harkeld finished his drink and caught Petrus's eye. "Help me dig her grave?"

INNIS TOOK DOWN the tents and loaded them on the packhorses. "Rand?"

The healer glanced up from the horse he was saddling.

"Did you use your magic to kill Malle?"

Rand grimaced.

"How did you do it, sir? Did you stop her heart?"

He buckled the girth strap. "It's not the sort of magic I want you learning."

"I may need it."

Rand sighed. He looked away, scrubbed a hand over his face, looked back. "I ruptured her major arteries. Carotid. Jugular. Aorta. It's a quick death. Almost instantaneous."

Innis met his eyes. "Thank you."

Rand nodded. He checked the girth strap and tightened it another notch. Innis watched him, seeing the lines of exhaustion and strain on his face. "Are you all right?"

"As all right as any of us are, right now. Don't worry about me, Innis. Worry about keeping him alive." Rand nodded in the prince's direction. "If we all worry about that, we may make it."

# CHAPTER FIFTY-NINE

THE ARROWHEAD STAYED in Britta's pocket all morning. The road traversed a barren hillside scattered with rocks and thorn trees and bisected by the occasional steep gully. There was nowhere to run to, nowhere to hide. Cutting the ropes now would achieve only one thing: alert the Fithians to the arrowhead.

Two of the assassins—Curly and Pox—dropped back. By mid-morning, they were so far behind that Britta couldn't see them when she turned in the saddle. She pondered their disappearance, turning it over in her head, gnawing at it as a squirrel gnaws at a nut. Why had they fallen behind? Did Leader expect trouble of some kind? None of the assassins seemed anxious. Red was even whistling cheerfully under his breath.

They crested the hill. A cold, damp wind blustered in her face, snatching at her cloak, making her eyes water. Britta blinked and squinted, examining the terrain ahead. Rocks, and stunted thorn trees, and nowhere to hide.

The road descended into a valley. Her ears caught a muffled roar that wasn't the wind. It took her several minutes to locate its source: a creek rushing down a steep gully in a series of foaming waterfalls. A hundred yards ahead the creek turned abruptly east, running alongside the road.

Britta peered into the gully as they passed. Nowhere to run to. Nowhere to hide.

The creek stayed with them all morning and into the afternoon. Other creeks joined it, swelling its waters. By mid-afternoon, it was wide and deep and swift enough to sweep a person away. But jumping in would serve no purpose. The road ran alongside the river. The Fithians would just ride ahead, splash into the water and haul her out. And even if she clambered out on the other side, the hillside was barren, with little cover.

The road wound its way down the valley. The hillside to the north grew higher, the hillside to the south dwindled. When Britta twisted in her saddle, she still couldn't see Curly and Pox. They were out of sight beyond the endless, thorny flank of the hill.

Refugees passed from time to time, heading west. Some called greetings, but most were silent, weary. They came in oxcarts, in farm wagons, on horseback, on foot.

Britta watched a family pass, in a dray drawn by two huge draft horses. The woman was nursing a baby. *How far to the curse?* she wanted to call out.

She wondered, yet again, how the Fithians were planning to use her.

Something that would separate Harkeld from the witches?

If she was an assassin, that's what she'd use bait for: to detach him from his guardians, and kill him when he was unprotected, like a pack of wolves taking out a lone sheep.

The road turned again. Ahead, Britta saw a pinching in of hillsides. The road turned north, winding its way up the flank of a stony hill, vanishing over its shoulder. The river turned south, falling away from the road in a series of cascades before plunging into a steep gorge. Britta followed the river's course with her eyes, from road, to cascades, to gorge.

She examined the gorge. It was a deep gouge on the rock. On either side the ground rose in steep, stony ridges. The river flowed swiftly out of sight, foaming around boulders the size of wagons.

Was now the time to use the arrowhead?

Two men leading a long string of packhorses approached. One was elderly, slumped in his saddle, the other was little more than a lad. Grandfather and grandson?

The old man stirred and raised his head. 'Turn back!' he cried, his eyes fierce beneath jutting white eyebrows. "Sault has the curse!"

Red stopped whistling. He touched his forehead, a gesture of respect. "We know, father. Thank you for the warning. We're not going far."

Not far?

The old man and his grandson passed. The long string of packhorses trailed after them.

Britta stared at Red. Had his words been a lie, to shut the old man up? Or were they the truth? Was Harkeld close?

"Where is my brother?"

Red glanced at her. So did the boy, riding alongside him. So did Plain, holding her reins.

Red grinned. "That's not something you need to know." He pursed his lips again, whistled again, a jauntier tune than before.

"How far to the curse?" Britta demanded.

Red ignored her.

Britta didn't waste her breath asking more questions. Her gaze swung back to the river, the gorge. What if Harkeld *was* close? What if he was over the brow of the next hill?

The answer was easy: if Harkeld was close, she needed to act now. And if Ivek's curse was close, she needed to act now, too. Once they reached the curse, everything would change. At least here, if she escaped, there was a chance she'd survive.

Britta bent awkwardly to rub her nose with her bound hands. Then, she fumbled with her cloak, drawing it closer around her. She groped the arrowhead from her pocket, straightened, and stared ahead. Red was still whistling. Plain was still holding her reins, his gaze on the road.

Britta clutched the arrowhead tightly, frozen with indecision. If Harkeld was a week from here, there *would* be better chances than this.

But if he was a mere day away, or worse, a few hours...

Five hundred miles. One hundred miles. Or on the other side of the ridge. There was no way of knowing. But what she *did* know, was that the Fithians would use her to kill Harkeld. They'd take his hands and his blood back to Jaegar, and Jaegar would hold the other kingdoms to ransom: death, or subjugation.

She had to act as if Harkeld was close. As if this was her last chance. Because it could be.

Britta took a deep breath. She pressed the arrowhead to the rope, and began to saw.

The coarse strands parted easily. In less than fifty yards, she'd cut through the rope securing her to the pommel. Fifty yards more, and the rope binding her wrists together was severed. Another party of refugees passed them, a man and his wife, with three daughters and a flock of white and black goats.

Fear tightened her chest. Breathing became difficult. In a few minutes, the road parted company with the river. In a few minutes, she had to jump. The cascades seemed to grow in size, the water in the gorge to seethe and boil as it bullied its way past the rocks. *I'll die.*

But hadn't that been her vow? Escape, or die. So she couldn't be used to catch Harkeld.

And perhaps the river changed just beyond what she could see, became wide and gentle?

*And perhaps cows will grow wings and fly.*

Escape, or die. That was the vow she had to hold true to. *Had* to. For the sake of the Seven Kingdoms and all the people who dwelled in them. And if she wasn't such a coward, she would have killed herself when she'd escaped into the forest. The Fithians would have found only her corpse. Harkeld would be safe from her.

But she had wanted to live. Still wanted to live.

Britta clenched her jaw and lifted her chin, but clenching her jaw didn't dissolve her fear, lifting her chin didn't erase her indecision. It was still possible to change her mind and take the coward's way out, to stay seated on the piebald mare and let the Fithians find the severed ropes and the arrowhead this evening.

The gorge snagged her gaze again. It looked like a gullet, overhung by cliffs, clogged with boulders, roaring and spitting spray. There was no telling what lay round the first bend—sheer waterfall or meandering river—but what she could tell was that the Fithians would have to throw themselves into the river to follow her. And once in the river, they'd be as helpless as she was.

Thirty yards to make her decision. Twenty.

Panic rose in her chest. The cascades were too high, the gorge too narrow, the churning water too frightening.

*You can do it, princess*, Karel's voice said in her mind, full of certainty. *I know you can.*

Britta tucked the arrowhead into the waistband of her trews; she might need it on the other side of the gorge. She slipped her feet from the stirrups.

Ten yards. Five yards.

She gulped a breath, and launched herself from her saddle.

# CHAPTER SIXTY

BRITTA PLUNGED INTO shockingly cold water, clawed her way to the surface, slid over the edge of a cascade and plummeted, plunging deep again. Water churned her, tossed her, pressed her down, pulled her sideways. She was desperate for air. Which way was up?

Britta flailed to the surface and gulped deep breaths. She couldn't see the road, couldn't see the Fithians. Her cloak dragged her down, the ties wound chokingly tight around her throat. She tore it off. *Keep swimming away.* Over the edge of another cascade, sliding and falling, plunging deep. The river caught her, tumbled her end over end, sucked her under, seemed to want to hold her in the bottom of this pool until she drowned. She fought the water, clawed at unseen rocks, tried to find a way up, out. Her lungs burned. Panic caught her. *I'm going to die!*

She burst to the surface, sobbing for breath, and grabbed for a rock, but the river had her in its grip, pulling her into a long, sliding fall, as if she was caught in a sluice. This time, she didn't plunge so deep. Water churned around her, blinding her, deafening her, filling her mouth and nose. Britta collided with a rock, and clung to it. Each breath she inhaled seemed as much water as air. She had no thought of the Fithians or the gorge. All that mattered was breathing, surviving, not being sucked under to drown.

But as breathing became easier, coherent thought returned. Britta raised her head, trying to see past the froth of spray. Where were the Fithians? It took several seconds before her eyes sorted the confusion of water into a scene she understood. There, through the spray, was the rocky riverbank, and there, running, were the Fithians. Leader and Red and Plain and Gap-Tooth. Leader's mouth was open, as if he shouted, but she heard only the roar of water.

Britta released the rock, and pushed away. The river caught her, buffeted her against rocks, dragged her down the next cascade. She plummeted, plunged deep, clawed her way to the surface, gasped for breath. The water turned her slowly over, showing her the sky, the rocky riverbank, Leader.

He stood thigh-deep in the water a scant half dozen yards from her. A snarl curled the lips back from his teeth. He looked more beast than man.

The fury on his face paralyzed Britta for a moment, froze her lungs. *He'll kill me.*

Leader's gaze slid past her. He opened his mouth and shouted, gestured with an arm.

Britta jerked her head around. Someone bobbed in the water behind her, hair slick to his narrow skull. Killer.

Panic burst in her chest. Her fear crystalized, became needle-sharp. She clawed frantically at the water, trying to get away from Killer. The river grabbed her, tipped her over the edge of the next cascade, a long slide and then a short drop into deep water. She swam desperately, kicking hard, but the river had her in its grip. It wanted to roll her over, to tumble her left and right. A rock loomed out of the water, as jagged as a broken tooth. Britta struck it hard, knocking the air from her lungs. The water sucked her down. A hand grabbed her ankle, fingers digging in. Britta kicked frantically, striking something soft and yielding. Killer? She kicked again. Kicked and kicked and kicked. The grip on her ankle released, the hand sucked away.

Britta tried to find the surface, but the river pressed her down, jammed her against a rock and held her there.

# CHAPTER SIXTY-ONE

JAUMÉ WATCHED THE Brothers haul the princess from the river. Her body was small and limp. *She's dead*, he thought, and was surprised by the grief he felt.

The Brothers laid her on the rocks. One of them bent over her, lifted her arms, lowered them, lifted them again. Jaumé couldn't tell who it was from this distance, but he knew what the man was doing; he'd seen Nolt and Ash do it in the jungle. The Brother was trying to make the princess breathe.

"Accident?" someone said.

Jaumé looked over his shoulder. A farm cart had halted alongside him. A man and a woman sat on the driver's box, peering down at him.

"My cousin fell in."

The woman's face creased with concern. "Oh, the poor dear."

"Need help?" the man asked.

"No, thank you," Jaumé said. "My uncles are soldiers. They know what to do."

The farm cart moved on. Jaumé turned his attention back to the river. The Brothers looked like tiny dolls at this distance. They were no longer pumping the princess's arms. They stood in a cluster. Talking?

Jaumé frowned, squinted, counted the men standing on the riverbank. Four?

He scanned the rocks, but saw no one scrambling up towards the road, scanned the river, saw no one in the long tumble of water. He counted the men again. Four.

One Brother was missing.

His heart seemed to clutch in his chest. Not Bennick!

No. It wouldn't be Bennick; it would be the one who'd jumped in after the princess. The one whose eyes he didn't like. Krey.

The Brothers picked up the princess's body and began carrying her towards the road, clambering over the rocks. She couldn't be tied to a stake any more and used to catch Prince Harkeld.

If the Brothers had no bait, would they decide to turn back?

Jaumé hoped so.

The men moved slowly, choosing their route with care. Jaumé saw red-blond hair. Bennick.

Their slowness, their care, made him wonder. Was the princess alive after all?

She couldn't be. No one could, after jumping into that river. It leapt from ledge to ledge, spitting up spray, fiercer than surf in a storm.

She was brave to jump into that. Braver than he'd ever be.

The Brothers were close enough that he could make out their faces. Vught and Luit and Doak and Bennick.

"Something wrong?"

Jaumé glanced sideways. Another farmer, another cart laden with possessions. "My cousin fell in. But it's all right. He's alive."

"Give the All-Mother thanks," the man said.

"Yes, sir. We will."

The man clicked his tongue, urging his horses forward.

Jaumé peered back down at the Brothers. The ground fell steeply away from the road, a jumble of boulders and great slabs of rocks. The Brothers climbed slowly, pausing to choose the easiest route, passing the princess carefully between them.

She *must* be alive. No one took that much care with a corpse.

Jaumé ran back to the packhorses. He unstrapped a bundle of blankets, tucked them under his arm, curled a rope around his hand, and trotted back to the edge of the road. Bennick liked it when he didn't have to be told what to do.

Vught scrambled up onto the road, panting.

"Need a rope?"

Vught held out a hand, not bothering to speak.

Jaumé watched silently as Vught lowered the rope, as Bennick tied it under the princess's armpits, as Vught hauled her up onto the road and laid her in the dirt. Her eyes were closed, her skin corpse-white except for the fading bruise on her cheek.

"Here." Jaumé held out a blanket.

Vught took it and began drying the princess. His clothes were wet, plastered to his body, and his hair stuck to his scalp, seal-pelt sleek.

The other Brothers hoisted themselves up onto the road. Bennick was wet too, and Luit. Jaumé gave them blankets. "She'll need dry clothes," Bennick said, wiping his face.

"I'll look for some," Jaumé said. He cast a quick glance at the princess. She looked dead, but he knew she wasn't. Not if Vught was drying her. Not if Bennick wanted clothes for her.

He hurried back to the packhorses. Part of him was glad the princess was alive, but part of him was sorry. He didn't want her to be tied to a stake. He didn't want Prince Harkeld to die.

# CHAPTER SIXTY-TWO

PETRUS TOOK OVER from Justen at noon. "See any people?"

Justen pulled a face. "There's a farm about three miles south of here, got a mill wheel. Don't go there. It's nasty."

"How nasty?"

"Worse than you want to see." Justen pulled on his trews, grabbed his boots. "There was a whole family there. Children."

"The children are alive?" Petrus said, startled.

Justen shook his head. He shrugged into his shirt in silence, pulled on his jerkin, wrapped his cloak around himself. "There was a girl on the ground, and this man, he was raping her, and... I had to stop him, you know? Even if she was cursed. Except when I got close, I could see she was dead. Long dead. Half of her had been eaten. But he was still raping her." He met Petrus's eyes, grimaced, shook his head. "Worse than you want to see. Don't go near that farm."

"I won't," Petrus said soberly. He stripped out of his clothes and flew up into the sky. Innis was already there, keeping watch over their cavalcade—wagon, riders, packhorses. He dipped his wings to her and began scouting, flying in ever-widening circles, looking for movement below.

The plateau was dry, rugged, almost barren, cut by eroding gullies, dotted with rocks and thorn trees twisted by the wind. The farmers had scraped a poor living from this land.

Smoke smeared the sky. Hamlets and villages burning. One large fire smoldered to the south and west, pushing up great plumes of smoke. The town of Andeol, he guessed. Where the elderly Fithians had probably come from.

Petrus flew in great sweeps across the plateau, investigating the road ahead, checking that no one followed them. The few hamlets were mainly charred rubble, but he inspected them carefully. He found hens and geese, goats, two black-faced sheep, cats and dogs, but no people. Always, at the center of his circles, were the wagon and long line of horses. Their progress seemed terribly slow, the roads endlessly long.

Mid-afternoon, he found a donkey grazing on sparse grass at the edge of the road. It was bridled, the reins dragging on the ground, and someone's possessions were strapped on its back.

Petrus glided down to land and shifted into himself. "Lost your owner, have you?"

The donkey flicked its long ears at him.

It took him a minute to catch it—the beast kept sidling away—but finally he was able to grab the reins. "Stand *still*, curse it," he told the donkey, shivering. "I'm trying to help you."

Quickly, he removed the packsaddle and bridle, piling them to one side of the road. The stones were sharp and cold beneath his bare feet and the wind seemed to eat into his skin. "There, you're on your own now." He slapped the donkey's rump, watched it trot away.

He found a body a few miles down the road. An elderly woman, several days dead. The donkey's owner? Her throat was slit open. Blood had dried in a great pool around her. She'd been raped. Had the rape come first, or the murder?

For her sake, he hoped she'd been dead first.

Something had pecked out her eyes. Maggots writhed in the gaping ruin of her throat.

Petrus pulled the woman's coarse gown down over her legs, covering her. He crouched and touched her bony, wrinkled hand with his fingertips. "All-Mother," he whispered. "I give this woman to your care, that she may rest peacefully."

# CHAPTER SIXTY-THREE

THE PRINCESS WOKE late in the afternoon. Doak, who was holding her, slid hastily down from his horse. The princess fell to hands and knees on the road, coughed several times, and then vomited. When she'd finished, Vught lifted her back onto Doak's mount and they continued. The Brothers rode silently. No one said anything. Bennick didn't whistle.

Jaumé didn't dare look at the princess. He was afraid Bennick would see his secrets on his face: that he admired her courage; that he wanted Prince Harkeld to live.

When they halted for the night, he tended to his pony and then made haste to start a fire and lay out smoked sausages and thick slices of rye bread and brew the bitter tea the Brothers liked to drink.

"Good lad," Bennick said, ruffling his hair. He sat down with a groan alongside Jaumé. "What a day."

Vught grunted sourly and reached for a sausage. "It'll give me great pleasure to kill that bitch."

Someone muttered agreement. Luit, Jaumé thought. Doak was watchman.

"That arrowhead," Bennick said, around a mouthful of bread. "Did she say where she got it?"

"Last night. In an old campfire."

Bennick chewed, swallowed, nodded. "We need to stop her pulling any more stunts like that. Slows us down."

"Punish her," Luit said. "Tell her we'll whip the skin off her back if she does it again."

"Cut off a hand," Bennick suggested. "She doesn't need both of 'em, does she?"

Jaumé stopped chewing. He tried to see Bennick's face in the dark. He was joking, wasn't he?

"Rape," Luit said. "There's six of us. Bet she wouldn't like that." He grinned, his missing teeth black holes in his mouth.

"We're not Sarkosians," Vught said flatly. "We have a code." He finished eating the sausage in silence, then rose to his feet and crossed to where the princess sat, huddled in a cloak. He bent over her.

Jaumé watched tensely. He wasn't going to cut off one of her hands, was he?

The princess screamed, a high-pitched sound of pain.

Jaumé jerked convulsively and almost dropped his bread.

"Pressure point," Bennick said. "To get her attention."

Vught's hand was fisted in the princess's hair, his mouth pressed against her ear. After a moment, he stood and walked back to the fire. He sat, reached for another sausage, shoved it in his mouth, chewed.

Jaumé looked past Vught to the princess. There was a tight, uncomfortable feeling in his belly. Horror? Pity? Whatever it was, he had lost his appetite.

# CHAPTER SIXTY-FOUR

AFTER THE TENTS were pitched, Harkeld went looking for Rand. The healer was at the fire, heating water and opening bundles of dried meat. "Those Fithians, the two old men... did you keep their throwing stars?"

Rand glanced up. "Petrus did. He thought you might want to practice burning them."

"I do." Harkeld turned on his heel, scanned the campsite, and found Petrus with the horses.

There were eight throwing stars, in two worn leather pouches. "Want me to chuck them in the air for you?" Petrus asked.

"Sure."

They clambered over the stone wall to the next paddock. Gretel came, too. A chilly wind whipped their cloaks around their legs.

Petrus took one of the throwing stars from its pouch.

"Don't throw that one," Harkeld said. "Put it on a rock. I need to make sure I don't use too much magic, otherwise I'll incinerate us all."

Petrus laid the throwing star on a rock and stepped prudently behind Harkeld.

Harkeld scanned the sky for shapeshifters, and found Innis hovering over the horses, a safe distance away. He flexed the fingers of his left hand and stared at the throwing star, concentrating on what he wanted to do. A burst of hot fire, the hottest he could summon, but small and focused.

White-hot. Small. Focused.

He put his right hand behind his back, raised his left hand, took a deep breath. *Burn.*

There was a loud crack of sound and a bright white flash of flame.

'Is it gone?" Petrus asked. He stepped forward and examined the rock from all angles. "It's gone."

"I need to try that again," Harkeld said. "I used too much magic." If he'd done that when the one-eyed Fithian had attacked, he'd have burned his own face off.

Petrus laid another throwing star on the rock.

It took three more attempts before Harkeld was satisfied. "All right," he said. "Throw them."

Petrus opened the second pouch, took out a throwing star, and held it by one blade.

Harkeld gripped the back of his belt with his right hand, and nodded.

Petrus tossed the star in the air. It arced up, the blades reflecting the orange sunset.

*Burn.*

A bright flash, a small clap of sound, a scattering of ashes.

Petrus tossed a second throwing star up.

*Burn.*

"Gretel? Could you throw one, too, at the same time as Petrus? I'd like to see how fast I can do this." Speed could save his life. Or someone else's.

Gretel took the last throwing star and stood opposite Petrus.

Harkeld tightened his grip on his belt. He flexed the fingers of his left hand and shifted his weight, leaning a little forward.

"One, two, three," the shapeshifter called. They flung the weapons in the air, Petrus's almost straight up, Gretel's curving in a parabola.

*Burn. Burn.*

The wind whipped the ashes away.

There was a moment of silence, and then Petrus said, "If we meet any more Fithians I'm sticking close to you."

Harkeld released his grip on his belt.

"Safest place to be," Gretel agreed. She put her hands on her hips and observed Harkeld. "Have you tried burning stone?"

"Stone?" He shook his head.

"Meant to be harder to burn than metal—it's raw, hasn't been worked—but your grandfather could do it. I'd say there's a good chance you can, too."

"My grandfather?" Harkeld scowled.

Gretel's eyes narrowed. "What?"

"Nothing." Harkeld bent and picked up one of the Fithian pouches. The leather was soft, supple.

"You dislike your grandfather?"

"Dislike?" Harkeld straightened. "My grandfather was a lying son of a whore. He pretended to be someone he wasn't. He corrupted my mother's bloodline. He bred *me* like I was a prize hound!"

"Your grandfather was a hero."

"Hero?" Harkeld snorted. "He was a *liar*."

Gretel took a step towards him. Her expression was fierce. "Your grandfather left his home knowing he would never, *ever* be able to return. Knowing he'd *never* see his family again. Knowing he could *never* be a Sentinel again. He lived the rest of his life unable to use his magic, hiding who he was, pretending, and yes, lying. Do you think he *enjoyed* that? Do you think he was happier in Vaere than he would have been in Rosny? Do you think it wasn't painfully hard for him?"

Harkeld opened his mouth, and then shut it again.

"Linus gave up *everything* so that your mother could be born. So that you could be born. And he did it for kingdoms filled with people who would have killed him if they'd known he was a mage. How *dare* you despise him!"

Harkeld looked away from Gretel's fierce gaze. He turned the leather pouch over in his hands. "I never thought about it from his point of view."

"*That's* obvious."

Harkeld flushed. He felt shame, and a sharp, unexpected grief for the grandfather he'd never known.

Gretel stepped closer. "You are the fruit of Linus's sacrifice. *You* may despise him, but he would have been proud of you."

Harkeld glanced up, met her gaze.

"Linus was a hero."

Harkeld nodded. He couldn't find his voice.

For a moment Gretel looked as if she'd like to say more, then she turned away and headed back to the camp.

Harkeld stayed where he was, gripping the leather pouch. He glanced across at Petrus. The shapeshifter was standing half a dozen yards away, his expression neutral.

Petrus crouched, picked up the second leather pouch, walked across to him. "You all right?"

Harkeld nodded.

"You look like she hit you with a battle-ax."

*I feel like it.*

"Want to practice some more? I could throw sticks."

Harkeld shook his head. "No, thanks. I, uh... I need to think."

Petrus's glance was appraising. "Think at the fire. You do it here, you'll freeze to death." He punched Harkeld's shoulder. "Come on, whoreson."

# CHAPTER SIXTY-FIVE

SOLL AND HETCHEL arrived while Jaumé was unrolling his sleeping mat.

"See them?" Vught asked, his voice low. He jerked his head warningly in the direction of the princess.

Soll nodded. "Twelve of 'em," he said, his voice equally quiet. "Big bastards, well-armed. Soldiers for sure."

"How far behind?"

"Less than three miles. They're camped at that last crossroad." He looked around. "Thought you'd be further ahead than this. Had some trouble?"

Vught grimaced. "Bitch jumped in the river. Nearly drowned."

Soll grunted. He blew on his hands, rubbed them together, warming them.

"Where's Krey?" Hetchel asked.

"Drowned."

Hetchel pulled a face, shrugged. "We come, we go."

"Three miles, you say?" Vught scowled, raked a hand through his hair. "We'll have a second sentry tonight, at the half mile mark. Standard signal. Luit, you're first."

Luit nodded, and disappeared into the darkness.

Jaumé helped Soll and Hetchel unsaddle their horses, but when he came back to the fire, Bennick pointed at the sleeping mat. "Bed."

Jaumé obeyed silently. He curled up in his blanket, listening to the wind, listening to the murmur of voices. The four Brothers were dark silhouettes by the fire, leaning close to one another, their voices low.

*Twelve of 'em. Big bastards.*

Jaumé shivered. He was afraid. Was he going to die tomorrow?

# CHAPTER SIXTY-SIX

BRITTA LAY AWAKE for a long time, staring up at the sky. Leader's voice echoed in her ears. Horror reverberated inside her.

Gradually the horror faded. Leader's voice dwindled to a whisper and was blown away by the wind. The coolness of the night seemed to fill her.

She gazed up at the sky, at the stars wheeling slowly overhead, the half-moon. The stars and the moon were the All-Mother. The dirt she lay on was the All-Mother. The air she breathed, the All-Mother.

*Dead or alive, I lie in the All-Mother's bosom.*

With that thought, came calmness.

# CHAPTER SIXTY-SEVEN

THEY ROUSED BEFORE dawn, ate a hasty meal, saddled the horses.

"After we rescue Brigitta, what then?" Prince Tomas asked.

Karel checked the gelding's girth strap, and tightened the buckle a notch. He heard King Magnas's voice clearly in his ears: *Bring Brigitta back if you can. Help Harkeld if you can. The curse* must *be stopped.*

"Depending on our losses... maybe some of us can push further into Sault, try to help Harkeld."

"I'd like to go," the prince said. He scuffed one boot in the dirt. "I didn't part well with Harkeld. My father is right: he's Harkeld first, not a witch, but I didn't see that then. I saw only the witch."

Karel glanced at him. Was this more than a heroic quest to Tomas? Did he have something personal at stake? "Certainly you can go, sire."

He swung up into his saddle and watched the armsmen mount. Daylight crept over the horizon. He could see the crossroads where they'd camped, could see everyone's faces. Some of the men looked determined, some grim, some flashed grins when they met his gaze.

The horses had caught the tension. They sidled and tossed their heads, put their ears back.

"We're only a couple of miles behind them," Karel said, once everyone was mounted. "Once we see them, we'll split in two; six overtake, six stay behind. Sire, you and Gunvald grab the princess and get out of there, fast as you can." He waited until he saw the two men nod.

"The boy?" Lief asked.

"Don't touch him—unless he engages us."

More nods.

"Strike hard and fast. No hesitation. And remember—we outnumber them. This is a battle we'll win."

But some of these men would die today. He knew that. They knew that.

A good commander would launch into a rousing speech now, fill the armsmen with confidence and optimism, but he didn't have a rousing speech. Karel glanced at Dag. "Got a joke for us?"

Dag grinned, his teeth catching the faint light. "Got a good one, if we've got time."

Karel nodded.

The armsmen jostled their mounts closer to hear.

"Once upon a time there was this queen, a real beauty she was, with the most bountiful breasts you ever saw." Dag cupped his hands in front of his chest, miming the size. "An armsman called..." his gaze skimmed the watching faces, "Solveig desperately wanted to touch 'em, but he knew he'd be put to death if he did."

Solveig grinned good-naturedly.

"One day Solveig told his friend, Eivor, the Royal Physician, that the queen's breasts were driving him mad. Eivor thought about it for a bit, then said he could arrange for Solveig to touch the queen's breasts, but it would cost him ten gold pieces.

"Solveig agreed, and the next day Eivor made a batch of itching powder and put some in the queen's breast-band while she bathed. Soon after she dressed, the itching started, and grew and grew until she was nearly mad with it. The king summoned Eivor to provide a cure, and Eivor said he knew of only one thing for an itch like that. Saliva. But—" Dag held up a finger. "It had to be *special* saliva, and the only man he knew of with such saliva was one of the king's armsmen, Solveig."

Karel glanced around. The armsmen were grinning as they listened.

"So the king summoned Solveig, who declared he was loyal and ready for any task the king set him. Eivor gave Solveig the antidote for the itching powder, and he put it in his mouth and set to work curing the queen's itch."

Prince Tomas snorted a laugh.

"It took an hour for the queen's itching to stop, and a more pleasurable hour Solveig had never spent. He went back to his rooms feeling very pleased with himself and not a little lusty, keeping an eye out for a likely serving maid, but when he got there he found Eivor demanding his ten gold pieces. Now, Solveig had a name for being tight—" a quick grin at Solveig, "... and he knew Eivor could never tell the king what had happened, so he just laughed and told Eivor to rut off."

Dag paused for a long moment, and looked around at the faces of the listening armsmen. His gaze came to rest finally on Solveig. His grin widened. "The next day, Eivor slipped a large dose of itching powder into the king's breech-clout. When the itching started, the king immediately called for his most loyal armsman, Sol—"

The shout of laughter cut off Solveig's name. It was so loud it startled the horses. Karel's mount half-reared. He soothed the gelding, laughing, stroking his hand down the creature's neck.

It took a few minutes to settle the horses. Tall Lief was still chuckling. Karel caught Dag's eye, gave a nod of thanks.

THEY RODE EAST from the crossroads, into a cold, blustering wind. Daylight spread across the sky. Karel glanced back at the armsmen. He wasn't the only rider still grinning. He urged the mare from a trot to a canter. Eagerness filled him, flowing like blood in his veins. Today was the day. They were so close he could taste it on his tongue.

The sky lightened further. The hills were no longer formless black shapes. He saw rocks, saw thorn trees. The wind moaned, but beneath that was memory of the armsmen's laughter. An excellent way to start a day like this, with a belly laugh.

Karel took it as a good omen.

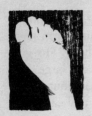

# CHAPTER SIXTY-EIGHT

THE BROTHERS DIDN'T seem worried that twelve soldiers were only a few miles behind them. They packed up the camp with the same unhurried efficiency as always, rolling up the sleeping mats, loading the packhorses, saddling the riding mounts.

Jaumé climbed up on his pony and waited beside Bennick. Bennick was watching Soll tie the princess's wrists to her pommel, frowning thoughtfully.

Vught came up alongside them. "You still as good as you were with that bow and arrow?"

"I'm even better."

Vught snorted. His mare pranced sideways a few feet and he dug his heels into her flanks, brought her back. "When we find a good place I'll put you to picking off those bastards. The more you get, the better."

Bennick grinned. "Maybe I won't leave any for the rest of you."

Vught snorted again.

Bennick's grin faded. His gaze returned to the princess. "Whatever you threatened her with, it didn't work."

Vught stared hard at the princess. His mouth twisted sourly. "Hetchel!" he called.

Hetchel looked up from checking the packsaddles.

"Ride with that bitch today," Vught said. "You and Soll both. I want a Brother on either side of her."

Jaumé stared at the princess. What? What was different about her?

Nothing that he could see.

Vught gestured sharply. It was a gesture Jaumé had seen Nolt make. He thought it meant, *Time to go.*

They left the campsite. Luit and Doak dropped behind them. Soon, Jaumé couldn't see them when he looked back.

Vught rode first, then the princess with Soll and Hetchel. Jaumé and Bennick were last, leading the packhorses. The skin on the nape of Jaumé's neck crawled. He didn't like being at the back, not with twelve soldiers behind them. He shivered and tried to think of something else, tried to fasten his attention on the princess two horse-lengths ahead. Her hood had blown back, exposing her face, but she hadn't bothered to pull it forward again.

Jaumé stared at her, trying to see what Bennick and Vught had seen. The bruise on the princess's cheek had faded to a grayish yellow, but other than that, he couldn't spot anything different about her. Finally, he asked Bennick, "Why do you think Vught's threat didn't work?"

"Why?" Bennick flicked a glance at the princess. "She's changed."

"Changed?" Jaumé stared at the princess again. She looked the same as she had yesterday. And the day before. Short hair. Bruised face.

"It's..." Bennick paused.

Jaumé glanced at him quickly. Had he decided it was one question too many?

No. Bennick looked like he was trying to choose words.

"In battle, there's four types of men. Well, there's more'n four, but there's four main ones. One, the men who're more cowards than fighters. You scare them enough, or hurt 'em enough, they'll run.

"Two, the ones with courage. For whatever reason, they've committed themselves. For honor, or for their families, or their kingdom, whatever. They'll fight to the death, but they're hoping they won't have to, because deep down, underneath their courage, they want to live." Bennick glanced at him. "Most men want to live."

Jaumé nodded.

"Three, the berserkers. You heard of 'em? Men that go mad on the battlefield? They have no fear, none at all. Don't feel pain, either. They'll fight till they're chopped to pieces. Dangerous, berserkers are. Don't know what they're doing. Don't care. But the thing with berserkers is, they're not thinking straight. They don't look at a battlefield and think, 'If I do that, it'll win this battle.' They just fight until someone kills 'em.

"And then there's the ones like her." Bennick nodded at the princess. "They're not scared of dying any more. They've accepted it's going to happen. They *know* it's going to happen. But they're still thinking, still planning, and because of that, they're more dangerous than berserkers. They'll take risks no one else will, because they know they're already dead. Risks that'll win battles."

"How do you know she's like that?"

Bennick shrugged. "I can see it. She's not scared of dying. She's made peace with it."

"She'll try to escape again? Is that why they're guarding her?"

Bennick shook his head. "She'll try to kill herself. That's why Soll and Hetchel are there. It's much harder to stop people killing themselves than it is to stop them escaping."

Jaumé frowned, not understanding.

Bennick saw his confusion. "Yesterday, when she jumped into the river, she still wanted to live. That was her mistake. That's why we were able to catch her."

"But she almost drowned," Jaumé protested.

"She did, but not because she wanted to. You know why Krey caught up with her? Because she was holding on to a rock, trying to breathe. She didn't want to die."

"Oh."

Bennick nodded ahead at the princess. "If she jumped in today, she wouldn't do that. She'd let the water take her. She'd drown, and there'd be nothing we could do about it."

"Oh," Jaumé said again.

"She sees a chance to kill herself, she'll take it. Jump off a cliff, throw herself under the wheels of an oxcart, whatever. Makes her dangerous. Means she has to be watched carefully."

"Will you cut off one of her hands now?" Jaumé asked, dreading the answer.

"Won't matter if we cut one off," Bennick said. "Won't matter if we cut both off. She doesn't care any more."

Jaumé shivered. *I'd care if someone cut off my hands*.

They rode in silence for half a mile, then Jaumé risked another question. "What did Vught mean last night, about Sarkosians and a code?"

Bennick snorted, a contemptuous sound. "Sarkosians. Mercenaries. Haven't you heard of them?"

Jaumé shook his head.

"Mercenaries are soldiers for hire, but they're not like us, not like Brothers. They're rabble. No discipline. Not much training. They're like those hillmen. Remember them? Remember what they did to those farmers?"

Jaumé did. The butchered children, the murdered woman lying half-naked. His stomach tightened. He swerved away from the memory.

"That's what Sarkosians do," Bennick said. "Worse'n animals, they are."

Jaumé's stomach felt queasy. He tried to ignore it. "What's a code?"

"A code is a set of rules you swear to live by."

"Brothers have a code?"

"Yes. You'll learn it in Fith." There was a note of finality in Bennick's voice. Jaumé knew what it meant: enough questions for now.

He let the pony drop back and rode next to the lead packhorse, digesting everything Bennick had told him. He wasn't sure he understood it all. One thing he was certain of: Bennick thought the princess wanted to die.

He stared at her, trying to see what Bennick saw, but he wasn't sure what he was looking for. Determination? Acceptance?

She had a calmness, Jaumé decided after several minutes' observation. The way the ocean sometimes had on a still day. A deep, peaceful calmness.

# CHAPTER SIXTY-NINE

HARKELD EYED GRETEL'S back. She rode a horse-length ahead of him, wrapped in her cloak. He took a deep breath and nudged his horse up alongside her. "Um... Gretel?"

She glanced at him.

"I'd like to try burning stone tonight, if... if you'll help me?"

"Of course."

His request was an apology of sorts. Did she understand that? Maybe she did. Gretel wasn't smiling, but nor was she hostile.

Harkeld squinted at the mountains through the haze of smoke, then looked at her again. "I don't know much about my grandfather," he said awkwardly. "He died before I was born, and my mother died when I was a baby."

"I know," Gretel said. "Look, Flin... I probably should have told you before, but your grandfather and mine were brothers."

Harkeld stared at her. "You mean... we're related?"

Gretel nodded.

He looked at her more closely, trying to find a note of resemblance. Gretel was short and stocky, sandy-haired, blue-eyed, none of which he was, but her face was square. *Like mine.*

Harkeld blinked, and sat back in his saddle. Gretel was his cousin? They shared some of the same blood?

"I know a lot about your grandfather. And your mother. Linus was never able to return to Rosny, but he wasn't abandoned. Sentinels visited him. Our family was able to exchange messages with him. We knew when his daughter was born. We knew when she married into the Rutersvards. And we knew when you were born."

"But he was dead by then."

"Rosny has been watching you your whole life, Flin. Any news about you was passed on to us. Because we're your family."

Family. A word that made his eyes sting slightly. Harkeld looked down at his reins and wound them around his fingers. "Was my grandfather unhappy in Vaere?"

"Unhappy? Not desperately. He didn't like living in the royal court. He'd been trained as a Sentinel, trained to *do*, not to sit back and be fawned over all day—but he had an amicable marriage; he was genuinely sad when the princess died. And he loved his daughter very much. When she married Esger..."

Harkeld glanced at her.

"Linus said it broke his heart, marrying her to a monster like Esger. But he knew he had to do it. And he couldn't tell her why."

A monster. *Yes, that's an accurate description of Father.*

"Linus lived long enough to know your mother was pregnant, that a child who could end Ivek's curse would be born."

*Me. A Rutersvard who carries mage blood.* Harkeld looked down at his hands again.

"I like to think he died happy," Gretel said.

*I hope so.* "I wish I could have met him."

"I wish you could have, too. You have lots of cousins, you know. We're a big family."

Harkeld's eyes stung again. He cleared his throat. "Are they all Sentinel mages?"

"Sentinels? About ten, twelve. There's some healers, couple of green mages, half a dozen fire mages. There's been no one who can burn steel or stone since Linus. Except for you."

"I may not be able to burn stone."

Gretel shrugged. "We'll find out tonight."

# CHAPTER SEVENTY

VUGHT HALTED. "THIS is as good a place as any."

Jaumé peered around.

They were in a broad rocky hollow off to the side of the road. It looked like a huge cavern with the roof taken off it. People had camped here, out of the wind, sheltered by outcrops of rock on three sides; he saw boot prints and hoof prints and the remains of campfires. Ahead, the road curved out of sight, winding its way in and out of folds in the hillside. Behind them, it vanished around a tight bend.

"Soll, Hetchel..." Vught's fingers moved too fast for Jaumé to make out the gestures.

Soll and Hetchel understood, though. They moved further into the hollow, taking the princess with them.

Vught turned to Bennick. "Should be able to pick them off from up there." He nodded at one of the outcrops.

"Easy." Bennick dismounted. "Want me to leave any for you?"

Vught shrugged. "Wouldn't mind a couple. Luit and Doak will want some, too."

310 The Blood Curse

Suddenly Jaumé understood. Vught and Bennick were going to ambush the soldiers here. Horror congealed in his belly.

Vught's gaze moved to Jaumé.

Jaumé stopped breathing. Was Vught going to ask him to help kill the soldiers?

"You, boy, stay right back. Out of the way." Vught jerked his thumb towards where Soll and Hetchel and the princess had dismounted.

Jaumé breathed again.

Bennick unstrapped his bow and quiver from one of the packhorses and checked them. He was slinging them over his shoulder when hoofbeats sounded and two horsemen came round the bend. Jaumé's heart kicked in his chest before he recognized them. Luit and Doak.

"They're half a mile behind," Doak said, sliding from his saddle. "Coming fast." He glanced around the basin and nodded, as if he liked what he saw.

Vught turned to Jaumé. "Boy, take all the horses. Get over there."

Jaumé obeyed hastily, grabbing the reins, leading the animals to where Soll and Hetchel stood. A creek trickled in a narrow slot of rock.

The princess's eyes fastened on him. "What's happening?"

"Bandits," Hetchel said.

Jaumé clutched the reins and watched Bennick scramble up the rocky hillside, find a spot he liked, and hunker down. He could imagine Bennick whistling under his breath.

Vught and Doak and Luit fanned out across the basin until they stood twenty or thirty yards from each other. They stripped off their cloaks and tossed them aside.

An oxcart lumbered from the west, its wheels creaking. The family in it stared at them. Jaumé glanced at Hetchel. What would the Brothers do if the soldiers came around the corner now? Kill the people in the oxcart too?

He heard Bennick's voice in his head. *We all go to the All-Mother, Jaumé. Doesn't matter where or when.*

Which answered his question. Yes.

Jaumé gazed urgently at the oxcart. *Hurry up!* he wanted to yell. *Hurry! Or they'll kill you too.*

The cart lumbered slowly around the corner, and disappeared.

Jaumé's grip on the reins was sweaty. The last time men had attacked them, he'd disobeyed Nolt and tried to see the battle—and earned himself a mark for disobedience. This time, he didn't want to see it. He didn't want the soldiers to die. Not if they were trying to save the princess.

He shifted his weight from foot to foot. He felt desperate and slightly sick. What should he do?

Bennick would tell him to shut up and stay where he was, but he was pretty sure that Mam and Da would want him to run down the road and warn the soldiers.

If he warned the soldiers, did that mean Bennick would die?

Jaumé imagined running towards the corner, imagined Vught reaching for the big bone-handled throwing knife at his waist—

A troop of horsemen rounded the corner with a clatter of hooves. They took up the road, their billowing cloaks making them seem the size of giants.

Before he could decide whether they were the soldiers or not, an arrow plunged out of the sky. A rider fell from his horse and cartwheeled on the road, arms and legs out-thrown.

Time seemed to freeze. Jaumé stood with his mouth half-open in horror, his eyes unblinking, his breath caught in his throat. But time didn't freeze for the soldiers. Or for Bennick. More arrows came from the ridge, too fast to count. Horses swerved, three more men fell.

One of the packhorses took fright. It reared, snorting, jerking its reins from Jaumé's grip.

Jaumé lunged for the reins and grabbed them again.

Riderless horses plunged across the road, but most of the soldiers were still mounted. Someone was shouting orders, his voice a loud bellow. The horsemen swung into the basin at a gallop, swords drawn. The man in front had a dark, fierce face.

Vught took a step forward and gave a flick of his wrist. A Star flashed through the air.

"No!" The voice was the princess's. It was a shriek, filled with an emotion Jaumé couldn't name. The packhorse didn't like it. It reared again, jerking Jaumé off his feet. The reins slid through his fingers, burning. Jaumé landed on his backside in the dirt. He scrambled up and snatched the reins he'd dropped. Across the basin, the Brothers were throwing Stars. The dark soldier brushed one aside with his sword. Behind him five other horses thundered, their riders bellowing battle cries.

The dark soldier bore down on Doak and raised his sword.

*He's going to cut off Doak's head!*

An arrow speared the soldier in the shoulder. He lurched, almost fell, but the sword was still in his hand and he swung it, striking Doak in the throat.

Jaumé eyes winced shut for an instant. When he opened them, Doak was on the ground.

The dark soldier hauled his mount around and charged at Vught. Only two other riders were still in the saddle, slashing at Luit with their swords.

Someone shouldered Jaumé aside. Soll. He had a Star in his hand. The blade sliced through the air towards Luit and buried itself in a soldier's skull.

"No!" the princess screamed again. She was wrestling with Hetchel, struggling to free herself. She didn't look calm any more; she looked frantic.

Hooves thundered. The dark soldier was upon Vught. He raised his sword—

His horse went down in a tangle of limbs, hurling its rider from the saddle. The soldier hit the ground hard and rolled several times, his cloak flaring. *He's dead.* But no, the soldier was pushing up on one elbow, groping for his sword. Blood streamed down his dark face.

"No!" the princess screamed. "Don't kill him!"

Vught stepped closer to the fallen soldier. He reached for a Star, twirled it between his fingers.

Someone shoved past Jaumé, almost knocking him off his feet. The princess.

Soll snatched at her and missed.

But the princess didn't run for the road and freedom; she ran towards Vught. "Don't kill him!" she cried, her voice desperate. "*Don't kill him!*"

# CHAPTER SEVENTY-ONE

LEADER TURNED HIS head. She saw his surprise, and then his amusement. He looked back down at Karel and kicked him in the head.

"No!" Britta shrieked. She shoved Leader aside with all her strength and flung herself over Karel, shielding him with her body. "Don't you dare kill him!"

Karel lay motionless. Had Leader's kick killed him? Britta fumbled at his throat, searching for his pulse, her fingers slippery with blood. *Don't be dead, Karel. Don't be dead.* Tears streamed down her face. She was breathless with grief, choking with grief.

Karel was alive. His pulse beat beneath her fingertips.

Hard fingers dug into her hair, into her scalp, wrenching her head up. Leader. His lips flattened against his teeth in a smile. "Know him, do you?"

She tried to jerk free, to turn back to Karel.

Leader's fingers tightened. "What will you give me in return for this man's life?"

"Anything!" Britta cried. "Anything!"

Leader's smile broadened. "Your word, princess. Your word of honor that you won't try to escape, you won't try to kill yourself."

"Yes!" she said. "Yes! Anything!"

Leader released her hair.

Britta turned back to Karel. Behind her, Leader's boots crunched in the dirt. She heard his voice, giving orders.

Britta blocked the sound. Leader was irrelevant. The Fithians were irrelevant. All that mattered was Karel, that he didn't die.

A gash sliced across his brow, bleeding freely. Blood pooled around his closed eyes, sluiced down the planes of his cheeks, puddled on the dirt. Britta tried to stem the flow with her hands. What was Karel doing here? He was supposed to be safe in Lundegaard. *Trying to protect me. Because that is what he does. What he has always done.* Her tears came faster, almost blinding her.

Footsteps approached. "You want me to patch him up?" The voice was ironic, amused.

"Keep him alive. We have an agreement, the princess and I. His life, for her obedience."

"Then I'll do what I can." Someone crouched on Karel's other side. Red. She understood his irony. It was his arrow in Karel's shoulder. His arrow that had killed the horse and brought Karel down. "How hard did you kick him?"

"Not hard."

Red slid his fingers through Karel's bloody hair, probed gently, gave a grunt of approval. "Well placed." He felt beneath Karel's jaw for his pulse, then bent his head and listened to Karel's breathing. He seemed to know what he was doing. Britta's panic-stricken grief eased slightly. Her breathing became easier, the tears stopped flowing so fast.

Red sat back on his heels. "Let me see."

She lifted her hands briefly and let him see the long slash.

Red peered close at the wound, then nodded. "Keep the pressure on."

Britta watched as Red examined Karel's right shoulder. The arrow was buried deep, the shaft snapped off. Red grimaced.

"Bad?" she asked.

Red glanced at her. For a moment, she thought he wouldn't answer her, then he shrugged. "The arrowhead's not barbed. Should come out in one piece."

He checked each of Karel's arms, articulating the joints, then moved on to his torso, feeling his way along the ribs, pressing lightly. "Some broken ribs. Nothing we can do about those."

The tears had stopped. Britta rubbed her face on her shoulder. Blood leaked from beneath her hands and trickled down Karel's brow. Horses and men moved around them, but she ignored everything except what Red was doing.

Red shuffled sideways, laid a hand on Karel's thigh. "This will be hard to get out. It's deep in the bone."

She opened her mouth to ask what he was talking about, and then saw it. A throwing star. Shock made her blink. She'd seen Karel swipe two throwing stars from the air with his sword, but she'd not seen this one hit him.

It had struck the front of his thigh and gone in deep. The tips of two razor-sharp blades protruded from his trews, the rest of the weapon was buried.

Red took careful grip on one blade, and tugged. The throwing star didn't move. He grimaced, released the weapon, and checked for broken bones in Karel's legs.

"Well?" someone asked curtly. Britta started. She hadn't heard Leader return.

Red looked up. "Hardest thing's going to be getting the Star out. If we can manage that, he should be fine. Long as his back's not broken."

"We'll get it out." Leader crouched, and studied Karel's face. "Not Lundegaardan. Who is he?"

"My personal armsman."

"From Esfaban."

"Yes."

Leader stared at Karel a moment longer, narrow-eyed. "Saw him at the Hook. He's the one who killed Bly." He stood, and reached down and grabbed her arm, pinching flesh to bone, pulling her to her feet. "Come on."

"What? No!" She started to struggle.

"Bennick'll look after him."

"But I have to stay with him!" she cried frantically. Karel's brow was bleeding again, blood streaming down his face, dripping to the ground.

"Your cooperation for his life. That was our agreement."

Britta dragged her gaze to Leader. His eyes were as cold and hard as granite. There was no humanity on his face. He'd kill Karel in a heartbeat.

She stopped trying to pull free, stood quiet and docile.

A thin smile touched Leader's mouth. He eased his painful grip on her arm. "Come along."

Britta cast a desperate glance back. Red's hand was pressed to Karel's brow, stemming the flow of blood. Gratitude brought tears to her eyes. She blinked them fiercely back. No more crying.

Horses milled everywhere. It took her a moment to realize it was intentional. Anyone passing on the road would see a mob of animals, not a battleground. It took her another moment to realize that there were no corpses. The only body she saw was Karel's mount, an arrow jutting grotesquely from its eye. Of Karel's dead companions, there was no sign.

Leader led her through the horses. A steep outcrop jutted out from the hillside. At its base was a jumble of rock, fanning out, and behind that, hidden in the shadow of the outcrop...

Britta's breath caught in her throat. She turned her head away, squeezed her eyes shut.

"Who are they?" Leader said.

Her obedience, for Karel's life. That was the agreement. Britta opened her eyes and looked at the dead men. They lay tumbled, limbs out-flung, as if thrown by some giant force. "I don't know." She shook her head. Too many men. Too many faces.

"Look again." Something in Leader's voice penetrated the fog of horror in her brain. He expected her to recognize at least one of these men.

Britta took a deep breath and tried to calm herself. The number of dead seemed to shrink. Eleven. Eleven men. She looked at each one in turn, her gaze flinching from face to face, examining them, trying to answer Leader's question. Who were these men?

They had tanned faces and fair hair. Strong bodies. Callused hands. They looked like soldiers or armsmen.

Britta's gaze stopped on the last body. Her breath caught in her throat. She stepped forward, pulling free of Leader's grip, and knelt.

"You know him." It was a statement, not a question. Leader knew who he was, too.

"Prince Tomas," she said numbly. "Youngest son of King Magnas of Lundegaard." A bloody hole gaped in Tomas's temple. Arrow, she guessed. Britta knelt and touched his hair lightly, touched his cheek lightly. *Ah, Tomas, what were you doing here?*

"And the others?"

Britta looked at the dead men again, resting her gaze on each face, trying to see the details that made each man individual. They had come to rescue her. And now they were dead. *I'm sorry.* "To my knowledge I have never seen them."

She had promised herself no more tears, but it was impossible not to weep silently.

# CHAPTER SEVENTY-TWO

Jaumé had waited with the Brothers' horses. He didn't want to earn a mark for disobedience. He watched Vught issue orders, watched Hetchel and Soll drag the soldiers' bodies from the road and carry them behind the rocks. Vught turned to him and beckoned. "Bring the horses." Jaumé hurried across to him, listened carefully to Vught's instructions, and carried them out as swiftly as he could, hobbling the horses, placing them so that they blocked the basin from view. Two wagons trundled past. Their drivers didn't seem to notice they were passing a battlefield. They were more concerned with the loose horses Hetchel and Soll were rounding up. "Need a hand?" one of them called.

Soll shook his head and gave a cheerful wave. "No, thanks. Nearly got 'em all."

Jaumé worked as fast as he could, but his gaze kept sliding sideways. He saw Bennick come down from the outcrop and talk to Vught. They crossed to the fallen soldier. Bennick crouched by the man's side. A few minutes later, Vught led the princess away. Jaumé craned his neck to see where he was taking her.

Hetchel and Soll hobbled the soldiers' horses. Only one horse was dead. The one the dark soldier had been riding. Hetchel's hand was bleeding and he couldn't use his thumb properly.

A farm cart rattled past, piled high with possessions. The cart slowed. "Got a lot of horses," the farmer said.

Soll turned to him, smiling. "Too many. Want some? I can give you a good price."

The farmer laughed and shook his head. The cart rattled onward.

Soll went back to hobbling the horses, the smile gone from his face.

Jaumé glanced again at where the dark soldier lay. Vught and the princess had returned. The princess knelt beside the man, but Vught was striding towards him. "Boy, light a fire and get some water boiling."

Jaumé hurried to obey.

# CHAPTER SEVENTY-THREE

THE BOY BROUGHT a pot of steaming water and some shirts torn into strips. The shirts were forest green. Lundegaardan. He set both water and shirts down carefully alongside Red.

Leader tossed something on the dirt. A roll of leather. Red reached for it, unrolled it. Britta saw bright needles and long, slender pincers and thin knives as sharp as razors.

"You're going to stitch him up?" the boy asked, wide-eyed.

"I am. And you're to help me."

"And I will, too," Britta said firmly.

Red glanced at her, and shrugged. "Wipe his face, then. Clean the blood off, so I can see what I'm doing."

Britta took a piece of cloth, dipped it in the steaming water, wrung it out. She wiped Karel's forehead while Red threaded a needle. The gash bled sluggishly. The edges had curled back. She could see Karel's skull.

"Jaumé, take the cloth, keep wiping. You, push the edges together for me like this." Red demonstrated, placing his palms on Karel's forehead.

The boy hurried to obey, taking the cloth from her, coming to kneel at Karel's head.

Britta took a deep breath and laid her hands carefully on Karel's face, one almost covering his nose, one near his hairline, and gently pushed. Karel's skin didn't seem to want to close over the wound. She pushed harder.

Red leaned over Karel. Britta winced as the needle penetrated Karel's skin. She looked away, at Red's face. He was concentrating hard, his brow furrowed, the tip of his tongue caught between his teeth.

It took Red almost twenty minutes to sew the wound together. Karel didn't stir. He was still alive, though. His pulse twitched beneath the skin at his throat, faint and steady.

Red sat back and surveyed his handiwork. The line of stitches curved across Karel's forehead, rising from his left eyebrow to bury itself in his hair near his right temple. Red shrugged and gave the needle to the boy. "Got a pot of water boiling on the fire? Put this in it."

Britta picked up the cloth the boy had abandoned, wet it, and carefully wiped Karel's face. Dark, sticky crusts of blood had dried around his eyes and on his cheeks.

"Right, let's look at this shoulder."

The arrow had caught Karel side-on, at the top of his right arm. The shaft jutted out a couple of inches; the arrowhead was buried deep in the muscle.

Extracting the arrow took less time than stitching Karel's forehead. Red sliced into the flesh on either side with one of the razor-sharp knives and yanked the arrowhead out. It left a deep, bloody hole. Red scowled at it thoughtfully. "Jaumé, fetch that needle again, will you?"

The boy ran off, darting through the horses, and came back holding the needle.

"Good lad." Red stitched the edges of the hole together and bound Karel's arm and shoulder with strips of torn shirts. "Not too tight," he said, whether to her or the boy, Britta wasn't sure. "Don't want to stop circulation. But we want to hold it all in place. Don't want the stitches to pull out when he moves." He frowned. "Infection's going to be the problem. Not much we can do about that, 'cept keep everything clean."

Karel still hadn't stirred. Britta checked his pulse—beating steadily—and felt through his bloody hair, trying to find where Leader had kicked him. Her fingers found a large lump. "What if his skull's broken?" *What if he's dying as he lies here?*

"Can't do anything for a broken skull. Don't think it is, though." Red reached over and lifted Karel's eyelids. "Pupils the same size, see?"

Britta's fear subsided slightly, burrowed beneath her breastbone and sat there like a clenched fist.

Red turned to Karel's leg, and grimaced. "This'll be difficult."

He cut Karel's trews away from his left thigh and examined the injury. The tips of two blades were visible, protruding a few inches. Red carefully gripped one blade and tried to wiggle it from side to side. The throwing star didn't move. "Stuck deep in the bone." He grimaced again, thought for a moment, pushed to his feet and walked off.

The boy busied himself cleaning the instruments Red had used, tidying them away. Britta reached for Karel's hand and held it in both of hers. A large hand, lean and brown-skinned, with a swordsman's calluses. A fighter's hand.

But there was no strength in Karel's hand, only a frightening limpness. *Don't die*, she begged him, her eyes on his face. Even bloodied and unconscious, Karel looked stern. It was the winging black eyebrows, the hawk-like nose, the slant of his cheekbones. Britta stared hard at him, willing him to stir, to groan, to blink his eyes open. But he didn't. He lay as if dead.

Red returned carrying a short, stiff piece of wire and a loop of rope. He bent the wire into a crude hook at one end and twisted it into an eye at the other, his fingers white-knuckled with effort, then he tied the rope through the eye and knotted it firmly. "All Stars have a hole in the center." Red opened a round leather pouch at his waist, held a throwing star out to the boy. "See?"

The boy nodded.

Red slid the weapon back into his pouch. He bent over Karel's leg and inserted the hook into the wound. Blood welled as he probed, trickling down the curve of Karel's thigh. "If I can just... ah, there it is. Now it becomes a matter of brute force." He stood, placed one booted foot on Karel's thigh, and yanked upward on the rope. The throwing star didn't move.

Red muttered a curse under his breath, wrapped the rope around his hands, and yanked again.

Still, the throwing star didn't move.

Red yanked a third time, his teeth gritted. A fourth time. A fifth, grunting with effort.

"It moved!" the boy cried.

"You think?" Red was red-faced, panting.

"Yes," Britta said, gripping Karel's hand tightly. The tips of the throwing star were a quarter of an inch further out. Blood flowed from the wound.

Red yanked again. Another quarter-inch of the weapon emerged. Another yank, another quarter-inch. "Almost out of the bone." He bent, took hold of the rope just above the wire's eye, and pulled upward firmly. For a second, the throwing star held fast in Karel's leg, then it slid free.

Red staggered slightly, but kept his balance. Blood began to flow swiftly from the wound. Britta released Karel's hand. She grabbed a cloth and pressed firmly down, stemming the blood.

"You did it!" the boy cried.

Red blew out a breath. "Not finished yet. We need that needle again."

By pressing hard on either side of Karel's thigh, Red managed to close the gaping slit where the throwing star had been. "Hold it like this while I stitch," he told Britta. "Lad, wipe away that blood."

Britta put her hands where Red's had been, and pressed hard. "Did you boil the wire in water?" she asked, while the boy mopped up the blood.

Red glanced at her, and nodded. He threaded the needle and crouched opposite her. This time, Britta didn't wince from sight of the needle piercing Karel's skin. She watched Red stitch, her arms shaking with the effort of holding the wound closed.

Red placed the last stitch, and laid down the needle. "Keep pressing," he said, reaching for the pile of torn shirts. "Those stitches won't hold otherwise."

Britta gritted her teeth and obeyed. Her arms burned, but she would do this until they fell off, if it meant Karel lived.

Red chose some bandages, slid them under Karel's knee and worked them up his thigh. "Keep pressing," he said again.

Britta and the boy watched as he wrapped the bandages around the wound, sliding his fingers under the fabric, checking the pressure. Firm, but not too tight. At last Red was satisfied. He sat back on his heels. "Done."

The boy was gazing at Red with something akin to awe.

"Thank you," Britta said.

Red shrugged. He pushed to his feet, rolled his shoulders, stretched.

Britta lightly touched the bandage. "When it heals... will he be able to walk?"

"Maybe." Red's expression said, *Maybe not.* He looked away from her. "Right, lad, let's clear this up."

*This* was more than the items Red had used on Karel. There was a pile of bloodied arrows she'd not noticed before. Red gave them to the boy to wash.

For each of those arrows, a man had died. In her mind's eye, she saw Prince Tomas lying sprawled among the rocks, a bloody hole in his head.

She glanced at Red. He stooped and picked up the throwing star. If Karel died, it would be because of him. And if he lived, it would be because of him.

\* \* \*

MORNING RIPENED TOWARDS noon. Britta sat in the dirt, holding Karel's limp hand. The Fithians set no one to guard her. She watched Leader and Red remove the dead horse's bridle and saddle and wrench the arrow from its eye socket, watched Leader go through the soldiers' saddlebags, watched Red examine the cleaned arrows and strap them on a packhorse, watched the boy trot to and fro, scattering handfuls of dirt on the ground, hiding the bloodstains. Leader crossed to her once—she braced herself—but he ignored her, bent and picked up Karel's sword, carried it over to the rubble of rock, and flung it away. She saw Pox a few times through the milling horses. His task seemed to be to keep passersby away.

The only sounds were the horses snuffling and shifting their weight, the wind moaning through the rocks, the crunch of wheels when the occasional wagon passed, Pox's voice as he exchanged greetings with people. How could everything be so calm, so quiet, so normal? And why were they still here? What was Leader waiting for?

Britta frowned and looked around, peering through the horses' legs. There were Leader and Red and the boy, and Pox. Plain was dead—Karel had killed him—but she couldn't see Curly, and she knew he was alive. And where was Gap-Tooth? Was he dead? If he was, his body hadn't been with the soldiers. But then, Plain's hadn't been, either.

Belatedly, it occurred to her to count the horses. Seven mounts for the Fithians, plus the piebald mare and the boy's pony, and the packhorses. Twelve mounts for the Lundegaardan soldiers... No, there were only five. And Karel's dead mount. Which left six missing horses.

The boy brought her bread and cheese and a waterskin. "Thank you," Britta said.

His gaze flicked to her and quickly away. He looked like a wild animal, wary. *I don't bite, child.* And then she remembered sinking her teeth into Pox's hand and huffed a faint laugh. The boy didn't hear it; he'd already gone, running back through the horses.

The sun reached its pinnacle in the sky, and still they waited. Red crossed to her, the boy trotting at his heels, and crouched and checked Karel's pupils, his pulse.

"Is Gap-Tooth dead?" Britta asked.

"Gap-Tooth?" Red tilted his head. "You mean Luit?"

Britta shrugged. "He didn't have a lot of teeth."

"That's Luit." Red looked amused. "Gap-Tooth, huh?"

"Is he dead?"

Red ignored the question. "What do you call the rest of us?"

They matched gazes for a moment. Britta debated the merits of antagonizing him. "Leader," she said. "Curly. Red. Pox."

"Pox?" Red laughed. "I'll have to tell him that."

Britta blinked. The killer had a sense of humor?

Red pushed to his feet, and turned to go.

"Is Luit dead?"

Red looked down at her. The laughter was gone

from his face. He was a Fithian again, cold-eyed. "He's dead."

Britta met his gaze squarely, refusing to look away. "What are your names?"

Red stared down at her. After a moment, he shrugged, as if it didn't matter whether she knew or not. "Bennick. And Jaumé." His hand rested briefly on the boy's hair. "Vught. That's Leader to you. Hetchel." A jerk of his head indicated Pox, standing on the other side of the horses. "And Soll."

BRITTA REPEATED THE assassins' names silently, fixing them in her memory. Vught. Hetchel. Soll. Bennick. And the boy, Jaumé.

Not long after her conversation with Red—Bennick—a wagon approached with a rattle of wheels. This time the wagon didn't pass. It halted. Britta peered through the horses' legs, saw Hetchel's boots, and another man's. Vught strode to join them. The horses milled, moved, parted. She caught a glimpse of Vught, Hetchel, and Soll. Behind them was an open wagon.

The horses moved again, blocking her view.

So that was where Soll had been: selling the horses, buying a wagon. She looked down at Karel. *To carry you.*

Even though she'd cleaned his face, blood still crusted Karel's eyelashes and the corners of his eyes. He looked as lifeless as the Lundegaardan soldiers, his stillness the stillness of death. Only the pulse fluttering in the hollow of his throat showed he was alive.

Britta bent her head and whispered fiercely in his ear. "You *have* to live, Karel! Do you hear me? Don't you dare die!"

There was a stir of movement among the horses; Hetchel and Bennick and Soll were removing the hobbles. Vught brought the wagon closer. "Boy, get some blankets, make a bed for him."

Karel didn't stir when he was laid in the wagon. Britta scrambled up after him. "Is he all right?" she asked Bennick. "Shouldn't he be awake by now?"

Bennick fastened the tailboard. "He'll wake when he wakes."

The wagon lurched forward, jolting and rattling. Hetchel trotted past, holding his reins in his left hand. His right hand was bandaged. For a moment Britta wondered why, and then she remembered.

It seemed like a lifetime ago that she'd bitten him, and yet it had been only a few hours.

The world had stopped when she'd seen Karel fall—stopped and turned itself upside down—and when it had righted itself everything had changed. The world was a different place; she was a different person. Her plunge into the river and Vught's whispered threats were things that had happened to someone else. What was real—the only thing that truly *was* real—was Karel's hand, warm and limp, lying in her clasp.

They rounded the corner. Britta glanced back, past Bennick and Jaumé leading the long line of horses. Nothing remained of the carnage except the horse's carcass lying abandoned in the dirt.

# CHAPTER SEVENTY-FOUR

IN THE AFTERNOON, Justen glided down to land. "There's a farm about a mile ahead, with someone still alive. A child." His expression was grim.

"Cursed?" Rand asked.

Justen nodded.

"How old?"

'I'd say... about three. Maybe four."

"Ah, All-Mother," someone muttered behind Harkeld. He glanced over his shoulder. Serril.

"Do we kill her, or leave her?"

There was a long moment of silence. Harkeld examined the faces around him. Rand driving the wagon, Serril and Petrus and Gretel and Adel on horseback. Everyone was as grim-faced as Justen.

"If we don't kill her, she'll starve," Gretel said. "Which is worse?"

"Starving," Rand said.

THE FARM WAS a poor place, with a farmhouse built of wood and stone and a lopsided barn. Harkeld dismounted in the dirt yard, dread tight in his belly. Justen landed again.

"Where is she?" Rand asked.

"In the barn."

Harkeld glanced at the hawk circling above them. Innis. He was glad she wasn't down here. She didn't need to see this.

Rand drew his sword, pushed open the barn door, and entered. Harkeld fumbled for his own sword and forced himself to follow.

The barn was dark. He paused inside the door for his eyes to adjust. The stink of putrefaction filled his mouth and nose.

Gradually his eyes made sense of the shapes in the dimness—the empty stalls, the rusting farm implements, the stack of chopped wood, the pile of straw.

The nauseating smell came from near his feet. He looked down and blinked for a moment, not understanding what it was he saw—as if his brain blocked it—and then understanding came. A dead baby. The plump flesh of arms and legs had been eaten away, the belly torn open, but the baby's face was still there. Mostly.

Harkeld lurched back, banging into someone. Serril. "What?" the big shapeshifter said, and then he saw the baby. "All-Mother." His voice sounded strangled.

"Serril, why don't you wait with the horses?" Rand said.

Serril didn't argue. He turned and pushed out the door.

Harkeld gripped his sword more tightly. "He all right?"

"He has young children." Rand advanced into the barn, his sword extended. Harkeld followed.

He was aware of someone behind him, and glanced back, saw Petrus and Gretel.

"Where is she?" Petrus said, in a low voice.

"Must be in one of the stalls."

But the stalls were empty except for wisps of old straw and goat droppings dried as hard as pebbles.

"Could have got out that hole easy enough," Gretel said, pointing with her sword.

"Indeed." Rand headed for the door. "She must be in the house."

Harkeld heard a rustling in the straw to his left. He halted. "Rand..."

The healer paused in the half-open door and looked back.

"She's here."

The little girl had made a nest in the straw. Harkeld stood frozen as she crawled out. Black curse shadows, yes, and a blood-smeared mouth, but also dimpled hands and hair in lopsided pigtails and a coarse cotton smock stitched with flowers.

He watched, unable to move, unable to swing his sword, unable to kill her, as she trotted past him, hands outstretched for balance, past Gretel, past Petrus, towards the open door and the sunshine.

Rand raised his sword—and then stepped back, out of the child's way. She disappeared through the doorway.

No one moved. He heard Rand swear softly. The healer sheathed his sword and hurried after the girl. Gretel followed.

Harkeld exchanged a glance with Petrus. *That's what my face looks like. Shocked. Horrified.*

He rammed his sword into its scabbard and ran for the door, Petrus at his heels.

The little girl was halfway across the dirt yard, tottering towards Serril on unsteady legs, her arms still outstretched, like a child running to her father.

The shapeshifter backed away, but the little girl grabbed hold of his trews in both fists and stood swaying, staring up at him. She uttered a gurgling, laughing sound.

The laugh wasn't delight; it was madness, bloodlust.

Serril held his sword away from the child. Beneath the tan and the close-cropped black beard, his face was ashen. "Rand, I can't."

"None of us can," Rand said. "I'll use my magic."

The little girl uttered the gurgling sound again, swaying on unsteady legs, and buried her face in Serril's trews and bit his knee. Serril didn't move. He stood rock-solid, staring down at the child, grief on his face.

Rand crossed to them and reached for the girl's nape. His touch looked gentle, but it startled her. She stopped biting Serril, released his trews, and ran for the house, tottering, surprisingly fast.

"I've got her." Gretel caught the girl in her arms.

The child began to thrash and shriek. Not with fright, but fury. Madness distorted her face. There was no fear in those eyes, no sanity. She sank her teeth into Gretel's hand.

Rand hurried to her and touched the nape of her neck. His expression was grim, jaw clenched.

The girl convulsed once and went limp.

"She's dead," Rand said. "You can put her down."

Gretel laid the child on the ground.

Harkeld couldn't look away. All he could do was stare at the girl. Her parents had been poor, but they'd loved her. Someone had combed her hair and tied it into pigtails, someone had spent hours stitching flowers onto her coarse little smock.

*We killed a child.*

The scene had the quality of a nightmare. The sky was too big, the sunlight too harsh. The dirt yard seemed to curve up at the edges, like paper curling in the sun.

"Where are the rest of her family? In the house?" Rand's voice sounded hoarse. It tore Harkeld's attention from the child. Were those tears in the healer's eyes? Rand was a father, too. How much had it hurt him to kill the little girl?

"Yes," Justen said. "Parents and another child."

"Put her with them." Rand rubbed his face, rubbed his eyes. "Did she bite you, Gretel? Is it bleeding?"

Gretel didn't answer.

Harkeld glanced at her. The fire mage was staring at her hand. It was dark with curse shadows. Darker than it should be.

Gretel turned to Rand, holding out her hand. "Rand..." There was a note of panic in her voice.

Harkeld's gaze jerked to Gretel's face. The shadows covering it were thickening, growing blacker.

The sense of nightmare became stronger. Harkeld couldn't move. His legs had rooted into the dirt. Gretel's face twisted, her lips pulling back in a snarl.

Someone shoved Harkeld aside. Petrus.

The shapeshifter swung his sword. The blade flashed in the sunlight, sliced obliquely, buried itself in Gretel's throat.

The impact flung Gretel sideways. She tumbled to the ground. Blood spilled from her throat.

Petrus lowered the sword, let its point touch the dirt.

The scent of fresh blood drifted across the yard.

No one spoke. No one moved. The only sound was Petrus's breathing, harsh, almost sobbing. The dirt yard seemed to tilt under Harkeld's feet. *I'm going to fall over.*

Rand stepped forward and gripped Petrus's shoulder. "Thank you, son. Be careful with your sword. Don't touch the blood."

"What happened?" Justen sounded as stunned as Harkeld felt.

"Blood." Serril's voice was rough, almost unintelligible. He cleared his throat, spoke again, "Blood or saliva. You think, Rand?"

"Yes." Rand rubbed his face again, pressing so hard his skin whitened, then lowered his hands. "Get rid of those trews you're wearing, Serril. Carefully. They're wet where she bit you."

Harkeld walked to where Gretel lay. He looked down at her. *My cousin.*

Petrus still stood there, the tip of his sword digging into the dirt. The shapeshifter's face was as bloodlessly pale as Gretel's.

"Petrus..." He touched Petrus's arm, waited for the shapeshifter to meet his eyes. "She would thank you."

Petrus swallowed, and nodded.

# CHAPTER SEVENTY-FIVE

THEY PASSED THROUGH the village where Soll had bought the wagon. Half a dozen men in dusty, travel-stained uniforms were rousting everyone out of their homes.

"King's Riders," Bennick muttered to Jaumé.

"You!" one of them barked peremptorily, when the wagon rattled towards the eastern gate. "You can't go that way. Ivek's curse is coming." He rode forward and blocked the road, forcing Soll to halt.

Jaumé tensed. Were the Brothers going to kill this soldier, too? He glanced at Bennick, at Vught, but neither man was reaching for his sword. In fact, Vught seemed to have shrunk. He sat round-shouldered in his saddle. "We're fetching m' sister," Vught said. His voice was different: the vowels rounder, the consonants less guttural, the tone submissive. "Soll here's wife. She's 'bout ready to breech. Can't get 'er on an 'orse."

The King's Rider frowned. "How far?"

"Farm 'bout five miles from 'ere." Vught nodded east with his chin.

The King's Rider stepped back and waved them on. "For the All-Mother's sake, *hurry*. Curse isn't no more'n a day or two from here."

"We will, sir." Vught ducked his head respectfully.

\* \* \*

THEY FOLLOWED ROADS that wound up valleys, climbing, always climbing, reaching a plateau as the sun sank towards the horizon behind them. Jaumé peered ahead. He saw mountains in the distance, and smudges of smoke. The sky was hazy, orange-tinted.

They turned off the road into a field with a creek running through it. The wagon lurched over the stubbly ground in a wide half-circle and came to a halt.

Bennick dismounted. "Let's check him."

Jaumé jumped down from his pony and hurried after him.

The soldier lay exactly as they'd left him, in the bed of blankets. The princess sat alongside him, holding one of his hands in both of hers.

"Thought you got carriage sick," Bennick said.

The princess looked at him blankly, and then blinked. "Uh... not in an open wagon."

Bennick made a sound like he didn't believe her. He climbed up into the wagon, knelt at the soldier's side, and touched the back of his hand to the man's cheek. "Getting feverish. Did he wake at all?"

The princess shook her head.

"We need to get him to drink," Bennick said. "I'll brew some feverwort. Jaumé, get a fire going."

JAUMÉ GATHERED WOOD and made a rough fire pit while Bennick and the rest of the Brothers tended to the horses. When the fire was burning, he put a billy of water on to boil. Bennick fetched a leather pouch from one of the packsaddles. Inside it, were lots of smaller pouches. Bennick found the one he wanted. "Not much left." He held it out for Jaumé to sniff. "Feverwort. You know what this is?"

Jaumé nodded. "Mam used it. She said the leaves make you well, and the roots make you sick."

"She was right." Bennick emptied the pouch of dried leaves into the billy.

"The alderman's son ate some feverwort root once," Jaumé said. "On a dare. He threw up for a whole day and night."

Bennick grunted. "Not surprised. It's a strong emetic."

"Em... Emmytic?"

Bennick pulled the boiling billy off the fire. "Emetic. Something that makes you throw up."

The feverwort leaves steeped while the water cooled. When it was only lukewarm, Bennick picked out the leaves. "Right, let's get him to drink. Fetch a mug, will you, lad?"

Bennick propped the soldier up slightly, his arm under the man's shoulders, and trickled feverwort into his mouth. The soldier's dark face was flushed with fever, stained with blood. He choked once, coughed, came close to rousing.

"Karel?" the princess said, leaning close to him. "Karel? Can you hear me?"

For a moment it seemed that he did. His head turned towards her, his eyelids flickered—and then he sank into unconsciousness again.

Bennick got almost a mug of feverwort into him. "Better than nothing," he said. "We'll try again later." He poured the rest of the billy into a waterskin.

"Thank you," the princess said. She hadn't stopped holding the soldier's hand. Jaumé wondered if she was afraid he'd die if she let go.

Bennick jumped lightly down from the wagon.

"Jaumé?" the princess said.

Jaumé paused on the edge of the wagon and looked back at her.

"May I have some warm water? I'd like to wash the blood off him properly."

Jaumé waited until he had Bennick's nod, then hastened to heat more water. He found some of the bandages that Bennick hadn't used and took them and the water to the princess. "To clean him with," he said, offering the cloths.

The princess released the soldier's hand and took the billy and the bandages. "Thank you, Jaumé."

The princess was dressed like a man and had short, scruffy hair and a bruised face, but her smile made him feel warm inside.

THEY ATE SMOKED sausages, tough and chewy, with whole peppercorns in them and coarse chunks of fat. After the meal, Vught unrolled a map and scowled at it. "The Brother in Andeol was going to have water barrels and a wagon for us. But we're not going to make it. Not if the curse is as close as that Rider said."

"We can get barrels," Bennick said, "at the next village we pass. Empty 'em out, fill 'em with water."

Vught grunted, and rolled the map up again. He looked at Jaumé. "You've been in cursed land before, boy. What's it like?"

Jaumé shivered. "Lots of blood."

Vught made an impatient gesture—*Tell me more.*

Jaumé glanced at Bennick, and saw his encouraging nod. He took a deep breath. "My Da killed my Mam and my sister," he said, in a rush. "And then he came after me." The smell of blood was in his nose—Mam's blood. "I ran to the village, but the curse was there, too, so I hid. They burned it, the village. I heard people screaming and laughing. And at night, I ran away."

"Laughing?" Vught's mouth turned down in a frown.

Jaumé shivered again. "Not good laughing. Like... like an animal would laugh."

"Huh." Vught shrugged with his face, with his shoulders. "Guess we'll find out soon enough."

Jaumé looked away. He couldn't smell the sausages any more, or the woodsmoke; all he could smell was blood. He remembered the sounds Da had made as he chased him: thudding feet, hoarse grunts of breath. His ribcage seemed to squeeze around his lungs.

Bennick stood. "Let's get some more feverwort down his throat. Come on, lad."

Jaumé scrambled to his feet.

Bennick rested one hand on the top of Jaumé's head for a moment. The panic retreated. Jaumé gulped a big breath. As long as he was with Bennick, he was safe.

# CHAPTER SEVENTY-SIX

THEY HALTED WHEN the sky shaded into another smoky orange dusk. Harkeld dismounted stiffly. He unsaddled his mount, then turned to the packhorses. He felt numb inside.

First Bode, then Malle, and now Gretel.

"Don't put up tents tonight." Rand's voice sounded too loud in the silence. "There's enough space for us all to sleep in the wagon."

*Now that Gretel's dead.*

Harkeld helped unsaddle the horses. Far too many horses for seven people. He carried bedrolls to the wagon, and two armfuls of blankets, and looked around—Adel and Serril hobbling the last of the horses, Innis and Justen circling overhead, Rand going through the packsaddles, Petrus gathering gnarled thorn branches in a pile.

He crossed to Petrus and crouched, lit the fire with a flick of his fingers. "How are you?"

Petrus glanced at him, shrugged. "Fine."

*No, you're not.* But if Petrus needed to talk with someone, he'd talk to Innis.

Petrus set up the iron tripod. He hung the stewpot over the flames and half-filled it with water from

his waterskin. Rand came over, carrying several
bundles. He tossed Petrus one. "Goat's meat."

Harkeld watched Rand open the other bundles,
sorting out herbs and dried yellow tubers. Deep
lines of strain were carved into the healer's face. He
seemed to have aged a decade since Hansgrohe.

Rand reached for a knife and started cutting the
tubers into chunks.

"Rand?" He waited for the healer to look at him.
"Gretel was going to help me try to burn stone
tonight. I'd still like to do it."

Rand put down the knife he was using. "Stone?
It's risky. You could harm yourself."

"My magic won't burn me," Harkeld said.

"Not on purpose, no. But an accident—"

"Sir... it might be a good idea for him to try,"
Petrus said.

Rand glanced at him, frowning.

"In Ankeny, the anchor stone wouldn't let him go.
It took all the skin off his palm."

Harkeld had a flash of memory: his palm flayed
raw.

"I'd forgotten that. I was more focused on the
arrow." Rand's frown deepened. "What happened
at the first stone, Flin?"

"Nothing. It just sucked up my blood. It was the
second one that wouldn't let me go. It was... I don't
know... stronger."

"What if the third stone's even stronger?" Petrus
said. He emptied the dried goat's meat into the
stewpot. "What if he can't get his hand off?"

"The stone will disintegrate," Rand said. "Like
the others."

*And what happens to my hand, then? Does it disintegrate too?*

Rand must have been thinking the same thing. He gave a nod. "All right, you may try. But I want to be with you when you do." He gave the knife to Petrus and climbed to his feet. "Where do you want to do it?"

"That stone wall over there."

They crossed the paddock together, the icy wind whipping their cloaks around them, and halted at the dry-stone wall. Harkeld picked up a pale gray stone the size of a plum and turned it over in his hand. It seemed impossible that he could burn it, impossible that anyone could. And yet his grandfather had been able to.

Linus. *Who gave up his life as a Sentinel so that I could be born.*

Harkeld put the plum-sized stone on the top of the wall and stepped several paces back. He felt nervous, uncertain. "I don't know how to do this," he told Rand.

"Do whatever seems most natural."

Natural? Could burning stone be natural?

It had been, for Linus.

Harkeld raised his right hand and called up his magic, let it rise in him, fierce and hot. *Burn.*

There was a sharp crack of sound and a bright flash of fire. The plum-shaped stone jumped in the air and tumbled to the ground. Harkeld lowered his hand. He walked across to the stone. It was black, hissing in the cold air. He stepped on it, hoping it would crumble like charcoal beneath his boot, but it was still rock-hard. He remembered what Gretel had said: it was harder to burn stone than metal.

"Well?" Rand asked.

Harkeld shook his head. "Didn't work." He chose another stone, balanced it on top of the wall, stepped back again. He shook out his right hand, flexed his fingers, and stared at the new stone, determined to burn it. Not for himself, but for Linus. For Gretel.

He summoned his magic again, let it build again. Hot. White-hot. Hotter than white-hot. Fire crackled and sizzled in his blood. He gritted his teeth and let the heat and the pressure build even higher. When it was almost too much to bear, when he felt as if he was about to explode, he released his magic. *Burn.*

There was a loud *whoomp* and a blinding burst of fire. Tiny shards of something sharp stung Harkeld's face.

He turned to Rand, blinking, squinting to see past the imprint of flame on his vision. "You all right?"

"Yes."

Harkeld crossed to the wall. There was a black scorch mark where the stone had been, and tiny black flecks that looked like glass. He touched the wall, felt the heat there. Some of the flecks stuck to his fingers. He rubbed them between thumb and forefinger. Gritty. Sharp.

Smithereens. He'd burned the stone to smithereens.

He turned to face Rand. "If I do that to the anchor stone..."

"If your hand is on the anchor stone and you do that, you'll blow your arm off."

Harkeld grimaced. He turned his hand palm-up, looked at it. *Better to lose the skin again.*

Rand walked across to him, his boots crunching in the dried wisps of grass. "And it's not just the risk to you that worries me. Ivek bound his curse to the anchor stone. Your blood is meant to destroy it, but if you do *that* to the stone..."

"You think the curse might not end?"

"There've been fire mages strong enough to burn the anchor stones, but they've never dared risk it. The only way of being absolutely certain of destroying the stones *and* the curse is to do it the way Ivek intended."

Harkeld stared down at his palm. He remembered how the first anchor stone had greedily swallowed his blood, how the second one had held on to his skin. What was going to happen at the third anchor stone? *Will it take my whole hand?* He'd said it as a joke, back in Ankeny, with his hand dripping blood, but it wasn't a joke.

"If you could burn stone with control," Rand said. "If you could burn *only* enough of the anchor stone to free yourself... I would consider allowing you to do it."

"If I practice—"

"How much practice do you think you'll need?"

Harkeld looked at the scorch mark, at the tiny shards of glass. A crude explosion. Fire wielded with no precision and very little control. He met the healer's eyes. "A lot. And I think... I need a fire mage to instruct me. Someone who knows how it should be done."

"I agree," Rand said. "Fire magic is a dangerous discipline. You could have a serious accident. Something Innis and I can't heal. I'm sorry, Flin."

Harkeld nodded.

They walked back across the paddock. Harkeld looked at the mountains. They were much closer now, looming against the sky. The third anchor stone nestled somewhere in those snowy peaks. *What will it do to me?*

Rand halted. "I don't know a lot about fire magic, but... what if you don't throw your magic? What if you try to burn stone by contact?"

Harkeld halted, too. "Contact?"

"Could you *melt* your hand free?"

Harkeld stared at the healer, thinking. "Maybe. I learned to burn wood by touching it."

"Want to try?"

He nodded.

They went back to the wall. The sky was almost dark, streaked with fiery orange streamers of cloud.

Harkeld laid his hand on a large block of stone. He blew out a breath and called up his magic again, let it hum warmly beneath his skin. How to do this?

He wished Cora was here. Or Gretel. Or even Bode. He closed his eyes. Melt stone. How?

He let the heat build in his hand, but didn't hold it there, let it flow out through his palm. Hotter. Even hotter. Intensely hot. Magic crackled and smoked in his blood, spilling out into the stone.

"I think you've done it."

Harkeld opened his eyes. Only one cloud glowed orange now, catching the last of the daylight.

He looked down at his hand. Steam wisped around his fingers. Or perhaps it was smoke? He heard a faint hissing sound.

Harkeld snuffed his fire magic. He lifted his hand. A handprint was burned into the stone—four fingers, thumb, palm. The print shimmered slightly, catching the light, seeming to move.

"Molten," Rand said.

Without his magic to heat it, the stone cooled swiftly, losing its sheen. It dulled as it hardened. Tiny cracks snaked across its surface.

Harkeld touched the handprint. It was rock-hard. "You think it would be safe to do that to the anchor stone?"

"I'm not a stone mage, or a fire mage, but I think... yes. If you need to."

"TRY NOT TO worry about the anchor stone," Rand said, as they walked back across the paddock. "I don't think Ivek intended it to harm you."

"I doubt he even thought about me. He didn't think I'd ever be born. I'm... impossible." A Rutersvard prince with mage blood in his veins. Ivek's joke against the Kingdoms.

"Fortunately for the Seven Kingdoms, you're not." Rand glanced at him, his face half-shadowed in the gloom. "Innis and I will be with you at the anchor stone. If your hand is damaged, we'll heal it. I promise you."

*If I still have a hand.*

They walked in silence, their boots crunching in the dirt and wisps of dried grass. Cora had made him a promise, too. To have one of the healers strip his magic from him once the curse was broken. Harkeld tried to imagine it: the gland in his skull dead, no more fire magic in his blood.

He looked for Innis, and found her sitting on the tailboard of the wagon. Petrus was with her. She was holding one of his hands in both of hers. They were talking, their heads bent close together.

A month ago he'd wanted nothing more than to be rid of his magic, rid of Innis and Petrus and the rest of the mages.

Now, he no longer wanted that.

HARKELD WENT TO sleep in the back of the wagon, with Serril on one side of him and Rand on the other, and dreamed that he sat on the driver's box. He saw stars, saw the black shape of a mountain range. Night was silent around him. There was no smell of smoke, no smell of anything. No wind. No icy chill in the air.

Someone sat alongside him. He felt the warmth of a shoulder, an arm, a thigh. His recognition was immediate: Innis.

"Are we sharing a dream?" His voice sounded loud in the silence. "Are we sleeping close enough?"

"Must be."

Harkeld took her hand. With that touch came the familiar sense of bone-deep contentment. It trickled into the hollow space inside him, filling him as rain filled a dry pond after drought. Despite everything that had happened today—the cursed child, Gretel's death—he found himself feeling happy. Truly, deeply happy. And Innis was happy, too. He sensed it through their handclasp, sensed her grief and exhaustion—and her happiness.

Happy, because she loved him. Because he loved her.

\* \* \*

THEY SAT IN silence, holding hands, while the stars moved leisurely overhead.

"How's Petrus?" he asked, after several hours had passed.

"More upset than he's letting on."

"He loves you, you know."

"I know." He felt the sharp pang of her regret. "He didn't used to. Not like he does now. It's new. Since he went on his Journey."

"Would you..." Harkeld closed his mouth, decided not to ask the question, but Innis heard it anyway.

"Would I love him back that way, if you weren't here?" She was silent for a moment. "I don't know. Maybe. Probably."

STARS ROSE FROM behind the dark bulk of the mountains and traced slow paths across the sky. The cool calmness of the night sank into Harkeld's skin, and the warm contentment of holding Innis's hand hummed in his blood. "Gretel's grandfather and mine were brothers. She told me today."

Innis hadn't known. He felt her surprise, and the rush of her emotions as she remembered Gretel's death, and knew she sensed his own emotions: grief, regret.

"She said I've got lots of cousins."

He'd lost one family, lost his birthright and his name, but that no longer seemed such a terrible thing. "The deal I made with Cora—to be stripped of my magic once this is over—I've changed my mind. I want to study at the Academy. I want to learn to use my fire magic properly, see what kind of healer I am."

"Truly?" He felt Innis's swift hope, her cautious delight.

"Truly." He let go of her hand, put his arm around her shoulders, pressed a kiss into her hair.

There were other things he wanted, too. But he wasn't going to discuss them with Innis while they were dreaming. When he asked her to marry him, he wanted to be awake.

# CHAPTER SEVENTY-SEVEN

Towards dawn, Karel began to stir, to twitch his head from side to side, to mumble. Britta threw back her blankets and knelt, trying to see his face. "Karel? Karel, can you hear me?"

But it seemed that he couldn't. The mumbling continued, the twitching.

It was a relief when dawn grayed the sky and the Fithians unrolled from their blankets. Bennick crossed to the wagon, the boy at his heels. "He's talking in his sleep," Britta told the assassin. "But he won't wake up."

Bennick climbed up into the wagon and bent over Karel for a moment. "It's the fever. Feel how hot he is?" He unwound the bandages and checked Karel's injuries.

"Are they all right?" Britta asked anxiously.

"A little swollen. Not too bad." Bennick retied the bandages.

"But the fever—"

"If these start seeping pus, *then* we worry. Hold his head up; I'll get some more feverwort into him."

# CHAPTER SEVENTY-EIGHT

THEY STOPPED AT the first village they came to. Wind blew through the empty market square, rattling the shutters, kicking up dust. Jaumé shivered. The village felt dead, as if even the straggling weeds around the well had stopped growing.

The Brothers searched for barrels and found two in the tavern. They knocked out the bungs, letting ale spill onto the straw-covered floor. Bennick saw Jaumé's shocked expression. "Easier to get the barrels outside if they're empty. Come on, lad. Let's look for feverwort. Someone here must've had some."

BENNICK CHECKED THE houses around the market square. In the sixth house, he made a sound of satisfaction. "Herbalist. Look."

Herbs hung drying from the ceiling. Some were whole plants, roots and all, others were bundles of leaves, twigs, flowers, grasses.

Bennick prowled the room, looking up. "Here's what we want. Feverwort."

The feverwort still had its roots. Jaumé eyed the pale tubers.

Bennick saw his expression and laughed. "Don't worry, lad. Can't hurt you unless you eat it. Or better yet, boil it and drink the water." He handed Jaumé the dried plants and turned his attention back to the hanging herbs. "Wonder if there's any boneknit...? Ah, yes." He pulled down a bundle of twigs with tiny dried leaves on it. "And something for a poultice..."


JAUMÉ'S ARMS WERE full by the time they left the house. In the market square, Vught and Soll were heaving the empty barrels into the wagon. Hetchel was at the well, filling buckets.

Jaumé helped the Brothers fill the barrels, trotting back and forth between the wagon and the well until his arms ached from lugging buckets. Afterwards, hot and panting, he guzzled water, slurping it greedily, but once on horseback, he quickly grew cold. This was the sweeping, icy wind that he remembered from when he'd crossed Sault with Nolt. He huddled into the sheepskin jacket and pulled his cap low over his ears.

The wind smelled of smoke. Something large was burning to the south. Jaumé wondered what it was. Stubble fields? He didn't think so. All the farmers would be gone by now, chased out by King's Riders.

He kept a nervous eye on the smoke. He'd seen two things burn: Girond, when the curse took it, and the farm the hillmen had raided.

Smoke meant death.

# CHAPTER SEVENTY-NINE

INNIS FLEW IN great concentric sweeps, checking anywhere a Fithian might be hidden—ditches and gullies, tumbledown barns, the charred ruins of farmhouses. In an abandoned hamlet, she landed and changed into a dog, searched for fresh scents, and found nothing. Two miles west of the hamlet, on a narrow track that wound up a dry gully, she found someone alive—a young woman, crawling.

Thick shadows almost obscured the woman's face; she was cursed.

The woman headed up the gully, crawling painfully, slowly. She wore a tattered, bloodstained gown. One leg trailed awkwardly. Broken?

Innis's head told her to keep flying—she couldn't heal the woman, couldn't uncurse her—but her heart told her to stop. Cursed or not, the woman was suffering.

Innis changed into a sparrow and landed on a nearby rock. The woman didn't notice. She crawled onward, her attention utterly on her task. Her palms and knees were lacerated, leaving bloody marks in the dirt. Innis heard her breaths—harsh, gasping.

This close, she could see the woman's face beneath the curse shadows. She was younger than Innis had thought; girl, not woman. Fifteen? Sixteen? A long braid of brown hair dragged in the dust. There was dried blood around the girl's mouth, dried blood on her chin and throat, dried blood crusting her bodice.

Innis listened to the gasping breaths. Her tiny sparrow's heart seemed to contract in her chest. Not horror, but sorrow.

A swift end to this painful, crawling death—it was all she could give the girl.

Innis took a deep breath, fixed in her mind's eye what she needed to do—carotid, jugular, aorta—hopped off the rock and glided down to land beside the girl.

The girl didn't notice. She dragged herself forward, grunting, gasping, leaving her blood on the cart track.

Another breath—a swift change into herself—her hand gripping the girl's shoulder—the girl turning her head...

Carotid, jugular, aorta. Innis sent her magic into the arteries fiercely, rupturing them.

The beginnings of a snarl distorted the girl's face—and then her body spasmed.

Innis released her grip and scrambled back as the girl collapsed on the track. "All-Mother," she said, and she wasn't sure whether it was a prayer or a plea for forgiveness. *All-Mother, what have I done?*

The girl lay still, unbreathing. Her face was turned towards Innis, open-eyed.

Innis knelt on the stony track. Her heart beat fast, her breath caught in her throat with each inhalation.

The curse shadows covering the girl melted away. Innis saw her face clearly. There was a dimple on her chin, beneath the crusted blood. Her eyes were golden brown.

"All-Mother," Innis said again, and pressed the back of her hand to her mouth. She was shaking. Rand had been right: it was a quick death. But it was brutal use of healing magic.

Innis lowered her hand, and made herself look at the girl's face.

She'd felt the curse in the girl, in that second before she'd died. There had been nothing left of the girl's personality, no human emotions, no pain, no fear, no despair, just a howling lust for blood. Innis could still feel the howl, reverberating in her fingertips.

She rubbed her fingers until the howl was gone, then reached out and carefully closed the girl's eyes. "All-Mother, I give this girl to your care, that she may rest peacefully."

# CHAPTER EIGHTY

KAREL'S FEVER GREW as the afternoon progressed. His skin became hotter, his sleep more restless. Sometimes her voice seemed to calm him and he sank back into quiet slumber; sometimes it made him agitated, and he tossed and turned as if trying to free himself from the blankets. Britta trickled feverwort into his mouth whenever she could. By the end of the day, the waterskin was empty.

When they halted for the night, Britta didn't wait for Bennick to come to her. She scrambled down from the wagon and hurried across to him. "The fever's getting worse. And I've used up all the feverwort."

Bennick's gaze swung to her. He seemed amused by her distress. Alongside him, Jaumé slid down from his pony. The boy didn't find her distress funny; his eyes were large and serious.

"We'll do what we can," Bennick said. "Jaumé, fetch those herbs."

The boy ran to the packhorses.

BRITTA WENT BACK to Karel and sat clasping his hand. After a while, Bennick and Jaumé came, carrying two steaming billies and some bandages. "Feverwort and bone-knit," the assassin said. "Brewed together. And a poultice. Not comfrey, but similar."

He unwound the bandages and scooped a paste of mashed leaves out of one billy, explaining what he was doing to Jaumé. "It's the moistness and heat that make a poultice work. Draws the infection out. If I put the leaves on cold and dry, they wouldn't do much."

The boy listened, his face grave, nodding.

Bennick deftly tied the poultices in place. "When you use poultices, you need to keep changing them. You want the wound to stay clean."

Britta eyed him. He knew a lot about herbs. "Are you a poison master?"

Bennick glanced at her. "What do you know about poison masters?"

"I saw one, once."

Bennick snorted. "I doubt it."

"He had one leg."

Bennick looked at her again. This time, he didn't dismiss her words.

"He killed my father."

Bennick shrugged. "Killed your father. Killed your brother."

Brother? For a second, the word didn't make sense, as if her ears didn't recognize the sound—and then alarm kicked in. "Brother? Which one?"

"The new king. Got him, too." Bennick's smile was wolf-like.

"When?" she demanded, and then: "If Jaegar's dead, then the bounty on Harkeld's head is—"

"Not dead yet," Bennick said. "Got a few months left in him. Long enough to pay out the bounty."

Britta frowned. "What do you mean, he's got a few months left?"

Bennick reached for the second billy. "Meffren got him with Five Moons. Means your brother's got five moons till he dies. Course, the last couple aren't going to be pleasant."

"Not pleasant, how?"

Bennick shrugged. "He'll be impotent by now. By the end of next month he'll be blind and incontinent."

Britta stared at him, open-mouthed, horrified. She had wished Jaegar dead, but not like *that*.

Her horror seemed to amuse Bennick. He grinned. Jaumé wasn't grinning. He was looking at Bennick as if he didn't recognize him.

"Why poison Jaegar?" Britta asked, and then she answered her own question: "Because he refused to pay for Father's murder?"

"Refused, did he? Well, Meffren's made sure he'll pay the All-Mother."

"Five Moons..." She looked at the billy Bennick held, struck by a sudden, terrible thought.

Bennick's grin widened. "Don't worry. Five Moons isn't a poison you drink."

"Then how...?"

Bennick put down the billy. He held out his hand to her.

Britta looked at it, and then at his face.

His eyebrows rose—*Come on*. He continued to hold out his hand.

Warily, she took it. They shared a brief handclasp, palm to palm, then Bennick released her hand. "Take a look."

Britta looked at her palm, found a damp spot on it. Water.

"Oh..." Her mouth stayed open for a second. "Oh, I *saw* that. I saw them shake hands!"

Bennick shrugged. "There you go."

Britta stared at her palm, remembering. Jaegar and the peg-legged man had shaken hands, and then... "He patted my shoulder, Jaegar did. And the next day my maid found a mark on my cloak. She said the fabric had been eaten away." She looked up and met Bennick's eyes. "*That* was it. The poison. It wiped off on my cloak."

Bennick's eyes narrowed. "When did your brother touch you?"

"Oh, maybe... five minutes after he shook hands." Had she unwittingly saved Jaegar's life?

"What about his face?" Bennick said. "See any marks on it? A couple of days later?"

"Marks?" Britta blinked, frowned. She'd only seen Jaegar twice afterwards. Once on the morning of his coronation, and once— "Oh! Blisters. Three of them. Below his eye. Here." She showed him with a finger.

Bennick's face relaxed into a smile. "The Five Moons took."

She hadn't saved Jaegar's life. He was dying. Horribly.

Instead of grief, Britta felt relief.


BENNICK FILLED AN empty waterskin from the billy, lifted Karel's head, and trickled the feverwort and bone-knit infusion into his mouth.

"Are you a poison master?" Britta asked again.

"No."

"Then why do you know so much about healing?" Bennick was a killer; the exact opposite of a healer.

"The sooner a Brother gets better, the sooner he can fight again."

BRITTA SLEPT ALONGSIDE Karel, her blankets spread over them both. The night was cold, almost freezing, but the sides of the wagon sheltered them from the worst of the wind. Towards dawn, Karel became restless, tossing his head. "Britta!" His voice was frantic.

"I'm here." She pushed up to sit, leaned over him. His eyes were still closed. He was dreaming, a nightmare that twisted his face with anguish. "I'm here, Karel," she said, more loudly.

His eyes sprang open. He stared at her for several seconds, then his face relaxed and he slid back into unconsciousness.

Britta sat back on her heels. Had he seen her in the light of the half-moon? Recognized her?

KAREL WOKE TWICE more before the sky lightened, both times distraught, calling her name—woke, and looked at her, and sank back into sleep.

At dawn, Bennick unwrapped himself from his blankets, pulled on his boots, and came across to the wagon, Jaumé at his heels.

"He awake?"

Britta shook her head.

"Thought I heard him."

"Nightmares," she said. "It's the fever."

Bennick climbed into the wagon and felt Karel's face. "Worse'n yesterday. Hoped it would have broken by now."

"If it doesn't break... will he die?" Tears rose in her eyes.

Bennick saw them. He looked amused. "So much agony over whether a person lives or not."

Britta blotted the tears with her sleeve. "Life is important."

Bennick shrugged. "We come, we go."

"Life is important," Britta said, gripping Karel's hand tightly. "And what we *do* with our lives is important. Whether we're kind or cruel. And Karel is *kind*. Kinder than anyone I know. He deserves to live!"

Bennick snorted, a sound of amusement.

Her temper sparked. "I pity you," Britta said contemptuously. "Your lives are empty. *You're* empty. All you do is kill people."

"Pity?" Bennick snorted again. This time, he didn't sound amused.

"'We come, we go,'" Britta said, her tone mocking. "What way is that to live life?"

Bennick's eyes narrowed. His face had gone stiff. *Will he hit me?* But she was too angry to care.

Beside him, the boy crouched, wide-eyed, alarmed, his gaze darting from her to Bennick.

Bennick's face relaxed. He shook his head. "Sentimental maundering. All one can expect from a female. Come on, lad, let's heat up more poultice." He paused on the edge of the wagon, and said,

"That's if her highness still *wants* me to heal him?"

Britta ignored the sarcasm. "Yes, I do."

The boy followed Bennick silently. He glanced back at her once. His expression was impossible to decipher.


BENNICK REMOVED THE poultices once the horses had been saddled. He had more than one face, this man. The smiling face he showed the boy; the cold assassin's face he wore right now.

He stripped the pads of crushed leaves from Karel's upper arm and thigh and retied the bandages, then sat back and observed her for a moment. Britta returned the stare, refusing to be intimidated.

"I killed your brother in Ankeny," Bennick said. "Arrow through the heart." He reached out and tapped her above the heart, so hard it hurt. "But the mages healed him. Next time I kill him, he'll stay dead." He jumped down from the wagon, fastened the tailboard, and strode to his horse.

Britta stared after him, rubbing where his fingers had struck her. Harkeld had been dead. An arrow through the heart.

She shivered.

She understood that Bennick's words were punishment for saying she pitied him.

# CHAPTER EIGHTY-ONE

THE ROADS WERE empty. The farms were empty. The villages were empty. Jaumé kept as close to Bennick as he could. "Is the curse here?" he whispered.

"I reckon so." Bennick didn't seem scared. He was relaxed as he rode, one hand resting on his thigh.

Near noon, they came to a crossroad. A covered wagon waited there, a handful of horses—and two men wearing long, hooded cloaks that flapped in the wind. Bennick stopped looking relaxed. He sat up straight in his saddle and touched the pouch of Stars at his hip.

Jaumé glanced around. Vught and Soll had stiffened too, and Hetchel, driving the wagon.

One of the hooded men moved his fingers in a series of gestures.

The Brothers' postures altered. Still alert, but not ready for battle.

They halted at the crossroad. The man who'd gestured pushed back his hood. Jaumé recognized his sleek black hair and slanted dark eyes. It was Steadfast. But Steadfast was dead in the jungle. He'd seen him die.

"Fortitude," the man said. "And Valor."

The second man nodded and pushed back his hood. He had sleek black hair and slanted eyes, too.

Jaumé stared at them both. He remembered what Gant had told him. *Everyone in the Dominion looks like Steadfast.*

These two men were from the Dominion.

He tried to find differences between them. Fortitude was older than Steadfast had been. Valor had a rounder face.

"You're a week later than Tancred expected," Fortitude said.

Vught scowled. "She's slowed us down."

"Andeol's fallen. Tancred asked us to wait for you. He took the northern route out, week and a half ago, with the Brother from Fenal. Reckoned they'd run into the prince and his party, thin their numbers a bit."

"Tancred and Udo? They'll thin them all right." Vught's grin was sharp and nasty.

Fortitude reached under his cloak and took out a piece of vellum, folded into a small square. "Tancred drew you a map." He handed it to Vught. "No point trying to cut the prince off at Delpy. You're too late. Have to head for the mountains. Try to catch them in the valley. It's going to be touch and go. Today's the last day we were going to wait for you."

Vught nodded, and tucked the map inside his shirt.

"What's in the wagon?" Soll asked.

"Water."

"The curse is here?"

Both men nodded.

"You seen any cursed people?" Hetchel asked, leaning forward on the wagon seat.

368  *The Blood Curse*

"A couple," Valor said. "We killed 'em."

"What're they like?"

"Madder than rabid dogs."

Vught flicked his fingers, the *Let's get moving* gesture. "If the prince is past Delpy, we got to make up time."


FORTITUDE DROVE THE covered wagon. Valor rode alongside Bennick. Jaumé listened to them talk. Valor told Bennick about his last contract, in a place called Noorn, and killing someone called a Sentinel mage. "She got in our way. Cree took her out. Didn't realize she was a Sentinel until later. *Big* mistake. Five of 'em came after us. Got Ferris and Dobin and Cree. *And* Brock. I only got away by a hair's breadth."

Bennick then told Valor about Nolt and the jungle and the breathstealers.

Valor laughed when he heard Bennick had killed the prince, but the witches had healed him.

Bennick's expression was part grin, part scowl. "I'll get the whoreson. Just you wait."

Valor's sideways smile was sly. "Maybe *I'll* get him."

Bennick snorted. "The way you shoot?"

Valor shrugged. "Mightn't come to arrows." He glanced ahead at the wagon carrying the princess and the soldier. "Who's that with her?"

"Armsman. Vught reckons he saw him at the Hook. Reckons he killed Bly."

"Bly?" Valor looked doubtful. "Is an armsman that good?"

Bennick shrugged. "If he was, he's not any more."

"What's an armsman?" Jaumé asked. "Is it a soldier?"

"A personal soldier," Bennick said. "Trained as a bodyguard."

"Better than an ordinary soldier?"

"Meant to be. But not all of them are."

Jaumé wanted to ask more questions, but he looked at Bennick's face and decided not to.

They rode in silence for half a mile, then Bennick said, "It's been easy pickings, here in the Seven. Lots of safe houses. No mages. Don't have to look over your shoulder the whole time."

"Easier than the Allied Kingdoms, that's for sure," Valor said. "Those cursed Sentinels, always interfering... But it makes it more of a challenge, don't you think? You come up against one of them, that's a *true* test of skill. And if you kill one..." Valor grinned, showing his teeth. "There's nothing better than killing a Sentinel."

Bennick considered this, and nodded. "True." His gaze fastened on something on the hillside. "Fancy fresh goat meat for dinner?"

# CHAPTER EIGHTY-TWO

KAREL GREW MORE restless, more frantic, as the afternoon progressed. He tossed and twisted in his bed of blankets, calling her name, gripping her hand fiercely. It was a relief each time his eyes opened and—for a few seconds—he knew he'd found her. His face smoothed free of anguish, his whole body relaxed, and he slept—twenty minutes, thirty minutes—before it started again.

Britta tried to make him drink in the moments when his eyes were open, but he was never fully conscious. He saw her face and recognized her, but that was all. Her pleas that he drink had no effect. By the end of the day, she'd managed to trickle most of the contents of the waterskin into his mouth, but his lips looked parched and he was growing gaunt before her eyes. She could almost see the flesh melting away beneath his skin.

"How long will this go on for?" she asked Bennick, nearly in tears, when they halted for the night.

He shrugged. "As long as it goes on for."

"It's killing him! He's too weak for this. He needs food, broth. Please, let me make him some broth!"

Bennick looked amused. "You know how to cook?"

"I can learn."

Bennick shrugged. "I'll make some broth."


TWO MORE ASSASSINS had joined their party. They had a covered wagon. "Can we move Karel to the other wagon?" she asked Bennick, when he came with fresh poultices. "He'd be more sheltered there. Warmer."

"You want to travel in that? Thought you got sick in a covered wagon."

"Not always."

"Not ever," Bennick said.

Britta ignored this comment. "Can we move him?" The mountains were shrouded in snow cloud and the wind stabbed like icy needles.

Bennick shrugged. "Don't see why not." He turned his head. "Soll! Val! Give me a hand, will you?"

Karel woke when they lifted him. "Britta!" he cried, his expression frantic, and she grasped his hand and said, "I'm here, I'm here."

His eyes clung to her face. She saw relief flood him before he slipped back into unconsciousness.

Britta gathered up the blankets, scrambled down to the ground, and hastily made up a new bed in the covered wagon. Once Karel was settled into it, Bennick unwound the bandages. "Looking good. See?" The comment was to Jaumé, but Britta leaned close to look. "Reckon we're on top of the infection. Poultices are working."

The smell of herbs mixed with the smell of roasting goat's meat. Britta's mouth watered. "The broth?"

"Broths take time. Got to boil the bones for at least an hour."

372 The Blood Curse

"Bones?"

"You boil bones to make broth. The more meat on the bones, the richer the broth."

"Oh," Britta said.

Bennick tied the fresh poultices in place. "Don't know if Vught told you, but we've reached the curse."

The curse? Every hair on Britta's body seemed to stand on end. She shivered, hugged her arms, shook her head. "He didn't tell me."

"Well, now you know. Don't drink anything but water from the barrels. Unless you want to die." Bennick smirked as he said the last words.

Jaumé, kneeling alongside him, didn't smirk. His face was solemn. How old was he? Eight? Nine?

"You shouldn't have brought Jaumé here," Britta said, suddenly angry. "This is no place for a child! He should be somewhere *safe*."

Bennick shrugged. "He chose to come. Didn't you, lad?"

The boy nodded.

"Does he know what you are?" she demanded. "What you'll make him into?"

"He knows. He wants to be a Brother. Don't you, Jaumé?"

The boy nodded again, but his eyes slid away from Britta.

Bennick clapped him on the shoulder. "Come on, lad. You can get in some practice before dinner. That goat'll be a while longer."

Jaumé scrambled down from the wagon and gathered up his bow and small quiver of arrows. Bennick set up a pale log as a target. Jaumé practiced first with the bow, then his throwing knife. The boy was good. Britta could barely see the ghostly shape of the target in the gloom, but Jaumé struck it every time.

She understood that this was a show, for her. Bennick was telling her the boy belonged with the Fithians.

Jaumé sheathed his throwing knife. He fetched a long object wrapped in hessian from the packsaddles. A sword. Britta narrowed her eyes. This was a weapon she could use if she had to. Small and light enough for her to wield. She took note of how Jaumé held the sword, how he stood, how he moved.

Bennick gave instruction patiently. She saw how intensely Jaumé wanted to please him, saw his fierce concentration, saw the way his face lit with joy when Bennick praised him. After the lesson was over, Bennick grinned down at the boy and ruffled his hair. Britta watched thoughtfully. She understood why Jaumé rode at Bennick's side all day, why he sat beside him at the fire, slept alongside him at night. The assassin was father, teacher, friend, protector.

But for all those things, Bennick was also a cold-blooded killer, and Jaumé's place *wasn't* with him.

JAUMÉ PUT AWAY the sword. Britta observed which packsaddle it went in. She wanted that sword.

She'd given her word of honor not to escape, but if she could save Karel, save Harkeld and the Seven Kingdoms...

Some things were worth breaking one's word for.

# CHAPTER EIGHTY-THREE

"WE SHOULD REACH the foothills tomorrow," Rand said, once they'd eaten. "There's a track over the first range, but we can't take the wagon on it. We'll need to go around." He unrolled a map and anchored it with rocks. "See, we're here..."

Harkeld leaned close.

"The anchor stone is between these two ranges of foothills. We need to go around the end of this first range, join with this road here, and follow it up the valley."

"There's a road to the anchor stone?" Justen sounded skeptical.

"It wasn't there three centuries ago. These mountains were the remotest part of Sault. Snowstorms. Wolves. People who ventured into them tended not to return. Hence their name."

Harkeld squinted at the map, trying to read the name written between the saw-tooth serrations of the mountains.

"The Widow Makers," Rand said, and Harkeld's eyes suddenly made sense of the tiny letters. The words leapt out at him, the spikes of W and M and K. "Least, that's what they call them here. Down in Vaere, they're called the Furies.

"Farmers have moved up the valley in the last half-century, so there's a road of sorts. We believe Ivek intended to go deeper into the Widow Makers, but he ran out of time. This was the last anchor stone he made."

"He was caught near here," Serril said. "Beheaded. Burned."

*By my ancestors.*

"Tomorrow, I want a shapeshifter to fly ahead and look for the anchor stone, check everything's all right there, check for Fithians."

"I will," Justen and Innis said at the same time.

Serril shook his head. "I will. That's a strong headwind."

"But—" both Innis and Justen said.

"I'm the strongest flier."

Innis closed her mouth. So did Justen.

"I want you all to be familiar with this map," Rand said. "If anything should happen to Serril and me, you need to know where to go and what to do." He looked up into the darkness, raised his voice: "Petrus? Come down here a minute, will you?"

Serril wrapped one corner of his cloak around his forearm and held it out.

Petrus glided down and landed on Serril's arm. He folded his wings and stared at Rand with yellow owl eyes.

Rand traced the route with his finger again. "South-west, around this range of foothills, then join with this road and head east."

Innis pointed. "Is that a river?"

"Yes. The road follows the river down to Andeol. Now, pay attention. Where the road ends, you need to head north, up into this side valley." He looked around, caught everyone's eyes. "North. Got that?"

Harkeld nodded.

"When you reach the end of the valley, there's a meadow. That's where the anchor stone is. This one's red. It may be under snow. Serril will find that out tomorrow."

"Red?" Harkeld thought back to the two anchor stones he'd destroyed. One had been black, one gray.

"Mostly red. It's sandstone."

"Sandstone?"

Rand tilted his head. "Has no one explained to you how the anchor stones were made?"

"Dareus said..." Harkeld frowned, trying to remember. "He said Ivek anchored the curse in the east, west, and north. And that the stones have been drawing power from the kingdoms they're in."

"True," Rand said. "But there's a lot more to the anchor stones than that." He tapped the tiny cross on the map that marked the anchor stone. "Now, do you all understand how to get there? Petrus? Adel?"

Everyone nodded. Petrus took off from Serril's arm with a great sweep of creamy-white wings, making the flames in the fire bow sideways and then flare high. Rand rolled up the map and put it to one side. "Anchor stones," he said, looking at Harkeld. "What happened is that Ivek took rock from each of the kingdoms—thirteen kingdoms there were, then—and used that to make the anchor stones. So each stone is bound to more than one kingdom. The black stone, that was basalt. It came from Ankeny and Roubos and two of the kingdoms Osgaard seized. Esfaban and..." His eyes narrowed. "Lomaly, I think." He counted on his fingers. "Four kingdoms. The gray was granite. That's Vaere, Sault, Osgaard and... what's that first kingdom Osgaard invaded?"

"Karnveld."

"Vaere, Sault, Osgaard, Karnveld, and some marble from Horst worked through it." He counted on his fingers again. "Nine kingdoms. And the sandstone is from Lundegaard and two more of the kingdoms Osgaard took, the ones west of the desert."

"Brindesan and Meren."

Rand nodded. "Them, and Lundegaard and the Urel Archipelago. All of it red, except for the stone from Urel, which is white and yellow. Thirteen kingdoms, bound to three anchor stones. Extremely complex magic. No stone mage has come close to replicating it."

"Why isn't there a stone mage with us?" Harkeld asked.

"They can't do anything with the anchor stones, except examine them," Serril said. "And they've done that."

"A day to the foothills," Rand said. "A couple of days to go around them. Three days, maybe four, all up. And then we're done."

Harkeld glanced around at the fire-lit faces. Five mages. Six, counting Petrus. *Seven, counting me.*

No one said anything. He wondered if they were all thinking what he was.

*How many of us will be alive in four days' time?*

# CHAPTER EIGHTY-FOUR

BRITTA ATE ROASTED meat dripping with fat and afterwards carefully spread goat grease on Karel's parched lips. Bennick changed the poultices. "I reckon that broth'll be cool enough for him to drink. Fetch the billy, will you, lad?"

Jaumé hurried to obey. The broth was warm, fragrant, glistening with fat.

Bennick filled an empty waterskin and lifted Karel's head. The armsman swallowed a mouthful, then turned his head away.

Bennick tried again—and again, Karel swallowed a bare mouthful.

"Armsman!" Britta said, leaning over him. "I order you to drink!"

Perhaps Karel heard the command. This time, when Bennick pressed the waterskin to his lips, he drank obediently, not one mouthful, but ten, twelve.

"You've got him well-trained," Bennick said. "Like a dog."

# CHAPTER EIGHTY-FIVE

"BED," BENNICK SAID, with a jerk of his head.

Jaumé obeyed. He lay down on his sleeping mat, wrapped himself in his blankets, and pulled the rabbit-fur cap low over his ears, but he didn't close his eyes. He kept his gaze fixed on the campfire, on Bennick drinking the bitter tea the Brothers liked.

How could he close his eyes when Ivek's curse was here?

He almost imagined he could see the curse, see dark shadows creeping across the ground, almost imagined he could hear it, a sound like ants gnawing on grains of dirt. He could definitely smell it. Smoke and blood.

Bennick finished his tea and crossed to the sleeping mats. He picked up his blankets, shook them out, moved his mat close to Jaumé's, so they almost touched. "Go to sleep, lad. Nothing to worry about."

And with Bennick alongside him, he found he could close his eyes.


JAUMÉ DREAMED OF blood and screams, and jerked awake. The night was dark, the campfire a pile of glowing embers. Alongside him, Bennick's sleeping mat was empty.

Panic surged through him. He sat up, clutching his blankets. Had the curse taken Bennick?

He saw the hulking shapes of the wagons, saw the low, dark humps of the Brothers on their mats—Vught and Hetchel and Soll, Valor and Fortitude—but no Bennick.

Fingers tapped the top of his head. Bennick's fingers.

Jaumé's panic evaporated. He knew what the tap meant. *Go to sleep.* He lay back down on the sleeping mat.

Bennick soundlessly moved away. His sleeping mat was empty because he was watchman for this part of the night, guarding them. Keeping them safe.

Jaumé curled up tightly in his blankets, closed his eyes, and slept again.

# CHAPTER EIGHTY-SIX

PETRUS PATROLLED THE plateau, searching for danger, for cursed people, for Fithians. The morning was cold, gray. A layer of clouds spread across the sky, too thick for the sun to break through. An hour into his shift, he found a farmhouse close to the road. Petrus circled, examining it. The farmhouse looked like it had been looted; the windows and doors stood open. It also looked like an excellent hiding place for Fithians. An archer, standing at one of those windows, would be able to pick off passersby with ease.

Petrus changed into a sparrow—dropping several feet in the air—and swooped down to land on the sundial in the yard. He settled his feathers, cocked his head, and looked around, alert, wary.

A sound caught his attention, a brittle *crunch*. Petrus hopped around to face this threat, ready to change into a lion and spring—and relaxed.

A dog, that's all it was. A dog lying in the half-open barn door, chewing on a bone.

The dog was lean, shaggy, larger than a wolf. Petrus looked at the size of its teeth, and decided not to explore the farmhouse in canine form. A sparrow would do just as well. And then he looked more closely at the bone.

It was a human forearm, with the hand still attached.

Petrus recoiled, almost falling off the sundial. He grabbed the air with his wings, caught his balance, steadied himself, but his heart was still beating too fast. He looked at the dog and the bone again, hoping he'd been mistaken... but, no, the bone was a human forearm, and the things at the end were fingers and a thumb.

*All-Mother*, he whispered in his head.

Petrus hopped into the air and cautiously explored the farmhouse and yard. The house was empty, cupboards hanging open, crockery lying on the floor. The yard was empty, too. Which left the barn.

The dog still lay in the half-open barn door, chewing on the bone. Petrus flew warily over its head.

It took a few seconds for his eyes to adjust to the darkness—and then he saw the carcass. Adult, from the size. Male, from the short hair and the large boots it still wore. A rat sat on the man's head, eating what was left of his face. Two more rats were feasting in the cavity of his abdomen. Rats and dog had been busy; the clothing was shredded, little meat remained on the bones.

Petrus jerked his gaze away. He made himself examine the animal stalls and the loft—found nothing—and darted thankfully back out into the yard.

The dog was crunching on something, rolling it around in its mouth. The dead man's thumb, Petrus realized.

He felt his stomach heave—and veered fast out of the yard, flying hard, putting distance between himself and the farm. Half a mile down the road, laboring against the wind, he remembered he was still a sparrow. He changed back into a hawk. His vision sharpened, flying became a lot easier. The nausea didn't alter, though. It sat in his belly.

He had a feeling the memory would stay with him for the rest of his life: the dog chewing the thumb, rolling it around in its mouth, crunching...

# CHAPTER EIGHTY-SEVEN

Midway through the morning, Karel's eyes opened—and stayed open.

"I'm here," Britta said, bending over him. "You found me."

Karel blinked, tried to focus on her. "Princess?" His voice was weak, hoarse.

"Yes." She swallowed a sob of relief and tightened her grip on his hand.

His fingers flexed weakly back, returning the clasp. "Where...?"

"We're in Sault." Could he feel the rattle and jolt of the wagon? Hear the clop of horses' hooves and jingle of their harnesses? "In a wagon."

He frowned. She saw him struggling to form a question, and tried to guess what it was. "You were injured. We're with the assassins."

She saw his alarm. His lips parted.

"We'll escape." Britta bent her head and whispered the words fiercely in his ear. "We'll escape before we reach Harkeld. I promise. Now drink this broth. You must get your strength back."

\* \* \*

KAREL DRANK, AND slept again, and when he woke an hour later he was still lucid.

"What happened?" he whispered.

Britta told him, watching his face, holding his hand. How much did he understand? His cheeks were flushed. His gaze kept drifting away as she spoke.

Still feverish, but better than he had been.

He listened, and then he slept, and when he woke again, he told her with embarrassment that he needed to relieve himself.

KAREL COULDN'T WALK. He could barely stand with help. It took two men, Bennick and one of the new assassins, the one Bennick called Val, to get him down from the wagon.

Watching him, Britta knew that there would be no escape. Not for Karel. She also knew that she couldn't leave him. Abandoning him with the assassins would be the same as killing him, and killing Karel was something she couldn't do.

The three men returned, the assassins half-carrying Karel. His face was tight with pain.

Bennick and Val heaved him up into the wagon. Britta helped Karel lie down, and drew the blankets up. He was shaking. His breathing was shallow, a groan in each exhalation.

"Do you have something for the pain?" she asked Bennick, as he turned back to his horse. "Willowbark?"

"Willowbark? You pamper your pets, highness."

"Do you have any willowbark?" she demanded.

Bennick shrugged. "Maybe. Got no time to brew it now, though. He'll have to wait until nightfall."

"But—"

"He may be your dog, but I'm not." Bennick swung up into his saddle. He didn't see the way Jaumé was looking at him. "He'll have to wait until tonight."

Britta opened her mouth to argue further.

Karel touched her hand. "Leave it, princess. I'm fine."

She turned to him fiercely. "You're not fine!" Tears stung her eyes. "You're hurting."

The wagon jolted forward. Pain spasmed across Karel's face. He seemed to stop breathing for a moment.

She took hold of his hand. "Is it the ribs?"

Karel's face had been flushed only a few hours earlier; now, it was pale. "Yes."

Britta touched his cheek. His skin was damp; he was sweating. Pain this time, not fever. She tried to think of something to distract him with, but he'd heard her story. "Tell me what happened to you, Karel. After I was abducted. How did you find me?"

"Find you? We followed your trail."

"No, silly." She smiled at him. "Tell me it all, from the beginning."

Karel groaned. He inhaled a shallow breath. She saw his eyes narrow, saw him try to remember back. "I saw them." His voice was hoarse, tight with pain. "I saw them carrying you away. I tried to stop them, killed one of them..."

"You killed a Fithian?"

He nodded.

"And then what?" she prompted.

Karel's story unfolded slowly, with ragged pauses. Gradually, his voice became stronger, less hoarse, his grip on her hand less painful. By the time he'd finished, he was no longer sweating and his face had lost its grayness.

"Feel a little better?" she asked, stroking his cheek lightly with her knuckles.

"Yes."

Britta released his hand. "Here, have something to drink."

She helped him drink from the waterskin, then tucked the blankets around him and told him to sleep.

Karel didn't close his eyes. They were dark, serious. "Do you know how they plan to use you?"

She shook her head.

"Highness, you have to escape without me."

"No."

"I can't walk—"

"Karel, I'm not leaving you behind."

"But, highness—"

"No!" she said, her voice sharp. "I'm not leaving you!"

"You have to." His gaze was stern, his jaw uncompromising.

Britta blew out an exasperated breath. "I'm not leaving you, all right? And stop calling me highness. You called me Britta before."

"I did? I beg your pardon, princess. I didn't mean to."

Britta almost thumped him. "This isn't the palace. I'm not a princess any more. Call me Britta."

Karel stared at her, frowning.

"Call me Britta." And then, because his jaw was still stubborn. "That's an order, armsman."

"If you're giving orders, you're still a princess."

Britta did thump him, on his left shoulder, where it wouldn't hurt. "You're as stubborn as an ox—and just as witless!"

Karel gave a short laugh, then groaned, pressing one hand to his ribs.

"Will you please call me Britta?"

He sighed, and capitulated. "All right. But only when no one can hear. Whether you say you're a princess or not, you *are* one, and—"

"No, I haven't been a princess since they cut off my hair." She held up a hand to forestall his response. "And I don't want to be one, Karel. If we get out of this—*when* we get out of this—I'm not going back to King Magnas's court. I want to be *me*, Britta, not a princess wearing a crown."

His expression was dubious. "If you don't go to Lundegaard, were would you go?"

*To Esfaban, with you and Yasma.* And then she remembered— "Oh! I didn't tell you! Jaegar's been poisoned!"

Karel's eyebrows snapped together. "What?"

She rapidly told him what Bennick had said. "Five moons, so he's got three left. And then..."

*And then everything changes.*

"If Jaegar dies, there'll be civil war," Britta said. "Won't there? Unless King Magnas gets there first."

"Half the nobles in the kingdom would make a grab for power." She saw horror and hope mingled on Karel's face. "But if Magnas steps in first... He can claim Osgaard in the boys' names. Take control of the kingdom as regent."

Britta nodded. "And if he does that, he'll break Osgaard up again, give back the annexed kingdoms. And Esfaban will be free."

She saw tears rise in Karel's dark eyes, saw him blink them back.

"We *have* to get out of here!" he said. "We have to get back to Lundegaard and tell Magnas!"

# CHAPTER EIGHTY-EIGHT

THE ROAD PASSED through a small hamlet. The hamlet looked empty, but when Innis landed and changed into a dog, she smelled a human scent. Male. Very recent.

She followed the scent trail cautiously. It led her to a small cottage built of dried mud and stone. Shutters covered the windows. The door was latched.

Innis circled the cottage, sniffing, listening. Her ears told her it was empty; her nose told her that someone was inside.

Fithian?

She circled the cottage a second time. A Fithian would have opened the shutters, the better to launch his ambush... wouldn't he?

Innis shifted into lizard shape. Nervousness tightened her ribcage. *If I'm attacked, I become a lion. Rip out his throat.*

She slipped through the crack underneath the door.

It took a few seconds for her eyes to adjust to the dimness. She saw a fireplace, a table and stools—and an open door into another room.

Innis scuttled across the floorboards and peered into the second room. It was a bedchamber. The bed was wooden, with a mattress and pillows. The blankets were the floor. Nesting in them, like an animal, was a man. All she could see was his forehead and one closed eye. It was enough to tell her he was cursed.

Innis sidled warily closer. The man was cursed, yes, but was he also a Fithian?

Assassin or not, she had to kill him. The wagon would pass through this village shortly, and if he woke, he'd attack.

Innis changed back into herself. For a long, terrifying moment, the room was pitch black— then her eyes adjusted. Faint light leaked through cracks in the shutters. She dimly saw the nest the man had made, dimly saw his forehead, his closed eye.

She reached out and touched his forehead with her fingertips, sent her magic into him, killed him.

It was easier this time—there was a terrible familiarity to it: the rupturing of carotid, jugular, aorta. Innis snatched her hand back, curled it into a fist, pressed it to her chest. Her stomach turned over on itself. Bile burned up her throat. She clenched her jaw, clenched her teeth, and stopped herself from vomiting by sheer willpower.

When she had control of her stomach, she opened the shutters, and unwrapped the man from his blankets. His body was limp, heavy, warm. He was dark-haired, younger than Serril, but older than Petrus. Thirty?

The man was naked from the waist down. Had he raped someone? Been raped? Or simply forgotten what trews were for?

Innis peeled off his sheepskin vest and rough cotton shirt and examined his chest, his arms, the nape of his neck, his back. No five-bladed throwing star had been inked into his skin, no rows of dagger tattoos.

Not an assassin. A peasant.

Innis touched the man's forehead, a gesture of respect, of sorrow, and spoke the words to the All-Mother for him. She covered his body with a blanket, and checked the hamlet a second time. Empty.

She shifted into hawk form and flapped upwards. The hamlet fell away. She saw stony paddocks, hillocks and gullies, looming foothills. Innis followed the dry, dusty line of the road with her eyes, looking for the wagon and the horses. They were a mile from the hamlet, Justen flying guard above.

FAT SNOWFLAKES BEGAN to fall. Harkeld pulled his hood up. Ahead, Rand halted the wagon, jumped down, and crouched, peering at the road.

"What?" Harkeld stopped, too.

"Take a look."

Harkeld dismounted and squatted alongside the healer. "What am I looking at?"

"The snow."

Snowflakes were gathering in the ruts on the road. Harkeld peered closely at them, white and delicate and... shadowed with Ivek's curse. He jerked back, almost lost his balance, and stood hastily. "The curse!"

A brown mare halted alongside them. Its rider looked down. Petrus. And behind him was Adel, leading the packhorses. "Something wrong?" Petrus asked.

Rand straightened. He rubbed a hand through his hair, dislodging snowflakes. "What we expected. Soon as the snow touches the ground, it carries the curse."

"But it's snow, not water!" Harkeld said.

"Most strong water mages have an affinity to water in both its frozen and liquid forms," Adel said.

Harkeld had a sudden, horrible thought. "It won't spread upwards, will it? The curse? To the snowflakes in the air?"

Rand shook his head. "The curse is bound to the soil, not the air." He scuffed a drift of snowflakes with the toe of one boot. "The snow'll only carry the curse once it's touched the ground."

"As long as snow doesn't start falling *upwards*, we're safe," Petrus said. His tone didn't quite manage to be flippant.

"Steam might carry the curse," Adel said diffidently. "If the water it came from did."

Harkeld remembered the boiling pools in Ankeny, and the thick sulfur-scented steam. He shivered.

"No steam here," Petrus said. "Thank the All-Mother."

Rand tipped his head back and frowned up at the sky. "Hope there's not too much of this."


ON INNIS'S NEXT pass over the wagon, Rand waved her down and held his arm out for her to land on. Snowflakes dappled his cloak, his hair, his eyelashes.

"Find us somewhere sheltered for the night. Say, another twelve miles. And Innis... be careful. The snow's cursed once it's on the ground."

Innis dipped her head in a nod, spread her wings, and launched into the air again.

She found a farm at the base of the foothills. The farmhouse was a blackened, burned shell, but the barn was still standing. It had a loft with dusty straw, and a woodpile. "We'll try to reach that one," Rand said, when she told him.

# CHAPTER EIGHTY-NINE

THEY CAME TO a village. Half the houses around the market square had been razed. The stink of smoke was strong. Jaumé rode warily, tensely, pressing so close to Bennick that their legs touched.

"Nothing to worry about, lad. No one alive," Bennick said, but he didn't move away. He let the mare and the pony walk close together.

Long after they'd passed the village, Jaumé could taste the smoke on his tongue. It made him think of Girond burning. He wondered what Girond looked like now. Was the alderman's house still standing? The fishermen's homes? The boatsheds?

As evening approached, they came to a river. On the far side was a range of steep foothills that marched east to the mountains.

Jaumé eyed the river. *Those who drink the water shall thirst for blood. They shall be as wild beasts.* He remembered the yelping laughter he'd heard in Girond.

Bennick squinted at the sky. "Looks like it could snow. We should find some shelter."

"There's farmhouses along the river," Valor said. "Fortified, most of 'em, from what Tancred said.

Meant to be wolves in the mountains, and some kind of tribesmen in those hills."

"Hillmen," Bennick said. "We've met 'em before, haven't we, lad?"

Jaumé nodded, and shivered.

"Course, they'll be dead now," Valor said. "Or cursed."

"Madder than rabid dogs? The hillmen already were. The curse won't've made much of a difference to them."

THEY RODE IN silence for a while, following the river, then Valor asked, "What are we going to do with her and her armsman afterwards?" He pointed at the covered wagon with his chin.

"He's more than her armsman," Bennick said. "He's her lover."

"You reckon?"

"She ran right in front of Vught and a Star to protect him, screeching her head off. You should have seen it."

Valor grunted a laugh.

"And you heard the way he kept calling for her. Definitely lovers." Bennick glanced at the covered wagon. "We got a good hold on her now. She's not going to run without him. And with *her*, we got the prince." There was something in his grin, something cruel, that Jaumé didn't like.

"What're we going to do with them afterwards?" Valor asked again.

"Vught's choice. Kill them. Leave them." Bennick shrugged. "I reckon we should leave them. They won't last long. Probably kill each other, once the curse gets 'em."

Jaumé looked away. He didn't like Bennick when he grinned like that, or when he joked about people dying.

He let the pony drop back, so he couldn't hear Bennick and Valor any more. Jealousy nibbled inside him like a maggot in an apple. He wasn't sure he liked Valor. Bennick talked too much to him, and he made nasty jokes.

As DARKNESS WAS falling, they came to a tall, square building made of stone. The walls were two stories high, with slit-like windows near the top. There were two doors—a small one at the back, by the river and a jetty with an upturned boat—and a large one at the front, solid and iron-studded and as wide as a barn door. "Is it a fortress?" Jaumé asked, tipping his head back and staring up at the high wall.

"A small one," Bennick said.

The door was barred on the inside, but Hetchel brought the uncovered wagon close, and Vught and Bennick stood on it and tossed Valor high. Valor pulled himself up onto the roof, and disappeared. Five minutes, later the big door swung open. "It's empty," Valor said.

They trooped inside—wagons and horses. There was a large, square dirt yard in the center of the fortress. On two sides were rooms with doors and windows, on the third side were stalls for a stable, and the fourth was a barn.

Jaumé gazed around, his mouth dropping open. "It's a farmhouse." A farmhouse inside a fortress.

"The sort of farmhouse you have if you live near hillmen," Bennick said, dismounting.

Valor barred the door again, and they set to work tending the horses. Hetchel explored the house. He came back, grinning, holding up a haunch of smoked ham. "Dinner."

Hetchel built a fire in the middle of the yard, and cut the ham into thick slices and fried it in lard he'd found in the farm pantry. He'd found a heavy iron skillet, too. The ham spat and crackled as it cooked. Jaumé's mouth watered. Bennick heated up the last of the broth for the soldier, and brewed an infusion of bone-knit. "What about willowbark?" Jaumé asked.

Bennick shrugged. "If you can find some, he can have it."

Jaumé ran to the packsaddles and hunted for the leather pouch of dried herbs. He brought it back to Bennick. "Maybe in here?"

Bennick went through the pouch. "That's willowbark."

Jaumé examined the stiff little curls of dried bark. "Will it stop him hurting?"

"A little."

# CHAPTER NINETY

INNIS SWAPPED WITH Justen, dressed, and went to help
with the horses, but Petrus said, "We're good. Go sit
by the fire and get warm." And Prince Harkeld heaved
a packsaddle off a horse and nodded agreement.

Innis helped Adel bring in firewood, then lugged
the bedrolls and blankets up the wooden ladder to
the loft. The straw smelled of sunshine and autumn,
safe things that had nothing to do with blood curses
and death.

Below, Rand and Serril were preparing the meal,
talking in low voices. Innis watched them while she
laid out the bedrolls. What were they saying? Why
did they look so worried?

She climbed down the ladder and crossed to the
fire. Adel crouched there, digging at his palm with
the tip of his knife.

"Thorn? Let me do that."

She sat cross-legged and took Adel's hand. A big
hand, long-fingered, bony. "Relax. It won't hurt."
But Adel didn't relax. She felt his tension, radiating
through his fingers.

Innis sent her healing magic into his hand and
blocked the nerves. A dig with the knife, a squeeze

between fingers and thumb, and the thorn slid out. "See? No pain."

"Thanks." But Adel's tension hadn't eased at all.

Innis studied his face. He looked hollow-cheeked, almost gaunt. "What's wrong?"

"Nothing." Adel pulled his hand free.

Innis recaptured it. "Let me just seal it. What with the curse and all."

Adel shivered, and didn't protest.

Innis healed the tiny wound. It took half a dozen seconds. She didn't release his hand; she let her magic expand into Adel, let herself detect his emotions. Fear rushed at her. It was like a slap on the face. She almost jerked backwards, almost dropped his hand. Adel's fear was so intense that her ribcage constricted and her own heart beat faster.

Innis swallowed and tried to relax, tried to slow her heartbeat. It was impossible with Adel's fear beating at her. "Adel, we're safe here."

Adel shook his head.

She tried to soothe him with her healing magic. *Calm. Relax.* Her awareness of Adel grew. She sensed the jittery panic underlying the fear. And the shame underlying that. The shame was almost as intense as his fear, deep and miserable, curdling inside him.

"We're all afraid, Adel."

His mouth twisted. He shook his head.

"Of course we are! Everyone is. Even Serril and Rand."

Adel shook his head again. His eyes fastened on something past her shoulder.

Innis followed his gaze. Serril. The shapeshifter crossed to Petrus and Prince Harkeld and said something, a pouch of supplies dangling from one hand. Petrus and the prince were tall and broad-shouldered, but Serril was taller, broader.

"Serril might be as big as a bear, but he's still afraid."

"He's not afraid of dying. He's just afraid we'll fail." Adel pulled his hand from hers. "When we get back to Rosny, I'm not going to take my oath."

She stared at him, shocked. "Adel..."

"I should never have trained to be a Sentinel. I'm not brave enough." Tears stood out in Adel's eyes. "Bode asked me to kill him and I couldn't. Serril had to do it for me."

"I couldn't have done it either."

"Yes, you could have. You've changed. You used to be like me, but you're different now. You're like them." A jerk of his head indicated Petrus and the prince, Serril.

Innis was silent for a moment. Adel was right. At the Academy she had been shy, diffident. She remembered Petrus poking her in the back once, pushing her forward when a tutor had asked for a volunteer. *Don't be so timid. You know you can do this better than any of us.* "Maybe I have changed a bit, but the thing is, Adel... I couldn't have killed Bode that night either."

"I'm not taking my oath," Adel said again.

Innis studied his face, saw his shame. "Why did you want to become a Sentinel?"

Adel shook his head, didn't answer. He stared down at his hands, clenched in his lap, bony and white-knuckled.

"I made a mistake in Ankeny, Adel. A *really* big mistake. I broke a Primary Law without permission. For no good reason."

Adel glanced at her.

"When I told Cora, she said that everyone makes mistakes, and that our mistakes make us better Sentinels." *If they don't kill us.* "I know she was right, but I still feel like my mistakes are failures. When I make a mistake, I feel like I've let everyone down. Especially my parents. Even though they're dead."

She had Adel's full attention now.

"And then, Cora asked me why I wanted to be a Sentinel. Was it for me? Or was it because of my parents? And she said it was important that I chose to be a Sentinel for *me*. That otherwise, I shouldn't be one." She held Adel's gaze. "Why did you train to be a Sentinel? For yourself, or for someone else?"

Adel looked away. His face twisted, as if he was trying not to cry.

"If you wanted to be a Sentinel for yourself, then there's no shame in not taking the oath. None at all. And if you're doing it for someone else, then you shouldn't be a Sentinel." Innis touched his tightly clasped hands. "Adel? Why did you train?"

"My village has never had a Sentinel before. They were so proud—" His face twisted even more.

"If you did it for them, then you shouldn't be a Sentinel. You have to do it for yourself."

A tear trickled down Adel's cheek, catching the firelight. He scrubbed it away with the back of one hand.

"Adel, there's no shame in not taking the oath."

"Isn't there?" he said bitterly.

"No. No one will think any less of you. I won't. Petrus and Justen certainly won't. No one at the Academy will. Or any of the Sentinels. And if the people in your village *do*, then tell them to rut off."

Adel uttered a choked laugh. "You don't know them."

"Then don't go back there. You have to do what's best for *you*, Adel. Not them."

Adel looked away from her, at the fire. "They're not bad people. They'd never say anything. They'd just..."

"Adel, there's *no* shame in not taking the oath."

Adel knuckled his eyes, wiped his face. He gave her a lopsided smile and pushed to his feet. "Thanks, Innis."

She watched him go. Adel had always been friendly to her at the Academy. She liked him. He was quiet and self-effacing, but also kind-hearted. Not as brave as Petrus, perhaps, but no coward either.

"Well done."

She looked across the fire and found Rand watching her.

"You think... I said the right thing?"

Rand nodded.

"I don't know if he believed me."

Rand thrust another thorn branch into the fire. "Serril and I'll have a talk with him, once this is all over."

# CHAPTER NINETY-ONE

WITH THE PRINCESS's help, Karel managed to sit up. He gritted his teeth and swallowed a groan. "How do you feel?" she asked. The fire was half a dozen yards distant, but firelight caught her face and showed him the anxious crease between her eyebrows.

"Fine," he lied.

"Fever?"

He shook his head. "Don't think so."

The princess touched his cheek lightly and seemed satisfied with the temperature of his skin. "What about your forehead?"

"Feels tight. Doesn't hurt too much." Which was actually the truth.

"Your arm?"

"It aches. Like someone punched me." More than once, and in more than one place. He hoped it wasn't broken.

"What about your leg?"

"The same." The same, but worse. A deep, raw ache that encompassed his whole thigh, including the bone. When he'd tried to walk, it had felt as if someone was cutting his leg in half with a blunt saw. The savage pain had taken hours to fade.

"Your ribs?"

"They hurt a bit," he admitted. Breathing was agony, moving was agony.

Her frown deepened. She touched his cheek again, then his brow. "I'll ask them to move you inside, tonight. There must be beds."

Move? Karel swallowed another groan. "I'd rather stay here."

The princess shook her head. "You'll be warmer inside—"

"Not much warmer. Not if we put the flap down. I've got blankets. I'll be fine here."

"But—"

"The less I move, the sooner my ribs will heal. And my leg."

The princess stopped arguing. "All right, we'll stay here."

"*You* sleep inside—"

"No."

"Princess... I mean, Britta, if you sleep here with me, they'll think we're, um..." He fumbled for words that wouldn't offend her. "They'll think I'm more than just your armsman."

Her eyebrows twitched up. She looked almost amused. "Who cares what they think?" She turned her head. "Ah, good."

The assassin with the red-blond hair, Bennick, and the young lad, Jaumé, were headed their way.

"Broth," Bennick said, taking a billy from the boy and putting it on the floor of the wagon. "And fried ham." He shoved two plates across the floor towards them.

"What about willowbark tea?" the princess said.

"The deal was that I save your lapdog's life, not pamper him. What do I care if he hurts? He killed two of my Brothers."

"Killed two of your brothers?" The princess snorted, a contemptuous sound. "What do you care if he killed ten of them? We come, we go. Isn't that what you said?"

Karel stiffened. Was she trying to get herself killed?

But Bennick didn't fly into a rage. He grinned. "That's what I said." He plonked a second billy down beside the first, and an empty mug. "Willowbark tea. For your lapdog." He turned and went back to the fire, whistling, Jaumé trotting at his heels.

Karel slowly released the breath he'd been holding. "All-Mother."

"What?"

"I can't believe you said that to him." The humor of it struck him. He began chuckling.

"What's so funny?"

"You, talking back to a Fithian," Karel said, wheezing with laughter and pain. "You never talked back to your father, or Jaegar, but you'll talk back to an *assassin*."

She grimaced. "Father and Jaegar didn't need me alive. The Fithians do."

Karel sobered. "You've changed."

"Yes," the princess said seriously. "I think I have."

With the ragged hair and too-large man's clothing, she should look like a waif. She didn't. "You look strong. Fierce."

"I do?" Pleasure lit her face. "Thank you. Now, which would you like first? The broth or the ham?"

"The willowbark tea."

Britta looked at him sharply.

*Yes, it hurts. A lot.*

He watched her face while she poured tea into the mug. Tea for her lapdog. Britta had heard the insult to *him*, but he didn't think she'd heard the insult to herself, the insinuation Bennick had made. A lady's lapdog. A lady's lover.

If he was strong enough, he'd climb down from the wagon and shove Bennick's head in the fire. As it was, it was all he could do to hold the mug when Britta gave it to him.

# CHAPTER NINETY-TWO

"THE ANCHOR STONE'S right where it should be," Serril said, tapping the *x* on the map. "Easy to find. Far as I can tell, no one's been there for months. No scents. No footprints. Nothing. I had a good scout around, saw some wolf tracks on this first range of foothills, but not many. Maybe one or two loners. There're a lot more wolves in the second range, on the other side of the river. Several packs, I reckon."

Innis examined the map—the short range of foothills between them and the anchor stone; the river; then a second, longer, range of foothills extending west. It looked like a thumb and forefinger, with the river running between them.

"There are people in that second range of hills." Serril pointed. "Here."

"People?" the prince asked.

"Bandits. Or maybe outlaws. They have shaved heads, 'cept for a—I don't know—a *mane* down the middle. I found their camp, way back in the hills. It was pretty big, quite a few families, but crude. Primitive. They either didn't know about the curse, or didn't care. Doesn't look like anyone tried to flee. There's lots of bodies. And I mean *lots*. Some of the men are still alive, running in a pack, down by the river."

The place Serril indicated was three-quarters along the forefinger of hills. Innis measured distance with her eyes. How many leagues away was that? Twenty? Thirty?

"I reckon they'll have killed each other by the time we reach the river, but... they're not the only people out there." Serril looked around the circle of faces, took a deep breath. "There's a party of Fithians."

Innis stiffened. The warm, smoky air in the barn seemed to take on a brittle quality.

"Six men and a young boy, and a wagon. Here." Serril planted his finger on the map. "I reckon they'll reach the anchor stone at least two days ahead of us. So we need to plan what we're going to do. We have four shapeshifters—"

"That'd be suicide," the prince said.

Serril looked at him. "You got a better idea?"

"I'll burn them."

Innis jerked her head round to stare at Prince Harkeld.

"Can you?" Rand asked.

"If I have to."

Innis shook her head. She'd seen the prince's nightmares.

"It would be safer," Prince Harkeld said. "I could do it from a distance, not like the shapeshifters. They'd have to get close. The Fithians will *slaughter* them."

"As I understand it, you burned a Fithian once before," Rand said. "Cora said—"

"I told her I'd never burn anyone alive again. That what she said? Well, I've changed my mind. If it's them or us, I'll do it."

Innis shook her head again.

Rand studied the prince for a long moment, his gaze assessing, shrewd. "Cora said she promised we'd never ask you to do it."

"Well, you're not asking; I'm volunteering."

"Flin..." Innis said. "Last time—"

He turned to her. "Don't."

They matched gazes for a moment. She knew him well enough to hear his unspoken words. *Don't tell them.*

The prince looked tough—the grimy clothes, the dark stubble, the dagger at his belt—but she remembered the way he'd cried in his dreams. That distress had been private, something he'd not known he was sharing. What had Cora called it? *A violation of trust.*

Innis looked down at her hands. This argument was his. She wouldn't interfere.

After a moment, the prince spoke again: "I'm doing it. You think I'd let the shapeshifters try to take on *six* Fithians when I can kill them half a furlong away?"

"I think it will be harder than you realize to burn a man to death in cold blood," Rand said.

"You killed Malle," the prince said flatly. "Serril killed Bode. Petrus killed Gretel. It'd be easier than that."

Innis glanced up, and saw Rand's face twitch in a spasm of pain and then stiffen. She looked at Petrus, at Serril. Petrus's expression was almost identical to

Rand's. The black beard hid Serril's jaw, but the muscles in his cheeks were tight.

For a moment no one spoke, and then Rand said, "Very well, the Fithians are yours."

# CHAPTER NINETY-THREE

IN THE MORNING, Bennick helped Karel down from the wagon. A frost lay on the ground. "Try not to put any weight on that leg," Bennick said. "Don't want the stitches to pull out."

Karel leaned heavily on Bennick, hating that he had to. "Any chance of a stick, or a crutch, or something?"

He felt Bennick shrug. "Jaumé, see if you can find something."

Karel limped awkwardly across the yard, Bennick taking most of his weight. How many ribs had he broken? Every single one, it felt like. They stabbed and grated with each breath, each slow, lurching step.

By the time he'd gone to the privy and limped back across the yard, Karel was shaking, gasping for breath, close to passing out. He looked at the wagon, and almost closed his eyes in despair. *I can't climb up into that.*

"Hard to believe you killed Bly at the Hook," Bennick said. "You couldn't kill a flea now."

"I gutted him," Karel said, gasping, shaking. "And I'll gut you, too, if I get the chance."

"I saved your life, lapdog," Bennick said, his voice amused. "Where's your gratitude?"

"Rut you."

Bennick laughed. Around them, the yard was a quiet bustle of activity. The horses were being harnessed to the covered wagon, the packsaddles buckled into place. It looked as if the open wagon was to be abandoned here; it had been pushed to one side. Jaumé hurried towards them, several sticks clutched in his arms. "Will these do?"

Two were walking sticks, and one was a stave. Karel chose the stave. It was strong and sturdy and he could lean his full weight on it without it buckling. Then, Bennick and the princess helped him climb up into the wagon. It hurt as much as he'd feared. For a moment he lost track of where he was—the world narrowed to the struggle to breathe, the struggle to cling to consciousness. When the wagon came into focus again, they were rattling out through the gate.

The princess had tucked his blankets around him. She was holding his hand. "It hurts a lot, doesn't it?" she said.

"Sometimes." His voice sounded rusty. "It's better now, though." Better, but not a lot. He tried to find something to concentrate on, something that would take his mind off the pain. "Would you mind telling me how you got here again? I don't remember it all."

Karel remembered even less than he'd thought. He forgot how much breathing hurt as he listened to Britta describe her journey. She'd tried to throw herself out of her cabin window? Been manacled to the floor? But it was her account of almost drowning in the river that appalled him the most. He'd *seen* that river. Seen the foaming cascades, seen the fierce chasm the river flowed into. She'd jumped into *that*? He couldn't comprehend the courage it had taken— or the desperation.

When Britta finished, he stared at her. She'd almost succeeded in killing herself twice. "Britta..." He was at a loss for words, horrified.

She was even braver and more resourceful than he'd thought. *Terrifyingly* brave and resourceful.

"What?" she said.

Karel tried to find words that would express his pride in her, and not his terror at how close she'd come to death. "You didn't need me to rescue you. You're capable of doing it by yourself."

She pulled a face and shook her head.

Karel tightened his grip on her hand. "You have to escape, Britta. Soon."

"We will."

He shook his head. "No. *You* have to escape."

"What?" Her expression became horrified. "Leave you? No!"

"You have to." He said the words as if they were an order. "You have to leave me and *go*. Head west, get ahead of the curse. I know you can do it—"

She pulled her hand free. "No."

"I'll create some kind of diversion—"

The princess placed her hand over his mouth. Her face was fierce, her eyes bright with tears. "Karel, I'm not leaving you. They'll *kill* you." And then she pressed her face into his left shoulder, and began to cry.

"Britta..."

"I won't leave you," she said, her voice choked with tears. "I *can't*."

Karel held her close, stroking her hair. His ribs ached, his right arm ached, but most of all, his heart ached. *I love you, Britta.*

Her tears were because she was afraid; and because he was her armsman and she didn't want him to die, not because she loved him.

Karel stroked the princess's hair, and felt his heart ache, and knew that once she stopped crying, he had to persuade her to escape without him.

# CHAPTER NINETY-FOUR

THEY WOKE TO blue sky and sunshine and a foot of snow. Oily curse shadows lay on the snow, puddling in the dips and hollows. "Be extremely careful," Rand warned. "If any of that snow gets flung up... if you inhale it..."

Harkeld helped hitch the horses to the wagon and lead them from the barn. Everyone mounted: Justen and Petrus flew overhead. The wagon rattled across the yard, negotiated the bend into the road—and halted. Rand, driving it, jumped down. "That didn't feel right. Something wrong with the back wheels." He strode back, crouched, peered under the wagon.

"For the All-Mother's sake, be careful," Serril said, dismounting. "That snow..."

Harkeld watched as both mages cautiously examined the back wheels of the wagon.

"Axle," Serril said, straightening. "Lost a few bolts. Looks ready to fall off. Let's get it back into the barn, unhitch the horses. We're going to have to fix it before we can go anywhere."

They searched for the bolts in the yard, in the barn. Adel found one, and Innis another, but two more bolts were nowhere to be found, and all four nuts were missing. "Must've fallen off on the road yesterday," Rand said, shoving a hand through his hair. "Rut it."

They went through the barn and the ruins of the farmhouse, looking for tools, looking for something to replace the missing nuts and bolts with. "I'll fly back to that last village," Serril said. "There was a smithy—"

"No need," Adel said. "Look what I've found." He'd been rooting through the clutter of broken farm implements and old buckets in the farthest corner of the barn. He held out a leather bucket. It held a jumble of nails, nuts, tacks, latches, hooks, hinges, bolts, and clasps.

"All-Mother bless you!" Serril said. He took the bucket, emptied it on the floor, and rummaged through the contents. "Here. I think these are what we need." He crossed to the wagon, slid under it. "Yes. These fit. Rand, where's that wrench?"

"Shouldn't we unload the wagon first?" Adel asked diffidently. "The barrels are heavy. What if it collapses?"

"Take too much time to unload it all." Serril's voice came hollowly from beneath the wagon.

"No, he's right," Rand said. "Better to lose half a day than lose you."

Serril rolled over, grumbling.

Harkeld frowned at the back wheels. "Are those wheels splaying?" He bent to look more closely.

The wagon gave a tiny half-inch lurch, like a drunk man trying to find his balance.

"Serril, get out from under there!" Harkeld yelled, but the sound of the wagon collapsing swallowed his voice. The back wheels came off. The rear of the wagon hit the ground with a *crack* that made the stone floor shudder. The tailboard fell open. Harkeld scrambled out of the way as barrels tumbled and rolled, splintering, spilling water.

Serril's legs protruded from beneath the tailboard.

"Get it off him! Get it off him!" Adel screamed, hauling at the wagon.

Harkeld grabbed the closest edge, but something shoved him aside. An oliphant. The creature wrapped its trunk around the end of the wagon and heaved.

Harkeld seized Serril's legs and hauled him out. The shapeshifter lay face down, unmoving. "Is he alive?" But even as he asked, he saw Serril's head twitch slightly.

Innis crouched alongside him. "Get him off the ground. The water's cursed now."

Wood groaned and cracked as the oliphant— Petrus or Justen, he couldn't tell which—lowered the wagon. Harkeld took a careful grip of Serril's legs, and together he and Adel lifted the shapeshifter and carried him to the back of the barn, staggering under his weight.

"Here." Innis hurriedly spread her cloak on the stone floor.

"Face down?"

"For now, yes."

They lowered Serril, grunting with effort. Innis knelt and cupped Serril's head in her hands.

"All-Mother!" Adel said suddenly, and hurried back to the wreckage of the wagon.

Rand half-lay amid the splintered remains of the barrels. The healer was clutching his leg, an agonized grimace on his face. Petrus crouched alongside him, naked. "Get away from that water, Petrus!" Adel yelled. "Now!"

"But—"

"*Now*. And don't walk! Fly. You get one splinter in your foot and you're done for."

Petrus shifted into a sparrow and flew to the rim of one broken barrel, perching there.

"Come on, Flin." Adel crossed to Rand, treading carefully. "Don't slip."

They crouched beside the healer. He was sweating with pain. "Broken leg?" Harkeld asked.

"Kneecap and shin," Rand said, his words a groan.

"Flin and I'll carry you." Adel glanced at Harkeld. "You got any cuts on your hands?"

Harkeld checked his hands. "No."

They carried Rand to the back of the barn and put him alongside Serril.

"Help me turn Serril," Innis said. "Try to keep his spine straight. I'll hold his head."

They rolled Serril over carefully. His body was as heavy and limp as a dead man's, but his eyes were moving. They focused on Innis's face. "How bad?" he asked, his voice a hoarse whisper.

"Spine broken in three places."

Harkeld saw denial on Serril's face—and then, grim acceptance. "You have to leave me. Let me die."

Innis sat back on her heels, her expression appalled. "No!"

"Can you heal him?" Harkeld asked.

"Yes."

"How long will it take?"

"A couple of days."

"Then we're staying." Harkeld pushed to his feet. "Come on, Adel. Let's get a fire going."

"The curse—" Serril said.

"Rut the curse!" Harkeld said. "I'm not letting you die!"

"You have to."

"No!" Harkeld yelled, his voice echoing in the barn.

"Son, we've no choice—"

"Horseshit!" he said fiercely, leaning over the shapeshifter. "What about your wife and children? Don't you want to see them again?"

The muscles in Serril's face tightened. Harkeld saw anguish in his eyes.

"We're staying until you're healed," Harkeld said flatly. "Come on, Adel, let's get that fire going."

Adel climbed to his feet.

"How much water's left?" The voice was Rand's, wheezy with pain.

A sparrow fluttered down, and shifted into Petrus. "Half a barrel."

Half a barrel. Harkeld glanced at Adel and saw the same realization on the water mage's face. *We're going to run out.*

"We'll go over the hills," Petrus said. "Flin and me. The rest of you can stay here."

Harkeld met Petrus's eyes. "Over the hills? Can we?"

Petrus nodded. "There's a track. We'll take a few waterskins, leave the rest of the water behind. We'll be at the anchor stone in two days."

*And I can end the curse before the half barrel is empty.* Relief swelled inside him. "Yes. Let's go."

He turned towards the front of the barn, urgency thrumming in his blood. They had to move *fast*.

"No," Rand said. "You'll take Innis with you, and Justen."

"And me," Adel said.

Harkeld swung back. "But Serril—"

"I can heal him. And myself. It'll take a little longer, is all."

"But—"

"You'll go over the hills, but you'll take as much protection as possible. And a healer." Rand's voice was weak, but filled with authority. "Now, go outside and tell Justen what's happening. And if someone could help me into dry clothes, I'd be grateful."

# CHAPTER NINETY-FIVE

THEY CAME TO a crossroad and halted. It had snowed here overnight. There was snow on the roads and paddocks, snow in the ditches, snow on the branches of the gnarled old tree standing at the junction.

Vught unfolded the map Fortitude had given him, studied it for a moment, then pointed left. "That's the road from Delpy. The prince'll come that way."

Jaumé heard the words with a jolt of alarm. He peered anxiously along the road. It was empty as far as he could see.

He craned his neck and looked around. They'd reached the end of another range of foothills. The hills ran back to the mountains, steep and bleak. One thin snow-covered road came from the left, around the end of the hills. The road from Delpy. The one the prince would take. It joined the road they were on, heading for the mountains, following the river.

"Unless he's ahead of us," Fortitude said. He slid from his saddle, walked to the middle of the crossroad, crouched, and made as if to brush the snow aside with his hand.

"Careful," Bennick said. "The snow could be cursed."

Fortitude glanced up, his black eyes unreadable.

Bennick shrugged. "What's snow but frozen water?"

Fortitude stood. He began pushing snow aside with his boot.

Cursed snow? Jaumé's toes curled inside his boots. He shuddered, and hunched into his sheepskin jacket, and hoped Bennick was wrong. There was snow *everywhere*.

Bennick had his spyglass out. He looked along the road to Delpy. "Nothing."

"And nothing here," Fortitude said. He'd cleared a strip across the road and was examining the ground. "Nothing fresh."

"We're ahead of them," Hetchel said.

"Shall we use her here?" Soll asked. "It's just about perfect. There's even a tree in the right place."

Kill the prince here? Jaumé's heart gave a little skip of horror.

Vught examined the crossroad and the hills, the gnarled tree. He studied the map again, and rubbed his chin. Jaumé heard the harsh scratch of his whiskers. "They might go over the hills. Tancred's marked a foot trail. We can't risk it. We'll use her at the stone. Doesn't matter what route the prince takes, he'll end up *there*. We'll set up a welcome for him." He grinned his shark's grin.

Jaumé glanced at Bennick. He was grinning, too.

"How far to the stone from here?" Soll asked.

"We'll get there tomorrow," Vught said, and he looked even more like a shark.

# CHAPTER NINETY-SIX

THE TRAIL ZIGZAGGED upwards, winding its way around rocky outcrops and between black-trunked trees that looked like firs, but had lost their needles. Harkeld had never seen trees like them before, but Adel had. "Larch," he said. "We have them at home." Where the snow had melted, the ground was orange with larch needles.

Drifts of snow lay along the track, and on top of the snow lay the curse shadow.

The track became steeper. The horses began to have difficulty. Harkeld dismounted. "Let's lead them. Spread out, though. Leave enough distance between us so that if a horse kicks up some snow, no one gets a mouthful."

The larch needles were as slippery as the snow, Harkeld discovered. He climbed, slipping and sliding, sweating, swearing, panting. They had a mount and packhorse each, traveling light, traveling fast. If this slow uphill laboring could be called fast.

He stopped to catch his breath, to wipe his face, to unsling his waterskin and trickle some precious, uncursed water into his mouth.

Two zigzags ahead was Justen, and one zigzag behind, Innis. Trailing last was Adel. Harkeld stoppered his waterskin and stared down the wooded slope. Adel had let go of his horses. He was running up the track.

Harkeld couldn't see Adel's face—too many tree trunks, too much slanting light and shade—but he knew something was wrong. It was in the way Adel moved. There was nothing gangly or awkward about him, nothing puppyish. He ran like a predator. A wolf intent on his prey. Loping fast.

"Innis!" Harkeld called sharply.

"What?" She halted and looked up at him.

He ignored the track, ploughing through snow and larch needles to reach her. "Get back. Into the trees."

Above, a hawk screamed. Petrus arrowed down, landed on the track in front of them, and changed into a lion. Did he think he was going to rip out Adel's throat? Maul to death someone he'd trained with?

"No!" Harkeld shouted. "Get back, Petrus! I'll do it."

Adel was half a zigzag away now, running fast. He could see the water mage's face. See the thick curse shadow. See the snarl and the madness.

"Petrus, get out of the way!" Harkeld bellowed. "Or I'll burn you, too."

The lion stepped to one side of the track and crouched there, growling, tail twitching.

Harkeld raised his hand. *All-Mother, forgive me.*

He summoned the hottest fire magic he was capable of. Adel wouldn't die screaming like the assassin he'd burned in the gorge. His death would be instantaneous.

*Burn.*

Adel flared alight in a white-hot *whoomp* of flame. He didn't scream. One moment he was running, the next he was gone. No blackened, twisted body lay on the track. All that remained of Adel was ash, blowing in the wind.

Harkeld lowered his hand.

The silence lengthened—ten seconds, twenty seconds—then the lion turned its head and looked at him. It padded across to him and changed into Petrus.

They looked at each other for a long moment, and then Petrus gave a short nod.

Harkeld swallowed, and nodded back. He was shaking inside. If he spoke, he was afraid he might cry.

He heard someone running downhill towards them. Justen. He didn't turn to look. His eyes were fixed on the spot where Adel had been.

Innis slipped a hand into his.

Justen reached them, panting. "What happened?"

"Adel got the curse," Petrus said.

"How?"

"Don't know," Petrus said. "He slipped on some snow a minute ago. But he got right back up. His curse shadow was fine then."

Harkeld gripped Innis's hand tightly. He found control of his voice. "Maybe inhaled some snow."

"Maybe."

No one seemed to want to move. The terribleness of Adel's death struck him. There was no body to bury. It was as if Adel had never existed. *I didn't just kill him. I obliterated him.*

"We need to say words for him," Innis said.

But saying words for Adel, giving him to the All-Mother's care, didn't ease the sense of terribleness. Nor did walking back down the track to capture Adel's horses. Harkeld followed Adel's footprints back up the zigzags. Big footprints, long strides... that just simply vanished.

"You all right?" Innis asked.

Harkeld looked down at the last of Adel's boot marks. "It was better than Petrus doing it."

He crouched, and laid his hand on the final footprint. *Forgive me, Adel.*

# CHAPTER NINETY-SEVEN

JAUMÉ STAYED CLOSE to Bennick. The slow, placid river frightened him. The water in it was cursed, and his imagination told him that if he got too close, it would reach out with thin, watery arms and touch him and he would become as mad as Da. He tried to ride with Valor and Bennick between him and the river. The snow scared him, too. What if Bennick was right? What if the snow on the ground *was* cursed?

They were heading up a valley, with foothills on both sides and mountains ahead, and the valley and hills and mountains were almost as frightening as the river and the snow, because the curse stone was somewhere close by, and if the Brothers reached it before the witches, they were going to kill Prince Harkeld.

*I have to stop them.* But how?

The only thing he could think of was the feverwort roots. If the Brothers were ill, they'd have to stop. And maybe the princess and her soldier could even escape.

But if he did that and Vught found out...

Nolt had been tough, but Vught was tougher. He had an edge of cruelty Nolt hadn't had.

Vught would kill him, if he found out.

Agitation gnawed in Jaumé's chest. He didn't know what to do. His mind kept returning to the feverwort and its pale roots—

Vught, riding in front, gave a shout. The wagon halted. Bennick and Valor spurred their horses ahead. Jaumé's pony trotted to catch up.

"People on the road," Vught said. "You carrying that spyglass?"

Bennick fished it out from under his cloak. He extended it, held it to his eye, looked for a long moment. "Hillmen," he said, offering the spyglass to Vught.

Vught peered through it, and grunted. He gave the spyglass back to Bennick. "Six of 'em. We'll use bows. Bennick and..."

"Me," Valor said.

They rode at a slow trot, the wagon trundling behind them, and behind that, the packhorses. "I'm going to get all six," Valor told Bennick. "While you're still fumbling for your first arrow, so you may as well not bother."

Bennick snorted. "You? I'm twice as fast as you."

"Twice?" This time it was Valor who snorted. "You think you're better than you actually are. Always been your problem."

Bennick wasn't offended. He grinned. "All right, then. Let's see who's fastest. Three each."

Valor grinned, too. "You're on."

Jaumé looked away. They made it sound like a game, killing people.

\*   \*   \*

MOUNTED AND BEARING weapons, the hillmen had been terrifying, but they were even more terrifying running in a pack, naked and unarmed, their skulls shaved except for long, matted manes of hair. They looked inhuman. Wild beasts, not men. They bounded through the snow, each straining to pass the others. Their eyes bulged from their skulls. Sinews stood out in their throats. They made no wolf howl this time. Their eagerness to kill was savage, silent.

The Brothers halted. Jaumé unsheathed his throwing knife and gripped it nervously. He glanced back. Soll was with the packhorses. Vught and Fortitude had gone back to the wagon. Did they think the princess might try to escape now?

Bennick and Valor dismounted. Bennick was grinning. He nocked an arrow, drew the bowstring back until his fingers touched his jaw. "Ready?"

"Ready."

Bennick released the arrow—reached for another one—and another one.

It was over before Jaumé had time to draw breath. The hillmen lay dead. Silence echoed between the hills.

Bennick lowered his bow. "I won."

"Did not—"

"One of yours is still alive." Bennick pointed, and Jaumé saw he was right: one of the hillmen was twisting on the ground.

"Rut it." Valor slung his bow over his shoulder and trudged through the snow. He took his knife from its sheath, crouched, and grabbed the man's mane of hair.

The hillman didn't try to pull away; he lunged, like a snake striking, his teeth fastening on Valor's hand.

Jaumé yelped and almost dropped his knife.

Valor didn't yelp or drop his knife. He put his knee on the hillman's throat, pressed down until the man's jaws opened, yanked his hand free, then wrenched back on the mane of hair and sliced the arching throat in a quick movement.

Jaumé looked hastily away. He sheathed his knife. When he looked back, Valor was climbing to his feet. He shook his hand, spraying blood.

"I'll get a bandage," Jaumé said. He slid off the pony and ran back to the packhorses.

He was rummaging through a packsaddle, when he heard a shout. He looked up. Bennick and Valor were fighting, grappling with one another, arms locked, swaying.

Jaumé watched with his mouth open. He saw Hetchel leap down from the wagon and pull them apart, saw Valor turn on *him*, saw Valor and Hetchel roll in the snow. And then Soll was there, too, and Fortitude and Vught, and they were all fighting.

And then he understood. It was the curse.

Someone screamed. A high, mad sound. Vught slashed at the ground with his sword, and the screaming stopped. Only Vught and Bennick were standing. The other Brothers were lying down. Dead?

Vught threw away his sword. Bennick turned and jogged towards Jaumé.

*Is he coming for me?* Panic flared inside him. Jaumé fumbled for his bow, hastily nocked an arrow, and drew the bowstring. His heat hammered in his chest.

But Bennick paused at the back of the wagon and said something, a brusque order, before jogging back to the packhorses. He stopped and looked at Jaumé, at the nocked arrow, and gave a curt nod. "Good lad."

Jaumé stared anxiously at his face. Bennick looked hard-eyed and grim, but not mad.

He lowered his bow. "The curse got Valor?"

"And Valor got Hetchel, or the snow did. And they got Soll and Fort."

"But... but Valor didn't drink the water."

"He was bitten. Seems that's enough."

"He didn't bite you?" Jaumé asked anxiously.

"No." Bennick's face relaxed fractionally. He reached out and ruffled Jaumé's hair. "Vught and I are fine. Now, I need you to ride with the packhorses while I drive the wagon. Can you do that?"

Jaumé nodded.

"Good lad. Go fetch your pony."

Jaumé hurried to obey. He tried not to look at the dead Brothers, but his eyes kept turning that way. He saw that Vught hadn't pointed the Brothers to face north, or taken their pouches of Stars to send back to Fith. Bennick hadn't gathered the arrows from the hillmen, and Vught's sword lay half-buried in the snow, where he'd flung it, blood on the blade.

Jaumé scrambled up on his pony, trying to figure out why. Were they afraid they'd catch the curse if they touched any blood?

*If it doesn't snow again, Prince Harkeld and the witches will see the bodies and know we're ahead of them.* He glanced at the sky. It was gray. The kind of gray that brought snow.

# CHAPTER NINETY-EIGHT

"FOUR OF THEM dead," the princess said, peering out between the flaps. "Looks like they killed each other."

"The curse?" Karel asked.

"Must have been."

He thought about that for a moment, while the wagon rattled and jolted. The Fithians knew not to drink the water. They were smart, cautious—and yet in a matter of minutes, the curse had got *four* of them. And then he stopped thinking about *how* and *why*, and started thinking about what it meant. Four dead. "There are only two left."

"Yes." Britta crawled back to him. "Bennick and Vught. And Jaumé."

*Much better odds.*

"If I set the wagon on fire and distract them, you can take one of the horses and—"

"No."

THEY WERE STILL arguing when the wagon lurched to a halt. The princess peered out again, and then held the flap back for Jaumé. The boy scrambled up into the wagon. He had two empty waterskins slung over his shoulder and a bundle under one arm. "Lunch."

Jaumé dumped the waterskins and pouch on the floor, turned to go, and paused. He looked back at the princess. "Vught reckons we'll get to the curse stone tomorrow."

And then he jumped down from the wagon.

Karel and the princess looked at each other. "Was that a warning?" she asked.

"I think so."

The wagon lurched forward again.

The princess opened the pouch. "Dried goat's meat. Are you hungry?"

The pouch was full. Enough meat to feed ten men. Karel looked at the pouch, and at the waterskins, and at the barrels of water. "He wants you to escape."

Britta frowned swiftly. "What?"

"We already have two waterskins, and yet he gives us two more. *And* enough meat for a week. And tells us we'll reach the curse stone tomorrow. He wants you to escape, Britta." He pushed up to sit, ignoring the pain from his ribs. "If he helps us, we can do it. I can set fire to the wagon, and while Vught and Bennick put it out, *you* take a horse and go. Jaumé can let the other horses loose, scatter them. That'd give you a head start. If you get a couple of miles' lead, they'll never catch you."

"But what about you?"

"Forget about me."

"But—"

"Britta, didn't you hear what he said? Vught reckons we'll reach the curse stone *tomorrow*."

Britta clutched the pouch, distress furrowing her face.

"You've got to escape. Today or tonight. If Jaumé helps…"

Karel rubbed his face with his left hand, trying to think. It all hinged on the boy. *Maybe I can persuade Jaumé to go with her? She'd be safer.* "You said Jaumé has a small bow? How big is it?"

Britta put down the pouch and silently showed him with her hands.

"If my right arm's strong enough, I could kill Vught and Bennick—"

"Jaumé will never help you kill Bennick. He loves him."

"But I could kill Vught…" *And that would leave just me and Bennick.* No question who would win *that* contest, but the princess would be gone. She couldn't be used as bait to kill Prince Harkeld. The Ivek Curse would be broken, the Seven Kingdoms saved. And Britta would live.

A wagon fire. The bow. Horses let loose.

Ideas spun in Karel's mind. Possibilities that hadn't been there half an hour ago.

It all hinged on the boy.

# CHAPTER NINETY-NINE

THE MOUNTAINS DREW nearer. Peaks as sharp and white as wolf's teeth speared the gray sky. Jaumé saw crags and ridges and gullies. The valley they rode up narrowed. Steep foothills crowded close on either side. Everything was white or black or gray—the mountains, the hills, the trees, the road, the abandoned farmhouses, even the river, with its black water and white ice-rimed banks. Wind blew from the mountains, ice-cold, ice-sharp, but other than the river and the wind, nothing moved.

The emptiness made Jaumé shiver. It gave him a dull, hollow ache in his chest.

In the late afternoon, Vught halted at a fortified farmhouse. It was like the one they'd stayed at last night: square, windowless, a jetty by the river, and a wide, iron-studded door facing the road.

"Give me that spyglass," Vught told Bennick. "I want to see what's up ahead."

The solid wooden door was barred from the inside, but Vught climbed up on the wagon seat, and put one foot in Bennick's cupped hands, and Bennick heaved Vught high enough to catch hold of the top of the wall.

Vught swung himself up, grunting with effort, and walked across the roof and put the spyglass to his eye, peering up the valley.

Jaumé looked at the mountains, at the sky, at the desolate white and black and gray emptiness. He hoped they were going to stop here.

"We'll keep going,' Vught called down.

He didn't swing down off the roof, but disappeared from view. A couple of minutes later, Jaumé heard the rasp of a door bar being removed, and one half of the big door swung open. Vught came out. He carried slab of ham in one hand and a string of dried sausages in the other. "There're a couple more farmhouses ahead," he told Bennick. "We'll stop at one of them for the night."

THE NEXT FARMHOUSE hadn't been shut up. One half of the main door stood open. The air smelled faintly of old smoke.

Jaumé stared at the open door and smelled the smoke and felt his skin crawl. Something bad had happened here.

Vught turned in his saddle and signaled to Bennick.

Bennick jumped down from the wagon. He drew his sword.

Jaumé watched with horror as Bennick trod through the snow and eased cautiously through the door. He wanted to run after Bennick and stop him. He had a sudden, terrible certainty that something dangerous lay on the other side of that half-open door.

He almost scrambled down from the pony, but a glance from Vught stopped him. He stayed where he was, dread squeezing his chest.

And then he noticed that the only tracks in the snow were Bennick's. Had Vught noticed that?

Of course he had. Vught noticed everything. His eyes were as sharp as knives.

Bennick emerged from the door. His sword was sheathed. "Been burned," he said. "Couple of days ago. It's just a shell."

Vught nodded. He glanced at the darkening sky. "We'll go on to the next one."

THE NEXT FARMHOUSE had been burned, too, but they brought the wagon and horses into the yard, where the high stone walls gave shelter from the wind. The charred remains of barn and stables and living quarters made Jaumé uneasy. Had the farm been empty when it burned, or were there dead people in the blackened rubble?

It didn't smell like a campfire, or a stubble fire. It smelled of lots of different things, some burned, some rotting. The burned-and-rotting odor made him think of Girond, and Mam lying dead on the floor, and Rosa screaming.

Jaumé set to work unsaddling the horses, but his gaze kept sliding to the wagon, and he could almost hear Da speaking to him in his head. *You got to destroy the curse, son. You got to do what you can.*

Bennick and Vught heaved the door shut. Part of it was burned, so they took a great, fallen beam and wedged it across the hole. The back door out to the jetty wasn't broken. Jaumé crossed to it, opened it, looked out at the river. An upturned rowboat lay on the jetty. He closed the door again, drew the bar across, and went back to the horses.

The packsaddles were too heavy for him to remove, so he built a fire and took a pot and climbed up into the wagon to get water.

"Jaumé!" The princess gripped his arm. "Did you mean what you said, about reaching the stone tomorrow?"

"That's what Vught said."

The princess released his arm. She glanced at her soldier. "Jaumé," the man said quietly. "Will you help her escape? Please?"

Jaumé clutched the pot tightly. He heard Da's voice in his head. *You got to do what you can, son.* "I'll put feverwort root in their tea tonight. It'll make them both sick. So you can escape."

The princess's mouth opened, and then closed. She exchanged another glance with her soldier. "Feverwort root?"

"It's an emmytick."

The princess nodded. "I read about it in the *Pharmacopeia*. Do you think it will work? Is it strong enough?"

"The aldersman's son ate a little bit." Jaumé prized the lid from one barrel. "He couldn't get out of bed for two days."

The princess took hold of her soldier's hand. "If they're both sick, then you can come too, Karel. And you, too, Jaumé!"

Jaumé shook his head. "If Bennick's sick, I need to look after him."

"He'll be all right, Jaumé. You don't have to stay with him."

"Yes, I *do* have to stay with him!" Jaumé said fiercely. "He looks after me, and I look after him. That's how it works!" And for a reason he didn't understand, there were tears in his eyes.

"Stay with him, if you must," the soldier said.

Jaumé blinked back the tears and nodded. He ladled water into the pot.

"We'll take the wagon," the princess said. "I can drive it—"

"They've barricaded the door," Jaumé said. "With a big beam. You'n me couldn't move it."

Her frown was swift. "Then how can we escape?"

"There's another door, out to the river. And there's a jetty. And a rowboat."

There was a moment of silence, and then the princess said, "Rowboat?"

Jaumé nodded.

"But... the curse."

"The river's real calm. If you don't row, if you just steer with an oar and let yourself drift, you won't splash any water on you."

The princess shook her head, her expression appalled.

Jaumé finished filling the pot and put the lid back on the barrel, jamming it in place. "Boats are easy. Easier than horses. And you don't have to rest them. Vught'll never catch up with you."

But he could tell from the princess's face that she didn't think boats were easy, and that she was afraid of the water. He was suddenly angry with her. How could she be a coward now?

"You have to go!" he said, stamping his foot. "Or they'll use you to kill your brother and the curse will just keep *killing* people."

"I know," the princess said. She pressed her hands to her face.

"Will a horse fit through that other door?" the soldier asked.

Jaumé nodded. "Yes."

"Britta, take a horse and go."

She looked at the soldier, lowered her hands, and asked, "Can you ride?"

The soldier shook his head. "Couldn't get up on a horse, much less stay on it."

"But you could get into a boat?"

The soldier hesitated. "Maybe."

"And lie down, while it floats," Jaumé said, lifting the heavy pot. "You could do that, couldn't you?" He wanted the soldier to go. If he stayed, Vught or Bennick would kill him. "Bennick reckons the snow on the ground is cursed, too."

The soldier frowned, his black eyebrows winging together. "He could be right."

The princess blew out a breath. "All right, we'll take the boat."

# CHAPTER ONE HUNDRED

THEY ONLY PUT up one tent. "I think we should sleep as wolves tonight," Innis said. "It's safer." She glanced at the prince. "Do you mind sharing a tent with wolves?"

He shook his head.

She studied his face. He looked weary, grim.

Rand had sent them with Prince Harkeld for protection, but it was more than that. If the prince became cursed, someone had to kill him and take his hand and blood to the anchor stone. *That's why he sent us all with him.*

The prince wasn't stupid. He'd have figured it out.

Petrus landed. "We need to check on the assassins. See where they are. You want to do it now, Justen, while I keep watch here?"

"I'll do it," Innis said.

Both Petrus and Prince Harkeld turned to her, frowning. "Justen can do it," Petrus said, and the prince nodded.

"I'm a Sentinel, Petrus. Stop treating me like I'm a child, to sit at the fire and be kept safe."

Petrus had the grace to look ashamed. "Sorry." He changed into an owl again and flew up to resume patrolling.

Innis looked at Justen.

"Do whatever you want," Justen said equably. "Doesn't bother me."

# CHAPTER ONE HUNDRED AND ONE

JAUMÉ LUGGED THE pot to the fire and set up the iron tripod. Bennick and Vught were heaving packsaddles off the horses. Jaumé fetched the tea the Brothers drank each night, and all the herbs, and the billies. He set to work infusing willowbark and bone-knit and brewing tea for Bennick and Vught.

The feverwort plants were rolled up in hessian. Jaumé glanced at Bennick and Vught. They'd finished with the packsaddles and were unharnessing the horses from the wagon.

Jaumé unrolled the hessian, snapped off two pale roots, and dropped them into the billy of tea. Would that be enough? He snapped off two more roots, just to be sure, and hurriedly rolled up the hessian. Bennick and Vught were still busy with the wagon.

Jaumé put the herbs away. When he got back to the fire, the billy of tea was boiling. Feverwort roots were rolling over in the water like pale worms.

He pulled the billy off the flames. The water stopped boiling. The roots sank to the bottom. After a minute, the dark flakes of tea began settling. Jaumé watched, his stomach knotting with a combination of guilt and fear. There was still time to change his mind, to upturn the billy and tip out the roots and start over again.

But then the princess wouldn't escape. And Bennick and Vught would tie her to a stake and use her to kill Prince Harkeld.

He put the tea to one side to steep, and the willowbark and bone-knit, too, and looked around, seeing snow and soot. Where would they sleep tonight? Not by the fire; the snow was melting into puddles of dangerous water.

He hunted through the rubble and found some blocks of stone and a couple of singed planks and made two low benches by the fire. A half-burned chopping block and an upturned iron bucket made good tables. He got mugs and plates and the salted ham and smoked sausages Vught had found, and laid everything out.

Bennick gave a grunt of approval when he saw it. "You've been busy." He sat on one of the benches, sighed, scrubbed his whiskery face with his hands. "What a day."

Vught lowered himself onto the other bench. Jaumé eyed them both nervously. Would they choose to drink their tea now, rather than later?

"How much further?" Bennick asked.

Vught reached under his cloak and pulled out the folded piece of vellum. "I reckon we're only five or six miles from the end of the road. And from there it's only a couple of miles to the stone."

Both men bent over the map.

Jaumé turned to the billy of tea, fished out the feverwort roots, and threw them into the fire. They hissed and sizzled briefly, then turned black. He turned back to Bennick and Vught. His heart was thumping. It felt as if a horse galloped in his chest.

Bennick and Vught hadn't noticed anything; they were still looking at the map.

# CHAPTER ONE HUNDRED AND TWO

THE BOY BROUGHT food, and a billy of willowbark and bone-knit brewed together. He didn't meet their eyes, just shoved the plates and billy at them.

"Jaumé?"

The boy lifted his gaze.

"If you decide not to go to Fith, you'll have safe refuge in Lundegaard," Karel said. "You have my word, and Britta's, on that. And if Britta and I aren't there—if we don't make it—tell King Magnas what you did for us. He'll see that you're taken care of. He's a good man."

The boy looked down at his boots. "It costs a groat to sail to Lundegaard."

"There's gold in my saddlebags. Take as much as you need. It's not stealing; I'm giving it to you."

Jaumé nodded, not looking at them, and ran back to the fire.

"I hope he listened," the princess said. "I hope he realizes he has a choice."

"I just hope Bennick and Vught don't kill him."

Britta glanced at him sharply. "You think they might?"

"Vught'd kill him in an instant, if he thought he had anything to do with us escaping."

"But... Bennick wouldn't let him."

"Bennick's an assassin. He'd kill the boy, too. He's not sentimental about life and death."

Karel looked at Jaumé, sitting beside Bennick at the fire, eating, and sent a brief prayer to the All-Mother: *Let the boy live.* Then, he looked at the food Jaumé had brought them. Salted pork, and smoked sausages. "Only eat the sausages," he told Britta. "We can say the pork tasted off. That way they'll think that's what made them sick."

They ate quickly, watching the Fithians. Bennick and Vught were drinking something out of mugs. The tea Jaumé had doctored? If so, how long would it be before the feverwort root took effect?

"I need to be out *there* before it starts," Karel said, pointing at the yard. "I can't get out of this wagon by myself."

"I'll tell them you need to use the privy." Britta scrambled down from the wagon.

Karel watched her cross to the fire. Was he doing the right thing, going with her? Would she have a better chance of survival alone?

Bennick put down his mug, climbed to his feet, and strolled across to the wagon. "Lapdog needs to piss, huh?"

Karel ignored the jibe. He reached for the stave and awkwardly pulled himself to the edge of the wagon. The dried meat, waterskins, and blankets were bundled together by the tailboard, ready for Britta to snatch when the time came.

"What?" Bennick said, catching sight of the half-full plates. "Didn't like your dinner?"

"Pork tasted a bit off."

"You really are a lapdog, aren't you?" There was contempt in Bennick's voice.

Karel planted the stave on the ground and tried to lean some of his weight on it as Bennick helped him down. His ribs grated together. Breathing became difficult. He clung to the stave, squeezed his eyes shut, tried not to groan.

Bennick took him behind the wagon to pee. He needed the assassin's help to unbuckle his belt. *How can I escape when I can't even piss by myself?*

Bennick helped him back around the wagon. Karel stared hard at Vught. He'd seen the man drink two mugs of tea. When would the vomiting start? Or had Jaumé lost his nerve and not used the feverwort root?

"Mind if I sit by the fire for a while?"

Bennick shrugged.

Karel limped towards the fire, leaning on Bennick, leaning on the stave. When he put too much weight on his left leg, the pain made him grunt.

"Lapdog wants to sit by the fire," Bennick told Vught.

Vught looked sour, and shrugged.

Karel levered himself awkwardly down onto a burned chopping block. The princess came across and perched on an upturned bucket alongside him. A small tinderbox sat on the ground beside the bucket. The tinderbox Jaumé had used to light the fire? Karel caught the princess's eye, then glanced at the tinderbox. She understood; she shifted position slightly, nudging the tinderbox closer to the bucket with her foot.

Karel carefully didn't look at Jaumé. He held his hands out to the fire and glanced at Bennick, glanced at Vught. Did either of them look ill?

# CHAPTER ONE HUNDRED AND THREE

INNIS CIRCLED OVER the Fithians. This wasn't the party Serril had described—six men and a boy. She saw three men and a boy, but also a woman. The woman's hair was chopped short and she wore men's clothing, but everything about her—the way she moved, the shape of her face, the smooth, unbearded skin—proclaimed her a woman. Surely Serril wouldn't have mistaken her for a man?

One of the men was injured. His dark face was gaunt with pain. He carried no weapons. Nor did the woman. But the boy was armed.

Innis circled, studying the people around the campfire, observing who spoke to whom. The party was in two groups, she decided. Two of the men were Fithian. The woman and injured man were prisoners. The boy...

She couldn't figure out the boy. He was a Fithian recruit, that was obvious. The assassin with the red-blond hair was his mentor. The boy kept close to him and seemed wary of the other, older Fithian. But the boy also had some kind of connection with the prisoners. She could see it in his body language, in the prisoners' body language. All three of them were aware of each other—*very* aware—and yet the prisoners didn't look at the boy, and the boy didn't look at them. There was a nervousness in the boy's movements, and a tense watchfulness in the prisoners, and she had a sense that all three of them were waiting for something. But what?

Innis watched for several more minutes, then let the wind push her down the valley.

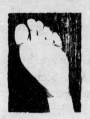

# CHAPTER ONE HUNDRED AND FOUR

JAUMÉ KNEW HE'D made a mistake. He'd not put enough feverwort roots in the tea, and not steeped them long enough. The emmytick wasn't working. He stared at the fire, unable to look at the princess or the soldier—

Vught abruptly pushed to his feet. He took half a dozen steps away from the fire, and vomited.

Jaumé's head jerked up. He looked at Vught, bent over, retching, and then at Bennick. Bennick's face was gray beneath the red stubble. His hands were pressed to his belly.

*It's working!*

Bennick stood, lurched across to a pile of rubble, and vomited.

Jaumé leapt to his feet. He ran to where the packsaddles were piled and grabbed the bundle of herbs. The princess and the soldier were on their feet, too. The princess was at the wagon, slinging the waterskins over her shoulder, and the soldier was limping towards the back of the ruined farmhouse.

Jaumé darted past him, shoved back the bar, and heaved the door open. He turned back to the soldier.

"Keep going," the soldier said, through gritted teeth. "I'll follow."

Jaumé ran down the snowy jetty. Above him, an almost-full moon hung in the sky. Someone ran behind him, feet thudding on the boards—the princess. Together they heaved the rowboat over. The oars were underneath the boat. Jaumé flung the herbs in, and the oars, and the princess threw in a pile of blankets and the pouch of dried meat. She turned to him. "Jaumé, may we have a weapon? Your sword?"

Jaumé hesitated.

"Please!"

He ran back through the door. The soldier had almost reached it.

Jaumé skirted the fire, wrenched open the packsaddle that held his sword, and hauled it out. Bennick and Vught were both bent over, still vomiting. Jaumé cast Bennick an anxious glance. He had to get him into the wagon. If Bennick collapsed on the snow, he could catch the curse.

He ran for the door. At the last moment, he saw the spyglass lying beside the fire. It must have fallen from beneath Bennick's cloak. He snatched it up.

The soldier was through the door and limping down the jetty, the princess helping him. Jaumé darted past and flung the sword into the boat. He wrapped the rope around his fist and cried, "Help me get it in the water!"

The princess stopped helping the soldier. Together, Jaumé and she lifted the boat and lowered it over the edge of the jetty. It hit the water with a soft *plish*. The rope began to tug.

Jaumé towed the boat to where a short ladder with six wooden rungs hung down. The black water reflected the moonlight. "Hurry!"

The soldier was two-thirds of the way down the jetty, leaning on the princess, leaning on the stave.

Jaumé jittered with anxiety. "Hurry!" he cried again.

It seemed to take an eternity for the soldier to reach him. Jaumé heard his breath, loud, hoarse, almost groaning.

The soldier did groan when he saw the ladder. "All-Mother," he said, under his breath. It sounded like a plea.

"Get in!" Jaumé cried. "Get in! Hurry!"

The soldier lowered himself to sit on the edge of the jetty. He released the stave and let it drop into the boat. To Jaumé's eyes it looked as if he didn't try to climb down the ladder, but just let himself fall, like the stave.

The boat rocked and the rope almost pulled from Jaumé's fist. He tightened his grip. The soldier's teeth flashed in the moonlight: a grimace of agony.

"Karel!" the princess cried. She scrambled halfway down the ladder, then turned and climbed back up again, hugged Jaumé fiercely, kissed his cheek. "Thank you. *Be careful!*"

Jaumé remembered the spyglass. "Wait! Spyglass!"

The princess shoved it under her cloak and climbed down the ladder. When she was in the boat, he said, "Use the oar as a rudder! In the stern. No, the other end of the boat. The other end!"

He until she'd clambered to the stern, then flung the rope into the boat and ran back into the farmhouse.

\*    \*    \*

BENNICK WAS STILL bent over, his hands braced on his knees, his head hanging. Vomit splattered the ground at his feet. Vught was kneeling, half-way to the door. His eyes followed Jaumé as he ran towards them. "Where's the princess?" he grated out.

"Ran away," Jaumé cried. "I tried to stop them!"

"Ran away?" Vught staggered to his feet, took several lurching steps towards the door, paused, and vomited.

"I tried to stop them," Jaumé said again.

Vught looked up, and wiped his mouth with the back of one hand. His eyes seemed to spear Jaumé. "Tried to stop them, did you?"

Jaumé nodded, and sidled past Vught, heading for Bennick.

Vught's arm snaked out. Hard fingers bit into Jaumé's arm. "Looked to me like you was helping 'em."

"No!" Jaumé tried to pull free.

Vught's grip tightened, pinching flesh against bone. He hauled Jaumé closer, shook him hard, making his head snap on his neck. "You helped." His other hand reached beneath his cloak, came out holding his heavy throwing knife. The sharp blade glinted in the moonlight.

"No!" Jaumé cried again, trying to twist free.

Vught released him suddenly and bent over, caught in a paroxysm of vomiting. Jaumé stumbled, almost fell, turned to run—and halted. Vught wasn't someone you ran from. Vught would throw his big knife and skewer him through the back of his skull.

Jaumé fumbled for his own knife, wrenching it from the sheath. He stepped closer to Vught and stabbed the side of Vught's neck as hard as he could—a punching blow, just under his jawbone—and pulled the knife out. Blood gushed blackly.

Vught staggered, half-turned, and slashed out with his knife. His mouth opened, but no sound came out.

Jaumé backed away. His heart thundered in his chest.

Vught lurched forward a step, raised his knife to throw, and collapsed to his knees. His eyes were fixed on Jaumé. His mouth was still open, as if he was roaring.

Jaumé turned and ran to the fire. There was no blood on his hand, but the knife blade was red with it. He put the knife on the chopping block and turned to Bennick. Bennick was on hands and knees, retching.

"Stand up! Stand up!" Jaumé screamed. "Get away from the snow!" He grabbed Bennick's arm, heaving him up.

Bennick stood, lurching and swaying. "Rutting lapdog was right," he gasped. "Pork was off."

"Into the wagon! Into the wagon!"

He guided Bennick to the wagon, pushed and pulled him into it, then ran to the packsaddles and got an armful of blankets. He looked across the yard. Vught had pitched forward and was lying face-down.

Jaumé climbed back into the wagon and made Bennick as comfortable as he could, wiping his face, wrapping him in blankets, giving him a mug of water to drink and the old bucket to retch into when he brought the water back up. Bennick was white-faced and sweating, shaking. *I'm sorry, Bennick. I'm sorry.*

Jaumé was shaking as much as Bennick. He'd stabbed a man before, a thief in Cornas who'd tried to steal his bread, but this was different. This time he'd killed someone. And then fear grabbed him: maybe Vught wasn't dead?

The fear was so strong that he had to creep down from the wagon and tiptoe across to where Vught lay. Vught didn't move, didn't seem to be breathing. Jaumé crouched cautiously. The smell of vomit and blood was strong. One of Vught's hands was out-flung, the underside of his wrist exposed. Jaumé reached for it with trembling fingers.

Vught's skin was cold. He didn't twitch, didn't rear up and grab him.

Jaumé couldn't find a pulse. He went back to the wagon, but he walked sideways, his gaze on Vught. Vught was dead, but, deep down, Jaumé knew Vught would come back to life and kill him if he could.

# CHAPTER ONE HUNDRED AND FIVE

INNIS FLEW UP the leeward side of the ridge. The pinprick of firelight that marked their tiny camp jumped out at her through the dark trees. A snowy-white owl hooted and flew to meet her. Petrus. No one sat at the fire. The tent flaps were closed. The prince and Justen were asleep.

Innis glided down and landed beside the fire, where a blanket had been spread on the snow. Petrus landed, too. "Well?" he asked.

"I found some Fithians with a wagon, but I don't know if they're the same ones Serril saw." She crouched close to the fire. "There are two assassins, and a boy... and two prisoners. A man and a woman."

"Prisoners?" Petrus frowned. "Fithians don't usually take prisoners."

"I know. And I feel like I've seen them before. I feel like I should recognize them."

Petrus crouched, too, and held his hands towards the fire. "What do they look like?"

"She's young. Younger than me, I think. With fair hair. And he's dark. Black hair, brown skin. Looks like he could be a soldier." She had a sudden flash of memory. A man with black hair and brown skin, wearing a scarlet tunic and burnished gold breastplate, hand resting on the hilt of his sword. "Oh…"

"What?"

Innis closed her eyes and let the memory replay itself. The palace gardens. The golden-haired princess. The armsman standing stern and watchful behind her.

"What?"

She opened her eyes. "It's the prince's sister. Brigitta. And her armsman."

Petrus stared at her, open-mouthed, and then shook his head. "No."

"Yes!" She stood, turned to the tent, and halted.

Petrus rose, too. He touched her arm lightly, warningly. "If we tell him…"

"They're hostages, aren't they?"

"Nothing else they can be. Innis… if he starts thinking about them and not the anchor stone…"

She met his eyes. "We can't tell him. Can we?"

He shook his head.

Wind gusted through the trees. Innis became aware of how cold she was. She shivered, and rubbed her arms.

"How close are they?" Petrus asked.

"Close. They'll reach the anchor stone tomorrow."

Petrus grimaced.

Innis shivered again, rubbed her arms again. "Go to sleep," she told Petrus. "I'll wake Justen when I'm ready to swap."

# CHAPTER ONE HUNDRED AND SIX

BRITTA GRIPPED THE oar. *Use it like a rudder*, Jaumé had said, as if it was easy, but it wasn't easy. It was more than a mile before she dared to raise her gaze from the oar and the black, dangerous river and look at Karel. The armsman sat slumped in the prow. She thought his eyes were shut. Unconscious?

The oar tugged. Britta jerked her attention back to the river. The water was opaque, ink-black, reflecting the moon.

It could have been tranquil—gliding soundlessly on a dark, moonlit river between ghostly white riverbanks—but she was almost afraid to breathe. An inch-thick wooden hull was all that protected them from the Ivek Curse.

She risked another glance forward. Karel hadn't moved. On the western riverbank was a hulking square shape: a farmhouse. They were almost level with the building when she realized it had a jetty, thrusting into the river.

Britta frantically manipulated the oar, trying to make the boat move to the left. Panic squeezed her throat. They were going to hit the end of the jetty—

The jetty drifted past, so close she could have reached out and touched it.

Britta let out a breath. Her heart was galloping in her chest. She stared up at the squat, square shape on the riverbank. It must be the last farmhouse they'd passed, the one that had smelled of burning. And in a mile or two, would be another farmhouse, with another jetty.

She stared intently ahead, watching for the next farmhouse, the next jetty, trying to keep as close to the middle of the river as she could. The four waterskins were still slung awkwardly across her chest and the tinderbox pressed uncomfortably into her hip bone, but she didn't dare try to remove any of them. The oar and the river required absolute concentration. If the rowboat hit the bank, or a jetty, or a rock, if they tipped over...

Britta gripped the oar more tightly. She shivered. Her hands were cold, her face cold, her feet cold—

With sudden horror, she realized that her feet were wet as well as cold. She peered at the bottom of the boat. Was that water, reflecting moonlight back up at her?

Yes.

Her panic thundered back.

"Karel!" she cried. "The boat's leaking!" But he didn't hear her, didn't react.

Britta looked wildly for somewhere to land, but the riverbanks sliding past were high and overhanging. "Karel! *Wake up!*"

He didn't stir, didn't answer.

Her eyes made out a dark shape on the riverbank. Squat and square. The next farmhouse.

How far ahead was it? Quarter of a mile? Half a mile?

Britta clutched the oar desperately, guiding the boat, feeling cold water slowly creep up her ankles. The farmhouse grew larger, taller. She saw the jetty, low and dark, jutting out into the river.

Britta aimed for the jetty. The rowboat was low in the water, sluggish. The jetty came closer, closer. At the last moment she saw she was going to drift past half a yard out.

Britta made a desperate lunge with the oar—digging deep into the dangerous water, hauling the boat to the right—and dropped the oar and grabbed one of the piles. The boat swung heavily round, wallowing like a pregnant cow in mud. A ladder hung down. Britta snatched for the lowest rung.

The rowboat came to a halt.

Britta groped in the boat for the rope. It was sodden. Sodden with cursed water. She threaded it carefully around the bottom rung, turned her head away so no drops could flick in her face, and pulled.

The rope wasn't attached to the stern, as she'd thought, but the prow. She had a moment of panic, when the rowboat swung into the current, stern first, and she almost fell in, but she didn't let go of the rope, and the boat stopped, and she realized she had to be in the prow if she was to tie it. Britta clambered cautiously through the calf-deep water in the rowboat, holding onto the rope. She stumbled over Karel's stave, over Jaumé's sword, and flung them both up onto the jetty. The blankets wound around her ankles like wet snakes, trying to trip her.

In the prow, she crouched alongside Karel, and hauled on the rope, and the bow of the rowboat came up snugly to the ladder. She tied a hasty knot. Karel still hadn't moved.

"Karel!" She shook his shoulder, slapped his face. "Armsman, *wake up*."

Karel jerked back to semi-consciousness.

"You have to climb the ladder," Britta told him, making it an order. She took his good hand and placed it on the lowest rung. "Climb it! Now!"

She heaved and pushed and got him halfway up the ladder, and then scrambled up herself and grabbed the back of his shirt and *hauled*.

Karel staggered onto the jetty and fell to hands and knees. The sound he made was agonized.

"No! The snow's cursed! Don't touch it!" And she hauled on him again, and got him to his feet and slung his arm over her shoulder. "Come on. Twenty yards. You can do it, armsman!"

She almost fell over Karel's stave, but managed to keep her balance. She left it where it lay; the armsman was barely conscious. He didn't seem to know where he was or what was happening. He moved like a sleepwalker, shambling and lurching. At the end of the jetty, where the riverbank started, he stumbled and fell to his knees. A sound came from his throat, almost a scream, high-pitched and breathless.

"Karel!" Britta grabbed him and stopped him pitching forward into the snow.

His breath was gasping, sobbing. He was crying with pain, she realized, an agonized, choking sound, as if he couldn't breathe.

"Karel." She knelt and put her arms around him, held him close. "Ten more yards, Karel. Please. I need you to walk. *Please*."

If he didn't walk, she couldn't carry him, couldn't drag him. He'd die out here, in the snow.

"Please, Karel." She was crying, tears sliding down her face. "Please, I need you to *walk*."

She got to her feet, bent and put his left arm over her shoulders, and said, "Armsman, *walk*," and hauled him upright. "Ten more yards! Karel, ten more yards!"

The ten yards took a slow, excruciating eternity, but finally they reached the door. The farmhouse loomed over them, tall and dark and safe.

Britta fumbled for the door handle, found a heavy iron ring, twisted it.

The door didn't open, but if she was right, this was the farmhouse where Vught had found the pork and sausages. The main door would be unbarred.

She slipped Karel's arm from her shoulder and tried to lean him against the wall.

"Stay standing. That's an order! Do you hear me, armsman? Stay *standing*." She wasn't sure whether Karel understood or not.

Britta ran around to the front of the farmhouse with desperate haste, slipping and sliding. *Hurry. Hurry.* She searched for the handle, found another iron ring, twisted it, leaned hard on the door. For a terrible moment she thought the door was barred, and then it swung grudgingly open.

Britta shoved inside, pelted across the moonlit yard, found the far door, heaved back the crossbar, and swung the door open. "Karel!"

He was still standing, leaning against the wall, panting with pain, his head hanging.

Britta guided him inside. The yard and the farmhouse were a confusing jumble of shadows and moonlight... and then her eyes made sense of the shapes in the dark. Stables to the left, barn at the back, living quarters to the right. "This way."

She got him through a door—their boots clumped on a wooden floor—and leaned him against the wall, unslung the waterskins, fumbled for the tinderbox, and struck the flint. Light flared for a moment, showing her a room with a table and stools and shelves and two doors. She struck the flint again— and saw a candlestick on the table. *Thank you, All-Mother.*

Britta lit the candle hastily and pushed open the nearest door. It led to a scullery and kitchen. She tried the other door, and found a bedroom.

"In here, Karel." She slung his arm over her shoulder again. "Come on."

They almost didn't make it. Karel staggered and lurched and half-collapsed—her knees buckled— and she got both her arms around his waist and heaved him onto the bed. "No! Don't go to sleep. Clothes off. I need to get you dry!"

He was almost as bad as he'd been three days ago, drifting in and out of consciousness. Britta stripped off his clothes and found a blanket in the chest at the foot of the bed and dried him with it. His legs were wet from the knee down, the backs of his thighs, his buttocks, one arm to the elbow. Karel's nudity was no more awkward than if she was drying her young half-brothers after a bath. He was too weak, too helpless, for her to feel embarrassed. She examined his injuries. His arm seemed all right, but the wound on his thigh had torn open and was leaking blood. The skin looked swollen and felt hot to touch.

His thigh was hot, but the rest of him was cold, shivering. Britta wrapped him in another blanket and piled furs over him. Wolf skins, thick and warm. Then, she took the candle and barred the door to the road and the door to the jetty. Now they were safe. At least until morning.

Back in the bedroom, she stripped off her clothes, dried herself, bundled another blanket around her, and burrowed under the furs with Karel. He didn't wake, didn't even stir. His breathing was shallow and painful.

Britta found his hand and went to sleep holding it.

# CHAPTER ONE HUNDRED AND SEVEN

BENNICK RETCHED OFF and on for another hour, before falling into a fitful sleep. Jaumé didn't sleep. He couldn't. Not with Vught lying on the other side of the yard. His imagination told him that if he closed his eyes for even one minute, Vught would clamber to his feet and come after him.

Jaumé cleaned the blood off his knife and sat gripping it, ready for Vught.

But Vught didn't come, and with dawn, Jaumé's imagination shriveled into dust and Vught became just a dead man.

Jaumé put away the knife and lay down beside Bennick. Bennick's face was the color of a fish's belly.

If Bennick was ill all day today, and maybe tomorrow as well, then Prince Harkeld might be able to reach the curse stone and break the curse.

Jaumé tried to imagine what would happen after that.

He thought about Bennick taking him back to Fith to train to be a Brother, and he thought about what the soldier had said: that he could go to Lundegaard instead. He didn't think Bennick would like that.

Jaumé turned it over in his head for a while, and decided that he'd look for the gold coins. He'd take just one, or maybe two—it wouldn't be stealing, the soldier had said he could take them—and then if he *did* decide to go to Lundegaard, he could.

Having decided that, he snuggled into his blankets and slept.

# CHAPTER ONE HUNDRED AND EIGHT

HARKELD WOKE AT dawn. Two wolves were in the tent with him. A large silver-pelted male, and a smaller, darker animal. Innis. The male was awake, watching him.

"Morning, Petrus."

The wolf blinked yellow eyes at him and yawned, showing sharp white teeth.

Harkeld yawned too, and sat up.

Petrus rose to all fours, pushed open the tent flap with his nose, and went out.

Icy air flowed into the tent. Harkeld shivered and groped for his cloak.

Beside him, the second wolf sat up. Harkeld touched her head, briefly stroked the soft fur on her skull.

They'd dreamed together, he and Innis, held each other, talked about Adel.

Innis pressed her nose to his cheek. Greeting? Kiss?

"You want to get dressed?" he asked her. "I'll get out of here."

He pulled on his boots, wrapped his cloak around himself, and crawled outside. The air was painfully crisp, stinging his face. He shivered convulsively.

"All-Mother, it's cold." The inside of his nose burned. Breath billowed from his mouth like smoke.

"Got quite a climb ahead of you today. You'll be sweating soon enough." Petrus crouched at the fire, bundled in several cloaks, chewing on a strip of dried goat's meat.

"You've got bare feet," Harkeld said, disbelieving. "For crying out loud, get dressed!"

"No point," Petrus said. "Swapping with Justen soon as I've eaten."

Harkeld hunkered down alongside him and reached for some meat. "Did Innis find the Fithians last night?"

Petrus nodded, chewing. "They're close. We'll check on them again in a bit."

"Will it be Innis who goes?"

Petrus glanced at him, and then at the tent. "We'll see."


PETRUS WAS RIGHT; it wasn't long before Harkeld was sweating. The track toiled upwards, even steeper than it had been yesterday. Snow crunched and squeaked beneath his boots.

Mid-morning, Petrus glided down for a drink.

"How much further to the top?" Harkeld asked, panting, wiping his face.

"Couple of hours, then the track follows the ridge for a while. Not as steep as this." Petrus rammed the stopper back into the waterskin. "Then it goes down the other side. Justen, Innis... one of you want to check on the Fithians?"

"I'll do it," Innis said.

"No, I will," Justen said.

Innis opened her mouth, but Justen held up a hand to forestall her. "You're the strongest healer we have left *and* a shapeshifter. If anything goes wrong, you've a better chance than me or Petrus of getting Flin to the anchor stone."

"But last night—"

"Last night it was dark. They couldn't see you. Today'll be different. They see a hawk checking them out, they'll take a shot at it. They're not stupid, Fithians. They know how we work." And then Justen shrugged, grinned. "And besides, I've had enough of climbing this rutting hill. I'm about to get blisters. So do me a favor, Innis; let me do it."

Innis closed her mouth.

Petrus met Harkeld's eyes and winked. "Be careful," he told Justen, then shifted back into a hawk and flew upward.

Harkeld sat on a rock. Breath misted in front of his face. His sweat chilled on his skin. He'd need his cloak if they didn't start moving again soon.

Justen stripped off his jerkin and shirt, bundled them together, and strapped them on a packsaddle. His Grooten amulet hung like a small round moon over his sternum. "All-Mother, will I be *glad* to stop climbing this hill," he said, bending to pull off his boots.

Harkeld grunted agreement.

Justen slung his boots over a saddle pommel. "In Margolie, when I did my Journey, we had this fire mage with us, fat old bastard. I remember once, he..." The shapeshifter paused, blinked, a look almost of confusion crossing his face. Then he shook his head. "Ach, what was I saying?"

"In Margolie..." Harkeld said.

But Justen didn't pick up on the cue. He stood barefoot in the snow, staring at Harkeld as if he didn't recognize him.

"Justen?"

The shapeshifter shook his head again. His brow creased, an expression of bewilderment.

"Justen?" Harkeld said again, standing. "Are you all right?" And then he saw the curse shadows. They crept upwards over Justen's skin in a dark, thick tide.

Harkeld froze. "Innis? Get behind me."

The shape of Justen's skull hadn't altered, his muscles hadn't shifted place under his skin, yet Harkeld could swear they had. The mage's face was fundamentally and profoundly different. Whatever looked at him out of Justen's eyes wasn't human; it was beast.

The shapeshifter's stance changed—a shifting of weight, a bunching of muscles. It was the same change he'd seen in Adel: predator.

Hair rose on the back of Harkeld's neck, on his scalp. He daren't look to see whether Innis had obeyed him, daren't shift his gaze from Justen. He gathered his fire magic in a sharp, searing rush and raised his right hand. "I'm sorry, Justen."

Petrus swooped down, shrieking a harsh hawk screech, startling the horses. He landed in the snow and became a lion.

Justen's gaze fastened on the lion. His lips curled back from his teeth in a snarl. There was no fear on his face, just a fierce, terrible madness.

"Out of the way, Petrus!" Harkeld yelled.

Petrus ignored him. He charged, knocking Justen backwards.

Man and lion rolled in the snow, scattering the horses, and then Innis was there too, grabbing Justen's bare shoulder.

Justen's mouth opened in a silent scream. His body arched, spasmed—and went limp.

Innis stepped back. The lion slowly rose to all fours. His mane was unbloodied. His teeth, unbloodied.

Harkeld lowered his hand.

The lion became Petrus. His face was as starkly white as Innis's.

"What did you think you were doing?" Harkeld bellowed at him. "I just about burned you!"

"He deserved a body to bury!" Petrus yelled back. Tears stood in his eyes. He turned to Justen and knelt, took Justen's hand, bent his head.

*He's crying.*

Innis knelt, too. She put her arms around Petrus and pressed her face into his hair.

Harkeld stood silently. He'd known Petrus and Justen were friends, but he'd not understood how close.

He turned back to the rock he'd been sitting on, lowered himself stiffly, sat with his head in his hands.

After a few minutes, he began shivering. Harkeld stood, even more stiffly, and found his cloak, and Innis's, and Petrus's. Petrus still knelt beside Justen, Innis still hugged him. She raised her head and looked at him silently. Harkeld gave her the cloaks—"Keep him warm."—and then trudged between the silent black tree trunks after the horses. They'd gathered, skittish, about fifty yards down the track.

He rounded them up, brought them back, found a shovel, and began to dig Justen's grave. Beneath the covering of needles the ground was rocky. Harkeld chipped and gouged a shallow trough. When he looked up, he found Petrus standing there. The shapeshifter had dressed, but his face still had a frozen whiteness.

"I can't dig any deeper."

Petrus nodded.

They laid Justen in the grave. His face was peaceful in death. He was no longer a predator, but Justen again. Petrus bent and removed the ivory amulet from around his throat.

Harkeld filled the trench with the dirt and stones he'd dug out. "Too shallow." Wolves would dig Justen up.

"We'll cover it with rocks," Innis said, and she made them bind their hands with strips torn from a blanket—makeshift gloves.

They gathered rocks and placed them on Justen's grave. Petrus still hadn't spoken a word. Every muscle in his face was tight. His eyes shone with tears.

"Who wants to say the words to the All-Mother?" Harkeld asked.

Innis glanced at Petrus. "I will."

She spoke the words, and then they each knelt and laid their hands on the grave and made their own silent farewells.

*Goodbye, Justen. We could have been good friends.*

Harkeld climbed to his feet again. Petrus had been right. It was better this way. A body to bury, a grave to say words over.

"I'll guard Flin," Innis said. "If you want to check the Fithians?"

Petrus nodded. He silently stripped and bundled his clothes onto a packsaddle.

Harkeld crossed to him. "Be careful."

Petrus gave a short nod.

"Don't take any risks. If you think they've spotted you, back off."

Petrus fastened the last strap and turned away.

Harkeld wished he could see inside Petrus's head, wished he could know what he was thinking. Was the shapeshifter so caught up in grief that his judgment was clouded? Would he take risks without even knowing he was doing it? He strode after Petrus and grabbed his arm, forcing the shapeshifter to halt. "It'll kill Innis if you die," he said, in a low voice. "So stop thinking about Justen and start thinking about staying alive. All right, whoreson?"

Petrus turned his head. His eyebrows drew together in a fierce glare.

"You can break my nose when you get back," Harkeld told him. "Just make sure you *get back*."

Petrus shook off his hand. Finally he spoke, "I will."

After Petrus had gone, Harkeld walked to where Innis stood at the grave. "He's taking this hard. Will he be all right?"

"He and Justen... they were best friends since their first day at the Academy. Twelve years."

Harkeld took her right hand, held her palm between both of his. She'd done to Justen what Rand had done to Malle: used her healing magic to kill. He wasn't dreaming, he couldn't feel her emotions, but he knew she was almost as upset as Petrus. "How did Justen get the curse?"

"He had a raw spot on one heel." A shudder ran through her. "I felt it when I touched him. The curse. He wasn't Justen any more. He was something else. Not human."

"Innis... if Justen had shapeshifted... could he have un-cursed himself? Animals can't get the curse, can they?"

Innis blinked. Her brow wrinkled. She thought for a moment. "Maybe, if he'd done it before his shadow fully changed. But once the curse took hold..." She shuddered again and shook her head. "He couldn't think, let alone shift."

Harkeld released her hand and pulled her into a hug, rested his chin on her hair. He looked at the mound of rocks that was Justen's grave. "When we were in the desert, whoever was Justen told me Grootens bury their dead at sea."

"That's why Petrus took the amulet. To return to his family. They'll have a ceremony and give it to the sea."

"Can we be there?"

"Yes."

"I'd like to." *If we're still alive*. Harkeld tightened his grip on her. "Keep close watch on me, won't you? All this snow... If it should happen to me, don't take any risks. Remember, I could burn you. I could burn you and Petrus just like I did Adel, so *be careful*."

Innis pulled back. She looked up at him, a frown on her brow, and shook her head. "I don't think you could burn us. I don't think Justen could even remember that he could shift."

"Just don't take any risks," Harkeld repeated. "Watch me closely and if it should happen... stay well clear of me until Petrus gets back." He stroked her hair back from her face. "Please?"

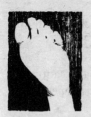

# CHAPTER ONE HUNDRED AND NINE

WHEN JAUMÉ WOKE, Bennick was no longer in the wagon.

Jaumé sat up hurriedly. Was Bennick lying sick on the ground?

No, Bennick was at the packsaddles, going through them. He looked like he always did: strong, well.

Jaumé squinted up at the sky. How long had he slept? The sun was high: noon.

Bennick looked up and saw him. "Hurry up, lad. We've got to get moving."

Jaumé scrambled down from the wagon. "But... you're sick."

"Not any more." Bennick glanced sharply at him, studying his face. "You all right? Didn't seem to take you as bad."

"I, uh... I only threw up once."

"Good." Bennick gave a curt nod. "Now get every waterskin you can find and fill it."

Jaumé hurried to obey.

Bennick saddled his mount and the pony, and loaded three packhorses. "Come here, lad." He made Jaumé try on some warmer clothes. Jaumé wondered whose they were. Valor's? Luit's?

"You seen my spyglass anywhere?"

"I think they took it," Jaumé said cautiously. "Um... do you want to know what happened last night?"

"I can see what happened. They took off while we were sick. In a boat." Bennick's gaze rested on Vught for a moment. "The lapdog took Vught out, or maybe his mistress did. Lucky kill, that one. Vught wouldn't have gone easily."

Had Bennick seen his footprints on the jetty? "I tried to stop them," Jaumé lied, twisting his fingers together. "But they'd already gone."

"I know. I saw the tracks." Bennick reached out and ruffled Jaumé's hair. "I mightn't be alive if you hadn't helped me into the wagon. You're a good lad, Jaumé. You'll make a good Brother."

Jaumé twisted his fingers even more tightly together. "Are we going to Fith now?"

"Fith? Not yet. Got to get the prince first."

"But... the princess is gone. There's no bait."

"Don't need her. Would have helped, I don't deny. Surprise can give you a powerful advantage: if you can make your target stop for even one second, you've got him." Bennick snapped his fingers, a sharp sound. "But I'll get him without her, easy enough."

Bennick crossed to Vught and stood looking down at him. "He get the curse before he died?"

"I don't know."

Bennick crouched, and cautiously rolled Vught over. He felt under Vught's cloak and took the folded map. "Right, let's be off."

"The other horses? There's no food for them here."

"We'll leave the door open. They'll get out." Bennick looked around at the sooty snow, the vomit, the rubble. "What a mess," he said disgustedly, and Jaumé remembered how clean the Brothers usually were. Clean, quick, tidy.

"No way of hiding this mess from the mages, if they're on the road behind us. Let's hope they're going over the hills."

# CHAPTER ONE HUNDRED AND TEN

THE ROOM WAS dim when Britta woke. Night? And then she realized that the window was shuttered.

She extricated herself from the nest of furs and opened the shutters. The window looked out on the central yard. Daylight.

She checked on Karel—deeply asleep—and then went in search of clothes and food. She found both, dressed and ate, and checked on Karel again. He hadn't moved.

Britta went out into the courtyard. She crossed to the back door, opened it, and went out onto the jetty. The rowboat had sunk. Only the tip of the prow showed above the water, held up by the rope.

Jaumé's sword and Karel's stave lay where she'd tossed them. She cut the rope with the sword, releasing the boat, and took both sword and stave back into the farmhouse and barred the door. Then, she checked Karel again. He still hadn't moved.

She explored the farmhouse further. Two families had lived here, she decided. She found six bedrooms, and a room with a tall loom that had a half-made blanket of undyed goats' wool strung up on it, and a wolf skin stretched taut on a drying rack. All the rooms had windows opening onto the central yard, but the upstairs rooms had narrow slits too, that faced outwards. For arrows, she thought. Britta found a slit that looked along the road, and pulled out the spyglass. The road was empty.

She put the spyglass back in her pocket and explored further, finding a selection of dried herbs in a room off the scullery. She examined the herbs. Which ones were for flavoring food, and which for healing? Those curls of dried bark could possibly be willowbark... or possibly not.

As well as the herbs, she found a small earthenware flask. Britta uncorked it, and sniffed. The smell jerked her head back, gave her a sharp memory: the palace, Duke Rikard.

Britta rammed the stopper back in. Poppy syrup. She'd drunk it every day of her marriage to Rikard. She thrust the flask back onto its shelf.

When she checked on Karel again, his eyes opened. After a long moment, his gaze focused on her. "Britta?"

"Yes." She sat on the bed and felt his face. Was the warmth due to fever, or the wolf skins? "How do you feel?"

"Where are we?"

She explained the river and the rowboat and the farmhouse. Karel's gaze drifted off several times. She saw the effort it took him to concentrate. "How do you feel?" she asked again.

"Tired."

And in pain. She could see it in his face. "Where does it hurt?"

"Hurts to breathe. And my leg."

She pushed aside the wolf skins, folded back the blanket, and examined his left thigh. It had bled during the night; blood crusted the blanket. His skin was hot to touch, a bruised-looking color, swollen.

"I'm going to make you some willowbark tea."

Karel's brow creased, as if he was trying to think. "How much water have we got?"

"Four waterskins."

His gaze drifted off again.

Britta had never cooked anything in her life, but there was a fireplace in the kitchen, and hooks for hanging pots over the fire. She didn't know whether to put the bark in before the water heated, or after. In the end, she decided it didn't matter.

It took her a long time, but eventually she had a pot of tea. The tea looked strong; she'd used a handful of the bark.

Britta put it aside to cool and went to see how Karel was. His eyes were closed. She went upstairs and checked the road again—still empty—and finished exploring the farmhouse and yard. She found a small smokehouse. Most of the racks were empty, but half a dozen strings of sausages hung near the back and two haunches of meat. At the back of the barn, was a stack of casks. Britta prized out the bungs and sniffed. Cider, and ale.

Back in the kitchen, the tea was lukewarm. Britta took it to the bedroom. "Karel? Karel, wake up."

He drank half a mug. "Does it taste all right?" Britta asked.

"Strong."

"But does it taste like willowbark?"

A smile touched his eyes. "Don't know what you're giving me?"

"Not really," she confessed. "It was the only bark."

"Tastes like willowbark, just strong." Karel drank another mouthful.

"Do you know what bone-knit looks like? Or comfrey?"

He shook his head.

Britta hesitated. "I found some poppy syrup."

Their eyes met, and then Karel shook his head. "No. I need my wits about me."

Britta nodded. Poppy syrup would dull his pain, but also his mind. Her marriage to Rikard was a blur, something she couldn't remember clearly even if she tried.

She got two mugs of willowbark down him, and most of a smoked sausage, then ran up to check the road again. Still empty. *But what will I do if it's not? What if Vught and Bennick come for me?* She decided to start wearing Jaumé's sword.

Britta found a leather belt in one of the abandoned rooms, and took it and the sword to Karel. With his help she managed to attach the scabbard to the belt and fasten it so the sword sat at her left hip. Karel looked at her, and his face became grim. "Britta, take it off."

"Why?"

"Because people who wear swords get killed. *Take it off.*"

He was so agitated that Britta unbuckled the belt. She sat alongside him on the bed and took his hand. "Karel, we're safe here."

"Maybe." His grip was tight, almost painful.

"The next people who come along the road will be Harkeld and the witches, and they'll destroy the curse, and then we can go home."

"Maybe," Karel said again. His voice sounded as if he wanted to believe it, but didn't.

Britta rubbed her thumb across the back of his hand. "Tell me about Esfaban."

"Esfaban?" His expression changed: sorrow. "It's the most beautiful kingdom in the world."

"Tell me."

She listened while he told her of blue-green seas and waves lapping on sandy beaches, groves of tall palm trees, warm breezes and heavy rains, tree frogs singing, and houses thatched with palm fronds. His grip on her hand relaxed, and so did his face, and then he told her about the people, and the muscles in his face tightened again. "Sending your eldest child to be a bondservant. Twenty years of slavery. How do you find the strength to do that? How do you send a child away, knowing what they'll have to endure?"

Britta shook her head.

"The families keep living, and sometimes they sing, and sometimes they laugh, but underneath that is guilt. You can see it in their faces. My uncle said it's like a rat eating away inside you. It sits in your chest, and it hurts, and it never goes away. Not even when the bondservants come home, because they're always broken. Always." Karel fell silent. He shook his head. "Osgaard has destroyed us."

Britta looked away. By Osgaard, he meant the Rutersvards. *My family.*

"If Yasma goes home, her family will never be able to look at her without feeling guilt. And she... I don't know. Maybe she can love them again. Maybe she can be happy. Maybe not." He released her hand and sighed, rubbed his face.

Britta tried to imagine it: the grief and despair of families sending a child into bondservice, the consuming guilt. How would it feel to welcome home a son or daughter who'd endured twenty years of slavery? How would it feel to *be* that son or daughter, coming home?

"What about you?" she asked. "Can you go back and be happy?"

"Me?" Karel glanced at her. "It's different for me. I wasn't a bondservant." He frowned, thinking. "If I went back after twenty years' service, my family would be joyful, because we'd all finally be free. But they think I'm dead, so... They'll feel guilt."

Britta took his hand again, squeezed it. "But if Jaegar dies, and Magnas becomes regent, and Esfaban is freed... *then* you can go back. Everyone can go back."

"Yes."

*And I can go with you, and Yasma.*

"Tell me about your family, please, Karel. If you don't mind talking about them?"

"My family?" He looked past her, at the wall. "I have two sisters, Elifira and Tamasin, and two aunts and three uncles and nearly a dozen cousins. My parents... My mother doesn't speak. She stopped speaking when she was a bondservant."

*Was she raped?* But Britta knew the answer: yes. All female bondservants were raped.

"My father served in the tanneries. His hands are broken, all scarred and misshapen, and he was whipped so badly he was practically flayed, but he's only damaged on the outside, not the inside. He smiles and he laughs. He was a good father. He loved us."

Did that mean his mother didn't?

Karel glanced at her, and maybe he saw the question on her face. "It's hard for the women when they come back. They need to bear a son, but they've been raped, and... it's hard."

Britta looked down at her hand holding his.

"My mother had two daughters before me. Father brought us up, and my aunts and uncles helped. Mother... she's not truly present. She's somewhere else, inside her head. It helps her to cope. But, she does like babies. It's the only time she smiles—when she's rocking a baby—and she makes a humming sound, like she's singing. When we were babies, I think we made her happy, for a time."

Karel fell silent. Whatever he was thinking about wasn't cheerful. Then, he seemed to give himself a shake, to turn his thoughts in another direction. "Father said the whole island celebrated when I was born. Everyone sang and danced. I saw it happen many times before I left. When a bondservant has a son, it's... It gives everyone hope that one day they'll be free."

A bondservant's son to bear arms for Osgaard, to give twenty years' good service, after which his family would be wholly free. Karel was the only Esfaban islander she'd seen as an armsman in the palace. "Were you the first one born? Son of a bondservant?"

"One of them. There are lots of boys behind me. The last few years I was home, it seemed like a bondservant's son was born every few months. In another fifty years, most of Esfaban's families will be free. If things stay as they are."

"They won't," Britta said. "Magnas will take control of Osgaard."

Karel shook his head. "We *hope* he will. We hope he *can*. All-Mother only knows what Jaegar's doing now, what changes he's making, what plans. And if Harkeld fails..."

"He won't," Britta said stoutly.

Karel released her hand. "I should have tried to kill Vught last night. And Bennick."

"Karel, you can't even *stand up* by yourself."

"No." He frowned. "Could you bring those herbs here? Maybe I can recognize bone-knit from the smell."

Britta brought the herbs, and Karel sniffed them all. "I don't think any of these is bone-knit."

She took the herbs back, and when she returned, Karel said, "Britta, I need to pee."

Britta fetched a chamberpot and put it on a stool beside the bed, and brought Karel his stave, but he wouldn't accept any help after that. She ran upstairs and checked the road—still empty—and ran down again.

Karel was back under the furs. His face was as gray as the wolf pelts and he was shaking. Britta emptied the chamberpot and gave him willowbark tea to drink and watched him fall asleep, then she picked the sword belt up from the floor, buckled it around her hips, and went to check the road again.

Still empty.

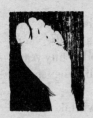

# CHAPTER ONE HUNDRED AND ELEVEN

AT THE END of the road, Bennick took out Vught's map and studied it. "Up that valley on the left. I think we're only a couple of miles from the stone." He urged his horse forward, into the foot-deep snow.

Jaumé trailed after him. There was a tight, anxious lump in his chest.

The valley was narrow and bare of trees. In summer, it would be a meadow; now, it was smooth and white and empty. Trees with black trunks clung to the steep hills on either side. They looked like firs, but had no needles.

Jaumé hoped there were witches in the hills and that they could see him and Bennick. He peered at the hillsides, searching for movement, for people, but saw nothing. *Hurry!* he told the prince urgently. *Or we'll get there before you.*

# CHAPTER ONE HUNDRED AND TWELVE

HARKELD CLIMBED THE ridge on horseback for several hours, beneath a blue sky, then the track veered east, zigzagging its way steeply down into the valley on the other side. He dismounted and walked, the horses strung out behind him. The snow was melting into slush. He moved slowly, placed his feet cautiously.

The sun tracked across the sky. Harkeld found himself glancing up often, looking for Petrus.

Had something happened? Had the Fithians seen him? Killed him?

Foreboding grew inside him. He found himself praying to the All-Mother: *Let Petrus come back. Let him be all right.* His relief, when he looked up and saw a second hawk circling with Innis, was intense. He halted, hurried back to the packhorses, grabbed a blanket and spread it on the ground. "Petrus!"

Both hawks glided down.

Harkeld rummaged for cloaks for them both, and a waterskin, and dried goat's meat. Questions bubbled inside him. He waited impatiently until Petrus had drunk. "Well? Did you find them?"

Petrus chewed on some goat's meat and nodded.

Harkeld almost reached out and grabbed him by the shoulders and shook him. "And? How many are there?"

Petrus chewed some more and swallowed. "One."

"*One*?"

Petrus nodded. "There's a body where they camped last night. A Fithian. The wagon's been left behind. There's just one assassin headed this way. Got his weapons with him, and the boy. They'll reach the anchor stone in the next hour or so."

"One," Harkeld said again. "Are you certain? Serril said he saw—"

"I followed the road back. Found the rest of 'em. Dead. And a bunch of... I don't know what they were. Outlaws. Bandits."

"From that camp Serril found in the hills?" Innis said.

"I reckon so. They had those manes he was talking about, looked pretty primitive. There were four dead Fithians there, and one further on, makes five. Plus the one still alive, makes six." Petrus reached for the waterskin. "I had a good look around—a really good look—and I swear there's no one alive out here but us, and that one Fithian and the boy. The assassin's an archer, by the way. Got a big bow."

Harkeld touched his chest, rubbed the ridge of scar tissue over his heart. "Only one Fithian. That's... better news than I expected."

# CHAPTER ONE HUNDRED AND THIRTEEN

THE VALLEY SWUNG to the right and ended in a large open space that was roughly circular. Hills rose up on three sides. Jaumé craned his neck. He felt as if he was in a massive arena.

A large, stubby thumb of rock stuck up out of the snow. Bennick dismounted and brushed some snow off. Jaumé saw grainy red stone speckled with white and yellow.

"This'll be it." Bennick slapped the rock and grinned.

The tight, anxious lump in Jaumé's chest grew bigger. He felt slightly sick.

BENNICK SURVEYED THE open space, and headed for the closest trees. Jaumé followed miserably. "Let's get set up," Bennick said. He glanced at the sky. "Hopefully it'll snow again soon. Hide our tracks."

They unloaded the packsaddles and then Bennick led the horses far into the forest. He dumped off the saddles and hobbled the horses. "What'll they eat?" Jaumé asked.

"Larch needles, twigs, snow. They'll be all right for a day or so. Long as no wolves come."

"Wolves?"

Bennick shrugged. "This is wolf country."

Jaumé hugged his pony tightly. "Be careful," he told her.

The pony didn't seem concerned. Jaumé glanced back as they left. She was investigating a tree. He heard a twig crunch between her teeth.


BENNICK HAD BROUGHT a tent. "Stand well back," he said, and then, "Even further, lad." He carefully dug out a patch of snow, working slowly, keeping his nose and mouth covered. Jaumé watched him pitch the tent and shovel the snow back again. When Bennick had finished, only the top of the tent showed. "All-Mother willing, it'll snow some more," Bennick said.

They put their supplies in the tent—food, waterskins, sleeping mats and blankets—and then Bennick prowled the edge of the trees, looking for the perfect shot. "Here," he said, finally. "This is the spot. Can't miss from here."

# CHAPTER ONE HUNDRED AND FOURTEEN

PETRUS WALKED THE last two hours of daylight. Fifty yards ahead, Prince Harkeld moved through the trees, leading five horses. The morning's icy crispness had given way to a raw dampness. The snow was melting, the orange of larch needles bright on the ground. Fog began to gather between the tree trunks.

At dusk, they halted. He and the prince put up the tent. Wet larch needles squelched beneath their boots.

"If I light a fire, you reckon that Fithian'll see it?"

Petrus sat back on his heels. "If we dig a pit, keep it small..."

The prince dug, frowning, and stopped with his boot resting on the shovel blade. "Why does the assassin have a boy with him?"

"Recruit," Petrus said. "Fithians always have an eye out for a likely lad. Situations like this— plagues, wars, floods—any time you've got children separated from their families, children orphaned... Fithians pick up a lot of recruits."

\* \* \*

THEY SAT BY the fire and ate leathery strips of dried goat's meat. Petrus hunted through the packsaddles and found a pouch of nuts. "Flin." He tossed the pouch over.

The prince took a handful of nuts and tossed the pouch back. "There's no reason to call me Flin any more, is there?"

Petrus shrugged. He chewed on a nut. "Can't see any harm in calling you Prince Har—"

"No." The prince winced. "Not prince, or sire, or highness. Just Harkeld."

Petrus shrugged again. "If that's what you want."

They ate the nuts in silence. "Look," the prince said, when he'd finished. "About what I said this morning—"

"You were right." Petrus veered away from memory of Justen. Now wasn't the time to mourn him; he needed to concentrate on keeping Innis and Harkeld alive.

The prince met his eyes. After a moment, he nodded.

"I reckon we'll be at the anchor stone by noon." Petrus remembered the second anchor stone, remembered the prince's flayed palm. "You want to practice burning stone tonight?"

Harkeld pulled a face; he was remembering too. "Yes."

PETRUS SWAPPED WITH Innis and flapped up into the sky as an owl. He watched Innis eat, watched the prince melt his handprint into half a dozen rocks, watched them sit together at the fire. The way they looked at each other—Innis, in shy glances, Harkeld, serious and searching—told him they weren't discussing the anchor stone. Their conversation was more personal than that. Personal, and important.

He wasn't stupid; he could guess what they were talking about: the future, their relationship.

Petrus veered away from the campsite, climbed above treetops, swung out over the valley. He wanted to hate the prince, wanted to *want* the prince to die tomorrow—but he couldn't. He liked the man.

Liked Harkeld. Loved Innis.

Rut it. Rut it. *Rut it*.

WHEN PETRUS RETURNED to the campfire, Innis and Harkeld were holding hands.

Bitterness caught him, and took him high above the treetops again, and in a fierce swoop down the ridge, and out in a wide arc over the valley. By the time he'd climbed back up to the campsite, the bitterness had ebbed to resignation and Innis and the prince were preparing for bed.

They couldn't have sex until Innis had completed her training. That gave Petrus sour satisfaction.

Innis looked up and waved goodnight—and he felt ashamed of himself. He did wish them happiness together, he *did*, it was just...

Rut it.

# CHAPTER ONE HUNDRED AND FIFTEEN

BRITTA CHECKED THE two outer doors, and retreated into the living quarters. Most of the doors had crossbars, which she slid across. She closed the shutters in Karel's bedchamber, moved the waterskins, some food, several unlit candles, the tinderbox, and the sword, in there, and barred that door, too. Karel was awake, watching her.

Britta took off her boots, blew out the candle, and crawled under the wolf skins.

"Britta, you shouldn't sleep in the same bed as me."

"So get out and sleep on the floor," she said, knowing he couldn't.

Karel laughed. The sound choked off painfully.

They lay in silence for several minutes. The bed smelled of wolf skins, and sweat and blood.

"I remember the first time I saw you," Karel said. "You looked like a doll."

"I did?" She tried to remember back to the day he'd been assigned to her. Three years ago? Three and a half?

"You were dressed in pink and silver, and you had that crown on your head, and you looked so *pretty*."

The way he said it, it wasn't a compliment. "Blue eyes and golden hair. Like a doll."

Britta lay very still. His words felt like a slap on the face.

"I hated you," Karel said. "Did you know that? I stood there and I looked at you and I hated you."

Britta swallowed. "Why?"

"Because you were a Rutersvard."

Britta bit her top lip. Tears were building in her eyes. She blinked them back.

"You went to see your father. Yasma came too, carrying your cloak. Do you remember?"

"No."

"The cloak touched one of your father's vases, one of the gold-embossed ones in the atrium, and knocked it over."

"Oh." Memory rushed at her: the smash of porcelain, her father's red-faced rage. *Have her flayed!*

"And then you stepped forward and said it was your fault. I thought he was going to hit you."

Britta shivered. "So did I."

Karel was silent for a moment. "Made me realize you weren't a doll. Weren't a Rutersvard."

The tears came back, filling her eyes. She blinked them away.

"Esger never saw who you are, or Jaegar. Or Duke Rikard. All they ever saw was your face and that crown. Harkeld saw it, though."

*And you did.*

She wanted to reach out and find his hand, but was afraid of his reaction. "I'm glad you were my armsman."

"I was almost assigned to Esger."

Britta shivered again. How different things would have been. For her, for him. "Why weren't you?"

"I think... because I'm from Esfaban. They didn't think I was good enough for the king."

"You're the only island armsman I've seen."

"There are several training, but it's tough. Not many get through."

"How tough?"

"Oh... We start at fifteen. My intake had more than two thousand boys, from all over Osgaard's territories. Two years training to be soldiers—both foot and mounted—then they pick out the best two hundred to train for the elite units."

Britta worked it out quickly in her head. The best two hundred of two thousand boys... The top ten percent?

"That's another year, and at the end of that, the best twenty go on to armsman's training. And at the end of *that*, the best half dozen are trained to be royal bodyguards. Only two of us made it all the way through."

"How long did it take?"

"All up, a bit more than five years."

Five years, and only two men out of two thousand made it. He'd not been exaggerating when he'd said the training was tough.

"I went to you. Bertolt went to Esger."

Bertolt. She could have had an armsman called Bertolt. If she had, her life would be quite different. She would never have escaped to Lundegaard, and her little half-brothers would be dead. Duke Rikard might even be alive—would Bertolt have killed him, as Karel had done?

Britta had a sudden, overwhelming, throat-choking awareness of just *how* great her luck had been.

She swallowed, and inhaled deeply several times. When she was certain she had control of her voice, she said, "Karel?"

He didn't reply. He was asleep.

Britta reached out underneath the wolf skins and found his hand. A swordsman's calloused hand.

Karel was badly injured, barely able to move, much less fight, but even so, he made her feel safe. He made her feel safe, and he made her feel strong. He made her feel as if she could achieve the impossible.

# CHAPTER ONE HUNDRED AND SIXTEEN

PETRUS STAYED CLOSE to the campsite, gliding silently through the trees. Clouds gathered over the mountains and blotted out the moon and stars. Was a snowstorm brewing?

Midway through the night, he swapped with Innis. She was curled up as a wolf, just inside the tent entrance. Petrus shook her awake. Innis crept outside and changed into herself. The fire had died down to a few glowing embers. Without owl eyes, the forest was pitch black. "Everything's fine," he said, in a low voice. "Didn't see anything moving."

Innis put a hand on his arm and leaned close. "What about the princess and the armsman?" she whispered. "Are they with the assassin?"

"They're not with him, and they're not where you saw them last night. I checked. There are no bodies, nothing. I reckon they escaped."

"Escaped?"

"I think they took a boat."

"A boat? On that river?" Her voice was appalled.

"We'll deal with it tomorrow. After the anchor stone. Maybe we'll find them." The chances weren't good. *They're probably dead. Or cursed.*

# CHAPTER ONE HUNDRED
AND SEVENTEEN

BENNICK CRAWLED OUT of the tent at dawn. He went
to the spot he'd chosen and stood there, watching,
waiting. Jaumé stayed in the tent, peering through
the opening. He could barely make Bennick out,
even though he knew he was there, and if he could
hardly see Bennick, how would Prince Harkeld and
the witches see him?

Agitation gnawed in Jaumé's chest.

Bennick had his bow and arrows, and his sword,
and his heavy throwing knife, and his Stars. Jaumé
knew how swift and deadly Bennick was. He hit his
target every time. Jaumé remembered the cursed
hillmen. Bennick had killed three of them faster than
he could blink.

Somehow, he had to stop Bennick killing the
prince.

Snowflakes began to drift down. The far hillside
retreated behind a haze of falling snow.

"Couldn't be better," Bennick said, cheerful. "The
snow will cover our tracks."

Jaumé's agitation grew. It jittered and twisted and
gnawed inside him. He kept his eyes fixed on the

snow-covered lump that was the curse stone. *Don't come*, he begged the prince silently. *Don't come!*

But he knew the prince would come. And he knew he had to stop Bennick from killing him. He just didn't know how.

# CHAPTER ONE HUNDRED AND EIGHTEEN

FAT, WHITE SNOWFLAKES floated down through the black trees. The flakes stuck to Harkeld's eyelashes, his clothes, the ground. By mid-morning, the orange larch needles were covered in a thick layer of white. And on top of that, was the oily stain of Ivek's curse.

The track wound its way steeply downhill. Beneath the fresh snow, yesterday's half-melted snow had refrozen into ice, slick and treacherous. Harkeld moved slowly, cautiously. *I wanted a snowy winter. What a fool I was.*

Another hour passed. The track became narrower, steeper. His boots slipped on larch needles, on ice, on snow. And each time he slipped, his heart lurched in his chest.

Innis was fifty yards ahead, five horses strung out behind her. Beyond her, the ground looked as if it flattened. *Almost there.* Harkeld took a big stride, skidded on needles, grabbed at the air, and tumbled backwards.

He lay where he'd fallen, afraid to move, afraid to inhale. Snowflakes spun down out of the sky and settled on his face. *Am I cursed?*

He didn't seem to be.

Slowly, Harkeld pushed up to sit. Cursed snow clung to his cloak, his sleeves, his hands. He breathed shallowly.

Petrus landed on the track and changed into himself. "Don't move. I'll help you up."

"My curse shadow hasn't changed?" His voice was thin with fear.

"No."

Harkeld took another shallow breath. "Careful. It's rutting slippery."

"No kidding." Petrus took a cautious barefooted step. "It's—ouch—" He stumbled, lost his balance, fell full-length in the snow.

Harkeld scrambled into a crouch. "Petrus?"

Petrus pushed frantically to hands and knees, shook his head, spat. "It got in my mouth!"

They stared at each other. He saw the terror in Petrus's eyes, saw his curse shadow began to darken.

"Petrus, *change shape!*" Harkeld yelled.

# CHAPTER ONE HUNDRED AND NINETEEN

HARKELD STARED AT the wolf. The wolf stared back at him. It was as motionless as he was, not one muscle moving. A shimmer of magic coated its thick fur—but no curse shadow that he could see.

Harkeld inhaled a shallow breath. He straightened from his crouch.

The wolf still didn't move. He'd never before realized how expressive a wolf's body language was. The set of Petrus's ears, the angle of his tail, the way he stood, stiffly, with splayed paws—his terror was plain to see.

Petrus's eyes were no longer green. They were golden, and anguished.

Harkeld swallowed, found his voice. "You don't have a curse shadow now." He shook the cursed snow from his cloak, brushed it off his sleeves, walked the two steps to Petrus, and crouched and hugged the wolf.

Petrus leaned against him and whimpered.

"I think it's going to be all right." Harkeld raised his head and bellowed, "Innis!"

Petrus was shivering. Not because he was cold; his fur was dense and thick.

Harkeld hugged the wolf more tightly, stroking the silvery fur. *Let him be all right, please, All-Mother. I beg you.* He knew he couldn't burn Petrus to death.

He heard Innis scrambling up the slope.

"Careful," he called. "Don't slip."

She reached them half a minute later, panting, anxious. "What's wrong?"

"I fell over and Petrus shifted shape to help me and he fell over, too, and got some snow in his mouth. His curse shadow started to change."

He saw her horror, saw her face grow pale.

"He changed into a wolf," Harkeld told her hurriedly. "Can't have been cursed more than a second or two. It hadn't got him properly. I think he's all right. His behavior's... he's not insane or anything."

Innis reached out to touch the wolf's head. Her eyes were as anguished as Petrus's.

"He's all right," Harkeld said again. "I'm pretty sure." He released the wolf, stroked its flank. "I just... I don't know what's going to happen when he changes back into himself. Do you think... he'll be all right?"

Innis blinked back tears. "I don't know."

"If he's not... I can't burn him, Innis."

The tears spilled from Innis's eyes. She shook her head, and hugged Petrus fiercely. "If he's cursed, I'll do it. It's... better."

The wolf whined and tried to lick her face.

Harkeld climbed to his feet. He walked back to the horses he'd been leading, found a blanket, brought it back to Innis and Petrus, and spread it on the ground. Snowflakes spiraled down. "Have him change on here."

Innis released the wolf and wiped the tears from her face. Petrus stepped onto the blanket.

"Check him over first," Harkeld said. "He stepped on something before he fell. Might have cut himself."

Innis checked the wolf, then sat back on her heels. "He's fine."

Harkeld blew out a breath. He crouched on Petrus's other side and stroked his head. "Don't stand up, Petrus, once you've changed. Just... just wait until we know."

Petrus glanced at Harkeld with golden, anxious wolf-eyes and nodded.

Innis laid her hand on the back of the wolf's neck. "Ready?"

Petrus nodded again.

*All-Mother, let him be all right. Please.*

"All right," Innis said. "Do it."

One moment, a silver-pelted wolf stood on the blanket, the next, Petrus was there on hands and knees.

Harkeld scrutinized the shapeshifter's skin— tanned, covered with curse shadows. He stared at the shadows, willing them not to grow darker.

Snowflakes drifted down and landed on Petrus's bare skin. Petrus shivered, the snowflakes melted, and still the shadows remained unchanged.

Harkeld glanced at Innis. "His curse shadow looks all right."

"I can't feel anything in his blood." She removed her hand from the nape of Petrus's neck, gave a shaky laugh.

Petrus raised up to kneel. His face was almost as pale as his hair. "I'm all right?"

Innis nodded. Tears shimmered in her eyes. "Yes," she said, and hugged Petrus tightly.

HARKELD FETCHED A cloak and a waterskin and a pouch of nuts. When he returned, Innis was still hugging Petrus. She released him, sniffed, and wiped her face with her sleeve. "Sorry, I can't seem to stop crying."

Petrus stood. Harkeld hugged him, too. "You scared the horseshit out of me."

"Scared the horseshit out of myself," Petrus said. He wrapped the cloak around himself. His face was still pale. "If you hadn't told me to change shape... Thanks. I was too panicked to think of that."

They ate and drank—not, Harkeld thought, because they were hungry or thirsty, but because they needed the normalcy of it. All around them lay cursed snow, but while they stood on the blanket and crunched nuts and swigged water, they could pretend everything was all right.

"How far to the bottom?" Harkeld asked.

"Maybe ten minutes," Petrus said. "And then it's two, three miles to the anchor stone."

"The Fithian...?"

"He's there."

Harkeld's stomach tied itself in a knot. He wasn't sure what he dreaded most: the anchor stone or the assassin. He rammed the stopper into the waterskin. "Let's go."

# CHAPTER ONE HUNDRED AND TWENTY

"Shapeshifter," Bennick said. "Hawk."

Jaumé held his breath and peered through the falling snow. Where?

He found the bird and watched it anxiously, hoping it had seen them. Was Bennick going to shoot it?

The hawk swung away and disappeared from view.

Bennick whistled a few bars of a tune. "The prince can't be far." Jaumé had to look twice to see him. He stood motionless beside a tree trunk, his cloak white with snow.

Jaumé crouched in the tent, in a state of agonized indecision. He looked at Bennick, and at the place in the sky where the hawk had been, and at the lump of the curse stone.

Da whispered in his ear, *You got to do something, son.*

Jaumé picked up his bow and quiver and crawled outside and went to crouch on the other side of the tree trunk from Bennick.

# CHAPTER ONE HUNDRED AND TWENTY-ONE

AT THE BOTTOM of the hill, the larch trees straggled into what must be a meadow. It was flat, white, pristine. "Reckon they graze their goat herds here in summer," Harkeld said. "Must be what the track's for."

Innis nodded.

They stayed in the trees, hugging the base of the hillside, heading up into the valley. Snow swirled down. The valley was less than half a mile wide, but the slope on the other side kept fading from view.

*If we can't see far, the Fithian can't either.*

Petrus swooped down from the snowy sky. Innis hurried to spread a blanket on the ground for him.

"Well?" Harkeld asked, handing Petrus another blanket to wrap himself in. "Did you see him?"

Petrus nodded. "He's in the trees directly opposite the anchor stone. Got his bow ready."

Harkeld rubbed the scar over his heart. "How far do you reckon he can shoot?"

"Further than the anchor stone. There's no cover. It's right out in the open. You'll be in full view maybe two hundred yards before you get to the stone. The last fifty of that, you'll be in range. Even with this snow, he'll see you."

Harkeld grimaced. "So, I'll stop before I get in range and burn him." *If I can see him.* "The boy?"

"He's there, too."

His stomach seemed to turn over.

"The Fithian... he saw me. Had to have known I was a shapeshifter. Hawks don't hunt in this kind of weather."

"So he knows we're close."

"At a guess, yes."

Harkeld glanced at Innis, and forced a smile. "Don't worry. I wager you a sword-weight in gold that I can throw fire further than he can shoot an arrow."

THE VALLEY ENDED in a natural amphitheater, ringed by larch-covered hillsides. They halted at the edge of the trees. Harkeld scanned the snowy ground. "Where's the anchor stone?"

"There." Innis pointed to the right.

"Where?" He squinted. "Ah... I see it."

It seemed almost too easy, that the anchor stone should be in this lonely little valley. Surely it should be hidden deep in the Widow Makers? Surrounded by precipices and crevasses and howling snowstorms. *Ivek ran out of time*, Harkeld reminded himself. *For which we should thank the All-Mother.*

He studied the anchor stone. It wasn't in the center of the clearing, but far off to one side, jutting up from the ground, waist-high, almost impossible to see in the snow. Thirty or so yards behind it, the larches started.

The larches where the assassin and the boy were.

Snow swirled in the air, drifting down, making everything indistinct. He couldn't burn the Fithian from here. He could barely see the trees.

Harkeld inhaled a deep breath. "Let's leave the horses here." He beckoned Petrus down, held out his arm for the hawk to land on. "You'll have to tell me where he is. Stop me before we get in range of his bow."

The hawk nodded, spread its wings, took off again.

Harkeld gathered two blankets, slung them over his shoulder, and turned to Innis. "You should shift. You'll be safer."

She shook her head. "Right now, I'm a healer, not a shapeshifter."

"But—"

"I can heal you or Petrus better if I'm dressed and not freezing to death."

"Yes, but—"

"I can always change shape, if I need to."

He sighed, and gave up. "Fine."

Innis tucked her hand into his. "Ready?"

Harkeld stared down at her face, at her dark gray eyes, at the freckles on her nose. *I don't want you to come. It's too dangerous.* "Ready."


THEY LEFT THE safety of the trees, their boots squeaking in the snow. Harkeld kept his eyes on the larches behind the anchor stone, searching for movement. Where was the assassin? But he couldn't make out the individual tree trunks through the falling snow, let alone see a man and a child.

The anchor stone grew closer, the trees became easier to distinguish, and he still couldn't spot the assassin. Harkeld's steps slowed. "We must almost be in range."

Petrus swooped low in front of them. Harkeld hastily shrugged the two blankets from his shoulder and spread one on the ground.

Petrus landed and changed into himself.

Harkeld gave him the other blanket. "You know where he is?"

The shapeshifter nodded, hugging the blanket around himself. "You see that spindly little larch that's furthest out into the clearing? Well, go back from it and left..."

It took five minutes before Harkeld was certain he was looking at the right tree. He still couldn't see the assassin, but he trusted Petrus. "And the boy?"

"Crouched down low, on the other side of the trunk."

"So I won't burn him?"

"If he doesn't move, and if you don't burn the tree... he should be all right."

*Should.* Which meant he might burn the child.

Harkeld took a deep breath. He shook out his right hand, flexed his fingers. Dread was tight and uncomfortable in his belly.

"I reckon you've got another ten yards before you're in range of his bow."

"Ten?"

Harkeld walked forward half a dozen paces, his eyes fixed on the tree. Snow squeaked beneath his boots, snowflakes whirled into his face. Still, he couldn't see the assassin. One more step—

His left boot sank deep in a hole. Harkeld staggered, fell, caught himself with his left hand, plunging elbow-deep in the snow. Something—rock or stick—stabbed the web of flesh between thumb and forefinger. "Ouch." He reared back, jerked his hand free of the snow, saw blood.

INNIS LUNGED FORWARD, grabbed his wrist, and squeezed it tightly between her fingers.

No one spoke. No one breathed.

The shadow covering Harkeld's left hand thickened and grew dark. The rest of his curse shadow remained unchanged.

Harkeld swallowed, swallowed a second time, tried to find his voice. "Can you hold it back?" The words came out thin and high-pitched.

"I think so."

Petrus dropped the blanket in the snow. "Get him to the stone. I'll take the assassin. Hurry!"

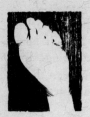

# CHAPTER ONE HUNDRED AND TWENTY-TWO

THE HAWK FLEW towards them, fast and low. Behind him, two people were running towards the curse stone. One of them was the prince. Jaumé *knew* it.

"I reckon that's the lot of 'em," Bennick said. "Three. Too easy."

Jaumé heard Bennick draw back the bowstring. His agitation burst into panic. Bennick had killed the prince before, from further away than this. He scrambled to his feet. "Wait!"

Too late. An arrow speared into the sky.

The hawk swerved at the last moment—the arrow caught its shoulder, not its breast—and plummeted, hit the snow—cartwheeled—and lay still, less than a dozen yards away.

# CHAPTER ONE HUNDRED AND TWENTY-THREE

THE PRINCE PLOUGHED through the snow. Innis hurried alongside, gripping strongly with her fingers and her magic, pinching closed the veins and arteries in his wrist. She could feel the curse in the prince's hand, feel the terrible *wrongness* in his blood. His heart was pumping fast, and with each beat it grew harder to block the curse. Fresh blood tried to force its way into his hand; tainted blood tried to force its way up his arm.

"Slow down," she cried. "Slow down!"

Prince Harkeld turned to her, desperation on his face. "The curse!"

"I can't hold it back if you run."

He gulped a breath. "Then we'll walk."

Walk they did, pushing through the snow. Innis glanced ahead. How far was the anchor stone? Thirty yards? Prince Harkeld's hand was turning purple beneath the thick, black curse shadows, and even though her fingers and her magic were tightly clamped around his wrist, she was aware of a change in his blood, a trickle of something that wasn't him. Savagery. Violence.

The prince felt it, too. His panic rose. "Be ready to kill me."

# CHAPTER ONE HUNDRED
# AND TWENTY-FOUR

BENNICK CAME OUT from the trees. He took half a
dozen steps, stopped, nocked another arrow.

"No!" Jaumé cried, fumbling for his throwing
knife.

The hawk on the ground turned into a naked man.
He pushed to his feet, lurched, caught his balance.
The arrow stuck right through his shoulder.

The witch stepped between Bennick and the curse
stone and stood there swaying, panting. "I won't let
you kill him."

"No?" Bennick sighted at him.

Jaumé desperately threw his knife. It hit Bennick's
right shoulder.

Bennick jerked, and the arrow whipped past the
witch's face, missing him by a hair's breadth.

# CHAPTER ONE HUNDRED AND TWENTY-FIVE

HARKELD GULPED COLD air. Snowflakes stung his face. His heart beat frantically in his chest. He kept his eyes fixed on the anchor stone. Another half minute and they'd be there. But could he last half a minute?

He was aware of fear and panic—and also rage. The rage built in him with every step he took, primitive and savage. It churned in his blood, fogged his brain.

His breath was coming faster, in quick pants. And with each inhalation, the rage built. His vision seemed stained with blood.

"Innis..." His voice sounded thick, unfamiliar. "We're going to have to run."

"We can't. Stay calm."

*Calm?* His control almost snapped. Rage almost bellowed out of him. He almost turned. Almost struck her.

Harkeld gritted his teeth and clung to his control. He concentrated on moving his legs, on walking. Walking. Walking.

Alongside the rage, was a rising hunger. Hunger such as he'd never experienced. He wanted blood.

Wanted blood on his tongue. Blood streaming down his throat. Blood in his belly. The hunger was intense. He almost groaned from the agony of it.

# CHAPTER ONE HUNDRED AND TWENTY-SIX

BENNICK SPUN ROUND. "What you doing, boy?"

"You can't kill the prince." Jaumé hastily unslung his bow and nocked an arrow. His hands were trembling. Behind Bennick and the witch, he saw the two people. They were walking. Too slow. Bennick would easily kill them.

"Can't I?" Bennick's face hardened. He reached beneath his cloak. A Star was suddenly in his hand.

Panic burst in Jaumé's chest. He released the arrow. It struck Bennick in the middle of his forehead.

Bennick pitched backwards. The Star spun over Jaumé's head in a lopsided arc.

# CHAPTER ONE HUNDRED AND TWENTY-SEVEN

"WE'RE NEARLY THERE," a woman said.

Harkeld turned his head and looked at her, didn't recognize her, didn't see anything but *female*. Black hair dusted with snowflakes. Smooth, pale skin. Soft lips.

Lust spiked in his groin, as intense as the hunger.

He halted, panting. The lust stabbed him again, so strongly that he almost doubled over in pain. He wanted to tear off her clothes. Wanted to bury his cock in her. Wanted to see her blood on the snow, taste her blood in his mouth.

The woman tugged his wrist. "Harkeld, come on."

Harkeld. The name sparked faint memory. *That's me. I'm Harkeld.*

And with that knowledge, came another spark of memory: the Ivek Curse.

A tiny sliver of sanity found its way through the blood-stained fog in his brain. He wrenched his gaze from the woman and fastened his gaze on the lump a dozen paces ahead of them in the snow. He knew what it was. Anchor stone.

*Get to it. Get to it.*

He stumbled alongside the woman, wrestling with his rage, with his lust. The curse bellowed in his blood: *Hurt her. Rut her.*

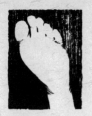

# CHAPTER ONE HUNDRED AND TWENTY-EIGHT

JAUMÉ STARED AT Bennick, at the outflung arms, the slack jaw, the arrow jutting from his forehead. Horror reverberated inside him. His heartbeat thundered in his head, pressing out all sound.

*I killed Bennick?*

The witch said something. Jaumé gulped down hysteria. He nocked another arrow, his hands hasty, trembling, and pointed it at the man.

"Are you going to kill me, too?" the witch asked.

Jaumé lowered the bow. Tears filled his eyes. He shook his head.

"Stay here," the witch said. "The prince has the curse." He turned and ran towards the curse stone, lurching and stumbling.

Jaumé looked at Bennick's body, and at the two people and the curse stone, and at the naked witch stumbling through the snow, the arrow sticking through his shoulder.

He ran after the witch.

# CHAPTER ONE HUNDRED AND TWENTY-NINE

INNIS SWEPT SNOW off the stone. The action sparked a memory: a smoky cavern, charred skeletons, ash. But that stone had been black; this one was rust red.

Prince Harkeld tried to jerk his hand free from her grip.

"No." She snatched the knife from the sheath at her waist, pressed the blade to his left palm, and slapped his hand on the stone.

The scent of blood rose in the cold air.

Prince Harkeld swung towards her. His lips curled back from his teeth.

"Harkeld!" Innis said sharply.

He didn't recognize his name. The curse shadows cloaking his face were almost as black as the ones smothering his left hand.

Her healing magic told her what the curse had done to him; she could feel the insanity and the bloodlust, the mad savagery. Innis searched frantically with her magic, trying to find some part of him that was unaltered, trying to find the bond they shared when they dreamed together.

The prince snatched at her with his right hand, the fingers hooked like claws.

Innis didn't release his wrist, didn't stop pressing his left hand to the anchor stone, didn't stop searching with her magic.

His fingers snarled in her cloak. He hauled her closer.

Innis tried to pull free while keeping her weight on his left hand. How much blood did the stone need?

Teeth snapped together half an inch from her cheek.

Innis recoiled. She wrenched free and released his wrist, scrambling back.

Prince Harkeld snarled and tried to follow her—and jerked to halt.

His left hand had stuck to the anchor stone, just like it had in Ankeny.

The prince uttered a baffled roar. He turned back to the stone and tugged. Tugged again. His hand didn't come free. It was sinking into the sandstone as if it was mud, not rock.

Prince Harkeld raised his head. They stared at each other, both panting. Black curse shadows covered the prince, covered the stone, covered the snow. Killing lust was in his eyes.

"Harkeld," she said. "It'll be over in a minute."

The prince didn't seem to hear her. He tried to wrench his hand free again.

A faint groan came from within the anchor stone. A crack snaked across its surface.

The prince tried to free his hand again. The expression on his face changed. Not madness; but panic.

"Harkeld?" Innis moved warily closer.

The prince didn't try to grab her, didn't try to bite her. He uttered a wordless cry of panic, of pain.

Innis laid her hand on top of his. She felt what the stone was doing to him. Gulping down his blood. Greedy. Killing him.

"Melt your hand free!" she cried. "Like you did last night."

But Prince Harkeld didn't hear her. He was too caught by the curse, too maddened.

Innis grabbed his hair and hauled his head down. She thrust healing magic into him, and screamed in his ear: "*Melt your hand free!*"

For a fraction of a second she felt something—a bond as thin and fragile as a strand of cobweb. A tiny spark of sanity must have remained somewhere inside him. Fire magic coursed down the prince's arm. His hand came free from the stone. He staggered back, and fell.

"Harkeld!" She dropped to her knees and reached for his bleeding hand, but he rolled towards her, snarling, snatching at her.

Innis scrambled backwards. "Harkeld! No!"

He grabbed her legs, hauled her towards him. Black curse shadows still covered him. Bloodlust was still in his eyes.

The anchor stone gave a loud, splintering *crack* and disintegrated. Gritty red dust sprayed out over the snow.

Prince Harkeld released her. His body spasmed, every muscle going rigid.

The ground beneath them groaned and trembled. The hillsides and the larches groaned and trembled, the very air seemed to groan and tremble—and then the groan died to a whisper and the whisper died into silence. Innis heard the snowflakes falling. It was as if the world held its breath.

The curse shadows melted away. Snow lay white and clean in all directions, uncursed. She saw Prince Harkeld's skin clearly.

"Harkeld?"

Another spasm racked his body. He screamed, a raw, agonized sound.

Innis grabbed his arm and thrust her healing magic into him. She felt his pain, as if every vein and artery in his body had been slashed open with a knife.

She held him while he convulsed, while he screamed. Held him while his body went limp and he slipped into unconsciousness. He'd lost more blood than she'd realized. He was shockingly weak, his heart struggling to cope.

Innis kept his heart beating with her magic and hastily sealed the cut on his palm. But something else was wrong. Seriously wrong. She could sense damage, somewhere...

She searched frantically, sending her magic through his body, and found the injury inside his skull. Blood leaked from burst capillaries in his brain. Not just one hemorrhage, but scores of them. Tiny, seeping, fatal.

Innis worked with feverish haste to heal them, but for every one she mended, there were a dozen more. "Curse you, Harkeld," she whispered, weeping, frantic. "You have to *live*."

\* \* \*

"INNIS!" PETRUS STAGGERED to a halt. The snow was red with dust, red with blood. Prince Harkeld lay sprawled, his face as pale as if he was dead. Innis crouched alongside him, cradling his head. The terrible screaming had stopped, but the sound still echoed in Petrus's ears. "Did he hurt you?"

Innis didn't look up, didn't reply.

Petrus grabbed her shoulder and shook her. "Did he hurt you?"

She raised her head, but didn't seem to see him, blinded by tears. "He's dying."

"What? How?"

"His brain. Bleeding."

Petrus released her shoulder. Brain injuries required more subtle healing magic than he possessed. He couldn't help her, couldn't help Harkeld.

A shiver racked him. He looked for the blankets and saw them sixty yards away, a dark patch in the snow.

Another shiver gripped him, so strong he almost fell. Petrus looked for the boy and found him standing behind him, eyes wide and frightened. "Help us, son?"

The boy nodded.

"I need those blankets." He headed towards them, weaving and stumbling. His feet were leaden, clumsy, numb. Pain radiated from his shoulder, stabbing with each step, each breath. The boy trotted ahead, grabbed the blankets, brought them back.

"One on the ground," Petrus said, through chattering teeth.

The boy laid one blanket down.

Petrus half-fell onto it, panting and dizzy. The boy wrapped the second blanket around him. The arrow snagged on the blanket, tugged in his shoulder, a jolt of pain that made everything go black for a moment.

Petrus blinked, and tried to focus. The snow was coming down more thickly. If they didn't get shelter, they'd all die. "Our horses. They're in the trees. Can you fetch them? We need the tents."

# CHAPTER ONE HUNDRED AND THIRTY

JAUMÉ FETCHED THE witches' horses and put up two tents. He helped the female witch drag Prince Harkeld into one of them. The prince didn't look like a prince. He was dirty and unshaven and his clothes smelled of sweat and blood. He also looked dead. As dead as Bennick.

The shapeshifter crawled into the second tent. He was shivering, his skin almost blue with cold. "Can you help me get this arrow out?"

Jaumé nodded. He cast a surreptitious glance at the witch's feet, afraid he'd see hooves, but the man had human feet. And his eyes were human, too. Green.

The arrow had gone right through the witch's shoulder. "We need to cut the fletching off," the man said. "You got a knife?"

Jaumé shook his head. His knife was sticking into Bennick.

"Harkeld's got one. On his belt."

Jaumé fetched the prince's knife and cut off the fletching.

"Pull out the arrow. Careful, the arrowhead's sharp. Wrap something around it, or you'll cut yourself."

Jaumé wrapped the hem of his cloak around the arrowhead and tugged. The arrow didn't move.

"Brace yourself against my back."

Jaumé took the arrowhead in both hands, braced his boots against the witch's back, and pulled *hard*. The arrow moved grudgingly—and then slid free in a rush. The witch gave yelp of pain. Blood trickled fast down his back.

Jaumé dropped the arrow and hastily pressed his cloak to the wound. He looked around for something he could use as a bandage, but there was nothing in the tent. *My shirt*, he thought. That's what Bennick had used; torn shirts.

"You can stop pressing," the witch said.

Jaumé cautiously lifted his hand. The wound was still there, in the back of the witch's shoulder, but the blood had slowed to a thin trickle. "Are you healing yourself?"

The witch nodded. His teeth were gritted.

"Can I help?" Jaumé asked.

The witch shook his head. He sat shivering, both hands pressed just below his collarbone.

"Um... I'll just put the blanket over you."

Jaumé draped the blanket over the man, like a shawl.

"Thanks," the witch said, and closed his eyes and frowned hard.

Jaumé sat back on his heels. This was how the witches had saved the prince in Ankeny. Magic.

He watched for several minutes, but there was nothing to see: just a man sitting with his eyes closed and his hands pressed to his shoulder.

Jaumé crawled out of the tent. The witches' horses were where he'd left them, huddled together, facing into the wind. *We need a fire. We need food.* But instead, Jaumé jogged through the snow towards where he and Bennick had camped. He veered around Bennick's body and hurried into the trees, slipping and sliding on larch needles, pushing deeper into the forest.

The pony was where he'd left her. Jaumé hugged her tightly, gulping back tears.

JAUMÉ BROUGHT THE pony and the horses back to where the curse stone had been, then he fetched his sleeping mat and blankets, and the food and waterskins. It took several trips. The path he made was a curve around where Bennick lay. Bennick's body was already covered by snow, but Jaumé could see the shape of him. And the arrow, sticking up out of the snow.

Next, he gathered branches for a fire. He didn't try to light it; the snow was still falling.

He looked into the first tent, where the prince lay like a dead man and the female witch held his head, and into the second tent. The shapeshifter opened his eyes. "Almost done. Come on in, son. Tell me your name. I'm Petrus."

Jaumé crawled in. "Jaumé."

"Where are you from?" The witch's accent wasn't like any he'd heard before. The *r* was throaty, the *s* soft and hissing.

"Girond."

"Which is where?"

"Vaere. On the coast. It's a fishing village."

The witch frowned. "East coast, or west?"

"East. As far east as you can go."

The witch's frown deepened. "And your family?"

Jaumé looked down at his hands. There was blood on one finger. He rubbed it off, and glanced at the witch. "The curse got them."

The man nodded, as if this was the answer he'd expected. "Tell me how you got here, Jaumé."

Jaumé told him everything. The witch listened, and sometimes asked questions, and once Jaumé asked the witch a question: "Bennick called you mages, and said witches and mages are the same thing, but... they're not, are they?"

"Means the same thing, but witch isn't a word we use. It's not polite."

"But..." Jaumé tried to find the words to explain his question. "But witches are *evil*, and they have hooves instead of feet, and goat's eyes, and some of them even have asses' heads, and... and you're not like that."

"No one's like that, Jaumé. It's a fishwives' tale."

"Oh." Jaumé thought about this for a moment, and then put it aside to consider later, and continued with his story. The mage asked more questions when he got to the bit about the princess and her soldier, and even more when he described their escape.

"I'll look for them tomorrow, first thing. And I'll help you bury Bennick."

"Brothers don't like to be buried," Jaumé said. "They just want to face Fith."

"Then I'll help you with that. Now..." The mage pushed aside his blanket. "Let me get some clothes on."

"Are you all healed?"

"I am. See?"

Jaumé looked closely at the pink scars on Petrus's shoulder, front and back. "Could you heal Karel? He needs it."

"If I find him, I will."

Petrus dressed, and went to check on Prince Harkeld. Jaumé followed. "How is he?" Petrus asked the female mage.

"Better, but not good."

Jaumé studied the man lying in the tent. He was thin and ragged and dirty, like a peasant. Jaumé didn't recognize him from Ankeny.

"Innis, this is Jaumé. He saved our lives."

The woman smiled at Jaumé, a sad smile. Like Petrus, she had human eyes. Hers were dark gray.

Jaumé didn't know what to say to her. He ducked his head awkwardly.

Petrus and Jaumé both crawled from the tent. The snow had stopped falling. The sky was darkening; night wasn't far away.

"Did you gather this wood?" the mage asked.

Jaumé nodded.

"Good work. Let's get a fire going and see to some food."

Jaumé hesitated. "Can we turn Bennick to face Fith, first?"

Petrus looked at him for a moment, and then nodded. "Of course we can."

They walked to where Bennick lay. Petrus crouched and brushed the snow from Bennick's face, and pulled the arrow from Bennick's forehead and put it to one side. The light was fading from the sky, and Bennick's hair looked brown, not red-blond, and the hole in his forehead was black. His eyes were open.

Petrus closed them, then he took Bennick's legs and dragged him around until his head pointed towards the tallest hills.

"Do you know where Fith is?" Jaumé asked anxiously.

"Somewhere north. No one but Fithians know exactly where."

"Is he facing north now?"

"He is."

Petrus picked up Jaumé's throwing knife. It lay in the snow, with Bennick's blood on the blade. "You want this?"

Jaumé shook his head. "It was Bennick's." His voice wobbled slightly.

Petrus laid the knife alongside Bennick and came to stand beside Jaumé. He rested his hand on Jaumé's shoulder. "You want to say words to the All-Mother for him, or shall I?"

"He wouldn't want us to," Jaumé said. His voice broke on the last word. Tears spilled from his eyes.

Petrus crouched, and hugged him.

Jaumé buried his face in the mage's shoulder and cried in great, wrenching, anguished sobs.

"Ah, son," Petrus said, and he stroked Jaumé's hair and picked him up and carried him back to the tents, just the way Da used to carry him, his arms strong and tight.

Jaumé clung to him and cried and thought about Bennick's body facing Fith. And then he thought about what Bennick had told him: *There's nothing wrong with dying. We come, we go.*

At the tents, Petrus put him down, and stayed crouching, looking at him. "You saved a lot of people, you know? Not just me and Innis and Harkeld, but people all through the Seven Kingdoms."

Jaumé sniffed, and gulped, and nodded.

Petrus stood. He rested his hand on the back of Jaumé's neck in a way that felt safe and warm. "I'm going to light the fire and get us some food. Want to help?"

Jaumé scrubbed his face dry with his cloak. "Yes."

While he was rummaging through the mages' packsaddles, he remembered more of Bennick's words. *We all go to the All-Mother in the end. Doesn't matter how, or when.*

# CHAPTER ONE HUNDRED AND THIRTY-ONE

KAREL WAS NO better or worse than he'd been yesterday. Britta brewed willowbark tea, and watched the roads, and wore the sword when she wasn't in Karel's bedchamber. At dusk, she closed the shutters and barred all the doors. The only thing that had changed from yesterday was that they had only one waterskin of safe water left.

"You know what I'd like most?" Karel said, when she was taking off her boots. "A bath. A bath and a razor." He touched the black whiskers on his jaw.

Britta sat on the bed with her feet tucked under her. "There's a bath tub here. I found it yesterday."

Karel lowered his hand. His gaze drifted to a corner of the room and he frowned. "Britta... Yasma once said, Harkeld told you Queen Sigren was murdered."

"Yes." Murdered in her bath tub.

"Did he say anything else?"

"About Sigren?"

"About the other queens."

The other queens? King Esger had had four wives, and they'd all died. "You mean... my mother was murdered, too?"

Karel glanced at her. "Harkeld told you?" She heard relief in his voice.

Britta shook her head. "No. I guessed. Did Father kill my mother?"

"Uh..." Karel looked away from her, to the corner again, as if he wished he could backtrack.

"Did he, Karel?"

"Uh... maybe. That's what some of the older armsmen said."

"Harkeld never said anything. Maybe he doesn't know?" She fingered a wolf skin. "Why would Father kill my mother?"

"He wanted a son."

*And mother gave him five still-born babes, and me.*

"It might not be true," Karel said.

"From what I know of Father... it probably is."

"I'm sorry," Karel said. "I thought—I hoped—Harkeld had told you."

Britta shook her head. She turned the edge of the wolf skin over, felt the thick, warm fur on one side and the supple hide on the other.

"I'm sorry," Karel said again.

"I'd rather know than not know." She looked at him and smiled crookedly. "It gives me another reason never to return to Osgaard." Osgaard, where her father had murdered her mother, and her half-brother had poisoned her father, and in turn, been poisoned himself.

Karel nodded. "Lundegaard would be safer."

Britta shook her head. "Not Lundegaard either."

"But—"

"I told you, I don't want to be a princess."

"Then where?"

"Esfaban."

"Esfaban?" Karel's eyebrows rose.

"With you and Yasma. If Esfaban is freed. If I may."

"Well, of course you *may*, but Britta, Esfaban's been conquered. It's... it's *broken*. It needs to be put back together. If that's even possible."

"It is possible." A kingdom that bred men like Karel would be able to rebuild itself. He had determination and courage and a far-sighted intelligence, as well as kindness and compassion. "If islanders are anything like you, Karel, you'll get Esfaban back on its feet."

"I hope so," Karel said. "I hope we get the chance." He fell silent, his gaze on the far wall, frowning slightly, and she thought he was thinking of Esfaban, and how it could be rebuilt.

After a while, he turned his head and said, "What about the boys? Will you take them to Esfaban?"

"I don't know. Maybe they'll come with me; maybe they'll stay with Magnas. It depends what's best for them."

Not long after that, Karel fell asleep. Britta blew out the candle and climbed under the wolf skins. She found Karel's hand and held it, thinking of Esfaban. Would the people accept her? A Rutersvard princess, daughter of the family that had conquered and enslaved them?

But she didn't want to go to Esfaban as a princess, or a Rutersvard: she wanted to go as Karel's wife. If he would have her.

# CHAPTER ONE HUNDRED AND THIRTY-TWO

THE FEMALE MAGE, Innis, stopped healing Prince Harkeld. There was nothing more she could do. "He's lost a lot of blood. His body needs to make more." She looked very worried. Jaumé thought that she'd been crying. Petrus hugged her for a long time and told her that *of course* the prince would be all right.

Jaumé peeked into the tent and looked at the prince and hoped Petrus was right.

"You're sharing with me," Petrus told him. "If you see a wolf, don't worry, it's just me. I'll be in and out all night."

Jaumé lay down on his sleeping mat, and wrapped himself in his blankets, but he didn't close his eyes. Ivek's curse was broken. No one else would die from it. Except maybe the prince.

He lay awake for a long time, thinking about Mam and Da and Rosa. For the first time since they'd died, it wasn't the blood and Rosa's scream that he remembered most, but all the other things. Da whistling while he hammered horseshoes on the anvil. Mam in the kitchen, kneading bread and singing. Rosa playing hide-and-seek in the barn. He remembered the wooden dolls Da had carved, and the tiny clothes Mam had sewed, and the look on Rosa's face when she'd first seen them. He remembered how Mam used to throw her head back and laugh at Da's jokes, and the way Mam and Da danced together on village feast days, holding each other close. And he remembered Rosa dancing too, skipping and clapping her hands, giggling.

He didn't think about Bennick.

# CHAPTER ONE HUNDRED AND THIRTY-THREE

WHEN HARKELD WOKE, he wasn't sure where he was. A tent. But which tent? And where? He tried to remember back, but his memory was a hazy, chaotic blur. Not remembering was alarming. He pushed his blanket aside and struggled up onto one elbow. His head swam dizzyingly.

"Here," someone said. "Drink some water."

Harkeld turned his head and saw Innis. His alarm snuffed instantly. If Innis was here, everything was all right. "What happened?"

"You destroyed the anchor stone."

"I did?" Relief washed through him. He lay back down.

"You lost a lot of blood. An awful lot of blood. The stone was just *sucking* it out of you."

"It was? I don't remember."

"Just as well. It was nasty. You almost died."

"Did I?" That must be why he felt so tired. "You saved my life again, huh?"

"Have some water," Innis said, and propped his head up and pressed a mug to his lips.

Harkeld drank several mouthfuls.

"Don't try to get up." Innis put the mug down and pulled the blanket up around his throat. "You need to stay in bed, build up your blood again."

Harkeld was fine with staying in bed. He didn't feel like moving; he was exhausted. He closed his eyes, and then alarm grabbed him again and jerked his eyelids open. "Where's Petrus? Is he all right?"

"Gone to look for Rand and Serril."

*I hope they survived.*

Harkeld fumbled for her hand, and held it, and closed his eyes again, and when he opened them, it felt like several hours had passed. Innis wasn't holding his hand. She was no longer in the tent. A boy sat beside him. A stranger.

"Hello?" Harkeld said cautiously. "Who are you?"

"Jaumé."

"Nice to meet you," Harkeld said. Who was Jaumé? The assassin's boy? He glanced around for a weapon. "I'm Harkeld."

"I know," the boy said. "I saw you in Ankeny. At the stone. When Bennick shot you."

"You did?"

Jaumé nodded. "Can I see where he shot you?"

"Uh... all right." Harkeld peeled back the blanket, undid a couple of buttons, and pushed his shirt aside.

The boy leaned close. "Right through the heart. Bennick said it was. He was really angry when the mages healed you."

"I bet he was," Harkeld said, doing up his shirt. He was amused, and confused. "Where's Innis?"

"We heard a wolf. She's gone to scare it away."

"Oh." He examined the boy. He was about eight or nine years old. Bright hazel eyes, dark brown hair, thin face. "How come you're here?"

"It's a long story," Jaumé said.

"I've got time."

Jaumé shrugged, and told his tale. Harkeld listened in astonishment. He forgot he was tired, forgot he was hungry and thirsty. Towards the end, he became aware the boy was skipping a few bits, skirting around something that he didn't want to tell, but then Jaumé got to the part with the anchor stone and he forgot everything else. The assassin had shot Petrus? This boy had killed the assassin?

"You had the curse and were screaming—"

"*I* had the curse?"

The boy nodded. "And you were screaming and *screaming* and Innis said the veins were popping in your head."

"They were?" Harkeld gingerly touched his forehead. He hoped the boy was exaggerating.

"And then you stopped screaming and just lay there. And that's the end."

"Huh." Harkeld stared at the boy. He had a lot of questions; he wasn't sure where to start.

The tent flap pushed open. Innis crawled inside. "You're awake. Good. Did you give him some water, Jaumé?"

The boy hastily poured a mug and handed it to him.

Harkeld raised up on one elbow and sipped it.

"Did you find the wolf and scare it away?" the boy asked.

"I did."

"How?"

Innis grinned. "Turns out wolves are afraid of lions."

"Wolves aren't dumb," Harkeld said. He put down the mug. "Veins *popped* in my head?"

Innis looked at Jaumé.

Jaumé shrugged. "He wanted to know."

# CHAPTER ONE HUNDRED AND THIRTY-FOUR

BRITTA AND KAREL argued about the last waterskin.
Britta wanted to share it; Karel was adamant that
she keep it for herself. "We don't know how long
it will be before Harkeld breaks the curse," the
armsman said. "If you're careful, you'll get another
two days from that skin."

"I'm sharing it with you," Britta said stubbornly.

"If we both drink it, it won't last the day!" Karel
was fiercer than she'd ever seen him.

Britta left the waterskin in the bedchamber and
went out into the yard. She looked at the well, and
the snow on the ground, and thought about the
casks of cider and ale in the barn. Sooner or later,
one of them was going to have to drink something
from this farm.

A shadow passed over the snowy yard. She looked
up and saw a hawk, with wide wings and a creamy
breast. The bird glided down and landed by the well.
It shook its feathers, folded its wings, and changed
into a naked man.

Britta snatched her sword from its sheath. She
brandished it at the man.

The man held his hands palm-out at his waist. "Princess Brigitta?" he said. "Jaumé sent me to find you."

Britta gripped the hilt tightly. "Who are you?"

"My name is Petrus. I've been traveling with your brother."

"Harkeld? He's here?"

"He's at the anchor stone. About a dozen miles from here."

Relief flooded her. There were suddenly tears in her eyes, tears in her throat. "The Fithians didn't kill him?"

"No."

"And the curse?"

"It's broken. Didn't you feel the ground shake yesterday?"

Britta shook her head. She lowered the sword.

"Jaumé said your companion is badly injured. May I see him? I may be able to heal him."

Britta fumbled to put away the sword. She wiped her eyes. "Of course."

The man smiled. He had a tanned, friendly face and untidy white-blond hair. "I apologize for my lack of clothes."

Britta shook her head again. What did clothes matter at a time like this?

She led him across the yard and into the farmhouse, and burst into the bedchamber at a run. "Karel! There's a witch here, and he says the curse is broken, and he may be able to heal you!"

Karel struggled to push up in the bed. Pain spasmed across his face.

"Ribs, huh?" the witch said. "No, don't sit up."

Karel frowned fiercely at him. "Who are you?"

"Petrus. Jaumé sent me to look for you." The witch crossed to the bed. "I apologize for my lack of clothes; hazard of shapeshifting. Now, let's have a look at these ribs."

BRITTA WATCHED FOR several minutes, until she was certain the witch was no threat to Karel, then she hurriedly searched the house and brought back an armful of clothing for the man, and some rags that looked clean enough for bandages.

"All-Mother bless you," the witch said, and dressed quickly. "Cold day."

"How is he?" Britta asked, looking anxiously at Karel.

"Not great, but he'll be a lot better by the time I've finished. I'm not a strong healer, but I'm good at bones, and he's broken a lot of them. Worst set of ribs I've ever seen, plus his collarbone and shoulder blade, and his arm's got two breaks. Came off that horse *hard*."

"His arm? His shoulder blade?" Britta was aghast. "We didn't know that!"

But perhaps Karel had known; he didn't look surprised.

"I'll mend his leg, too. Needs to be done soon, or he won't be able to walk. As for the rest..." The witch shrugged. "Innis or Rand can finish what I can't. Tomorrow or the next day."

"Thank you," Britta said, the words heartfelt.

\*   \*   \*

SHE PUT TOGETHER a tray of smoked sausages and salted pork, and a jug of cider, and carried it into the bedchamber.

"All-Mother bless you," the witch said again, his face lighting up. "I'm starving."

"I've forgotten your name," Britta confessed.

"Petrus."

"How long will it take, Petrus?"

"The bones? A couple of hours."

NEXT, BRITTA HAULED the bath tub into the scullery and heated water in pots on the fire. She found soap, and clean clothes, and a comb, and when the tub was full, she had a bath and washed her hair. It was better than *any* bath she'd had in her life.

She dressed, and combed her hair—it was all different lengths; *I need to trim it*—and headed for the bedchamber. She heard Karel say something, heard Petrus reply, heard Karel chuckle. They sounded like friends.

Britta paused in the doorway. Even though Petrus's coloring was almost the exact opposite of Karel's, the two men looked surprisingly similar—the same age, the same build, the same grin on their unshaven faces.

"How's it going?"

"Good," Petrus said. He stood and stretched, and Britta heard his spine crack. "I'm about to start on his leg. I'd like to cut the stitches. You seen any scissors here, or small knives?"

Britta found a pair of small, sharp scissors in the room with the loom. She took them to Petrus.

"Perfect," he said.

The tray she'd brought them was empty. Britta fetched more food and cider, and set water to heat for Karel's bath. She found clothes that she hoped would fit him, old and patched, but they smelled clean. After much hunting, she also found a razor blade. When she went back, Petrus was cutting the stitches out of Karel's arm.

"You're doing his arm, too?"

"Not completely, but enough that he won't need the stitches. And those ones in his forehead should come out, too."

Britta went back to the pots of heating water, emptied them into the bath tub, refilled them. Then, she looked for fresh sheets for the bed. By the time she'd found some, Petrus was carefully cutting the stitches on Karel's forehead. He snipped the final one and pulled it out. Two tiny drops of blood welled where the stitch had come out. Petrus pressed his thumb over them and narrowed his eyes briefly in concentration, then wiped Karel's brow with a rag, and examined the scar. "Whoever sewed that, did a good job. Very tidy." He stood and stretched, and Britta heard his spine crack again. "I'll see you tomorrow. Karel knows where to go."

"Harkeld will be there?"

Petrus nodded.

"And Jaumé's there, too? Is he all right?"

"He's unhurt. Karel'll tell you all about it." Petrus yawned, and Britta saw how tired he was.

"Would you like to stay here tonight?"

Petrus yawned again and shook his head. "It's only a dozen miles." He began to strip off his clothes.

Karel got out of bed and wrapped a blanket around himself and took the shapeshifter out into the yard. The daylight was fading. Britta watched Karel closely. He moved freely, strongly, as if he'd never been injured. When he came back inside, Britta said, "How do you feel?"

"A thousand times better."

"I've made a hot bath for you.

"You have?" Karel's whole face lit up. "Truly?"

"And I found a razor."

Karel laughed, and then he said the same words Petrus had: "All-Mother bless you."

# CHAPTER ONE HUNDRED AND THIRTY-FIVE

THE PRINCE WAS awake when Petrus glided down to land. He was sitting at the fire, playing a game with Jaumé that involved pebbles and twigs. He looked up and watched Petrus change shape, his face pale, tired, sharp with anxiety. "Well?"

"I found Rand and Serril. They're both up and walking. Rand said Serril's reflexes are good, but he wants to check him over one more time before he lets him shift. They'll set off tomorrow, meet us at the crossroads the day after."

The prince closed his eyes. "Thank the All-Mother." Petrus heard how deep his relief was.

Petrus caught Innis's eye. She followed him to his tent, her expression almost as anxious as the prince's.

"I found our missing princess, too," he told her, in a low voice. "And her armsman."

"Are they all right?"

"The armsman was in a bad way, but I spent the afternoon healing him. They're only a dozen miles from here. Their boat sank. They'll be here by noon tomorrow. Going to walk back to that last farm, then ride up on the horses the Fithians left behind."

"Noon?" Innis said, disbelief and hope mingling in her voice.

"Noon." Petrus looked at Harkeld, who was debating what to do with his last pebble. From his expression, he was losing the game. "You want to tell him now, or wait?"

Innis chewed on her lip. "Wait. Just in case."

"Nothing bad's going to happen." But Petrus understood her need to protect him. The prince was hollow-cheeked beneath the stubble. The bones of his skull seemed to push through his skin. Petrus watched him agonize over where to place the pebble. "Can't wait to see his face when he sees them."

"Petrus... did you find any survivors?"

He glanced at her, and shook his head. "Went all the way down to Andeol and back. Found some fresh bodies. No one alive."

"How fresh?"

He shrugged. "Looked like they died yesterday."

Innis nodded, as if that was the answer she'd expected. "I think what happened to Harkeld—the convulsions, the hemorrhaging—I think that happened to everyone who had the curse. I think they're all dead now."

Petrus thought about the contorted bodies he'd seen. "Reckon you're right." He looked at the prince again. "He's lucky you were with him."


PETRUS DRESSED, AND went to sit at the campfire with the others.

"... the refugees will all go home, now," Prince Harkeld was telling Jaumé.

"Not for a while yet, they won't," Petrus said, holding his hands out to the fire. "No one but us knows the curse is broken. They'll keep running."

"But—" The prince closed his mouth, frowned, and then said, "They can't see the curse shadows are gone."

Petrus shook his head.

"Curse shadows?" Jaumé asked.

Petrus half-listened to the prince's explanation. He thought about the King's Riders he'd seen in Nime. Those men would still be desperately emptying villages, turning people out of their homes. "The sooner we get word back to Sault's king, the better. We should find some King's Riders, tell them."

"Will they believe us?" Innis asked, adding another branch to the fire.

"If Rand shows them the diplomatic seal, they might." Petrus thought about the land he'd flown over today, the smoldering ruin of Andeol, the abandoned farms. More than half of Sault was empty, and all of the kingdom of Vaere. "You think everyone will come back?"

Prince Harkeld glanced at the dark shapes of the mountains surrounding them. "Some will, some won't. The ones who sailed to the Allied Kingdoms... they might not."

"Big task ahead of them. The ones who return."

"Sault will get back on its feet," Prince Harkeld said. "It's got a good king. Vaere will take longer. It was hit hard."

"The other kingdoms will help, won't they?"

The prince snorted. "My father will invade Vaere, if he gets the chance." And then he glanced at Jaumé, and said lightly, "But that's not going to happen. You hungry, son? Let's eat."

# CHAPTER ONE HUNDRED AND THIRTY-SIX

AFTER THEY'D EATEN, Britta pushed her plate away and studied Karel in the candlelight. He looked stern—his cheekbones and eyebrows made it impossible for him not to—but he also looked relaxed. She saw no pain on his face.

Five days ago he'd been close to death, slipping in and out of consciousness. She remembered the way he'd called her name—anguished, desperate—and the utter relief on his face each time he'd opened his eyes and seen her.

"Karel?"

He glanced up.

"There's something I need to discuss with you before we reach Harkeld."

His eyebrows rose. "Sounds serious." He pushed his own plate away and leaned his elbows on the table.

*It is serious.* And it needed to be sorted out now, before Harkeld and Karel could step into their familiar roles of prince and armsman: one giving orders, the other obeying.

Britta took deep breath and tried to ignore her

nervousness. "On the ship, you said you didn't want to marry Yasma."

His eyebrows rose even higher. "I don't."

"Is there someone at home—someone in Esfaban—who's waiting for you?"

He shook his head.

Britta took another deep breath, and clutched her hands together, and blurted, "Will you marry me?"

Karel blinked, and his expression went completely blank, and he pushed back slightly from the table.

"Please?" Britta said.

"Marry you?" He looked away, swallowed, looked back at her. "Britta, you're a princess—"

"So?"

"So, it's not... it's not..."

"My parents are dead. What does it matter who they were?"

Karel closed his mouth and frowned.

"If Esfaban is freed, I want to go back with you."

He stared at her for a long moment, and then said, "You don't have to be my wife to do that."

"Karel... I love you."

"Me?" Emotions crossed his face, too quickly for her to identify them.

"Yes. I need to know if you think you might possibly, one day... love me."

Karel looked away from her. She saw him swallow.

"Or, if you think you never will. If you'd rather wait for someone else."

Karel closed his eyes. What was he thinking?

Britta looked down at her hands, clenched together on the table, and waited.

"Of course I love you," Karel said, his voice low. "I've loved you for years."

Britta raised her head. Karel was looking at her, and the emotion in his dark eyes was so intense that she could scarcely breathe.

Karel wrenched his gaze from hers. He looked down at the table. "Are you sure you wish to marry? After Duke Rikard, I thought—"

"Rikard happened to someone else. It... it doesn't seem *real*. It's like a dream that I can't even remember."

"Probably the poppy syrup."

"Probably." But part of it was also that Rikard was dead, and that she was no longer in Osgaard, and that she'd changed so much in the past few months. She wasn't the submissive Princess Brigitta who'd married Duke Rikard. She was Britta, strong and confident and making her own decisions about her life. And Duke Rikard had never touched Britta.

Britta pushed back her stool and walked to where Karel sat. He watched her approach, his eyes black and wary in the candlelight.

She held out her hand to him. "Marry me? Please?"

He wanted to, and he thought he shouldn't. She could see the struggle on his face, so she bent her head and pressed her lips to his.

Karel became completely still. And then he groaned under his breath, and tried to pull back. "Britta..."

Britta grabbed his hair, held him in place, and kissed him again.

For a long, terrible moment, it seemed that Karel wouldn't respond, and then he kissed her back. His mouth was gentle, reverent, yet also fierce. His arms came around her and he pulled her down to sit on his lap.

They kissed, and kissed some more, and then Britta said, "I want to share your bed tonight."

"Share it?" Karel said cautiously. "You mean...?"

"I mean I want us to have sex. Because tomorrow we'll reach Harkeld, and if he orders you to leave me, I'm afraid you'll obey."

"I won't."

"You've been obeying orders for eight years, Karel. And if Harkeld tells you to—"

"I haven't obeyed every order. And I will never leave you."

"I know." And she *did* know it, but she also wanted to forge their bond so profoundly that no one could ever break it. *I am his, and he is mine.* And so she stood and pulled him to his feet, drawing him towards the bedchamber and the wolf skins and the clean sheets.

Karel resisted. "Maybe we should wait."

"Why?"

To her surprise, Karel blushed.

"Why?" she asked again.

"Britta, I've never lain with a woman. It was either bondservants or whores, and I didn't want either. And... I'm afraid I'll *hurt* you."

"You won't."

Karel looked at her, and she saw the conflict on his face—wait; not wait—and then he swung her up in his arms and carried her into the bedchamber.

# CHAPTER ONE HUNDRED AND THIRTY-SEVEN

THE TENT WAS empty when Jaumé woke. He yawned and rubbed his eyes and crawled outside. The sky was blue and the snow bright white. A large, silver-pelted wolf lay by the fire. It raised its head and looked at him with yellow eyes.

"Petrus?" Jaumé said cautiously.

The wolf winked at him, and stood and stretched and shook itself from head to tail, like a big dog, and changed into Petrus.

Jaumé ate breakfast, and helped Petrus gather more firewood, and then they went across to the creek and checked on the horses. The animals had found the grass beneath the foot-deep snow and were grazing. Mid-morning, the prince emerged from his tent. He was less tottery than yesterday.

Jaumé kept sneaking glances down the valley. When would Princess Britta and her soldier arrive?

Innis patrolled as a hawk, and came back an hour later.

"How far?" Petrus asked her, in a low voice.

"End of the road," Innis whispered back, and went to sit beside the prince at the fire.

Petrus searched through the packsaddles for a needle and thread to mend a hole in his shirt. Jaumé went to help him. When he looked up, the prince had his arm around Innis and they were leaning towards each other, their heads bent close together. Petrus caught his elbow. "Let's give them some time alone." His voice sounded funny. Jaumé looked at his face, and thought his expression was funny, too, as if Petrus didn't know whether he was happy or sad.

THEY STAMPED DOWN a large patch of snow, and Petrus gave him his first wrestling lesson.

"Size and strength matter, but so does this." Petrus tapped his forehead. "You want to be fast, and you want to be *smart*. You got to be thinking two steps ahead of your opponent."

Jaumé nodded seriously.

"But first, you have to learn the moves."

Petrus was teaching him how to grapple, when he suddenly stopped and looked down the valley. Jaumé stopped, too. "Is it...?"

Two riders had come into view.

"It is." Petrus put a hand on Jaumé's shoulder, and turned towards the fire, where Innis and Prince Harkeld sat, and called, "Here they come."

HARKELD LOOKED UP. Was it Rand and Serril? Already?

But the smaller rider was too small to be Rand, and the larger one wasn't quite large enough for Serril. "Who are they?" he said, baffled. He looked at Innis. She was grinning. So was Petrus, and so was Jaumé.

The riders drew closer, and they were wearing cloaks with hoods, and Harkeld couldn't see their faces, no matter how hard he stared, and then the smaller rider halted and slid down from his horse and ran through the snow towards him, and his hood slipped back and—

"Britta?" Harkeld stood so fast that he almost fell over. "*Britta?*"

Britta flung herself at him and hugged him hard, and Harkeld hugged her back, dizzy, more confused than he'd ever been in his life, and he said, "What?" and then, "What?"

Innis and Petrus were laughing, and Jaumé was laughing, too, and the second horseman dismounted and pushed back his hood. Harkeld stared at him, recognized the dark face, and grew even more confused. "What?"

Petrus laughed even harder. "You look like a fish with your mouth open like that."


THEY SAT AROUND the fire, and Harkeld held Britta's hand tightly. Questions tumbled in his mind. He didn't know where to start. Something had happened to Britta, that was obvious. Something momentous. She wasn't the girl he'd left behind in the palace. It wasn't just the short hair that was different. It was her face, her manner.

"What are you doing here? What's happened?"

Britta and her armsman exchanged a glance. The armsman had altered, too; he was thin, almost gaunt, and a long, fresh scar tracked across his forehead.

"From the beginning," the armsman said, and Britta nodded and said, "You tell it."

The armsman told the tale sparsely. Harkeld listened in growing horror. "Marry Rikard?" he said, and then "Invade Lundegaard?" He didn't say anything when he heard his father was dead, but he said "Execute the boys?" with such panic that Innis reached out to touch him, at the same time that Britta said, "Don't worry, we got them out."

He felt Innis's healing magic slide under his skin, and his heartbeat steadied. "You did?"

The armsman nodded and continued the tale—the escape from the palace, the voyage to Lundegaard—and then the story veered sharply. Harkeld stopped asking questions and just listened. Britta had been abducted by Fithian assassins? He flicked a glance at Jaumé. This was what the boy had been skirting around when he'd told his tale. The armsman filled in the gaps, and added his own story, told of Prince Tomas's death, and then he said something that focused Harkeld's attention absolutely. "One of the assassins said that Jaegar's been poisoned. It's slow-acting. He'll be dead in three months."

Harkeld stared at him. "All-Mother..." And then, urgently, "We *have* to get back to Lundegaard! Tell Magnas! If Jaegar dies..."

"We know," Britta said. "Civil war."

Harkeld frantically worked out the distances in his head. "If we leave here tomorrow—"

"We're hoping Magnas can claim Osgaard in the boys' names," Britta said. "Act as regent for them."

"He'll try," Harkeld said. "I'm certain of it!"

"And if he's regent, he'll break Osgaard up again, won't he? Give back the annexed kingdoms? End bondservice?"

"Of course." Magnas would rebuild Osgaard— *if* he had the opportunity. "We have to get back! The sooner Magnas knows, the better chance he'll have!" And then Harkeld's urgency deflated. "I can't go to Lundegaard with you. I'm... Did Tomas tell you I'm a mage? A witch?"

He looked at Britta, expecting to see fear and revulsion. "He told us," Britta said. She didn't pull her hand free.

"Magnas said that he regrets he can't offer you a home in Lundegaard," Karel said. There was no revulsion on his face either. "But you're welcome there for a time. He'll give you gold, if you need it. And he said... that in his eyes, you're Harkeld before you're a witch."

Harkeld's throat tightened. He looked away from the armsman, blinked, swallowed.

"So, that's settled?" Britta said, squeezing his fingers. "We're going to Lundegaard?"

"Yes."

"I'd like to bury Tomas and the armsmen," Karel said. "Speak the words to the All-Mother for them."

"Yes." Harkeld felt grief sting his eyes. "I want to say words for Tomas, too. Ah, All-Mother... it's going to be hard telling Magnas his son's dead."

"It's going to be hard telling all their families," Karel said soberly. "They were good men."

\*　　\*　　\*

INNIS MADE HIM rest, and then Harkeld talked with Britta and her armsman again. He might be a little shaky on his legs, but he wasn't blind. Britta was luminous with joy, and the armsman had the dazed, incredulous expression of a man who'd had an unattainable dream come true. It was obvious the pair were in love. Deeply in love. And if they weren't already having sex, he'd eat his saddle, buckles and all.

Harkeld looked across the valley and tried to decide how he felt about it. Britta, and an Esfaban armsman.

He'd wanted her to marry Tomas, but Tomas was dead, and if Karel had done even half of what he said he'd done, then...

*There is no one who deserves her more.*

Harkeld studied the armsman's face. It was a strong face, made almost harsh by the scar. He'd seen Karel fight in the training arena, knew he was smart and tough, not a man to go up against. But there was clearly a lot more to Karel than just his ability to fight.

The armsman met his eyes. "Highness?" he said. "There's something—"

Harkeld held up a hand, halting him. "Harkeld. Not highness, not sire, not prince. Just Harkeld."

The armsman closed his mouth, and then opened it again. "Uh... Harkeld, sir—"

"Not sir, either."

Karel closed his mouth again. Harkeld could see him wrestling with his training.

"Karel? Just spit it out."

The armsman took a deep breath. "Britta and I are getting married."

Harkeld looked at the wariness in Karel's eyes, at the defiant jut to Britta's chin, and said, "Good."

Britta blinked, and lowered her chin. "You don't mind?"

"Why would I?"

"I'm going to live in Esfaban with Karel. I'm not going to be a princess any more."

"Good," Harkeld said again.

Britta looked disconcerted, as if she'd expected an argument, and then her expression changed: worry. "We're not sure what will happen with the boys. We need to discuss that with Magnas, decide what's best for them."

"We'll figure something out," Harkeld said.

"What about you?" the armsman asked. "Where will you go, high—uh, Harkeld?"

Harkeld glanced at the creek, where Innis stood with Jaumé and the horses. "To the Allied Kingdoms. I'm going to train be a Sentinel mage. And I'm going to marry Innis." It was a future so different from any he'd ever envisaged for himself that he almost couldn't believe it. *Me? Be a Sentinel? Marry a mage?* And he wondered if he had the same slightly dazed, incredulous expression on his face that the armsman had.

Probably he did, because the armsman grinned. "Sounds good."

Harkeld grinned back. He liked this man; Britta had chosen well. And then he looked more closely at Karel's face. "You shaved," he said enviously. "Where—and how soon can I get there?"

Karel laughed. "Had a bath, too."

"Whoreson," Harkeld said, even more enviously. "Where?"

\* \* \*

INNIS SPENT SOME time with the armsman, checking his injuries. The bones were well-mended; Petrus had always been good at bones. She worked on the muscle fibers in Karel's thigh for half an hour, then turned her attention to his upper arm. As always, her magic brought her an awareness of who her patient was as a person. Karel was interesting. He was a striking man, dark and good-looking, with a hard, dangerous edge, but inside, he was... not what she'd expected. He had all the characteristics of a good soldier—courage, determination, intelligence, loyalty, honor—but he also had a strong core of kindness. An exceptionally strong core of kindness. And underlying all of that, shaping who he was, was an old and pervasive grief. Something had happened to him in his childhood, something that grieved him still. Something to do with his family?

"All done," Innis said. "Let me just check your forehead."

Karel buttoned his shirt while she examined the long scar. She wondered what his background was.

A hoot of laughter snagged her attention: Petrus and Jaumé throwing snow at each other. Innis watched for a moment—the snowballs spraying snow that sparkled in the sunshine, the laughter bright on their faces. *How safe we are, now that the curse is broken.*

She turned her attention back to Karel and ran her fingers along the scar, probing lightly with her magic. "I can't do anything with this, I'm sorry."

"Doesn't matter," Karel said. She saw him glance at something behind her and knew what—who—it was without looking. Her magic felt the surge of his emotions.

Princess Brigitta came to sit beside them. Karel's love for her, his deep joy, hummed beneath Innis's fingertips.

"How is he?" the princess asked. Her golden hair was even shorter than it had been two days ago; the armsman must have trimmed it for her. Instead of making Brigitta look boyish, the short hair emphasized the delicate beauty of her face.

Innis lowered her hands. "In perfect health." She looked at the princess, tilted her head to one side, examined her. "You don't look how I remember."

Princess Brigitta's brow furrowed. "You've seen me?"

"Both of you. At the palace. Karel looks the same, apart from that scar, and he's thinner. But you..." The princess had worn a crown, intricately woven into her long hair, but that wasn't the difference she'd noticed. Brigitta had an emotional strength, a confidence, that had been lacking in the palace gardens. She'd been a girl, then; now she was a woman.

Brigitta's frown deepened. "At the palace?"

"In the gardens. I was a black hound."

"Oh." Her brow cleared. "I remember."

Sweet Britta. That's how Harkeld thought of her in his dreams—sweet Britta—and there *was* a sweetness to Britta's face, something that had nothing to do with her physical beauty, but rather, seemed to come from inside her.

"Harkeld tells me that I—we—shouldn't call you witches; it's insulting. I apologize if we've offended—"

"You haven't."

Britta hesitated, bit her lip, then leaned forward and said, "And he said... he's asked you to marry him."

Innis met Britta's eyes, sky-blue, and bright with curiosity. *She wants to know who I am, as much as I want to know who she is.*

Karel grinned and stood. "I'll leave you two to talk."

PETRUS WENT HUNTING. Jaumé saw him come back, a great silver-pelted wolf with a goat dangling from his jaws. While the goat roasted, Princess Britta and her soldier talked to him. Karel sat on one side of him, and the princess on the other, her arm around Jaumé's shoulders. "Jaumé," she said. "We're all going to Lundegaard now, and then Harkeld and the mages are going to the Allied Kingdoms, and if everything works out, Karel and I will go to a kingdom called Esfaban. Have you heard of it?"

Jaumé shook his head.

"It's islands," Karel said. "A string of islands up near the equator. It's a lot warmer than this. Never snows."

Jaumé nodded, and wondered why they were telling him this.

"There are lots of refugees from Vaere in Lundegaard," Princess Britta said. "If you want, I'm sure we can find someone to take you back to Vaere. But I don't think there'll be anyone left alive from your village."

"You can stay in Lundegaard, if you want," Karel said. "King Magnas will make sure you have a good home. Or you can go with Harkeld and Innis and Petrus to the Allied Kingdoms. They'll find you a home, too."

"Or you can come with us," the princess said. "To Esfaban, if it's freed, or the Allied Kingdoms, if it's not. Wherever we go, we'd like you to come with us. If you want to."

"We wouldn't be your Mam and Da," Karel said. "But we'd be your family."

Tears rushed to Jaumé's eyes. He wiped them away with his knuckles.

"You don't have to decide now," Princess Britta said. "But think about it."

She stood, and brushed his hair back from his face, and dropped a kiss on his brow, and Karel stood, too, and looked down at Jaumé.

"Is there fishing in Esfaban?" Jaumé asked.

"Lots of fishing," Karel said, and then he smiled and held out his hand, and Jaumé took it.

JAUMÉ ATE ROASTED goat until he felt like he was going to burst, and then sat half-asleep, listening to the talk around the fire.

"Can't wait to see you wrestle with Karel," the prince told Petrus. "He'll flatten you."

Petrus grinned, the firelight playing over his face. "You reckon?"

"He's better than me. Better than you. I've never seen anyone beat him."

"I get beaten," Karel said mildly.

Petrus chewed for a moment, and then said, "You know, I've never seen anyone beat Serril."

"Karel'll beat him," the prince said.

"You reckon?" Petrus eyed the soldier, and said, "Looks a bit scrawny, to me. Serril'll snap him in two."

Karel grinned, unoffended.

"You *are* thin," Harkeld said, frowning at Karel. "We need to fatten you up."

"*You*'re thin, too," Britta pointed out.

Innis nodded. "Skinny."

"You look like a scarecrow," Petrus said, licking his fingers. "All dirt and rags."

"And that's a dreadful beard," Karel said, his face very serious.

Harkeld self-consciously touched his chin. "Rut you."

Everyone laughed, and Jaumé laughed, too, and hugged his knees, and looked forward to tomorrow.


THE END

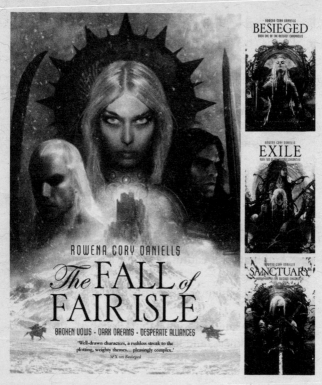

It has been six hundred years since Imoshen the First, Causare of the T'En, brought her beleaguered people across the seas to Fair Isle. The magical folk mixed with the natives, bringing culture and sophistication, and made the island one of the wealthiest, most powerful nations in the known world.

But all glory is temporary. The Ghebites, savage barbarians from the warm north, have rolled over the mainland, conquering all in their path, and now they have taken Fair Isle. Imoshen, namesake of the first Empress and the last pure-blooded T'En woman, is all that survives of that great heritage. Now, just seventeen years of age, she must offer herself to the Ghebite General, Tulkhan, and do what she can to ensure her survival, and that of her people.

One other T'En survives: Reothe, Imoshen's betrothed, newly returned from adventuring on the high seas. As the T'En warrior foments rebellion against Tulkhan in secret, Imoshen must choose, both as a woman and as a leader, between a past now lost and an uncertain future£

This volume collects *Broken Vows*, *Dark Dreams* and *Desperate Alliances* for the first time.